# BENEATH THE DRAPER MOON

# BENEATH THE DRAPER MOON

JULIUS PARKER

Charleston, SC
www.PalmettoPublishing.com



Hardcover ISBN: 979-8-8229-3148-0
Paperback ISBN: 979-8-8229-3149-7

*For my wife and my children for their unending and patient support for my time and late nights in this self-educational endeavor.*

*And for those I called by only one name growing up as a child in the Deep South, but who unknowingly taught me about respect for all – Bertha, Ruthie, Shorty, and Duffy.*

# Prologue

August 8, 1975
New River Railroad Line – Just
Southwest of Draper, Virginia

For those too adventurous to earn merit badges for helping old ladies with their groceries, or learning to properly wash their own hands – there was the YMCA sponsored Indian Guides. This group was made up of rugged young wilderness survivors and their "weekend away from the wife" seeking fathers. It was truly a bonding time for young men and their dads…and it was spectacular. Their arts and crafts activities revolved around usable items like creating tools from what nature had to offer – they didn't make pinewood derby racers, they made snares and traps to capture small game for survival. They didn't earn badges or wear uniforms – they wore camouflage and Levis and earned feathers for their headdress. They didn't shine their shoes, they wore boots or went barefoot. They didn't practice archery…they practiced bow hunting.

This morning, the fathers of the nine young braves were warding off the evil spirits from a late night pow-wow with bad firewater that carried names such as PBR and Schlitz and came out of steel cans. They were all lying along the banks of the New River with their feet in the water. A couple held fishing poles but didn't really hope for a bite. They would get it in gear for a cookout and campfire later that afternoon.

The braves ran about in different directions with most staying along the riverbank near their fathers. Jimmy, Chris, and Ricky climbed up the small cliff and through some bushes until they reached the abandoned Norfolk Southern Rail Line. They followed it east toward Draper and Claytor Lake, watching the tracks for railroad spikes or other collectibles from yesteryear. The goldmines of discovery along these tracks were the bullets from the Civil War – Minie balls and ringed .36 caliber Colt pistol rounds. The boys ventured around a bend in the track just underneath a large rock outcropping that rose seventy-five feet in the air. It was ringed by large Sycamore trees near the base and scrub brush grew like patches of hair at the summit. They had seen this rock formation many times - but today Ricky saw something unusual.

"Look at the hole up yonder," he pointed just up the slope at the base of the rock formation. "Behind the brush there," he pointed again with more emphasis this time.

"Ain't never seen that before," Jimmy started off the tracks and through the brush. "Let's check it out."

The other boys followed Jimmy through the scraggly bushes, scraping their legs without care as they went. They emerged at a pile of rocks that sloped up to a hole about three feet wide in the face of the formation. Jimmy scrambled to the top of the heap and peered into the hole, then he turned to the others with wide eyes.

"It opens up and goes deep – can't see the end of it."

"C'mon down," Chris said with a worried look on his face. He was scared of dark places and didn't want anything to do with this one for sure.

"Go get my flashlight from the tent," said Jimmy.

"I ain't goin' in that hole," Chris backed up as rocks slid under his feet.

"Me and Ricky will check it out," Jimmy grinned. "You can stand watch."

"There might be snakes," Chris warned again.

"Just go get the light, chicken."

It took less than five minutes for Chris to bring the flashlight. Jimmy had to knock it against his hand a couple of times to get it to come on, then he slid down two feet of rocks and into the cave opening…Ricky followed behind. He shone the light as deep into the cave as it would go but it didn't illuminate much more than they could already see.

"Let's go in a few feet," Jimmy encouraged Ricky.

"This looks dangerous."

"We won't go far in…"

Ricky got as close to Jimmy as he could and followed him, using shuffle steps until they were ten feet inside. The darkness had grown now, and the flashlight showed more as the sunlight gave way. They heard water dripping somewhere deep inside – it made a clicking sound – almost like a clock.

"That's enough, man," Ricky said.

"It curves to the right there – just ten more feet – we look around the corner and then get out."

They took two steps forward and the flashlight went out. Jimmy pounded it three times in his palm, and it came back on. Ricky grabbed his shoulder from behind and they shuffled forward until they reached the curve. Chris called their names but neither answered. Jimmy slowly turned the beam of light around the corner and then jumped back knocking Ricky to the ground.

"What the hell, man?"

"Did you not see that!"

"I was too busy falling, dumbass!"

"I – It was white."

"White?"

"Yeah."

"Moving?"

"No – I don't think so."

"Let's look again."

The boys hunched together and shimmied forward as Jimmy slowly raised the light from the floor. Ten feet away was the white object he had seen.

Ricky screamed and instinctively ran back toward the cave entrance as Jimmy's flashlight went out again. He beat it on his palm and the fourth time it came back to life. Jimmy felt his heart trying to pound its' way out of his chest. Five feet away was the skeletal remains of a man in uniform with a sword laying by his side. His skull looked crushed, and his mouth was opened in a horrible grin. The sockets where his eyes used to be were sunken and black. Jimmy dropped the flashlight as he joined Ricky's flight and scrambled out of the cave. The boys ran past Chris so fast he couldn't get a word out.

In the cave behind them the flashlight hit the floor and rolled slowly toward the far wall of the cave – like a macabre, silent, black and white movie it quietly revealed three more skeletons until it struck the rock wall and went out again.

*I, too, sing America.*

*I am the darker brother,*
*They send me to eat in the kitchen*
*When company comes,*
*But I laugh,*
*And eat well*
*And grow strong.*
*Tomorrow,*
*I'll be at the table*
*When company comes.*
*Nobody'll dare*
*Say to me,*
*"Eat in the kitchen,"*
*Then.*
*Besides,*
*They'll see how beautiful I am*
*And be ashamed –*
*I too, am America.*

**Langston Hughes 1924**

# 1

"Thomas Warren?"

"Can you hear me?"

Was that his mother? There was a dense bright fog in front of his eyes – or was it smoke…it was acrid. He thought he heard something but wasn't sure anyone was there. Then it was quiet again, and he fell back to Antietam and General Hood's regiment. He was walking along an old cattle road that had grown thick with weeds during the summer. His brothers were with him Stephen the youngest, John was next, and Dewey was his older brother. They weren't speaking to each other much but simply walking just as they had been for twelve long days. The later summer nights were getting cooler but the days were still scorching hot. Hundreds, if not thousands, of men and young boys spread out in front, behind, and all around them. A few were clothed in grey uniforms but many just wore their farm clothes – probably the same ones they had on when they left their mothers crying on porches all over the South. Stephen finally broke the silence.

"They say we might get to see Lee – that he might speak to us."

Thomas looked at him but for some reason was unable to answer.

John answered sullenly. "Would that make it a good day to die?"

Dewey turned to him with a scowl growing through his lightening beard. "I'm bringing you all back to mother alive! I promised," his voice trailed off.

They kept walking not knowing exactly where they were going or what would happen once they got wherever "there" was. Thomas knew Sharpsburg was somewhere nearby. He had ridden this far on a buckboard with his father once. His father, Dewey Summerlin Sr., was a hard- working Southern Virginia farmer who had done quite well for himself, having amassed a plantation covering some two thousand acres in the Western part of the state. But he was a nasty son-of-a-bitch. When his boys left to face the Yankees he didn't even say goodbye. In fact, that morning he got up early and left to go hunting before the boys were even in the kitchen. Thomas had wanted to see if his father would shed a tear for his boys that morning, but he didn't think he had. He would never find out.

The fog was lifted in front of his eyes ever so slightly and he thought he was glancing towards a window - it looked like snow was coming down hard outside. His eyes closed again without his permission. He was surrounded again by mostly young Virginians, North and South Carolinians and Georgians. Some boys walked next to their fathers; a few other older men stumbled along in solitude. Most of them have brought their own weapons. Thomas had one of his father's shotguns slung over his shoulder, but he also carried a Remington 1858 pistol given to him by his grandfather. Dewey carried a sword on his side – it had been in the family for a long time. It would be lost forever in the next ten minutes.

There was an angel in the room – or a demon. A dark-skinned woman with long straight black hair. Who was she? Candles flickered on the mantle above a dying fire. Was the paint peeling off the wall. Silence....again.

Thomas and his brothers were ordered to stay with the 500-man regiment from Georgia who were to hold off the Union army as long as possible to allow Hood to move west and join Lee and Jackson. They marched onward. A small bridge loomed in front of them – they were to protect the crossing. There was a steepled church across the river which looked big enough for a congregation of maybe twenty folks. Thomas smiled at the peaceful country scene as leaves scattered from the Sycamores and twirled about making him long for home – until blood from his brother Dewey's head splattered all across the front of his woven shirt. They had found what they left home in search of – was it glory? The blue coats were now swarming from behind the church and onto the bridge. The little country scene became complete chaos. Smoke filled the air and blood soaked the dirt. Thomas and his younger brothers were running toward the river even before Dewey's body hit the ground.

The angel was there again. Was she the angel of death? He heard dripping water as she squeezed a cloth and put it on his face. A bad smell hit his nostrils. It was putrid. He was back on the riverbank.

The shallow river was now filled with corpses. Men and boys screamed out for their mothers. Bullets whistled past both of Thomas' ears at once like a swarm of summer bees. He didn't know whether to shoot, cry, or run. A young boy of about sixteen was on top of him now preparing to stab a bayonet deep into his heart. Thomas instinctively whipped the shotgun from his back and fired it into the boy's chest. His blue eyes looked at first shocked and then saddened as his lifeless body fell halfway into the blood red river.

It was raining outside the window now. But flowers were blooming, and he thought he heard a bird singing. Then the sound of a scream shattered it all…

"Let's Go! Now!" Stephen screamed as he pulled Thomas from the ground.

They ran to the formerly picturesque country bridge. Bodies were hanging from the sides and men lay all over the decking, screaming and crying for help…and home. It was hard to run in all that blood. It was everywhere. Sticky. Slippery. The smell. John was in front, and Stephen was in back when he saw the flash. It was a huge puff of smoke just on the other side of the church. He never heard the explosion of the cannon, but he felt the heat and pain as the shell hurtled its' way through the crowded bridge tearing limbs and heads away. Then it was dark…so very dark. Was he dead? His Civil War action – and glory - had lasted all of eight minutes.

The angel was back. She had a slight smile on her lips and was singing as she swept the floor with a cornstalk broom. Then her back was to him. She was not a demon. Was she? Her hair was so beautiful and glimmering in the sunlight coming through the window. Where was Elizabeth?

The sounds of the battle rang in Thomas' ears for hours as he lay there dying. He wept for Elizabeth and his mother. They could never be together now. They could never have the acreage her father had set aside for them to raise tobacco, corn, cattle, and horses – and children. He had ruined it all. He clamped his eyes tighter shut and said goodbye to her. "I love you, my dear" he whispered to no one.

There was mushy food in his mouth now and he tried to swallow. He got some of it down. Then a little water. His eyes felt fastened shut.

Who feeds the dying on a battlefield he wondered? The taste of the mush awakened him a little and he opened his eyes. There, not three feet away was his brother Stephen staring wide eyed at him. He must have fed him and was now waiting for him to get the strength to move. The sounds of the battle seemed to be further away now. He laid still and closed his eyes again.

The angel was there again, but now she was surrounded by men in blue coats. They were yelling something at her, and she appeared to spit at one of them. He felt like someone picked him up and then dropped him on the floor. His body shuddered.

The smell…was horrifying. The dead around him on the battlefield were rotting in the late summer sun. Thomas rolled his head to one side and when he opened his eyes all he saw was bloated bodies, flies, vultures, and crows. There was a dead horse shot almost completely in half not ten feet away. He closed his eyes and rolled back to look at Stephen again. What he saw was his brother – he would recognize that eye anywhere. But where was his other eye? Stephen's belly was so swollen it looked like it was about to rupture. Thomas thought he was screaming but no real sound escaped his throat. Where was John? He was dying.

The angel was wiping his face once more with a cold cloth – it was sweltering in here. He looked past her to see the portrait of his mother on the far wall. Was he home? Was… this… heaven?

"This one's alive!" he heard in a woman's voice. He squinted slowly opening his eyes to see an older woman with a scarf tied tightly around her face offering him water. She was covered in sweat and blood.

"Let's see if we can get you home son." She whispered.

He opened his eyes again to see the angel sitting beside him on the bed. She was crying into a dirty apron that was tied at her waist. She must have realized that he had opened his eyes because she turned to look at him and smiled. One eye was the most beautiful deep reflection of gold and hazel he had ever gazed upon. The other was swollen closed.

"Mr. Thomas" she said softly. He closed his eyes again.

Thomas and his three brothers were walking slowly down an old overgrown cattle trail. They had been walking for twelve days and had been silent for much of this one.

"They say we might get to see Lee…."

Not again….

Not again….

Thomas forced open his eyes once more to see the angel sitting next to him again. Her eye was miraculously healed.

"Who…are…you?" he whispered.

# 2

Charlottesville and the University of Virginia were cooling off quickly in the early Fall of 1962. Leaves flew from the sycamores and hickories, gathered in piles on the ground, and swirled off into small twisters to other parts of the campus. Crunching sounds were echoing through the quad as students walked through the leaves heading to their early morning classes in the Academical Hall. Ladies in long skirts and frilly blouses with their hair mostly up and held firmly in place by hairspray and bobby pins, laughed and gossiped as they went. The boys, joking their way down the hill from their dormitories and fraternity row, mostly wore slacks with white or blue collared shirts – some wore bowties. The girls, all juniors and seniors who had come over from Mary Washington College in Fredericksburg, found the younger boys to be extremely immature.

Luke Montgomery came bounding out of the locker room door of Memorial Gym and rushed toward his dormitory. Class was in fifteen minutes and his books were 10 minutes away. He was still dripping from the early morning basketball practice, but the coach kept them late and there was no time to get cleaned up before class. He would have to go as-is. He started down the only paved path between the gym and the dorms. The path crossed into a "T" at the bottom of the first hill before it went back up the second hill into the trees beyond. The intersection became quickly too difficult for Luke to coordinate with his speed, and he barely avoided crashing into a group of girls who stepped to the side. The three white girls jumped into the path of a young colored girl who had to stop short, but still she bumped into the back of one of the other girls who quickly turned around.

"Watch it imbecile!" she spouted as she pushed the young girl's books from her hands onto the ground. The young girl slipped and found herself sitting in mud next to her books.

Luke heard the commotion and brought himself to a stop – quickly turning around.

"Seriously?" he said as he walked back to help the girl get back up. The other girls turned and continued up the walk toward the classrooms.

"I'm so terribly sorry. That was all my doing," he panted.

"Yes, it was," she said without looking up.

"Let me help you."

"I can manage."

Luke picked up her books by the strap bound tightly around them. "I'm really sorry, honestly."

"And I said I could manage." She stood up and reached for her books – pulling them from his outstretched hand as her eyes turned downward to check the damage on her clothing. She used the other hand to wipe dirt and leaves from her white sweater and black checkered skirt.

"You've got mud all over your skirt. Can I give you my shirt so you can clean it off?" he started to pull up on his white cotton jersey.

"A rich white boy taking off his shirt to hand to a poor colored girl in the middle of the Quad? No thanks." She finished brushing herself off and looked up into Luke's face.

Their eyes locked only briefly. She found herself looking up at the 6'2" point guard. Luke smiled at her before glancing uncomfortably back up the hill. He felt horrible about what he had caused.

"Do you have time to go back to Munford to get changed?" he said.

"I don't know what is more amusing to me, the fact that you think I have an abundance of nice clothing, or the fact that you think I am allowed to live in the dormitory." she had just about gotten herself together and was turning to head up the walk.

"I didn't mean anything by it," he said. "I'm just ignorant, I guess."

"I guess so," she smiled at him ever so slightly.

"I know we will be great friends," Luke said slyly.

"Since there isn't much chance of us running in the same circles, I don't need to worry about that too much," she started to walk away.

"Are you a student here?" he asked.

"Of course, I am."

"I'm a student too...that's at least one circle,"

"Our circles would have to be concentric," she said.

"Don't try to trick me with your Geometry talk," Luke laughed.

The dark-haired beauty left Luke standing where he was and started to shuffle through the leaves and up the sidewalk toward the UVA Hospital. Another brisk breeze came through and leaves flew up between them.

"My name is Luke. What's yours?" he called after her.

"Doesn't matter," she said.

"Come on – I told you mine."

She turned to look at him and to enforce her point she clearly pronounced each word, "It...doesn't... matter."

Luke looked up the walkway and into her soft brown eyes, "I hope you have a fantastic day, Emmaline Foster."

She glared back at him.

"You wrote it on your notebook," he said.

Emmaline cringed as soon as she said, "My mother wrote it!"

Luke almost fell over laughing as Emmaline spun around and scurried up the sidewalk.

Luke turned, and smiling, ran up the hill toward his dorm.

# 3

"Who are you?" Thomas said again, but he couldn't hear his own voice.

The angel gently put both hands on his cheeks and leaned slightly closer to him. He could smell smoke and maybe rose water on her fingers. The sense of the smell overwhelmed him, and he closed his eyes again.

"Thomas?" she said.

He opened his eyes again and was met with a burning in both eyes and in his throat. She squeezed the cloth and placed it gently over his eyes. He felt a small teacup brush against his lower lip, and he drank in the cool water until it was gone. Swallowing was so difficult at first, but each sip eased the pain more and more. She removed the cloth, and he opened his eyes again into a squint.

"My name is Gracie, and you are at home – Waverly," her voice was soft and kind. "Welcome back."

"Where is my Mother?" he asked. "Elizabeth?"

"We need to get your strength back so I'm going to fetch you some soup and a piece of bread if you can swallow it down," Gracie stood and started toward the open door leading to the hall. The room itself was expansive with twelve-foot ceilings and a slow burning fire in a large fireplace framed by a marble hearth and mantle. "I have to get more wood too."

She stopped at the door and turned, "I'm so happy you are awake – I've been waiting for you. It's good to finally hear your voice." She smiled a warm, beautiful, youthful smile at Thomas and was gone.

Thomas Summerlin did his best to look around the room, but his eyes kept watering and burning so he closed them very often. The curtains on the windows were drawn but he could tell by the bright white light framing them that it was daytime. His mind drifted in and out of sleep, but he didn't lose consciousness again. He wondered why his normally bustling plantation home was so deathly quiet. The only sounds he heard were the popping and sizzling of embers in the fireplace and the ringing in his ears. He tried to lift his head a few times but gave up – it was the same with his arms, he couldn't lift them at all, but he could move his fingers back and forth but not clinch a fist. Every muscle that he could feel was on fire. He closed his eyes and tried to block out the ringing by listening for birds chirping, cattle lowing, or horses whinnying outside, but he heard nothing in the stillness. He started to doze off again.

Gracie interrupted his sleep with an armful of poorly cut firewood that she dropped from her arms to the floor in front of the hearth. Thomas watched as she placed five logs on the top of the smoldering cinders and pumped a cloth bellow to speed up the process of flame. She stood up and wiped her hands on her apron, turning to face Thomas.

"I'll be right back, sir" she said and before Thomas could protest, she was gone again.

It wasn't long before she returned with a wooden tray with a bowl of broth and a crust of day-old bread. She placed the tray on a small table next to the bed and pulled up a rickety looking ladderback chair. Thomas opened his eyes to look at her. She seemed younger than he first thought – maybe twenty or so, but her eyes were just as beautiful as he remembered from his dreams. Her black hair was long and straight

– unlike any he had seen on a slave girl before. Her features were very pronounced, and her skin was as light as the heavily milked coffee his mother used to give him on especially cold winter mornings.

"I'm going to put another blanket under your head so you don't get constricted," she said as she gently lifted his head and placed a thick woolen blanket underneath. "I didn't make the soup too hot 'cause I don't want you to get burnt."

Gracie gently held the silver spoon to his lips, and he felt the warm salty broth trickle across his tongue and into the back of this throat. On the third sip he coughed violently, and the pain almost caused him to blackout. She put a cloth on his head to cool him down some.

"We can try more later,"she said softly. "You need to get some rest."

Gracie offered him a sip of water from the small chipped teacup and he gladly gurgled it down. She stood up and moved the little table away from the bed and placed the chair behind it.

"I'm going to let you rest for a little bit while I go outside and do some things that need doin'." Gracie smiled at Thomas again.

"Can you open the curtain?" he said in an almost inaudible whisper.

"It's too bright out there with the sun glaring off all that snow. It's most up to the window panes – let's wait until sundown starts," she said.

"Seems early in the season for a snow that big," said Thomas as he rolled his head toward the window.

"Nothing early about it," Gracie leaned over and placed another log on the fire. "It's so very good to hear your voice."

"Can you tell my mother I'm awake?" Thomas whispered.

"All in time, Mr. Summerlin, all in time. It is so nice to hear your voice," she stopped at the doorway.

Thomas lacked the energy to argue, "Why do you keep saying that about my voice?"

She looked back at him with her beautiful blazing eyes. "I'm certainly glad you are awake, but I'm also a bit selfish. I haven't heard another human voice in four months."

Gracie went down the hall. Thomas closed his eyes and wondered if he had misheard her.

# 4

November of 1962 was a huge month for Luke Montgomery and the UVA campus. Basketball season was back and that meant the Memorial Gym being packed to the rafters and Thursday night bonfires with screaming fans. It was really all that kept him going. If it wasn't for basketball, he didn't think he would really fit in here. Sure, he had everything he could really ask for including a girl who thought he had hung the moon. Caroline Aubrey came from a prominent Annapolis family. Her father was a decorated Naval Officer who survived Pearl Harbor on the Oklahoma and then fought in the Pacific theater until Hiroshima in 1945. Caroline was born in 1943 and her father didn't see her until she was almost three. He now commanded the midshipmen at the Naval Academy – a well-deserved appointment. Luke and Caroline had been together for almost six months now after she decided they were an item and he decided to go along with it.

Luke probably should have gone to a smaller school closer to home. His grades and study skills were never the best, but he had the ability to remember most of what he heard in class - his problem was regurgitating it onto paper. He still carried the knowledge he heard with him for the most part. Caroline was way out of his league, and he was certain her only interest in him was the fact that he played basketball - and for some unknown reason he was liked by most of her friends. It was probably because he had a quick wit about him and could say what he meant without causing waves.

His blonde hair, blue eyes, and slight dimple didn't hurt his chances either. He was genuine, and quite frankly he had nothing to hide even though he wasn't overly open about his childhood. He couldn't compete with the upbringing most of them had - nor did he want to. So, Caroline and her friends stayed squarely focused on his boyish good looks and his ability to run the court and command the team. None of this bothered him much. He had met Caroline's father on Parents Weekend a few weeks ago and the report he got back was "he's a fine and strong young man who should probably consider a stint in the military when he graduates." That was not Luke. Not this version of Luke anyway.

The sparks were already crackling high into the air and blowing away into the brisk night sky when Luke got to the fire. He didn't have to look for Caroline very long as she came prancing towards him with her friend Audrey in tow.

"Luke! It's so cold out here tonight! So cold!" she exclaimed while throwing her arm around his waist.

He did as was expected and removed his third-year letterman jacket and wrapped it around her shoulders. He knew she was going to ask for it which is why he had put on a sweater underneath. She wanted him to give it to her permanently so she could wear it all over campus, but he lied to her by telling her that the coach wanted him to wear the jacket to every away game and he "just didn't need the hassle". Instead, he had given her his Woodrow Wilson High leather jacket to wear. But she never wore it because she did not want anyone to think that she was dating some high school boy – that would be gross.

"I told everyone we were going over to "TP's" later to hang out," she offered, and Luke winked at her.

"TP's" was a local drive-in diner called Tail Pipes. It was basically a bunch of teenagers sitting around in their parent's borrowed convertibles listening to Elvis Presley and Fats Domino while stuffing their faces with hot dogs, ice cream, and French fries. It was as close to heaven as these young folks could find in Charlottesville on a cold Fall weeknight.

The basketball bonfire had become a tradition in recent years, especially if there was to be a home game on a Friday night. The fans would cheer as Coach McCann introduced his starting lineup to the crowd. There was, of course, a rather stupendous rousing of applause when Luke Montgomery was introduced - he was now a third-year starter and people simply loved to watch him play basketball. Luke was actually a great basketball player who was garnering national attention, with some comparing him to the great Celtics star Bob Cousy. He played along with these moments, but being in the limelight really wasn't for him. He really was a guy who grew up playing ball on a playground with a hoop and no net and sometimes half a backboard.

Caroline stayed wrapped warmly in his jacket while clutching his arm and jumping up and down excitedly as his other teammates were announced. This moment seemed to be more about her than him. They were opening their schedule with Old Dominion the next night in the Memorial Gym in Charlottesville and the house was going to be packed. Luke loved basketball more than life, and he was looking forward to another exciting year on the hardwood. As the crowd began to thin, Luke, Caroline, and Audrey headed for Dominick Solomon's 1955 Chevy convertible to ride over to the drive-in. Dominick was Luke's roommate and he also played on the basketball team, although the vast majority of his time was done as a spectator from the bench. They were close enough friends, but Dominick hailed from Washington where his dad was a United States attorney and while they disagreed about a lot of issues, especially when it came to politics, they did their best not to discuss those matters. It seemed to make living together much easier if they just talked about basketball, school, music, and girls.

Tail Pipes was only about two miles from campus down West Main Street. When Dominick swung the big red and white Chevy into the parking lot it was already teeming with cars and there was a long line of students standing at the window to order. Joe Millstone had a habit of getting to TP's early and saving Dominick a spot right up front - tonight was no different and Joe was right there waving them in. They pulled up, parked, and left the radio humming to Elvis Presley's *Love Me Tender*. The rest of this evening was going to be about listening to tunes, eating some burgers, and watching the girls dance around the car in their skirts and bobby socks. As the evening wore on many of the other students came past the car to shake hands with Luke and wish him luck in the game against Old Dominion. Luke was very modest about the fandom, and it really wasn't something he lived for. He mostly smiled and nodded as folks came by.

The drive-in itself had a glass front with two windows, one on the left for ordering and one on the right for picking up food. The roof on the building curved upward and outward like the points on a crown. Cars lined the parking area in the front, and many had their lights still burning even though the lot was lit up like a Christmas tree by floodlights mounted on fifteen-foot-high poles all along the perimeter of the property. There were a few umbrella covered picnic tables near the building but almost everyone ate in or around their car. Like a gas station, the restrooms were hidden in the back and accessed by exterior doors. They were probably cleaned once per day – if that much. Shortly after nine, and after a large Dr Pepper, Luke excused himself from his friends and made his way around the back to find some relief.

He rounded the corner to the back of TP's just in time to observe a dark-skinned girl with her hair stuffed up under a hairnet attempting to hoist a garbage can and pour it into a dumpster. The can started to turn sideways on her, and Luke knew she was about to dump the contents all over herself and on the ground so he reached out, caught the lip with one hand and pushed the can up into the opening. When it was empty, he lifted it over her head and placed it on the ground by her feet.

"Don't they have men for this task?" he said as he turned toward the restroom door.

"Always my knight in shining armor, aren't you?" Luke heard a small but sarcastic voice from behind him that sounded vaguely familiar.

In the most ridiculous Southern accent he could muster Luke turned around and said, "Why Emmaline, my dear, I declare I did not know that was you. Had I known I would not have proliferated my assistance in this matter!"

"Well at least this time you didn't cause the problem, but thanks for your help," she grinned rather sheepishly. "I'm not sure you know what "proliferated" actually means do you?" This made her giggle.

Luke started to contemplate how a woman this beautiful could ever find herself dumping garbage cans, when she said, "How have you been Luke? We haven't run into each other around school lately." She put a huge emphasis on the word "run" and he got the point.

"Well Emmaline, you must not have been looking too hard because I'm there every day," he set himself up and she quickly retorted, "I didn't say I have been looking for you – more like looking out for you." This time she emphasized "out".

"So, you work here?" he asked, knowing immediately what a stupid question that was.

"I'm out of smart comments. Yes, I work in the kitchen and do things like what you just helped me with. Mr. Richard doesn't like us to take orders at the window so, you know, they reserve those spots for the white girls." Emmaline grabbed the garbage can by one handle.

"Or maybe you're just not good at taking orders," Luke thought he would try his hand at being smart – it didn't work.

"Well thank you for helping me dump the garbage can I'll send for you when I need to dump another one," she said as she began to drag the can toward the back door of the kitchen.

At that moment another colored girl came out the back door, removing her hairnet as she approached them. "I told Mr. Richard that I needed to study for a test, and he told me to go ahead and go and that you would finish up. I promise I'll cover for you tomorrow – I'm just so tired Emmie."

"It's alright." Said Emmaline. "I'll see you when I get done and I'll ask Mr. Richard about the heat again."

The girl walked between the two of them and went into a small white shed with a single door and two tiny windows about 30 feet away. She closed the door behind her and moments later a soft yellow light illuminated the windows which appeared to have sheets hanging in them for drapes.

"So, what is that like a changing room?" Luke said.

"No, genius, that's where Natalie and I live." She moved closer to the door.

"Can I call you Emmie too?" Luke had to struggle for words after what she had just told him.

"Only my friends call me Emmie." She said without turning around.

"Emmie it is then…" Luke smiled and closed the door to the restroom.

Emmaline grinned without turning around and went through the kitchen door.

# 5

It had snowed again overnight, and the house had gotten very cold, so Gracie stoked the fire in Thomas' room and prepared him a bed warmer by heating some clay bricks on the hearth and then wrapping them in cloth and placing them in the bed along both sides of his body. Her role of taking care of Thomas had never been easy, but it certainly seemed to be a little more difficult now that he was awake and asking questions. He had gotten so demanding over the past few days that she had been forced to walk out of the room and feign having "other duties to take care of" quite often. But she understood his anxiousness. She felt it too, and was honestly scared to tell him everything, so she did her best to put it off. Gracie rightly believed that he needed to regain at least a bit of his strength to handle what she had to tell him. It was going to be so difficult. Everything he knew was different now – even the world was different. She continued to bring him things that she thought he could handle like soup, mashed field peas, and soft bread with lots of water. She knew he needed to drink, but she also knew it meant emptying his bedpan more often. "No matter", she thought – she had made a promise that she meant to keep.

A few times each day Gracie would provide Thomas with a small glass of rye whiskey which she told him was for the pain, although he rarely complained of it. She really did it so he would sleep, and she could get a respite. Since beginning to care for him she had given Thomas a bath every three days when he was unconscious. Unfortunately, today was the third day since he had awakened – and he so clearly needed to be washed. She dreaded it. She had to roll him over with great effort, but she always kept a clean cloth underneath him to catch what the bed pan missed and to absorb his night sweats. Most days the sheet came out yellow and she would just throw it in the pile to scrub clean later. Washing him this time was going to be a different story.

She was heating some water up in a cast-iron pot hanging from a spit near the fire when Thomas Summerlin roused from his latest bout of nightmares, "Jesus, Gracie are you making soup in here now?"

"It's time for your bath Mr. Thomas," she said without looking at him.

"I think I can wait til' I get out of this bed and give myself my own bath, thank you very much," Thomas said in a grumpy but obviously muffled voice. He cleared his throat, coughed painfully, and spat up a large glob of mucous and blood which Gracie quickly wiped away with her apron.

"Believe me when I tell you Mr. Thomas, you're nowhere near ready to get out of that bed and besides that, you stink to high heaven. Ms. Henry used to say "you stink like two mules in a pigpen." Gracie picked up the small kettle with an iron fire poker and carried it over to the bedside where she placed it on a small rug on the floor. She then walked back to the hearth to retrieve the two cloths she had left there warming – one for washing and one for drying.

Gracie dipped one of the cloths into the steaming kettle, then she wringed it out and began to gently wash Thomas. First his forehead around his ears, then his gristly cheeks and neck trying not to scrub too hard. She began to hum, and Thomas thought conversation might help get him through this a little quicker – though it wasn't as bad as he thought it was going to be. He breathed deeply through his nose and enjoyed the lilac smell of his nurse. A bit distracted, he caught his wits and posed, "Now maybe you can tell me where my mother and father are?"

"I need to lift your night shirt up," was her reply. She began to scrub his hands while lifting each arm in turn. It saddened her to see how frail he was. She had lifted his arms and legs several times a day to keep his muscles from atrophying too much, but she couldn't help his body much with nutrition and when someone lays in the bed that long, getting up again is nearly impossible.

"Why am I so weak?" he asked nervously.

"Mr. Thomas, you were injured in Sharpsburg, and you've been in this bed for a while recovering." She lifted his shirt and slowly washed his chest in a circular motion which caused him to cough again. This time more than just a little blood came up and she used the cloth to wipe his mouth and cheek and then turned him on his side.

"I'm sorry, Gracie," he said with despair in his voice.

"You never mind that sir – it's part of getting well." She grabbed the clean drying cloth, soaked it quickly and scrubbed his backside and shoulders then gently lowered him onto his back again. She pulled the sheet down to his knees so she could continue.

"I don't know about this part, Gracie," Thomas complained.

"Mr. Thomas, I've really seen everything, and I've been giving you baths for a longer time than I can remember - this is no different than any other day - except you is awake now," Gracie looked into his eyes, smiled, and continued washing.

If Thomas could have lifted his own arm, he may have placed his hand on her cheek. Instead, he lay still, mostly because he didn't have any choice. She really was an angel he thought to himself, but the thought quickly escaped him when he realized just how confined to this bed he really was.

"Can you feel me touching this part of your leg" she asked.

Thomas replied, "Just barely - it feels like somebody's running a feather up and down my leg."

"I'm going to put another pillow and sheet under your head because I think you need to see something, and so we can talk about what we are going to do about it together." Gracie propped him so he was slightly angled looking down the bed at the sheet covering his lower legs. Something was wrong and he hadn't quite figured out what it was yet.

"I don't want you to be surprised by this when I'm not here with you so I'm going to show you something," she looked into his blue eyes with sweet compassion, but the anxiety didn't even begin to wash out of him. "We will handle this," she said.

She rolled the blanket and sheet down to expose his left leg which was completely bandaged from his knee down over his foot and to the extent of his upturned toes. "OK," he said. Then Gracie slowly rolled the blanket down over his right leg, but she didn't pull it down to his toes. She didn't need to. His right leg was gone from the knee down. He closed his eyes and let out a short but audible whimper as a tear rolled down his cheek. Gracie never saw Thomas cry again – well almost never.

"I need to change the bandages, Mr. Thomas. Your wounds have healed for the most part but I'm keeping them covered to make sure you can't get a fever in them," she began to slowly unravel the bandages from his legs and then she placed them with the cloths to be washed. She didn't have too many extra supplies just laying around this giant house.

Thomas lay still with his eyes closed while she gently wrapped him in clean bandages and rolled the wool blanket back up around his chin, leaving his arms exposed by his sides. The small tear had dried on his cheek and part of him – a huge part of him – just wanted to roll over and die.

"Well, no wonder my parents don't want to see me, I'm useless to everyone now," he said.

"Guess what, Mr. Thomas? You are alive and awake now and that's all that matters. There's plenty to tell you, and all will be said. But right now, I think you need to get some rest, so I'm going to go and prepare you something to eat, and I'll be back directly. Gracie picked up the cooling kettle, threw the cloths and bandages inside, and made her way to the door.

Thomas mustered the courage to speak. "Thank you, Gracie," he said as she turned to look at him with a gentle smile – her silky hair bounced around her perfect face. "By the way, you look so very young – how old are you?"

"I'm fairly certain that I am nineteen now" she giggled. "I think so, anyway."

"Well, that's a good age," Thomas said. "I've only just turned twenty-one myself, you know?"

Gracie smiled and looked long and hard at him with a wrinkled brow. She started to leave the room then she stopped and looked back at him again. "There are so many things I need to tell you Mr. Thomas," she started. "I feel so bad about being the one who had to tell you about your leg, and there are many more things you must know that are not going to make you feel any better." Gracie glanced to the floor "I know you just told me that you've just turned twenty-one, but one thing I need you to know now is that you're actually twenty-two now."

Thomas listened as she walked down the hall towards the kitchen and then he slowly closed his eyes again, but he didn't sleep. He couldn't let the war come back for him again – not right now. Spring was coming and he had work to do. He had to get out of this bed...and how the hell was he twenty-two?

# 6

Emmaline Foster had walked this road many times over the last two months. She walked it rain or shine, night and day. She put up with the racist jeers, the trash throwing, and the people going out of their way to hit puddles so she would be soaked and muddied to the core. It was impossible to get far enough from the edge because both sides sloped quickly into a drop off, so she had learned to deal with the puddle splashers by timing her strides so as not to be a target. It wasn't everyone, in fact it wasn't most of them, it was just a few angry people who had a big problem with her going to the University of Virginia. Most of the time she felt like she didn't actually attend the school – she wasn't allowed in the regular classrooms, dormitories, or the library, and her classes were held separately in the basement of the university hospital. When she was doing rotations in the hospital many white folks didn't want her in their room, and they definitely didn't want her to touch them.

Richard Johnson was the man Emmie and Natalie called Mr. Richard. Mr. Richard grew up with Emmie's father during the Great Depression in the city of Richmond, more notably in the area north of Broad Street. The area was rife with poverty and sporadic violence as segregation and Jim Crow laws took their toll on the Colored people there, but for the most part it was just an area where families tried to do better for their children. When Richard and Emmie's father, Anthony Foster, returned from the war they both got married, Richard to his high school sweetheart, and Anthony to Emmie's mother, who he met at the Colored USO. They both located their families in Church Hill, where the white population had begun to flee the city for the suburbs. Richard had been a cook in the army, so when he came back home his natural inclination was to open a restaurant. *Dickie's Smoke Shack* was a huge hit in the 1950's and Richard became quite successful cooking Barbecue for the fast-growing Colored population around Church Hill. He left his restaurant in the hands of his younger brother in 1959, and moved to Charlottesville to get his family out of the city, and as he told Anthony, "them rich white kids up that way love to spend their daddy's money." He also said, "they don't mind us cooking for them, they just don't want to eat with us." Richard had convinced Emmaline's father that he would keep an eye on her and keep her safe while she went to nursing school at UVA. So, she came to live and work at *Tailpipes.* Emmie worked there, studied there, and lived there, and it was as comfortable as it could afford - except the heater was still broken.

This was a typical morning in November for Charlottesville, the sky was overcast, and it was spitting a slight cold drizzle into the forty degree air. The only thing unexpected about this morning came jogging down her side of West Main Avenue wearing UVA shorts, a UVA sweatshirt and a pair of high-top Converse that were supposed to be white but were covered in orange mud. As they approached one another, and he realized who she was, he slowed down, and a broad grin spread across his face. Then he leaned his hands on his knees to gather a quick breath as he came to a stop in front of her. "Good morning to my beautiful Emmie," he declared between puffs of breath. "How are you on this fine morning?"

"First of all, it's raining on this fine morning, and secondly I told you my friends call me Emmie, and I barely know you." She kept walking but Luke turned and joined the quick pace alongside her toward the school.

"So, what are you studying?" He asked.

"You already know I'm in the Nursing School," Emmie kept looking at the ground in front of her thinking she'd dare not make contact with those blue eyes.

"Well, that's certainly an honorable profession," said Luke. "There's definitely a great need for caring nurses right now especially with things flaring up in Southeast Asia."

"Look Mr. Montgomery, I'm not trying to be rude, but I really don't think you and I should be having any small talk. I have so much work to do and I certainly don't need to help foster your misguided contact with me into some sort of a campus scandal. There is nothing in common about us." Emmie was trying to be stern, but it wasn't sounding that way to Luke.

"Of course, we have something in common." he said. "I'm always there to come to your rescue when you need it most."

"I certainly don't need your rescuing on a daily basis," she said.

They walked on towards the school in silence for a few minutes and Luke started to trail behind. Emmie thought he was sulking – or maybe he wanted her to think that he felt rejected. It made her so frustrated, so she turned and stopped him in his tracks and said, "Look you're the star of the basketball team, everyone knows who you are, and you don't need to be seen walking around campus with the likes of me – that's the way rumors are started, and it will end badly for me."

"I like walking with you, and talking with you," said Luke in an almost catatonic tone. She turned around and he shuffled along behind her before she stopped and turned again.

"Why are you out here on this road this morning? Don't you have basketball practice, or weightlifting or something else every morning?" she turned around and walked on.

"The coach had some family emergency and had to go to Maryland for a couple days. Jesus, I'm just doing my best to stay in shape while he's gone. Don't overthink this please."

"We are almost to campus, and I think we need to distance ourselves before we get there," Emmie said without looking back.

"I have to get back to the dorm and get cleaned up for class anyway," Luke said. "But I don't really know what your problem is."

Now she was angry. She stopped, turned around and started walking straight at him so fast he almost tripped over backwards. "Here's the problem, you can go back to your dorm, and you can change your clothes, and comb your hair, and you can come back outside feeling like a different person, but I am always the same person, I can't change anything about me or who I am, and I certainly can't change the color of my skin."

"And therein lies my problem Emmaline," he said softly. "Not only would I never ask you to change anything about yourself, but I'd be mad as hell if you did."

Emmie stood quietly for a moment looking into his eyes – those eyes, "I can't do this with you Mr. Montgomery, please just keep your distance. I'm begging you to." She turned and walked in the direction of the hospital.

Luke started back towards the dormitories and glanced back at her once just to see the back of her sweater as she headed up the hill. He turned back and smiled – and thought – "She likes me..."

# 

The Spring morning was warming nicely, and the last snow melt of the Winter was well underway. Gracie strolled into Thomas' room with a tray filled with bowls and teacups, placed it on the bedside table, and walked to the window where she threw back the gray curtains as the bright morning sunlight created prisms across the wall and onto the ceiling twelve feet above. Smoky steam evaporated away from the frosted panes and curled slowly upward and out into the courtyard before disappearing. She turned back to Thomas as he was grumbling awake and complaining about the light, but she cut him off before things went negative, "I've got us some porridge and toast to go with the fresh milk that I had in the well overnight, so it's nice and cold."

"When I get out of this confinement, I will see to getting us some fresh game," Thomas was getting better at propping himself up to eat. "My back is killing me!" he added as he pushed his head back against the headboard.

"We only have the one rooster, but we have ten hens, and they are setting pretty well – I'm expecting some additions to the flock soon so I can probably cull a hen too," Gracie placed his bowl of porridge next to him on the bed and he took a firm grip of the spoon to feed himself. "Feeling a might spry this morning Mr. Thomas - maybe some poached eggs for lunch. I can tell you are feeling better because your complaints are louder now," she smiled and took a sip of milk.

Gracie placed the cup back into the saucer and smiled at him with a white milk mustache which she quickly wiped on her apron. Her beautiful eyes worked to melt him just like the frost on the windowpanes was subdued by the new fuel in the fireplace. Her long silky black hair shimmered down her gray dress almost to her white apron. It took everything Thomas had to press her for more understanding of what had transpired while he was out cold. "So, your last comment to me last night didn't make any sense at all – I am twenty-one years old." Thomas mustered a little more courage and asked "where are my parents? Where is Samuel? Where is Elizabeth? And... Who are you and how did you come to be here?"

Gracie pulled herself closer to the bed and took the bowl from Thomas who was beginning to make a mess trying to eat while lying on his side. "First, let me help you with this. Second, those are all fair questions." Gracie gave him a spoonful of the porridge and wiped his lips with her apron, "Probably best if you know who I am before anything else is told."

Gracie crossed her hands and placed them in her lap and started to speak. "From what I recollect, and gathering from what your mother told me, your father came to my last farm in Roanoke a few days after you boys left to go off and fight. My master, Mr. Connally, he didn't have any food and no crops to speak of, so your father traded him a side of smoked beef, a few sacks of flour, some sugar, and a couple of guns for me and two others. He chained us in the back of a buckboard and brought us back here. The other two – I didn't really know them - they ran off within a couple of days, but I didn't have anywhere that I knew of to go to, so I stayed, and I was here about three weeks before the ladies brought you and your brothers back home."

"I have an uncle, David Connally who lives in Roanoke," said Thomas.

"Yes, I think it's the same man," she said.

"I saw you writing in a journal earlier, when you thought I was asleep – how do you know how to read and write so well?" Thomas was changing the direction of the conversation.

Gracie filled his mouth with a crust of bread. "I'll get there," she said. "My mother was a slave in Upper Maryland and there used to be a young Iroquois man who would come to the plantation where she lived. Mrs. Henry, that was the plantation owner's wife, she put my mother in charge of dealing with this man for household goods like linens, cast iron pots, flour and sugar – kitchen things. She oversaw making trades for everyday household items. She traded smoked pork and lamb to this man for a long time and he kept coming around to see my mother more often, and they found themselves in love. When Mr. Henry found out she was with child he had the Iroquois man hung from an oak on the plantation. That man was my father." Thomas started to speak so she put another spoonful of the hardening porridge in his mouth.

"My mother died giving birth to me and Mrs. Henry was so angry about the hanging and my mother's death that she demanded to raise me inside the house, even though she had just had a baby girl of her own. I was raised alongside Abigail Henry, and I even called Mrs. Henry "Mother". We did all the same things. We learned to read and write and draw. We learned poetry and even the piano. We learned etiquette and how to be a proper Northern lady. Until Abigail got sick when we were about twelve years old. She was taken away from me and held in an upstairs bedroom for a long while – years even. I would climb up the rose trellis and see her in her bed through the window. Then one morning she was gone. I went to Mother to try and console her, but she pushed me away and said I wasn't her daughter anymore. I stayed hidden in my room for a long while, and then I stayed around the ladies who worked in the kitchen. They taught me to cook, but they also taught me that I was really born a slave and shouldn't be thinking that I would ever be more than that again. One morning Mr. Henry had come back from an early morning ride, and he went upstairs only to come back down screaming and hollering and out the door he went. The other ladies wouldn't let me go upstairs but I watched them as they brought Mother's body down and she went off to the undertaker just like Abigail had done. One of the outside boys told me she had hung herself up there. Mr. Henry went to drinking all the time and one day he just decided to give up too – so he drank on the porch all day and night for weeks until he just decided to put a pistol in his mouth one morning. So, Mr. Connally came and bought all the slaves at auction, including myself, and I was brought to Roanoke, and Mrs. Connally, well she brought me inside the house to clean up and serve food to the family." Gracie was crying now as she dredged up her past for Thomas. It seemed like a story she had needed to get out for a long time but never had been given the opportunity.

"So, that's' how you ended up with my horrible uncle," Thomas stated as he tried unsuccessfully to pull himself up more. He winced in pain.

"Maybe I should go get us the whiskey bottle Mr. Thomas," Gracie sniffled and wiped her face on the overly used apron. "I can pinch off some birchbark for you to chew on for the pain too – I wish I could get you some morphine, but I don't know how," her voice was labored.

Thomas reached out and held her hand gently in his. "Just breathe Gracie - just breathe. We can talk more later."

Gracie didn't let go of his hand, but she shifted in the chair and continued. "Mr. Connally, your uncle, he was a cruel man. He never touched me, but I saw him whip others for no other reason than he thought they shouldn't be tired after fourteen hours in the field. Mrs. Connally, she found out I knew how to cook, and she brought me in the kitchen. But, they didn't have much food and she was always angry that we couldn't seem to put a proper meal out. I spilt some sugar once and she slapped me so hard across the face that I couldn't stand back up for a good long while."

"So, your father, Dewey, he came on the buckboard, and he traded Mr. Connally for the three of us. Mrs. Connally protested that she was going to have to work, but her husband yelled something about her either working or starving and she shut right up. We left Roanoke late one morning and we spent the night chained to the wagon before getting here late the next day. I saw the kindness in your mother's eyes as we were unloaded, so when she asked me what I knew I told her all about my work in the kitchens and cleaning the house. She said she would give me a try, but I still had to stay out in one of those little houses out back, so they told Samuel's wife Margaret to show me where to go. I got a small room with a straw cot and a door to both Ms. Margaret's room and the outside so I could go to the bathroom and not wake anyone. Margaret told me "You are a girl of age, so you need to have a little privacy is all," Gracie took a deep breath and squeezed Thomas' hand. "A few weeks later those ladies dressed in white showed up with you and your brothers in the back of a wagon…the smell had me covering my face and turning away. I looked back to see Samuel carrying you inside the house and into this front bedroom. Then they pulled the wagon to the barn and unloaded what I soon learned was your brother's bodies."

Thomas was clearly growing tired of trying to keep himself propped so he lowered his head back to the pillow. "Can we continue later if you don't mind," he said. "I'm not feeling well and need to close my eyes just a bit." Thomas was dizzy with fear more than anything else because he could almost feel how bad things must have gotten at Waverly.

"It's fine Mr. Thomas, this is a long story and most of it is not so good," Gracie raised the blanket to his shoulders. "Don't need your lungs catching a chill."

Thomas turned his head toward the window where the shadows were moving across as the sun began to move behind the house. "Have you seen Elizabeth?" he asked while staring blankly away from her.

"Not very many folks have been up to the house since I've been here. The doctor and his nurse, a man selling some bonds or something…your mother threatened to shoot him, and he ran down the road – "

"No, Gracie, this would have been a woman about my age." Thomas turned to look at her now.

"The girl with the golden hair…she was so beautiful," Gracie said this slowly as if to soften the blow that she was about to deliver.

"That sounds right," Thomas said.

"She came here a few days after you came home. She was dressed in a beautiful blue smock and her long golden hair was braided down her back and had a large white bow at the bottom...she had some flowers – daisies I think."

"Her favorite to pick from the pastures," Thomas listened on.

"She sat on the bed next to you for a while and she just cried and wiped her eyes on a handkerchief while your mother sat next to her. Your father stood outside smoking with another man – her father maybe," Gracie breathed deeply and sighed. "Then Mr. Thomas, she got up and went outside and dropped the flowers on the ground and headed down the hill. The man went after her in his carriage." She paused and then added, "I never seen her again."

"I need to send for her and tell her I'm awake," Thomas said in a low voice.

"Mr. Thomas, most people around here have either run North or fled South...there's too much fighting close by."

"How long ago was she here?"

"It was Autumn before last," Gracie put her hand on his shoulder.

"You have to be lying to me."

"I don't have any reason to lie Mr. Thomas," she said, "I'm stuck here just the way you are."

"You can go...I give you your freedom," Thomas was beginning to show beaded sweat on his forehead.

"Where would I go from here? I have nothing, nobody, and nowhere to go," Gracie wiped his forehead. "You need to rest."

"My God! How much time have I lost?" Thomas was growing more agitated.

"Mr. Thomas you've been awake from time to time and even had your eyes open, but always staring like you weren't seeing anything. Everyone finally decided that you were never coming back," she said.

"So, they just left me?"

"Weren't that simple." Gracie rose to her feet. "I'm going to let you rest now."

"What about my mother then?"

"I made her a promise after she saved my life," Gracie moved toward the door.

"To take care of me after I awoke?" Thomas asked.

"To bury you...after you died."

# 8

Election days played an important role in the lives of the students at the University of Virginia because Charlottesville was thought by some to be the birthplace of The Republic with the ghosts of Thomas Jefferson, James Monroe, and James Madison lurking about. Each had built magnificent estates in the area in the early 1800s as the school was being formed. There were no classes on Election Day, but there were plenty of students milling about on the mall and around the quad. There were tables set up everywhere covered with pins and posters for every candidate up for re-election or replacement. On the edge of the hill along West Main many of the exhibitors were set up to debate and inform on crucial topics of the day. One table had members of the Young Republicans protesting the Cuban Missile Crisis and the Cold War with the Soviet Union. Another protested flaring tensions in Southeast Asia, an area shortly removed from the Korean War where almost 36,000 Americans had lost their lives. Wesley Sharpe, a colored second year law student at UVA, was setting up a table to bring light to the racial injustice facing his world. Wes had borrowed a small folding table from the Johnsons, the colored family he lived with on the other end of town five miles from campus. He had prepared a hand drawn poster asking for donations and the signing of a petition to bring the Reverend Martin Luther King Jr. to campus to speak with students. Luke Montgomery was sitting on a blanket on the lawn enjoying an impromptu picnic with Caroline and her friends when he glanced up the hill toward Wesley's table and noticed that Emmaline Foster was helping him set things up. "Be right back," Luke said to the girls who paid him no attention as he headed up the path.

"Good morning, Emmie – how are you this morning?" Luke said sarcastically as Emmaline turned, saw him, and offered an overly obvious eyeroll.

Wesley raised his eyes from the table and said, "Wow! Mr. Montgomery, to what do we owe the pleasure of your presence? Huge fan – love to listen to the games on the school radio station. I wish I could handle the roundball like you."

"Come now, Wesley Sharpe," Emmie tried to prop him up. "You've got skills in your own right."

"So, tell me what you guys have going on here," Luke said.

Wesley stood proudly, "It's time for our rights to be the same rights as all men. It's time our voices were heard, and our suffering came to an end. Will you sign our petition?"

Luke looked around nervously, "I agree with everything you are standing up for, but I don't think I'd better put my name on that list – I'm on full scholarship you know."

"I understand – you can't be associated with our civil disobedience," said Wesley with a sarcastic grin. "You know, like getting signatures and trying to raise some expenses to bring the most important man of our lifetime to visit us with his message."

Luke ignored the not so covert hint of Wesley's sarcasm, "What are you studying here Mr. Sharpe?"

"I'm a second-year law student hoping to graduate next year and sit for the Bar. I'm planning to make waves in Washington." Wes straightened his clipboard and placed the pen in perfect alignment for the first signee.

"Is there something else you need then, Mr. Montgomery?" Emmie interrupted.

"No. It's just now that we are such close friends, I thought I would say hello, Emmie," Luke laughed and backed up a couple of steps, knowing she was going to come out swinging.

She was gentle in front of Wesley though, "I think you are more than well aware of my thoughts on that," she said.

Luke retaliated with his failing wit, "It's a darn good thing you're a law student Wesley - Emmaline here is a tough case to crack."

Wesley laughed, "I have always loved a good challenge."

Emmaline made eye contact with each man individually before bringing both down to earth, "Stop acting like I'm some kind of prize to be won, because neither of you are in the game."

"So, what you are saying is that I can sign up to be a participant?" Luke said.

"There's not even much of a chance that we will be friends," she said.

"But, there is a remote possibility?"

"Mr. Montgomery, I think you should go back to your friends now," Wesley imparted with an underlying tone of jealousy. "I'll ask you again before you go if you may sign our petition. What do you really think of our civil rights?"

Luke paused and then said thoughtfully, "My father always taught me that every man is flesh and bone, puts his pants on one leg at a time, and bleeds red. I think every man deserves to be treated the same, no matter the day - no matter the cost."

"I think your father is a wise man," said Wesley, "But not every man on the Virginia campus is as agreeable as Luke Montgomery."

Emmaline had just stood up from taping their poster when an egg struck the edge of the table and splattered upward and all over her blouse. Luke turned around quickly, "What the hell!" he yelled as three boys ran along the edge of the ridgeline and into the closest dormitory door.

"I'm really sorry about those jerks! I'll find them." Luke started toward the dorms then came back to the table, "It takes all kinds to screw up this world."

"Relax Luke it's not something we don't see every day out here," Emmaline offered, "we are on the outside of our fence, and it scares people."

Wesley pulled out his handkerchief and began wiping off the poster and his clipboard. Emmie was staring down at her blouse as the bits of shell and egg began to roll down the front in an effort to drip onto her shoes. There was a small blob of yolk on her cheek. Luke wiped it off with his finger and she looked into his deep blue eyes again. She had to stop doing this, she thought.

"This time you are getting my shirt," he said as he slipped off his UVA sweatshirt and handed it to her. He wore a white cotton tee underneath. She started to wipe her blouse and he said, "no, I have something else for that," as he pulled out his handkerchief and handed it to her.

Then Luke said, "You put the sweatshirt on over that and wear it home and you can just give it back to me the next time I see you at the drive-in,"

Emmaline looked at him and smiled like she was really seeing him for the first time, and it took a short awkward pause for her to come up with, "Thank you, Luke. When I return home, I will wash it for you and give it back to you when I see you at TailPipes later."

"Yes, that's what I said, Emmie. It's OK."

Luke turned to go back down the hill and then paused. Turning around he said. "You and I aren't really that much different. I know what it's like to be persecuted and looked down upon. These people here see me as their basketball star, but none of them really know me, they don't know where I really come from – I don't let them see that side of my world. You and Wes are so brave while I hide my past and my life away from here - because I don't want to be treated differently. Good luck in pursuing your goals – I support you," Luke reached down, picked up the pen, and signed his name at the first position on the form. "Watch this," he said and went back down the hill.

Emmaline watched as Luke reached Caroline and her friends. They had been giggling about the egging incident. He talked to them for several minutes out of Emmie's earshot but what happened next was nothing short of a 1962 miracle. The girls filed up the path to the table and one by one they signed the petition - line after line below Luke's name. Luke went to another group and another, and word of mouth took over and Wes and Emmie's petition was signed again and again below Luke's signature. When he got to the edge of the quad near the library, he looked back up the hill and saw Emmie smiling at him from ear-to-ear.

He walked into the library muttering to himself…" My God, she's so beautiful."

# 9

Two weeks after Thomas Summerlin came back from his 18-month ordeal, he started waking up in the middle of the night covered in sweat and screaming at the top of his lungs. Gracie had already been moved into a room directly across the hall from Thomas by his mother over a year earlier. It wasn't really a bedroom – Mrs. Summerlin called it a Butler's Pantry. When Thomas' night terrors came, Gracie would go to him and warm up a teacup full of milk for him to sip while she toweled him off with a cold cloth. She often found herself sitting on the bed next to him holding his hand like a small child while he drifted back off to sleep. Many times, he would be barely lucid, so Gracie would kneel on the floor by the bed while wiping his brow for over an hour. Whatever he had witnessed in Sharpsburg on Antietam Creek would be something that would haunt him for the rest of his life. This night was different – Thomas was trying to sit up in the bed with his eyes wide open calling for his brothers Dewey, Stephen, and John. Gracie lifted him hard under his shoulders and got him into a seated position with his back against the burled walnut headboard of his three-quarter bed. His eyes were wide open, and he clearly recognized her because he said, "Where are they? Where are my brothers, Gracie? What have you done to them?"

He started to slump toward her, but she pushed him back up and put pillows on both sides of him to keep him from rolling out of the bed. Again, he asked for his brothers as she calmly tried to wipe his forehead. Tears were rolling down her cheeks. Gracie hated this delirium – it frightened her to her soul. "My God, just tell me!" he said.

"Mr. Thomas, I've told you – you are safe at home in your bed," she repeated the story of how the wagon with the ladies in white came to the house and Samuel carried him in and took his bothers to the barn, only this time she added, "It was a horrible time, Mr. Thomas, we buried those two boys under the oak up on the hill with all the others who went before."

"Oh. My God." Thomas was whimpering now and seemed to be coming awake. "I saw them again - Dewey dead behind me, and Stephen lying next to me in the field. I think they are all dreams, but then I'm up and you are here, and I remember it all – all of it!"

Gracie realized he was fully awake, so she poured him some whiskey. "No sir, Mr. Thomas, those aren't dreams – they are memories. That was a terrible day for Waverly."

"Did you see them – I mean after they were unloaded." Thomas was shaking as he sipped from the glass.

"There wasn't anything really to look at Mr. Thomas, they were wrapped up in thick wool blankets and tied with rope in three places. They lay dead on the field for days and were mostly unrecognizable." Gracie sighed. She needed a good night's rest.

"How – how do they know it was them?" Thomas slowed his breathing.

"I remember the wagon pulling up and your mother collapsing on the ground. Your father bloodied his hand on the fence post. And, the smell, the smell was awful – it was the smell of death and it's all over the mountains now. I think many are used to it, but when I hear the train coming South through the hollow, I close the windows because the smell of the dead drifts up from the river and sometimes it lingers here. I bring in fresh flowers if they are growing, and sometimes I burn a fire even in the summer heat. Thomas closed his eyes and fought back tears. She wiped his brow again. "You want me to heat some milk, Mr. Thomas?"

"No, how about one more of those," he pointed to the bottle. "And pour yourself one."

Gracie did as she was told and poured out two small glasses. Thomas raised his glass and held it toward Gracie. She picked hers up and clinked it against his. "To my brothers," he said.

Gracie threw back the whiskey and winced with a shudder. "Something tells me this horrible substance doesn't touch your lips too often." Thomas smiled slightly.

"Only when it is so cold, I can't feel my toes, Mr. Thomas."

Thomas closed his eyes for a few moments and his breathing slowed as he started to doze. Gracie stared at him for a good long while as he slept. Two days earlier she had fully removed the bandage from his head, noticing that while his golden hair had started to grow back, she could still see the edge of the deep scar running from his forehead inward to the top of his skull. She thought about what he would look like once the scar was completely concealed by his beautiful hair, and she smiled. A few birds had started to chirp outside, and she was fairly certain she heard that damned rooster crowing in the root cellar. Welcoming sounds that meant Spring was here and she could plant some corn, beans, and tomatoes soon. She had done some canning with some old mason jars she found in the cellar, but she had almost run through all of those.

She also wondered if Thomas would ever really be ready to eat anything more than what she was feeding him. She lowered the sheet to his waist and pulled up his nightshirt to reveal the scars across his stomach. She remembered the day he came home, and Dr. Draper had come to the house and sown him up much better than the way the ladies had delivered him. The doctor had said "well, this part works better on the inside than the outside," and then he talked of infections, and fevers and things not working as intended anymore.

Gracie noticed the light was growing in the window, so she started to think about what she needed to get accomplished for the day. She covered Thomas back up with the blanket, pulled it up to his chin, and gathered the items to put back on the kitchen tray. She stood up, smoothed down her nightdress, picked up the tray and started out.

"Gracie?" came from behind her.

"Good morning, Mr. Thomas,"

"If they were wrapped up like that, how could you be sure it was them?"

"Your mother came up to the back of the wagon after she was able to stand again. She undid the middle rope on first one then the other. Then she put her hand inside and she felt around until she pulled out a scrap of paper from each body. Then she collapsed again. Samuel told me later that she had written each of you boys' names on a piece of paper and stuck them deep into each of your coat pockets the night before you left. She had a feeling it was the only way she would ever find you again." Gracie started tearing up again, so she walked out of the room.

Thomas listened as she walked to the kitchen - then her footsteps stopped. Then he heard the tray hit the floor and the glasses shatter. Then he heard Gracie's raised voice…

"Who is you! Why's you in dis' house! You's got ta go! My massa' gone be some'pin angry you in heh!"

# 10

There was no bonfire that Thursday night and Luke had told Caroline that he needed to do some serious studying, so he was going straight back to the dorm after practice. He headed for the dorms all right, but walked straight past them and turned right on West Main Street just as the last glimpse of daylight was sinking below the horizon in front of him. Luke started a light jog toward the drive-in as the cool night air filled him with energy, but it was his adrenaline that had him sweating before he reached the halfway point. He just kept kicking, after all he was the starting point guard for the Virginia Cavaliers and running two miles was nothing to him - so why was he getting so winded. Still as he reached the parking lot he had to stop for a moment and lean over with his hands on his knees, breathing deeply for almost a full minute. "What the hell?" he muttered under his breath – breath which was coming out in huge quickly dissipating clouds as he exhaled into the chilly night.

The parking lot was already filled with cars and kids, with varying songs blending unharmoniously from all different directions. "Good Lord, why can't just they install some speakers in the parking lot and pump music out of a jukebox?" he thought to himself for the twentieth time. Luke longed for the quieter times of his hometown as he slipped between two lines of cars and headed towards the back of the restaurant - and Emmaline. He heard his name once or twice, but he kept walking. He glanced up at the big clock which said 6:50 as he reached the back door of the kitchen, and after about twenty-five minutes of waiting he began to realize his run from campus may have been for nothing. Finally, Emmaline came out the back door, pulling away a hairnet and shaking her head to allow her beautiful black hair to flow over her shoulders and down toward her waist. She quickly untied her apron and pulled it away into a ball. She looked up and he thought she was immediately flustered. "Oh gosh, I'm sorry. I forgot you were coming tonight," she lied.

"It's OK – I was already here with some friends and remembered the sweatshirt," Luke returned the favor. "I think I caught you trying to look your best for me," he laughed.

"Fat chance of that," she said. "Just let me go get your sweatshirt from the backhouse."

"Sure thing," he said, as he followed her towards the small shack that she shared with Natalie.

Emmie opened the door and went inside while Luke tried his best to strike a nonchalant pose on the threshold. Peering inside he saw Natalie sitting at a small table with her books spread out in front of her. She had apparently taken the night off early again to do her studying, leaving poor Emmie to do extra work for Mr. Richard. "I have your shirt right here, Mr. Montgomery," she said as she picked up the folded gray shirt from the edge of the small table.

She walked back toward the door…and Luke. Then Natalie decided to throw in her two cents. "Mr. Montgomery," she said sheepishly, "You may want to wash that – you see our friend Emmaline has been sleeping in it for the past three nights."

"Nothing could be further from the truth," said Emmaline.

"Come on, Emmie-pie," Natalie giggled and flipped her pencil in the air.

Emmie looked Luke directly in the eyes – those deep blue eyes - he had such beautiful eyes and for a moment she got lost in them, but then she defended herself, "Yes, I did sleep in your shirt, but we don't have any heat, and it's freezing in here."

"Oh, Mr. Richard said the guys were coming to fix it in a few days, so you can give up the nightshirt," Natalie said. "Hopefully they'll get it fixed in time for the real winter weather."

"Well thanks for the shirt back," Luke said, "but in all honesty I'd rather you just keep it if you're cold, Emmaline."

Emmie looked toward the floor, "It's your shirt and there's no reason for you not to have it for the cold – I'll make do just fine."

"I have several just like this one – kind of a perk for playing basketball, and to be honest with you I wouldn't have missed it, so why don't you just keep it." Luke and Emmie both had a hand on the shirt in question.

"Yeah, Emmie, just keep it so you can sleep in it every single night and never wash it," said Natalie, and she laughed louder this time.

Luke feebly tried changing the subject, "Why do you guys live here again?" he said uncomfortably.

Emmie seemed more than just a little perturbed by this. "Do you really not know? Or are you just trying to be a horse's ass?"

"I do love horses."

"You know we can't stay in the dormitory - just as much as you also know that we don't go into the real classrooms, and our classes are held in the basement of the hospital," Emmie seemed ready for him to leave so he stepped back out into the night. "You shouldn't come here again."

Luke looked at her honestly and said, "I guess I should've known that, but I'm usually just too self-absorbed with my own world to see what's going on around me."

"Well, that's pretty much how most of you rich white boys are, isn't it?" Emmie said as she put one hand on the door to close it.

Luke started to respond. He wanted to tell her everything about himself - where he came from and how he got here, but he thought it would be better to save it for another time. "It's OK, Emmie," he said, "I wanted you to have the sweatshirt and I really just came here to see you again."

Emmie made the mistake of looking up at him again and once their eyes were locked it seemed very difficult to avert her gaze, "It's OK if we're friends, Luke, but you know we can't be anything more than that - ever." She wondered if she sounded a little sad when she said it.

"I'm not one to listen to people when they try to tell me what I can and can't do," Luke said with somewhat confidence.

"You know why we can only be friends, and besides, we shouldn't even really be seen together too much, or people will talk." Emmie clutched the sweatshirt with no intention of giving it back now.

"I don't care what people say," Luke said.

Emmie looked at him and tried to be as stern as she could muster, "You will care if it affects your reputation, and your standing at the school, won't you?"

Luke shrugged his shoulders and decided he was content to continue this fight another day, when she said, “I’m seeing Wesley anyway.”

“Oh, you mean the hero that was more concerned about his poster than your clothes and your face?”

“He’s very dedicated to our cause and that’s what I really like about him.”

Luke struggled for words now, “Okay, well I guess I should head back to school. Enjoy the sweatshirt, Emmaline. I hope it keeps you warm - you don’t deserve too ever be cold.”

Luke didn’t want to stop staring into her eyes, but she slowly closed the door in his face anyway. Then she turned around to face Natalie and slumped with her back against the door clutching the UVA shirt to her chest.

“Why did you lie to that boy?” Natalie asked.

“You know exactly why,” was the only response she had.

# 11

"Are you John Summerlin?" the first grey coated intruder asked Thomas.

"What if I am? You gonna charge me and my half a leg with desertion and hang me from that big oak out front? Thomas groaned as he pushed himself up to sit on the edge of the bed.

"I just asked a simple question sir. My name is Corporal Wagner. I'm with the 1st Virginia Brigade under the command of General Jackson."

"My family has given enough – two of my brothers are dead and buried outside and I will never walk again." Thomas reached for the whiskey bottle that sat on the side table. He pulled out the cork and took a deep drink.

Gracie was seated on the floor next to the now dying fire. The three men seemed to be struggling to figure out what to ask next. When the corporal came up with, "Where the hell is everybody else? There's four slave houses out front and one laying in ruins." He turned toward Gracie. "Got any answers girl?"

"No sah, I doesn't," she lowered her head and put her hands in her lap.

"Leave her be! She's nothing but a house maid and she ain't worth your time or mine," Thomas cleared his throat and felt a rush of blood which he swallowed back with another shot from the bottle.

"Dr. Draper told us you have been delusional for the past fifteen months or more – that is if you are indeed Thomas

Summerlin," the two rebels with the corporal stood uneasy with their hands on their sidearms.

"We were in the first group to be hit at Sharpsburg and were left with the Georgia regiment to slow the Yanks from crossing the bridge over Antietam Creek – so Lee could run west." Thomas took a deep breath and felt the cold hand of pain squeeze his lungs until he almost stopped breathing. "I'm Thomas Summerlin," he said slowly, "That's my coat hanging there – in the pocket you will find a slip of paper where my mother wrote my name so my body could be identified on the field. I guess my brothers got the easy way out."

"I'm from the University Battalion from Charlottesville, sir," said one of the boys with the corporal.

"You should have stayed in school," Thomas said.

Corporal Wagner retrieved the slip of paper from Thomas' coat pocket and read it aloud.

***Thomas Warren Summerlin of Waverly***
***Plantation***
***Born December 3rd in the Year of Our Lord 1840***
***Please return him home to his mother no matter***
***Pulaski County Virginia***
***Reward***

"Have you seen him?" he asked.

"I've only been awake for a few – "

"Not you, you." He pointed at Gracie who began to shake.

"Why are you after my brother so hard? Isn't there a war still going on?" Thomas diverted the attention back to himself.

"Sir, your brother was seen running Northward into Maryland while the rest of the Georgia boys turned West to follow Lee. The next day our forces were hit hard from two sides and hundreds of our boys died. Your brother was then seen six months later near Roanoke riding in a wagon with a woman and two children just before our boys were ambushed near Malvern Hill outside of Richmond. We believe he is acting as a Union spy and he's suspected of murder," Corporal Wagner walked slowly across the room to where Gracie was lying on the floor.

"My brother didn't have a wife, and certainly no children. You are mistaken" Thomas tried again to slow the Corporal. "How do you know it was him?"

"Your Uncle, David Connally, reported seeing him in town getting supplies – then heading West." The corporal turned back to Gracie who was rocking back and forth holding her knees."

"Alright, girl, he was asleep, so you are going to tell us where John Summerlin is." Wagner started to reach for her.

"Gracie, tell them what you know," Thomas pleaded with her.

Gracie stopped rocking and looked at Thomas as tears streamed down from her already swollen eyes and trickled down her cheeks. "I's sorry, Mr. Thomas – I's so so sorry."

"Speak girl!" The corporal was growing agitated as the two young soldiers stepped back.

"Tell them, Gracie."

"Do I need to beat it out of you?" Wagner grabbed her by the arm and started pulling her up.

"Gracie," Thomas pleaded.

"Dey's dead, Mr. Thomas. Dey's all dead! Evey one oh dem! All gone!" Gracie slipped from his grasp and landed on her side on the floor.

"Explain," said the corporal.

"Dey's barried in da back – back dare," She pointed toward the back of the house.

"Don't just stand there boys – go look!"

The two young soldiers scrambled back down the hall, through the kitchen, and out the side yard door. Corporal Wagner paced back and forth between Thomas and Gracie. "For your sake you'd better not be lying to me girl or there will be hell to pay."

"Take it easy, corporal," Thomas' head was on fire and sweat poured down his brow and into his eyes.

It seemed like an eternity before the boys came back into the room – they were both out of breath. Thomas noticed the holes in their boots exposing their toes for the first time.

"Report, please," the corporal said gruffly.

The boy who seemed proud to tell Thomas he was in the University Brigade began to speak slowly, "There's a bunch of graves out there marked with wood crosses and charcoal writing." The boy paused to catch his breath better.

"And?"

The boy started again, "Samuel on one, then Margaret, then one that just says "the boys" on it. Then further back – Dewey senior, Dewey Junior, and Stephen," he looked at Thomas and then back at the corporal, "and one behind them all – John."

Thomas felt his heart sink into the pit of his already painful stomach, but he gathered his strength. "Satisfied?"

The youngest boy looked at the corporal, "there's somethin' else, sir." The boy glanced at Thomas, "another grave, fresh dug…and empty."

Gracie stood up and walked to Thomas' bedside, "that un's fer you, Mr. Thomas," she said slowly as she lowered her eyes to the floor.

"Mr. Summerlin, The Confederate States of America thanks you for your sacrifice," announced the corporal.

"Please just leave so I can die in peace," Thomas fell back into the bed.

The soldiers were headed toward the hallway when Thomas stopped them with a word from his pillow.

"Wait. You two boys stop in the mudroom on the way out and see if any of my brother's old boots will cover your feet better than what you got on – and first chance you get you burn new holes in them getting back home."

# 12

The third Friday of November 1962, saw the University of Virginia Cavaliers men's basketball team visiting the Richmond Spiders at the Richmond Arena. The arena had been home to a US Army motor pool during World War II and later became a city garage – both facts which were still evident inside the large musty facility. Luke Montgomery had boarded the team bus about three o'clock that afternoon, with the rest of the team filing on behind him. The weather had turned wintry, so everyone was bundled up in heavy coats. A very small group of dedicated fans were there to see them off, including Caroline and Audrey. They were waving small UVA pennants as the bus departed. On top of the embankment, above the parking lot, stood Joe Millstone, waving one hand to the men, with the other stuffed into the pocket of his overcoat. Luke had known Joe for many years prior to coming to UVA in 1960. A friend of Joe's father owned a prestigious horse farm in Southwestern Virginia near the New River Valley, and he and Luke worked there every summer all through high school and into college. Luke's father was friends with the same man, and he had delivered Luke to the farm the day after school got out for the summer for six straight years. Luke counted the days until he could be back around the horses and be himself – not what everyone else wanted him to be.

The trip over to Richmond was quick, and they found themselves pulling into the parking lot by 4:30 for the 7 o'clock tip off. The University of Richmond had some similarities to the rich history of the University of Virginia, but even as Luke and his teammates pulled into the parking lot and walked toward the arena, it would still be another six years before the first colored student was allowed to walk the halls. The Cavaliers were in the locker room and fully dressed out by about five, so they had plenty of time to listen to their coach ramble on about how poorly they had played in the last game, which they had lost by double digits. Richmond was a small school, and they had a small team, so they shouldn't pose a big problem for the superior Cavaliers. But still, the coach was very concerned about the beginning of the Atlantic Coast Conference season, and the tough competition they were going to face in the winter months ahead. Coach McCann wanted to get out there, take care of business, and get back to Charlottesville early. Both teams hit the court to warm up around 6:15 and Luke Montgomery was on the floor for the tip at 7pm. The game was going just as expected in the first half, with Luke scoring twelve points with several steals and just as many assists. With two minutes left in the half, the Cavs had built a sizeable 22-point lead and headed to the locker room up by 18.

The beginning of the third quarter was when things really started to get interesting. Luke made a quick steal from the Spider's point guard and was headed for an easy layup when the speedy shooting guard for Richmond came in hard from behind and knocked the ball forward, out of bounds, and down the service tunnel into the darkness. Luke's momentum was already carrying him in that direction, so he slowed down but continued down the tunnel to get the wayward basketball. There were three figures standing just inside the shadows where the light from the arena couldn't quite reach them. One of them, a young colored man let the ball roll up his outstretched foot and into the air where he gingerly caught it and snapped a quick pass back to Luke from ten feet away.

"Thanks, my friend," said Luke as he turned and started to head back toward the floor and the fans. It only took him a split second to realize what he had just seen, and he stopped in his tracks and turned back to the trio. "Emmaline?"

She just stood there smiling at him – next to her on the left was the young man who had returned the ball – on the right an older balding colored man in faded grey overalls. "Hello, Luke," she said barely above a whisper.

"Son?" the referee called from behind him, but he just stood there staring into the shadows for another gruelingly long three seconds. "Son, we have a game to finish here," the ref was walking toward him now.

Luke barely gathered his wits, turned, and headed back to the floor. The rest of that quarter his game was a little off, but the Cavaliers still held onto a 20-point lead going into the fourth and they finished the game off in easy fashion without Luke on the floor for most of the quarter. The teams shook hands and headed off to their respective locker rooms as Coach McCann came up behind Luke with a clipboard in his hand. "Son, I don't know what caused you to lose your edge out there tonight, but we can't afford that in conference play."

"Yeah, Coach. Sorry just a little tired with classes and all," Luke answered in a manner which suggested he wanted the conversation to stop there – but it didn't.

"A lot of folks pulled a lot of strings to put you here, and they expect you to give it your all."

"It was one game Coach – I got it," Luke walked ahead of McCann and into the locker room. He hated being reminded of what "everybody did to get him here".

Many of Luke's teammates were already starting to jump into the shower for the quick change before the ride back to Charlottesville. Luke stood there for a moment then turned and went back out the door and onto the court. He headed for the tunnel at the far end and noticed it was now lit up. Emmaline and the others were still there, but the older man was standing next to a garbage can on wheels with a broom handle sticking out the top.

"Emmie, what are you doing here?" he asked. "It's great to see you outside of your element - thanks for coming all this way for my game." Sweat beads were forming on his brow – probably from the heat in the gym, or so he surmised.

Emmaline laughed, "don't flatter yourself, Mr. Montgomery. This is my Uncle Ernie - he gets to clean up the floor after all you white boys gone and got it all dirty with your basketball game."

"Emmaline Foster!" said Uncle Ernie in a scolding tone. She ignored him with a slight grin in his direction.

"I came home to see my parents for the weekend, because I have to stay in Charlottesville and work over Thanksgiving – something you wouldn't know anything about," Emmie continued. "And this is my cousin Alvin, Ernie's son."

Alvin thrust out his hand and gave Luke a firm handshake, "Man, I wish I could handle the roundball like you did out there tonight – it was like a work of art."

"Really, Alvin?" Emmie said.

"Wasn't my best game but we won anyways," Luke looked back at Emmaline.

"So, at the house this afternoon they were talking about tonight's game, and I had the misfortune to mention that you and I are acquainted," Emmie looked back at Ernie. "So, my uncle brought us down here so we could all stand back here in the shadows and watch your game – yay!" she threw up a disingenuous fist which quickly and limply fell back to her side.

Luke heard one of the assistant coaches call his name and he said, "I'd better get back to the locker room or I'm gonna get left here – you know playing basketball for the school is like a full-time job."

"So is dumping garbage", Emmie started but was interrupted by Alvin.

Alvin laughed and said, "Maybe you and I will get a chance to play together someday."

Luke looked at him and said, "I would love that, Alvin, and I regret that you guys couldn't sit out on the floor and watch the game like everybody else – it's not fair."

Uncle Ernie started to speak, and Emmie chimed in, "Here comes the history lesson - everyone get a chair."

Ernie ignored her. "No son, we're not allowed out there - not yet anyway, but we're working on it. The University of Richmond is not yet willing to allow us into the halls, or the field house for that matter, unless of course the floor needs cleaning. Did you know the entire student body formed into its' own regiment in 1861, and went to join with Robert E Lee against the North? The entire student body. That tells you a little bit about the history here – don't it?"

Luke just shook his head, "None of it really makes any sense to me he said - we all carry the same red blood." Luke looked at Uncle Ernie, "Believe it or not I know plenty of white people that are treated outside their circles the same way you are."

Ernie reached out and put his hand on Luke's arm and looked him straight in the eye, "That is surely true, son, but once they get out of that circle they have a chance to blend in just like you have – that's a chance we don't get."

Luke just nodded as the assistant coach yelled louder for him this time. "I'm sorry, I have to go. It was an honor to meet you gentlemen," He turned to go and then looked back, "And, Emmaline, I'm very happy we are acquainted." Luke sprinted back toward the locker room smiling.

Emmie looked at her uncle, "What did you mean by "just like you have"?

"Young lady, I have two pieces of advice for you," he gently grabbed her by both shoulders, "Firstly, I can see it in him, and if he ever decides to tell you, he will. Second, you'd best keep yourself, and that boy, out of trouble."

"What is that supposed to mean?" she said.

"That one…don't need any explaining," Ernie turned and rolled the garbage can toward the arena floor.

# 13

"Do you care to explain any of that?" Thomas asked as Gracie stood by the window watching the three soldiers walk down the long drive in the direction of the road leading to town.

Gracie shrugged her shoulders, "I guess, I can, if you really need me to, Mr. Thomas."

"Didn't you tell me you hadn't seen my brother John?"

"He's not dead Mr. Thomas – in fact he's very much alive as far as I know," Gracie was warming some water so Thomas could get cleaned up, an act which he was increasingly able to handle by himself as he grew stronger.

"The way you were speaking..."

"Mr. Thomas, the last thing the South needs is an educated negro woman. The ladies in the kitchen at Mr. Henry's taught me to know my place – and to act my place. It's safer that way." Gracie lifted the steaming pot from the spit and carried it to the bedside.

"Then why not keep up the act for me?"

"I've been here with you by myself for a very long time now, and I trust you not to judge me beyond who I am," She wet a cloth and handed it to him – he placed it over his face and let it rest there for a few moments. "I trust you because all I have is you...and all you have is me. We must trust each other."

She sat next to him on the bed, and he placed his hand on her arm – her skin was smooth and warm to his touch, "I do trust you, Gracie. I'm sorry if I was harsh before."

The weather was surely getting warmer, and tiny shoots of grass had started to turn green in patches around the yard. Many different types of birds had returned, including robins - and the first mayflies of the season were drifting about. Golden sunbeams streamed down through the sycamores as stage lighting for them all. Animals were emerging from their winter shelter where they had stayed hidden away from the cold, much like Thomas and Gracie had inside Waverly House. Gracie went out to the kitchen and brought back a fine breakfast for them both, consisting of poached eggs, several small, toasted crusts of bread, and some sassafras tea. Thomas was beginning to sit up on his own now, and every day Gracie was trying to tell him more and more of what had transpired at Waverly – she knew very little of what else was happening outside these two thousand acres. Thomas was longing to get out of the bed, and he kept telling Gracie how much he wanted to help her around the house. Gracie would just smile, her beautiful reassuring smile, and promise him it wouldn't be long now.

Thomas sat up on the edge of the bed and was able to feed himself for the most part, save for a few drops and crumbs that spilled down the front of his nightshirt. "The first thing I need to do is get myself to the latrine on my own, so you don't have this unnecessary mess to clean up several times a day."

"That would be nice, Mr. Thomas, but I don't mind, really," Gracie was as humble as ever.

"From what I can see from here the garden looks beautiful – you are doing such a great job out there, Gracie," Thomas kept his hand on her arm but turned his palm up so the back of his hand touched her soft skin.

Gracie glanced away nervously, " 'Taint me that makes a garden beautiful – it's God up in Heaven. He always has a plan despite what we do on this earth to ruin it all."

"God uses your hands to help paint his landscape," said Thomas.

"I guess, Mr. Thomas." Gracie stared at the beautiful little white flowers beginning to bloom outside the window, but she also saw the small buzzing flies lighting back and forth on the windowpane trying to get to the smell of death that was Thomas Warren Summerlin.

"When is the last time you have seen Dr. Draper, or better yet, when is the last time he saw me?" Thomas shifted uncomfortably, and his pain showed through a slight grimace.

"Dr. Draper got called to the Army Field Hospital in Lynchburg a while back, but I might be able to get his wife to come by and see you – I'll have to walk to town at night," Gracie said, and looked at the floor.

"I need some crutches – some good crutches," Thomas wriggled around and pulled his legs back up on the mattress. "I have to get out of this bed." He noticed she wasn't paying attention to what he said. "Gracie? Are you alright? You seem to be somewhere else."

"I'm scared, Mr. Thomas," she unfolded a clean blanket that had been hanging over the footboard and spread it out over his legs. "I have things to tell you that will make you angry – very angry."

"Look at my plight, Gracie. I can't stand up...I can't do anything for myself. Hell, I would be dead if you weren't here with me. Nothing you tell me could make me angry with you." Thomas folded his hands onto his chest and took a deep but little less labored breath.

"Everything that has happened… it's because I came here," Gracie sat back down on the edge of the bed as a single tear rolled down her cheek.

"You were brought here – there's a difference," he reached for her hand, but she pulled it back.

"Your father brought me here," she started. "From, I'm guessing it was your uncle's house – that Mr. Connally. And when we arrived here, he took me to Samuel and his wife, Margaret, and he asked them to do something with me. So, Samuel - he was a very nice man and he treated me with a respect and kindness I hadn't seen in some time. They lived in the second little house in the front, and it had a little room on the side which had a cot and a table and chair inside. I was told that would be mine. Ms. Margaret, she gave me some candles and a wash pan with some cloth to take care of myself." Gracie paused as Thomas tried to turn on his side to face her.

"Samuel was a good man – what happened to him?" Thomas asked.

"That answer lies with what I am going to tell you, so please be patient with me," Gracie continued, "So, I lived in the little room next to Samuel and his family. His wife, Margaret, was very kind to me and I loved playing with their two little boys, Jeremiah and Sammy in the garden - where your mother had me working at first."

Thomas was listening with little expression now.

"Your mother, she would come outside and sit nearby on the grass while I was tending to her vegetables. She figured out during our time together that I was educated, because somehow, she saw through my charade, and then things changed for me. She wanted me around her all the time. She brought me into the kitchen, we had tea together every day, and she was intrigued about my ability to use the English language in a finer manner than she – so she said. Our conversations for the first couple of days were mostly about you and your brothers, and I read her some poetry – then things got bad." Gracie poured some water from a pitcher into a small clay mug with a handle and took a sip.

"I used to write my mother little poems and read them to her before supper," Thomas didn't know what else he could say right now.

"She has those little notes in the cupboard in one of her tea kettles – she showed me." Gracie put the mug back on the table and wiped her lips with her apron, then she offered Thomas an easy smile. "One morning, after you had been brought back home, we sat in the kitchen, and she told me she had been coughing blood, and she knew she was going to die. That was the first day she brought me into this room to see you. I sat in this chair for hours that day, holding her hand while she cried on the edge of your bed. She told me Dr. Draper told her she was sick with consumption, and she didn't know how much time she had left. All I could do was ask her what I could do to make things easier for her and your father. Well, your mama, Ms. Mattie, asked me to work in the kitchen and do the house cleaning so I didn't ruin my delicate pretty hands in the dirt outside – her words not mine."

Thomas was beginning to fade on her – she could tell. It had been a long day already.

"Your mother used to say to me "this is my beautiful boy, Tom, he loves the outdoors, he loves his horses, he loves to read and write about the wonders of nature – I miss him so badly – please come back to me Tom Warren."" "I would sit with here with her by your bed for long periods of time, and only occasionally would I leave to get her some tea or more cold water to put on your head, or to fix food for your father," Gracie took a deep breath and drank another sip of water. "It was around that time that your father took notice of me and started "keeping his eyes on me" as he liked to say. I was thinking maybe he didn't trust me to be in the house, but he had other thoughts. The way he was looking at me was beginning to make me very nervous."

Thomas put his hand on Gracie's and squeezed it gently, "My God, you don't need to tell me this."

"You need to know the whole story, Mr. Thomas," Gracie let him keep holding her hand.

"One night – it was very late, and I was asleep – I was awakened by the side door opening and your father coming inside in his night clothes and sitting next to me on the bed. I pulled the blanket up around my neck, but he gently and slowly pulled it away from me." Gracie turned away from Thomas – she couldn't face him and tell him this. "Then, Mr. Thomas, he pulled my night shirt down from my shoulders all the way to my lap and exposed me. I said, "please don't, Mr. Summerlin sir", but all he kept saying was how beautiful I looked, and he needed to touch me. I could smell the whiskey on him. He reached for me, and I guess I must have screamed, because it wasn't long before Samuel was standing in the light of the doorway in just his night breeches."

Samuel said "Massah, I 'spect you best be go on back up to da house 'bout now."

Your father turned on him and said, "It ain't your place to tell me what to do with my own property now is it?" Then he said, "close the door and go back to your woman."

Samuel said, "I can't rightly do that sir – you got to leave dat youngun' lone."

"Your father yelled, "close the door" very loudly and Samuel grabbed him by the back of his shirt and his suspenders and yanked him out into the yard.

Then he said, "I tol' you to go back in dat house."" "I saw your daddy get up and dust himself off, then he told Samuel that he was gonna pay for this and pay harshly. He started towards the house, and I saw your mother standing in the light of the doorway, and he pushed right past her without a word."

"Margaret came into my room and got me back together and lay with me all night, but I knew the first chance Mr. Summerlin got, he was going to come for me again. I knew he wasn't going to quit."

Thomas was beginning to look angry and confused, "I can't see my father doing that," he said, "Sure, he was always very hard on us, and he could be bitterly nasty at times, but I've always known he loved my mother – that I've never questioned."

"Sickness and war changes folks, Mr. Thomas," Gracie turned back to him. "I don't know, Mr. Thomas, your mother became very frail, and she was very sick, and I don't know why he turned his attention to me, Mr. Thomas. I'm so sorry – I didn't do anything purposefully."

"It's Okay, Gracie. I'm sure it wasn't your doin'," Thomas began to think about how beautiful she was, but then he quickly blocked it from his mind with a shudder.

"So, the next morning, your father had Gunther - the "slave boss" is what they called him - drag Samuel to the cross rail by the barn and tie his hands with his back turned out toward the yard. He had us all seated in the yard. Your daddy told us we were going to have to watch the whippin' that Gunther was going to give Samuel for his actions." Gracie paused as Thomas loosened his grip slightly on her hand. He was beginning to sweat now.

"What happened to Gunther? He was my dad's foreman ever since I was a boy."

"You need to let me finish please, Mr. Thomas," Gracie was growing tired, and she took another sip of water. "So, your father told Gunther to give Samuel twenty lashes, and I heard Gunther ask him if this was necessary. Your father said, "hand me the damned whip and I'll do it myself". So, Gunther turned and swung the whip and opened Samuel's back, and a streak of red formed on his shirt. Your father told Gunther to hit him again and then give him eighteen more after that, then he turned to go into the house to eat his breakfast. Gunther said "you ain't going to stand here and watch with the rest?" Your father said, "do your job Gunther or you don't have one." So, your father went up the porch and into the house and I saw Gunther turn back toward Samuel and raise the whip. Then he said, "You scream loud, boy." He snapped the whip and splinters flew into the air next to Samuel's head. "I said to scream, boy!" Gunther yelled loudly again. He hit the post again and Samuel screamed this time. Then, all the other times he struck the post and Samuel screamed. Gunther laid off an inch of wood from that railing and then he walked up behind Samuel as your father started to come back outside. Gunther told Samuel to hold his breath as he smeared the blood from the one wound all over Samuel's back until it soaked his white shirt, then he whispered in his ear to fall on the ground and wait for his wife to get him once his hands were untied."

Gracie looked again into Thomas' eyes and said, "I'll get us through this," then she continued. "So, Gunther took the whip, and he walked up to where your father was standing on the steps with his tin coffee cup, and he told him "that was the worst thing you've ever told me to do – and the last."" Then Gunther raised that whip up and dropped it on the ground in front of your daddy's feet. Then he walked to the barn where he lived, and a few moments later he came out carrying a sheet with all his belongings rolled up in it, and he walked down the road, and over the hill and out of sight. Margaret helped Samuel back to the house. She was crying the whole time."

Thomas looked at her incredulously, "If what you are saying is true then Gunther is gone, and my father has gone mad."

Gracie clutched him by the hand and said, "Mr. Thomas, it's this war it's tearing families apart, and it's making men and boys do things they never thought they would do. Your father thought that he had lost all of his boys, and that your mother was dying before his very eyes. He'd lost everyone and everything."

"How can you just sit there and defend him after what he did to you – and to Samuel?" Thomas asked.

"I'm not defending him. He came after me again, and he had to answer for what he did," Gracie felt herself getting flush and didn't know if she could tell him the rest of the story.

Thomas rubbed his thumb across the top of Gracie's hand - her skin was as soft as silk. "Gunther taught me everything I know about horses and now he's gone. He didn't come back?"

"I haven't seen him since that day he walked off this farm, and it's been almost a year now, I'm guessin'," she said. "I know how hard this must be for you, Mr. Thomas, and I have much more that you need to know, but maybe I should go get another bottle of whiskey from the cellar."

"Maybe you should, but you probably shouldn't - I need to hear everything that happened and then I need your help to get me out of this damned bed!" He was growing more defiant.

She gripped his hand tighter and felt comforted as he continued rubbing the top of her hand. "I was in the kitchen later that day and I overheard your mother and father arguing upstairs. He kept saying he had nothing left, and she told him that was no excuse to lay his hands on me. They got quiet for a few minutes then I heard your mother yell at him – "She's a child, Dewey – she could be your own daughter!" Then she told him that she hadn't ever seen him whip Samuel or any other one of us. Your father yelled at her and said he had lost control of everything. Your mother said that losing Gunther was all his doing, and he needed to keep his hands off of all of us – that she weren't going to tolerate this sin at her house. Your father went out the door and stormed away to the barn. Your mother spent all afternoon telling me she was so very sorry, and that she wouldn't let it happen to me ever again – no matter what."

"So, that was the end of it?" Thomas rolled his body toward her and was clearly in pain again.

"It ended it for a while, but your father drank too much, and one evening he came after me again – this time he brought a pistol and told me to keep my mouth shut about it. But Samuel was expecting it, so he had been staying up and sort of listening out for me. He slammed open the door and your father told him to get out – or die. After that everything happened so fast – it was all a blur to me. It all happened so fast after that, Mr. Thomas. I heard your mother crying and telling Samuel to go to his family. Samuel looked at her and fell back down the stairs and into the yard. When he was out of the doorway, that's when I saw your mother standing there with that gun." Gracie pointed to the shotgun in the corner by the mantle.

Thomas stared at her in disbelief – afraid of what would come next. "Your father raised the pistol at your mother, and she fired the first barrel into his shoulder, and he dropped the pistol on the floor by my feet. He was on top of her so fast. She had gone to the ground with the shot, and he easily yanked the shotgun away from her. He raised it up and held it right in front of her eyes. I heard the click as he cocked the second barrel. Your mother looked at me and closed her eyes to let it happen." Gracie had tears streaming down her face now, and she had trouble even seeing Thomas through the haze.

Thomas held a cloth up to her and she took it and wiped her eyes. "My father – he – killed my mother?"

Gracie continued to sob uncontrollably, "Mr. Thomas, I am so sorry – he was gone mad," she took a deep breath and clutched his hand even tighter, "Please don't hate me for this." Thomas pulled her closer and brushed her hair away from her face – her deep beautiful eyes looked hopeless.

Gracie pulled in a quick breath and said, "I picked up that pistol and I shot your father in the back…he turned and pointed the shotgun straight at me…and I shot him in the chest…I dropped the pistol on the floor, and it clattered down the steps…and I felt a wave of calm pass through me as he hit the ground."

# 14

The team bus rolled back into Charlottesville a little after midnight, and Luke quickly grabbed his gear and walked with Dominick back toward the dormitory.

"Feel like rousting the ladies for a little while?" Dom asked. "It's still Friday night."

"We got that team meeting at 9 o'clock in the morning, and another game in the Gym tomorrow night that ain't going to be a cakewalk," Luke yawned. "I think it best to turn in."

"I think it best to turn in?" Dominick laughed. "What are you, my butler?"

Luke smiled and said jokingly, "Some of us actually played basketball tonight, so we are tired."

"Hurtful," Dominick replied.

"You will get your turn," said Luke.

"Doesn't matter, as long as they keep paying my partial. I'm going to call over to Munford and see if Audrey wants to meet me at the Union for a soda," Dominick trudged onward and up the hill ahead of Luke.

The game against Marshall was going to be a much tougher matchup than the one against Richmond, and Luke knew the whole team would have to be on their game. A tiring weekend of basketball was certainly on tap. As they got back to their cramped but "adequate" room, Luke threw his bag in the corner and collapsed on the bottom bunk. Dominick walked right back out the door to go use the hall phone. There were many thoughts running through Luke's head about tonight's game, but most of them had to do with seeing Emmaline

Foster. As he laid there contemplating his situation, Dominick came back in the door looking like a lost puppy, he kicked out of his Converse and climbed up to the top bunk where he hit the bed with a thump of twanging springs. Luke figured Audrey gave Dominick the cold shoulder. It was quiet for a few minutes and Luke closed his eyes, until Dominick asked the question of the night.

"What's with that girl – Emmie is it?" Dominick asked. "She came all the way to Richmond – so it must be getting serious between you two," he laughed.

"She's from there, and her uncle cleans the gym after "all of us white boys mess it up."" Luke said.

"Trouble in forbidden paradise already?" Dominick's smirk seemed to hit a nerve. "You looked like you had seen a ghost when you came back out of the tunnel tonight, so I would assume you didn't know she was going to be there."

"I don't control where people go," was Luke's answer.

"Does she go to school here, or just work up at TPs?"

"I really don't know that much about her," Luke lied, and thought to himself "but I want to know everything about her." Then he added, "We are just acquainted." He hated that choice of words.

"Acquaintances don't catch you off guard like that," said Dominick.

"I just didn't expect to see her there – that's all," Luke was growing impatient, but he didn't mind that the conversation was about her. "She does go to school here – she's becoming a nurse."

"Your subpar play in the third quarter tells me there is more to this story," Dominick leaned over the edge of the bunk and peered down at his friend.

"Subpar to say the least," Luke laughed before adding, "I told you she's a friend and she is just a really good person – there's really nothing more to add."

"Does Caroline know about your new friend?"

"That's it. Goodnight, dummy," Luke rolled toward the wall, and when he closed his eyes all he could see was Emmaline Foster's beautiful smile.

Dom interrupted his thoughts again a couple of minutes later, "Just be careful. You don't want any rumors starting about something like that. It's good to have a lot of friends, but you know what I'm saying."

Luke reopened his eyes for one last comment, "She is my friend – I'm white and she's colored…it doesn't mean we can't know each other. I won't go through my life letting others judge me for who I speak to."

"I'm sorry, Luke."

"Just go to sleep please," it took him a minute, but Emmie came rushing back into his head again as he closed his eyes, and a slight smile crossed his lips as he began to doze.

The next day was all about basketball. The temperature had fallen overnight and there was a definite feel of winter rolling into the valley. The team had a meeting in the morning to talk strategy, and then lunch with the coaching staff to watch some film on the Marshall Thundering Herd. Game time was late afternoon at 4 o'clock in front of a packed house, and despite taking an eight-point lead into the locker room at the half, Marshall's big men underneath the basket outrebounded and outplayed the Cavaliers front court in route to a devastating six-point home loss for Virginia.

As Dominick and Luke came out of the locker room, they ran straight into a small group of fans that included

Audrey and Caroline. Caroline came straight up to Luke, stood on her toes, and planted a kiss on his cheek. "Tough loss tonight, boys – you will get them next game." She had on his Woodrow Wilson High jacket – that was a first.

Audrey swept in and grabbed Dominick by the hand, "should we head to the diner for some hot apple pie and maybe some cocoa?"

"I've had a really long weekend so far, and I have a stack of books with my name on them," Luke looked at Dominick as if expecting his approval, but he really didn't feel up to dealing with Caroline and her constantly chattering cohorts tonight. "I'll make it up to you tomorrow – I promise."

"C'mon, Luke – just for a half hour?" Caroline put one hand on his forearm and the other on the bulging bicep of his right arm.

"Sweetie, I wouldn't be good company tonight – I'm not in the best mood," Luke gently broke her grasp and walked over to Dom. "Want me to carry your bag to the room?"

Caroline gave him puppy dog eyes and he said, "Why don't you go with your friends and have a good time?" she raised her eyebrows and put her head on his shoulder – he could smell the Aquanet in her hair and it almost overwhelmed him, but he finally said "Look I'm not going anywhere tonight - I need to get some rest and I have two tests on Monday - before the Thanksgiving Break starts. I'm already gonna be in the library all day tomorrow."

"You're a party pooper, Luke Montgomery," she pouted in her best Marilyn Monroe.

Luke leaned in and kissed her gently on the lips and got the reaction he expected – she was proud to be kissed by Luke

Montgomery in front of her friends – it validated her. "Again, I promise I'll make this up to you tomorrow."

The group headed for the parking lot as Luke headed for the dorms at the top of the hill. When he got in the door, he threw Dom's bag on the floor next to his laundry basket, dropped his next to it, and lay down on his bunk. When his head hit the pillow, he was sound asleep almost at once. The Saturday night noises of the dorm never phased him, and he slept all night.

The next day, Luke got up early and studied in his room, waiting for the library to open at one. Dom got up and went to Chapel at 10 am, and Luke knew he would face the wrath of the coach for missing it, but he was getting too far behind in Calculus and Biology. On the way to the library, he popped into the cafeteria and grabbed a cold bologna sandwich on Sunbeam and a Dr. Pepper which he quickly consumed and tossed the containers in the trash. He stayed in the library until he noticed the sun had gone down around 5:30, and he remembered Caroline and the promise he had made. He quickly stacked up his books, wrapped a strap around them, and ran out the front of the building and up the path.

As he entered the dorm and started towards his room, he saw Joe Millstone standing in his doorway talking to Dom. "Yeah there were three police cars down there parked on the side and one around the back."

"What's going on?" Luke said as he slid past Joe, threw his books on the desk, and pulled off his coat.

"Don't know exactly, but the gossip is that one of those colored girls that works down there got beat up pretty bad by some electrician or something." Joe shrugged his shoulders slightly.

Luke looked at Dom and didn't need to speak but Dom did, "On the desk."

Luke scooped up Dom's keys and almost knocked Joe down getting past him as he raced down the hall and slammed the bar on the exit door, and disappeared into the darkness.

"What the hell was that about?" Joe asked.

"Just an acquaintance," said Dom to a now obviously confused Joe.

Once Luke got out of the student lot, he was pulling into TPs less than two minutes later. He parked the car in a space in the front next to a convertible load of girls drinking pop and watching what was going on in the back. He jumped out and started toward the back between two local cop cars.

"Luke?" he heard from behind him and cringed – Caroline.

"Are you looking for me?" he heard her say.

"Sure, I've just got to go to the bathroom – I'll be back."

"My father is sending a car for us for Thanksgiving – you are still coming right?"

"Yes," he lied without knowing how he was going to get out of it – he had no desire to be dictated to all weekend by Caroline's regimental father.

Luke turned and continued quickly through the cars… and then he saw her. Emmaline was sitting on the stoop of the little house she shared with Natalie, rocking back and forth with a blanket wrapped around her. Her long silky hair was a bird nest around her shoulders, and it was pulled toward the back of her head. Luke got to within twenty feet and she looked up and saw him coming. At once she was up and running to him and he opened his arms to receive her. She thumped into his body and wrapped her arms around him – driving her face into his chest. He wrapped his strong arms around her and held her, and she felt the warmth of his comfort begin to spread through her.

"Well, this is a new wrinkle," said the sheriff.

"Yes…yes, it is," said Mr. Richard frowning.

Behind them, standing silently between the two police cars, was Caroline.

# 15

"I slipped down the step and landed on the ground next to Samuel and immediately burst into tears, telling your mother how sorry I was. Samuel stood up and then pulled me up off the ground and told me to "quit my caterwaulin'"", Gracie had been to the kitchen and gotten them some cheese and bread crusts.

"All your mother could say was "I told him not to…I told him not to…he never listened to me - ever," with Samuel and me just standing there looking over her. Margaret and the boys came slowly over to join us, and they sat on the ground next to your mother telling her it was gonna be alright. Samuel picked up the shotgun and the Colt and carried them up onto the porch. It was deafeningly quiet after the shots had been fired. Samuel got your mama up and helped her back inside the house, where he sat her at the kitchen table. I told her I would get her some tea and she asked for whiskey. Nobody said one word for a while."

Thomas was growing very weary, and his concentration seemed to be waning, but he tried to struggle through the pain.

"Do you need me to stop now for a while, Mr. Thomas?" Gracie asked. She was getting tired too.

"I just need a sip of water," he said.

Gracie held the tin cup to his lips, and he drank deeply. "That's better," he said. Gracie could tell she was losing him quickly.

"I need to put some ointment on your lips – they look like crow's feet," said Gracie. "I have a certain point of this story I need to get to before I quit, so let's keep going if you can handle it." She paused briefly, then started again, "So, your mother started speaking after a few sips of whiskey, and the first thing she said was, "I'm dying, and there is no reason y'all must stay here and watch that. She said "Samuel, I need you to bury Dewey up in the cemetery – get started on that tonight. People are so wrapped up in this war they won't notice he's gone for months." Then she looked at Samuel and Margaret and told them that they belonged to her now since her husband was dead, and as their new owner she was granting them their freedom. She told them to take one of the buckboards and a mule, and whatever they could carry, and what they thought they might need, and to go North, and not to stop until they reached Pennsylvania. Then she said for them to never set foot on this God forsaken blood-soaked Southern soil again. Samuel said to her, "Ms. Summerlin, you c'ain't run dis place by you lonesome so we's not goin' anywhere anyhow – we ain't leavin' you." Your mother took Margaret by the hands and told her that the only thing left here was her dying son and nothing more – they had a chance to be free and if they stayed here, they might be slaves forever. She said, "do it for those boys – you leave, and you never look back.""

Thomas groaned, "I'm sorry, the pain is trying to pull me down here. So, if Samuel and Margaret left with their boys then why are there graves marked for them? Some of this don't make any sense to me."

"Samuel and I made those grave markers so if anybody came here looking for them, they wouldn't be inclined to look no further," Gracie straightened the apron over her dress out of habit. "Also, turned out your mother had knocked her shoulder out of place, but Samuel used a rope tied around the post in the kitchen to pull it back in – but, boy, did she ever scream. Then we put her to bed, and she went right out."

"That was the night I started looking after all of your needs, because she no longer had the capability to handle it. She was in and out of her capacity over the next several days, and I sent Margaret to fetch Dr. Draper to come up here and look in on her. Ms. Katherine came here and looked upon your mother and told all of us that she was going to be unable to care for herself for much longer. She suggested we take her to the sanatorium in Roanoke because Richmond was too far, and the war was raging that way," Gracie stood up, reached over Thomas and fluffed up his pillow.

"This all…sounds so mad," said Thomas. "How do I know what you are telling me is the truth, Gracie?"

"Do you really think I would be here waiting on you hand and foot if I was lying." Gracie sat back down on the edge of the bed and wiped the sweat from Thomas' brow again.

"Why are you?"

"I promised your mother, but more importantly, and selfishly I suppose, I have no place else to go," Gracie sipped more water – her mouth was drying more with each word. "One evening, while we were making plans for her to go to Roanoke, she told me she wished she would die before you, so she didn't have to watch every member of her family die right in front of her. She was getting sicker and growing so weak by the day – she had lost half of her weight, and she couldn't keep any more food down. Dr. Draper came from town, and Samuel gathered her up in a quilt and carried her to the wagon, where she was placed next to another dying woman that I ain't ever seen before. I packed her a bag with all her ladies' necessities and some clothing. She could barely speak, but she had the strength to tell Samuel and Margaret again to take what they wanted and leave this place behind," Gracie paused for a moment and took a deep breath – then cleared her throat. "Mr. Thomas, I was scared for her because she lost her will to live. I had to take a knife away from her after she tried to cut her own neck, and Samuel caught her as she tried to throw herself down the staircase. We had to hide all the knives – and all the guns. I couldn't watch her and take care of you any longer. But she had talked so much about you, and how much she loved all her boys. She told me that when you were little you didn't understand why all the people lived in the little houses outside when the family had so much room in the house for everybody. She doted on your kind heart and gentle soul, and said you hated the idea of people being held against their will and forced to work," Thomas looked into her eyes, and she could feel his regret, so she asked him, "Why – why did you go off to fight this horrible war?"

Thomas looked at her sternly, but he wasn't angry at her question, "I didn't want to see this war come – I kept pretending it wouldn't. My life was here – with my horses and my family – on this farm," he paused to catch his breath – that was quite a few words for him in his condition. "My brothers were excited for it – except for John – he just followed whatever Stephen did. My father told me I would be considered a coward if I didn't go with them, and my mother made me promise to go and bring them back alive – and I failed her." Thomas rolled back on his side with a grunt.

Gracie put her hand on his arm, "It's okay, Mr. Thomas, I know times are bad, and men are doing things they will soon regret."

"What happened to Samuel and Margaret then?" Thomas asked.

"Samuel and his family - they left about six months back - but that's a story for tomorrow. I think we'd better get you comfortable for the night." Gracie went to the hearth to heat his bedwarmers up.

"They just left you here by yourself. Why didn't you go with them?"

"I told you Mr. Thomas, your mother saved my life, and I promised to stay here and bury you when you died." She leaned over the fireplace and pumped the bellows a few times.

"Then why don't you just leave now that I'm awake again?" Thomas was feeling sorry for himself now.

"You heard the promise, didn't you? With you sitting up, talking, and feeding yourself – I'm fairly certain I can't bury you yet, mainly because you're still alive."

# 16

"Are you okay?" Luke didn't want to let her go. "Did you get hurt?"

Emmaline pulled back her arms from around his chest and moved to his side. She was keenly aware that there were other people around, but they seemed to be not all that important to her right now, "I-I'm okay, Luke."

He began to walk her back toward the stoop of her little house, "I'm here now, everything's going to be alright," he felt strange saying that to her, but he felt it anyway.

"It's Nat," Emmie said. "She stayed here for the repairman – and he did something awful to her." She wiped her tears on the blanket and sat back down. "She's gone to the hospital."

"I'm so sorry," Luke knelt beside her. "Is she going to be okay?"

"Physically, I guess so."

"Son, we need to ask Ms. Foster a few more questions," the sheriff was standing behind them now.

"I said…I don't know anything. I wasn't even back here yet," Emmaline looked at Luke and just wanted to crawl away.

"You were in Richmond – is that right?"

"I already told you that – do you want my Mother's phone number?" Emmie was clearly agitated.

"Don't take an attitude Miss – I'm just doing my job," said the sheriff.

"Really? So, you are going to arrest this guy, Mr. Roberts? Why aren't you talking to him?"

"Because I'm talking to you," the sheriff stepped closer, "we could talk at the station where it's more private if you'd like."

"I don't really know what else I can tell you. I got back here and found her curled up in a ball on the floor by our bed." Emmaline looked at Luke, "We only have the one."

Luke straightened his lips but not quite into a smile. "Officer, maybe you should be speaking with Natalie or this Roberts guy." Luke looked up at him.

"I know who you are, boy" the sheriff stared down at him, "It might be best if you stand over there with your friend while I talk to Ms. Foster."

"It's okay, Luke, you can go," Emmie looked at the cop again. "okay – what else?"

"This may be a tough question, but it goes to Ms. Sharpe's character," the sheriff put his hand on his pistol grip as if to appear more serious. "Mr. Roberts says she offered herself up to him as a form of payment for getting the heat fixed. Has she done anything like that before."

"That's disgusting!" Emmie said.

"I paid to get that heater fixed," Mr. Richard stood closely behind the sheriff.

"I'll speak with you later, sir," the sheriff turned back to Emmaline, "Right now it's her word against his – and we know how things work with you people sometimes."

"Get – the hell out of my face!" Emmie said as she stood up.

"Emmaline…" Mr. Richard said.

"Maybe we should go to the station if you are going to get hostile."

"Are you arresting me?"

"Not yet," the sheriff said.

Luke walked back to her side, "Grab your shoes – let's get out of here."

"We will have more questions later, Ms. Foster," the sheriff closed his notebook and turned to Mr. Richard.

"Should we go into the kitchen and speak?" Mr. Richard led the sheriff away from the kids.

"I have a car," said Luke." Let's go for a ride."

Emmie walked toward the parking area between the two cop cars where Caroline was standing. Luke followed closely behind.

"What are you doing, Luke Montgomery?" Caroline said exasperated.

"This is my friend, Emmaline, she needs my help right now."

"How do you even know this person?" she asked. "She lives back here by the garbage?"

"Your friends knocked me down, and your boyfriend picked me up," Emmaline retorted.

Caroline looked at Luke and flipped her hair to the side as the moist night air was stealing her hairspray. "She lives back here in a cage – like the other animals."

It took everything in his power to not put her in her place right then and there. "She needs a friend – and that's all I am."

"I need my boyfriend – and he hasn't been available to me all weekend," Caroline said. "Do you know how embarrassing it has been for you to ignore me in front of my friends all weekend long?"

"This isn't about you," Luke walked past her.

"Go, take care of your pet, but don't call me – ever," Caroline was crying now.

Luke turned to her, "We all live in cages, Caroline – like animals. Thank you for freeing me from the one you kept me in." Luke turned and led Emmie to Dom's car, put her in the passenger seat, drove out onto West Main Street, and turned right, away from campus.

# 17

By late March of 1863, Thomas Summerlin had started to regain enough strength to prop himself up in a seated position and turn his body so that he was sitting on the edge of the bed with his good foot on the floor. He could also do an adequate job of feeding himself, but he hadn't quite gotten the nerve to get out of the bed yet. He had asked Gracie to bring him some short pieces of lumber from the barn so he could try to push himself up and out of the bed. This proved to be a colossal failure from the start, as he would get himself up about halfway and then come crashing back down onto the mattress, wincing in pain. One time he landed on the hard oak floor, and it took Gracie at least a half hour to get him back onto the bed. She came close to giving up and just leaving him where he lay. Gracie spent hours each day massaging the foot and calf of his left leg while he was sitting on the edge of the bed. She moved his foot up and down until he started to regain the feeling – she giggled, and he laughed when she realized he was very ticklish on the bottom of his foot.

This morning though, was different somehow. Thomas awoke to a cold bowl of porridge sitting on the rickety table next to the bed, and as he sat up to eat, he could see Gracie dancing in the sunlight through the window in her gray smocked dress. She appeared to be singing as she raked the courtyard and snipped at the rose bushes with rusty scissors. Thomas sat there for at least an hour after he finished his food, watching her dance and sing and pile up debris in the center of the courtyard. She leaned over at one point, struck a wooden match, and lit the little pile on fire – then she danced around the smoke like a wood nymph. All Thomas could do was smile and all the while wonder why she was so happy. He thought about how life had treated them both so unfairly, and how they were left in such a horrible plight together. He began to feel like something was different in the room, and as he looked towards the fireplace, he saw something leaning against the wall that wasn't there yesterday. Somewhere, Gracie had managed to scrounge him up a pair of real crutches, and this brought a broad smile to his face. There was a light tap at the window and there was Gracie peering in with her beautiful, inviting smile. She waved at him and laced the honeysuckle vines up onto the shutter latches, so they draped in front of the window for Thomas to see. Gracie seemed so very happy that Thomas could sit up and see the flowers and the beautiful courtyard outside of his window. Her smile was short-lived however as a sea of foreboding and dread swept through her like a tempest. The chore of keeping them both alive was growing more difficult by the day and her strength – and food supply - were both waning.

Once Gracie had the flowers just like she wanted them, she disappeared with a last smile toward Thomas. A moment later she came into his room. "I can heat up your porridge and- well you're not gonna believe this but I have some coffee - would you like some? She sat down next to him on the edge of the bed.

Thomas immediately thought to himself "why are you doing all of this?", but he said, "Of course I would like some coffee - it sounds like I haven't had any for a year and a half." He put his arm around her shoulder and squeezed it gently

– it made him feel a little awkward. "Better yet, where did you find these crutches, and how did you come across this coffee?"

"I am so glad to see you in better spirits today, Mr. Thomas," Gracie rose from the bed and sat in the little ladder-back chair. "After you fell asleep last night, I put on your mother's long coat and a hat – the black one - and I walked to the Mercantile to see Ms. Draper."

"That's a good five miles from here..."

"There was a fair moon last night and I was able to keep to the fields and ditches most of the way. I did see some of the blue coats on the road, but I hid real good in the ditch as they passed by. When I got to the Mercantile, I went around back to Dr. Draper's house and I knocked on the door and his wife answered. Ms. Katherine, she pulled me inside real quick and told me it was very dangerous out there. I was surprised to find Dr. Draper there too. I told Dr. Draper that you were awake, and he couldn't believe it. He told me that he thought I was there to tell him that you were dead." Gracie took a deep breath and continued. "I told him that you were trying to get out of bed, and he gave me this old pair of crutches - and most importantly he said he can come take a look at your leg and see if he can fit it with something to help you walk – isn't that exciting Mr. Thomas?"

Thomas just smiled at how excited she was and said, "I think you are a fantastic woman Ms. Grace."

Gracie shyly glanced at the floor and smiled, "Then Ms. Draper packed me up some coffee and some dry beans and some flour and some sugar - which I was more than happy for us to get, and I came back here in the dark of night after the moon had set down behind the mountain."

Thomas almost found himself unable to speak again, but he found the courage as he reached out to take her hands into his, and looked into her eyes, "You may be the most amazing person I've ever known," he said.

Gracie pulled her hands away and walked towards the fireplace, and then she turned back toward him, "There's a lot more that I need to tell you, and when I'm done you probably won't think I'm the most amazing person you've ever known," she turned and put her hand on the mantle and stared into the fireplace below.

"I think you're wrong there - I don't think there's anything else you can tell me that will top the last story – at least nothing that would make me think any less of you." Thomas shifted his weight on his arms and looked at her.

Gracie walked back toward Thomas, crossed her hands in front of her apron, and clasped them together, "Your brother John... he's very much alive as far as I know – he was here, and he left with Samuel and his family – and he wasn't alone. There was a woman and two children with him – just like that man said." Gracie lowered her eyes and said, "And your father – he ain't the only man I've had to kill here."

# 18

"You didn't need to speak to that girl that way," Emmie had never been in a car like this one. Her parents had an old 1952 Studebaker that her father had repaired a blown engine on – it got him to work and the family to church three blocks away. She was in great admiration of the radio, which Luke promptly turned off.

"I'm sorry – I will apologize to her later," Luke had one hand on the top of the wheel and the other at his side against the door. "I couldn't let her speak to you that way."

"I choose, and fight, my own battles, thank you," Emmie wrapped the blanket tighter around her shoulders. "Does this car have a heater?"

"Takes a little while to warm up."

Luke didn't really know where he was going because he really hadn't spent too much time in the actual city of Charlottesville. He knew what Monticello was, and he knew that West Main basically turned into Monticello Avenue, so he figured they could go that way and then turn around and come straight back to campus. He glanced over at Emmie and tried not to smile when he saw how beautiful she looked in the glow of the streetlights as they passed through town and headed out into the countryside.

"Where are we going?" Emmie asked.

"I don't know – I just figured you needed to get away from the mayhem is all."

"I probably shouldn't be here," she said.

"But you are – so make the best of it," Luke smiled this time. "Do you want to listen to the radio?"

"You probably don't like what I like, but sure if you want to," Emmie smiled back at him.

"I like Ray Charles and Etta James." Luke said.

"And I like Elvis Presley and Steve Lawrence – you don't need to just name colored singers for my benefit – just be yourself," Emmie giggled a little to herself.

"I'm really sorry about what happened to Natalie," Luke said as his smile faded. "If there's anything I can do for either of you..."

"There isn't anything you can do – we live this lie everyday – nobody believes anything we say. I mean – maybe they do, but they just don't care." Emmaline leaned back into the seat and got more comfortable. The car was finally starting to warm up some and she felt it on her feet. "I'll check on her as soon as I get to the hospital in the morning. They have her sedated and she will hopefully sleep through the night."

They drove on for a few minutes listening to "Twistin' the Night Away" and "Soldier Boy" playing quietly on the radio. The weather was really pushing for an early winter and the heater was doing its best to stave off the outside cold. Luke glanced over at Emmaline and saw she was laying with her head against the back of the seat looking at him. Despite the mess of her hair, he thought she looked like an angel sitting there. Her eyes danced and shimmered gold with each passing headlamp. He could see her sorrow and wanted to fix it. He wanted nothing more in the world. Luke brought the Chevy to a stop at a 4-way intersection. Coming across in front of them was an old, rusted Ford pickup with two white men in it. Luke caught the eye of the driver as they passed each other, and the bearded driver's animated expression caught Luke off guard. The man yelled something, but Luke didn't know what - or why. As they exited the intersection Luke saw the truck slam the brakes and begin to make a hard u-turn to come back their way.

"Damnit, hold on," he said and tried to remain calm.

"What's going on?" asked Emmie.

"I don't know yet."

Luke pushed the Chevy ahead, easily putting distance between themselves and the rickety old truck. A huge plume of white vapor was rolling from the car as it accelerated. The blacktop curved hard to the right and Luke saw what he was looking for – an old farm road that cut off to the right and disappeared into a cluster of tall trees. He maneuvered onto the road easily and killed the headlamps as he rolled under the trees and came to a stop seventy-five yards from Monticello Road. Thirty seconds later the rusty old green Ford lumbered past without seeing them.

"That – right there, is why you are better off not knowing me, Luke Montgomery," Emmie looked at him and placed her hands on the seat between them.

"You need to know one thing," he said. "I would never be better off for not having known you." Luke put his hand on hers and he could sense she wanted to pull away, but she didn't.

Luke's hand was freezing, but Emmaline dared not move her hand away. She wanted him to hold her hand. She wanted him to be right where he was – with her, in this car, on this dirt road – at this very moment. There was nothing else – no prejudice, no segregation, no hatred…just Luke and Emmaline. No person in this world could take away the butterflies flurrying in her stomach, nor would she want them to. But her mind kept going back to one thought and she couldn't shake it away - "this is not right."

"Luke, I think maybe you should drive me back now – I'm sure Mr. Richard will be wondering about me," Emmie pulled her hand away and turned her head to the window.

"I want you to know that I am your friend, and if you need me, I will always come as fast as I can," Luke wondered if he sounded like an idiot – he didn't just want to be her friend – that he knew for sure.

"I know you will," said Emmie.

Luke backed the car into a three-point turn and drove Emmaline back toward the diner. They rode in silence with the hum of the radio barely audible over the engine. The police had left, and he was able to pull straight up to Emmie's door. He parked the car, walked around to get her out, and escorted her to the stoop.

"Do you want to – maybe study together tomorrow?" Luke asked. "I'm done with practice by six and can be up here at six thirty or so." He opened the door to the little house and pushed it open for her.

"Probably not wise," she said.

"Probably isn't "no" – I'll take it."

"You can't come inside," she said.

"I have a blanket and we will sit up front at that unused picnic table and I will freeze with you if I have to," Luke laughed, and their eyes met again.

Emmaline fell into the pool of his deep blue eyes again – she couldn't stop herself, "We can sit in the back of the kitchen where Mr. Richard can keep an eye on me for my Daddy like he promised." She drew a shy smile and wondered what it would be like to run her fingers through his tousled blonde curls. She quickly pushed the thought away.

"It's a date," said Luke.

"No, it isn't," she said.

"You have your terminology, and I have mine," Luke turned to go.

Emmie called after him, "Thanks for taking me for a ride in your beautiful auto," she said. "It was definitely exciting."

"That it was," he said.

Luke drove Dom's car back to the dorm parking area and placed it back in the same spot. He smiled to himself, knowing he had never told her that the car wasn't his. He had never even come close to owning a car. Sure, he had his license -and he had driven farm trucks during the summer – but if he had to count the number of times in his life that he had driven an actual car like Dom's, he would only need to take off one mitten.

# 19

"What's your real name? Thomas had learned to prop himself up on the crutches, but it was usually short-lived, and he didn't get far from the bed.

"Mr. Thomas, you know my name is Gracie," she laughed as she stacked some small pieces of firewood next to the hearth. The days were warm, but the nights remained cool.

"No - I mean your full name - what's your full name – your given name? Thomas was sitting up now, with his legs swung over the bed and his only foot on the floor again. He arched the foot up and down to regain some muscle to help support his weight.

"I was named Grace by Mrs. Henry, and she gave me the middle name of Beatrice, which was her mother's name - so I guess my name is Grace Beatrice Henry, but everyone always called me Gracie," Grace turned and smiled at him as she walked to the little table and poured some milk into his porridge bowl. "Now, you need to eat."

Thomas smiled at her and said, "I haven't heard the rooster crowing in a while, but you said you were hoping to hatch some chicks soon – you do know how that works, right?" He took a spoonful of the porridge and swallowed hard – no wonder she put milk in it this morning – it was hard as a rock.

"Oh I keep that fella locked away down in the root cellar - he has a little bit of light coming in from the window and he crows something fierce down there," she looked down at the floor. "Mr. Thomas, if any of the soldiers on either side hear that bird hollering, they will come looking for him – and he will be in a stew pot by sundown. Those boys are so hungry that they are short sighted. My plan is for that rooster to provide us with many meals – not just one."

"You are a very smart and beautiful lady, Miss Beatrice Henry," Thomas laughed.

"If you please sir," she laughed and lifted him up onto the crutch – he grabbed onto it with both hands. "I'll be quick," she stripped the sheets off the bed from behind him and threw them in a pile on the floor. She had the replacements on in less than a minute. "That's better," she said.

"I don't want you to think that I'm not grateful that you're here," Thomas struggled to turn himself in her direction and almost fell over.

"Waverly really is paradise – even with all the war and killing going on around it - I wouldn't want to be anywhere else," Gracie laughed and bundled up the sheets from the floor into her arms. "You'd best be sitting back down now, Mr. Thomas."

"Gracie, why do you trouble yourself with the flowers and cleaning up the yard outside? Don't you think there are other things that are more important? Thomas tried to lower himself onto the bed, but it turned into an uncontrollable fall onto his rear end.

"Nothing is more important than taking care of God's beauty that we have all around us," she looked at him and her eyes all but melted him. "We are going to get you out of that bed and out of this house very soon!" Gracie knew he kept asking the same questions – but she would just keep answering them with a smile.

"That will be a fine day, Gracie, I've really missed my horses."

Gracie lowered her head and clutched the sheets closer to her, "I don't know how to tell you this, Mr. Thomas, but I haven't seen the horses since early winter. The blue coats came through here chasing the rebels, and they took most of the horses with them – except for the ones they couldn't catch."

"How many got away?" Thomas felt his heart sink. He lived for his horses.

"The black stallion with the lightning bolt on his forehead - he took off, and three mares followed him up and over the ridge and out of sight. A few of the Yankees went off after them but they returned empty handed, and one of them was bloodied up pretty bad," Gracie took a deep breath, and the smell of the sheets almost overwhelmed her. "I've seen the stallion up on the hill a few times, but he won't dare come back down to the house, and I haven't seen the mares at all. I need to go carry the wash out and then I can tell you more."

"Gracie, if you get me out of this bed, and out to the barn, we will find out if the horses are still out there pretty quick." Thomas smiled knowing *Lightening* might still be alive.

When Gracie returned from carrying the soiled sheets away, she spent the next hour trying to help Thomas hop around on the crutches, but his left leg wasn't strong enough yet and his upper body couldn't support his full weight, so they stayed near the bed. She would get him up for a few seconds before he would collapse back down onto the bed in pain and exhaustion. Thomas repeatedly complained about trying again, but she did not think this would be the day he moved around on his own. Finally, Gracie said that he had had enough for the morning and that he should lie down and rest until after dinner.

"I have got some salted pork hidden in the basement that the Yankees didn't find. When I come back inside, I'm going to slice some of that, and I'll make you those poached eggs you liked so much. But first I'm going to let you sleep for a few hours while I do some things outside."

Thomas had lost all his strength for the day and couldn't find it in himself to protest, so he laid back down and put his head on the pillow. Gracie put a blanket over him and pulled it halfway up "I'll see you very soon," she said and headed towards the door, "there's a glass of water on the table if you need it."

As she reached the door and started to go out, Thomas spoke to her, "Gracie," he said, and she turned around and smiled back at him, "Gracie, thank you – without you I would have nothing left."

Gracie allowed his piercing blue eyes to see into her soul, "And, without you I wouldn't either."

A few hours later, Thomas awoke from his slumber and sat up on the side of the bed to drink his glass of water. He rubbed his eyes and felt the scar running along his scalp line – it stung when he touched it. He ran his hand through his blond hair and put the glass back on the table. Out the window he could see Gracie in the garden surrounded by dandelions blowing through the air amidst twisters of oak leaves and small yellow butterflies. She was oblivious to the nature swirling around her as she dug another hole to plant a small tomato bush she had grown in the kitchen window sill from a seed. Thomas thought he could hear her singing. The sound gave him the strength he needed to pick up the crutches and push himself up from the bed. He teetered and wobbled at first, but he finally moved the crutches forward six inches and brought his good leg along with them. Thirty very small steps later, Thomas got to the window and saw and heard Gracie in all her beauty outside in the garden. What had been dreamlike serenity for a moment, was quickly turned into a nightmare of such immense proportions that each crutch practically flew from his arms as he collapsed with a giant thud against the wall. Thomas lay there curled up in a tight ball until Gracie arrived at his side.

"Oh, Mr. Thomas, you should have waited on me!" Gracie propped a pillow under his head and sat him against the wall beneath the window. "I'm going to get you an ice-cold cloth for your head."

"How?" he asked.

"Tomorrow," she said.

"It's always tomorrow, isn't it?" Thomas was struggling to sit up more.

"Tomorrow, I will show you my journal – and read to you from it," Gracie sighed and put her hand on his. "I don't want to leave anything out."

It was a full half hour struggle to get Thomas back to his bed – and another fifteen to get him in it and comfortable. He just lay there as Gracie left the room to get him a shot of whiskey and some bread – the other meal would have to wait. He couldn't believe what he had just seen… Gracie's Garden was spectacular to say the least, but behind it along the ridge, the trees were filled with black vultures and crows – and flies swarmed all along the fence line. It was at that moment that he had seen the handkerchief wrapped around

Gracie's face – but then he looked to the left and up the long drive which led out to the road to town – the fields were barren and brown, and vines grew all along the three-rail fencing. Glancing to the right was what shocked him into losing his balance. Two of the five little white houses sat charred and crumpled into piles - and worst of all – his beloved barn, where he spent most of every day with his horses, was a pit of broken black timbers and rotting wood – it was gone.

Waverly Plantation as he remembered it …was no more…

# 20

Luke walked to Tailpipes in freezing drizzle on Monday night and found himself thankful for the warmth and the smells of the kitchen. He sat with Emmaline at a small table with four chairs near the kitchen door which led out to the back where the dumpsters were...and Emmaline's house. Mr. Richard was acting as the fry cook that evening because a few of his employees had already left for Thanksgiving break.

"Got my eye on you two!" he announced from his position at the prep counter.

"I'm sure you do," said Emmie softly, without looking up from her Human Anatomy book.

"You know – I know quite a bit about Anatomy," Luke tried to make conversation over his copy of the *Illiad* that was being studied in his Lit 102 class.

"Is that a joke?" she asked.

"Not at all – well let me clarify – I know quite a bit about equine anatomy."

"Horses? Not the same as people," Emmie stared unimpressed over her textbook.

"Horses are much more complex animals than people. Did you know they have 205 bones in their body?" Luke was trying harder now.

"And humans have 206 – see more complex." She at least smiled a little when she said this.

"A horse's bones, ligaments, and tendons have to support over a thousand pounds of weight." Luke pressed further.

"Proportionate to overall body weight, the bones in a human take up a larger percentage of the mass," she had no idea if this was true, but it sounded good – and it briefly shut him down.

Luke changed the subject, "I have a game tomorrow night and then I'm heading North to my family for the break. Can I see you when we get back? We can study together again."

Emmie looked directly at him and found the courage to say, "We have exams when we get back – and my studying needs to be more studying and less nonsense…and you staring at me for two hours."

Luke thought about saying, "I am studying – I'm studying you," then he thought better of it, which was probably a good thing. "I'll just drop by to check on you then – maybe next Monday evening." Luke picked up his book -it was the only thing he had brought with him – and he stood up. "I should probably head back up the road," he said.

Emmaline looked into those blue eyes again – she really needed to control that, "Goodnight, Mr. Montgomery," she said.

"Goodnight, Ms. Foster – until we meet again," Luke left the kitchen through the back door and started the long cold trek back to the dorm – he didn't seem to mind.

Emmaline smiled and stared off into the space where he was just standing for a good thirty seconds before putting her nose back into the Anatomy book. Her fear and sadness welled back up almost at once, making it hard to concentrate. She found herself re-reading pages too often.

The next night Emmaline Foster was delivered to the Greyhound Bus terminal by Mr. Richard. She found herself waiting on a hard bench in the cold wind for what seemed like an eternity – until she heard a familiar voice.

"Well, if it isn't the number one nursing student in all of the state of Virginia - Miss Emmaline Foster," Luke had an uncanny ability to show up wherever she went.

"Are you following me now?" she said and wrapped her overcoat firmly around her waist with her hands stuck into the sleeves.

"I thought you were staying here to work," Luke dropped a small duffel bag on the ground next to her. "What's with the two big suitcases? We only have a five-day break."

"After what happened to Natalie – I think I'm just going to go back home – and stay there."

Luke sat down next to her, and she felt his warmth from two feet away, "You can't do that, Emmaline. This world has too many people like me and not enough like you. The world needs a nurse like Emmaline Foster. You are compassionate and caring in a country filled with angry people." He put his gloved hand on her arm, and for a moment she felt his sincerity. "Please don't give up on yourself – or the rest of us."

A tear rolled down her cheek and Luke brushed it off gently with the back of his glove. "I just don't know – I've kind of made up my mind. My dad needs me back in the hardware store anyway." She needed to stop talking about it now, "Why are you at the bus station? Where is your car?"

Luke smiled, "Emmie, I don't have a car – that was Dom's. I've never had a car – in fact my family has just one back home and my dad needs it for work – when it works."

"What do you mean?" She looked at him with a mix of bewilderment and doubt.

"If you go home and don't come back, I may never see you again, and I don't want that," Luke inched closer to her, almost out of necessity to fight off the eighteen-degree temperature.

"I wish life were simpler," she said, "but I can't change the reality of it all – things would be much different if I could – that I promise." Then she looked at Luke again, "It doesn't matter if I like you, Luke – we can never be together – it's just another harsh punishing reality of my life."

Luke took a deep breath, "Will you watch my bag while I go the men's room really quick?"

"Hurry up please, my bus leaves in a few minutes."

"Mine doesn't leave for an hour – but I'll be right back."

Luke took off in the direction of the facilities and Emmie pulled his bag closer, even though there weren't many other people in the terminal. He returned about five minutes later.

"Boarding for Richmond – colored first please," the bus driver called out to the few folks braving the nighttime chill for a ride home to see their families. Segregation on interstate buses had been made illegal by the federal government, but some intra-state bus lines in the South stuck to their last few remaining straws where they could.

Luke grabbed Emmie's bags and carried them over to the driver who placed them inside a compartment that was accessed from the outside. The man reached over and took Emmaline's ticket and said, "Anywhere in the back six rows ma'am."

"Thank you, sir," she said and turned to look at Luke. "I know we were destined to be good friends, Luke. You are so very thoughtful, and you have taken good care of me -whether I deserved it or not. I'm sorry if I was mean to you at times," she lowered her head. "It's just for the best." She said and went up the steps and disappeared into the back of the dark bus.

Emmaline found a seat against the far window in the second to last row where she collapsed and put her head against the glass and closed her eyes. There were many more tears working their way to the outside, but she did her best to stall their trip. A moment later someone sat down beside her, and she closed her eyes even tighter. The last thing she wanted was small talk with a stranger on a four-hour middle of the night bus ride.

"This seat taken, ma'am?"

"What are you doing?" Emmie blurted out at Luke.

"Son, your seat is in the front," the driver was standing two rows up from them.

"No sir, your seat is in the front – mine is right here next to my friend."

"Suit yourself – time to go – I ain't gonna argue with you at this hour."

"You are on the wrong bus, Luke," Emmie looked so beautiful to him, and he was looking forward to having her undivided attention for half the night.

"I'm on the right bus – I didn't go to the bathroom – I swapped my ticket for Richmond." Luke gave her a broad smile. "Do you think your parents will like me?"

Emmie smiled back at him, "I think they will disown me for bringing you home." She lay her head on his shoulder, and it felt so good – so good in fact that she was soon fast asleep as the bus rumbled eastward.

# 21

## December 1862 – The Journal of Grace Henry

*The grey coats limped into the courtyard three days back. Most of the two dozen or so could barely walk – they were missing boots and socks, and many of them didn't have anything to keep them warm from the horrible winter wind. Only a handful even had a rifle in their possession. I made a kettle of broth for them with some old soupbones I had been holding back from using. Mr. Thomas and I don't have much left to eat since the house was ransacked a few months ago. But I think we can make do until Spring with what I have hidden away. I kept a cloth over my face and my hair up under a bonnet – some because of the smell of them and some because I didn't want them to look on me as anything other than a slave. I hid inside the house from them at night – but they knew I was taking care of one of their own, so they mostly showed me respect for that matter. They gathered around the oak trees near the barn and tended to their wounded around a couple of small fires they had burning. I gave two of them a spool of thread so they could try to repair their clothes. They were a sad lot really – I think they were planning to try to move further South in the coming days. They may have been waiting on the New River train to come through.*

*I was awakened in the dawn hours of their fourth day at Waverly by shouting at first – and then distant gunfire. I crept to the window in Mr. Thomas' room, and I could see the soldiers trying to get to their feet and then they moved off up the ridge and headed toward the river. They left several dying men behind them piled like straw dolls around the oak trees. Some were almost dead, but others were just too badly injured to walk – let alone run – and they were screaming for help from the ones that left them behind. The Union soldiers surrounded the house and made their way into the yard just as the sun was rising over the eastern ridge. They approached the group of grays around the oak and one by one they stabbed them to death with their bayonets. It was over quickly, and the group moved out after the others that were running away. A few moments later several men on horses arrived in the front, and they dismounted as more soldiers on foot began to fill the yard. It seemed like over a hundred soldiers were around the house and barn. I knew they would come inside, so I just sat in the chair by Mr. Thomas' bedside, and I waited. It didn't take long until one of the young soldiers found me – and soon thereafter a man they called Captain Jensen walked up to me as I sat there.*

*He asked me if Mr. Thomas was a Confederate and I told him that he was just a young boy caught up in something he didn't know anything about. Then that man turned to another that he called Corporal and told him to send me North and burn the house. The Corporal asked about Mr. Thomas, and he said just leave him in the bed he made for himself – "he won't feel nothing, hell he's most dead anyway". They didn't seem ready for what I did next. I stood up and got in front of Mr. Thomas and I told those men that I promised his mother to stay here with him until he was dead, and I meant to do just that. The captain drew his pistol, and he pointed it at Mr. Thomas and said he could help hurry that along – so I stood in front of Mr. Thomas so the gun was pointed right into my chest and I told that man that I keep my promises, and I wasn't leaving. The captain turned to his corporal and told that man to hog tie me to the bed so I could stay with the traitor until the end. Then he told the corporal to take care of it all and meet back up down at the New River. Then I watched out the window as all the soldiers, save the corporal, streamed out behind the barn and flooded up over the back ridge.*

*Things got worse from that point. I asked the corporal to spare our lives and he told me not to worry because he had plans for me. He threw me down on the floor beside the bed and took out a knife and he opened my smock from top to bottom until it just hung wide open on me. The next part just happened so fast – he went to put the knife back in the sheath on his belt and I used my free leg to kick him back off me and his head hit the corner of Mr. Thomas' bed with a loud thud. I rushed to the hearth and grabbed the fire poker as he came for me again – and I just turned and drove it straight into the soft part of his belly just above his belt. He went to his knees calling me some unholy names and then he fell over on his side and didn't make another sound. His blood started to run and seep into the cracks of the floorboards, so I got one of Mr. Thomas' sheets and tied it tight around his ankles and with some effort I pulled him out of the house and dragged him down the footpath behind the rock to the river. I rolled him into the edge of the river, and I am guessing the shock of the cold woke him, because he grabbed what was left of my dress and pulled me down there with him – and I almost got pulled away. By God's grace my hand found a large stone and I drove it into the side of his head, and he let go. I watched him floating down the river face down until he disappeared around the bend toward Christiansburg.*

*I gathered myself up and somehow got back up the path to the house. I knew that captain would be looking back for the smoke, so I lit the slave house next to Samuel and Margaret's afire and it spread to the next one over. But I didn't feel it was enough smoke to be the main house – so I lit up the barn as well. If they were to come back this way, they'd kill us both for sure. Then I set to scrubbing up all the blood in the house and down the steps just as quick as I could, and I threw the sheets and cloths in the fire. Then I crawled under Mr. Thomas' bed with the shotgun – and I hid...and cried...and was scared they were coming back... and I begged God to forgive me for this day. After two days and nights I crawled back out to my miserable existence and resumed my death watch.*

# 22

Emmaline stepped down from the Greyhound at 1:45 am and into the arms of her waiting mother, Mathilde Foster. She had slept on Luke's shoulder the entire way, and truth be told she was a bit disappointed when they arrived in Richmond.

"Oh, Sweetheart- are you alright?" said her mother.

"I'll be okay," Emmie moved with her mother's arm wrapped tightly around her shoulder to where the driver had begun to unload their luggage.

"Foster," the man cried and threw out Emmie's first bag which was quickly followed by the second. Her mother picked up the first bag with her free hand, and then she saw a white hand reach in to grab the other.

"That's our bag, young man," she said to Luke.

"I've got it, and I can even carry the other one if you'd like."

"We will get along just fine, sir - I don't have money for a tip," Mathilde moved to retrieve the second bag.

"I don't require one," said Luke. "Just giving Emmaline some help. I've just got this small duffel."

"Where's Daddy?" asked Emmie in a vain attempt to stifle her mother's next question.

"Waiting in the car with the heat on of course," her mother started toward the pick-up area where Emmie's dad was waiting in their Studebaker. She eyed Luke suspiciously as they got to the car and Emmie's father got out and opened the trunk with a press of his thumb.

"This looks like every bit of your laundry, young lady. You must be trying to work your mom's fingers to the bone?" Anthony Foster was a tall but stout, formidable force of a man. He took Emmaline's bags from Luke and hoisted them into the car effortlessly. "Thank you, young man. We don't have money for a tip though," he echoed Mathilde.

"Glad you got home safe, Emmie," Luke smiled and put his hand on her arm.

"Ya'll meet on the bus then? Which one was in the wrong seat?" Anthony laughed.

Luke looked at Emmie to see how she wanted him to answer but she didn't give him the chance, "We know each other from school, Daddy" she said.

"Yes, we are friends - we met on campus," Luke saw the concern Emmaline's mother had in her eyes. "It was certainly nice to meet you folks – I know Emmaline's very tired and could use a good night's sleep, so ya'll need to get her on home. I'm just going to hang out here in the terminal and catch the next bus going my way in the morning," he smiled and opened the rear passenger door for Emmie.

"Are you not from Richmond?" Anthony asked.

"No sir, West Virginia," Luke answered.

"You rode all the way here with Emmaline for no reason?" Anthony seemed suspicious, but only slightly.

"I ran into her at the bus station in Charlottesville, and she seemed a little sad, so I just wanted to make sure she got home okay. It's nothing really," Luke looked squarely at Emmie's father.

The Foster family seemed to be having a conference with just their eyes. Emmaline was still absorbing the fact that she hadn't really known where Luke was from.

Emmaline's dad broke the awkward silence, "Nonsense, son, you come to the house and get some sleep - we'll feed you, and I'll bring you back to the terminal myself in the morning on my way to work. You can stay in Emmaline's brother James' room. He's off at basic training anyhow," Anthony opened the rear driver's side door. "Get in – it's cold."

The unspoken family conference began again, and Mathilde finally relented. "Throw your bag in and let's get out of this chill before we catch the death of cold," she said. "Boy's gonna look like a grain of rice in a bowl of black-eyed peas up in Church Hill," Emmie's mom laughed and climbed into the front seat.

Luke and Emmaline sat just about as far away from each other as was humanly possible in the back seat of Mr. Foster's car. Emmie could see both sets of her parents' eyes glancing into the mirrors to keep an eye on her. The ride home was quiet for a few minutes and Luke watched the city of Richmond roll by as they headed toward Church Hill. He could feel the tension in the car, but he did everything in his willpower to stay calm and not show the fear he had for Emmie's mother.

Anthony broke the silence again, "So, Luke – is it? What are you studying over at UVA?"

"I'm majoring in Biology – hoping to be a farm vet someday," Luke looked at Mr. Foster's eyes in the rearview mirror.

"Emmaline's scared of horses – did you know that?" Mathilde turned now to look at them both.

"I did not," said Luke.

Emmaline just rolled her eyes and gave her mother a blank stare. Luke could tell she was simmering. "We don't know each other all that well – he just seems to show up when I have a problem. He might just be bad luck."

"Really? Do tell?" Emmie's mother seemed invested now.

Luke looked at Emmaline and then offered, "I picked her up when she got knocked down…"

"Your fault."

"I helped her at Mr. Richard's when she almost dropped a garbage can on her head…"

"I would have managed."

"I gave her my sweatshirt when some idiots threw an egg at her and Wesley's table on the Quad…"

"Probably throwing it at you for talking to us."

"And – I went to check on her when I heard what happened to Natalie," Luke lowered his eyes.

"Yes," she said slowly, "…he was very sweet that night," Emmie looked at her mother who somehow managed a smile.

"Wesley is such a nice young man," Mathilde said, and Emmie ignored her.

The Studebaker pulled up in front of a small square house and parked on the street. The house was lap-sided and painted light blue with two windows in the front facing the street, two dormers protruding from the sharply angled roof, and a chimney at least six feet wide running up one side. A set of stairs ran parallel to the house just inside a rusted wrought iron gate and up to a small porch where the front door was waiting.

"Home sweet home," said Anthony as the girls climbed quickly out of the car to avoid further conversation. "You girls get inside, and we'll get the bags."

Emmaline walked ten feet in front of her mother and hurried into the house.

Anthony opened the trunk and with Luke's help they retrieved the three bags.

"Thank you." Anthony said.

"For what, sir." Luke looked at him – they were just about the same height.

"For watching out for my little girl – that's what," Anthony put his free hand on Luke's shoulder.

"It's really nothing, sir. Emmie's a very special person."

"It's something to me," Anthony continued. "Ain't too many white folk who pay us much attention – and you done something I never thought I'd see." He looked straight into Luke's eyes as they started toward the house, "You gave my little girl the shirt straight off'n your back."

# 23

Gracie slowly closed her journal and looked as if the sorrow would just pour straight out of her if she was held upside down. A single tear rolled down her cheek and she brushed it away, hoping Thomas wouldn't see it. "I'm sorry - for all this Mr. Thomas."

"So, you want me to forgive you for saving my life? For saving the Waverly House?" Thomas Summerlin continued to be overwhelmed by Gracie's strength and courage. "You owe me no apology – ever. I am the one who should apologize for doubting you earlier," he sat up on the side of the bed and took her hands in his. "You amaze me, Grace Henry."

She investigated his beautiful, and sincere blue eyes and her frown straightened slightly, "It happened so fast, Mr. Thomas, - I was out of my head…the dead Rebels – I dragged them in the same manner but with a rope…to the edge of the three-rail fence. Then I rolled them down into the ravine and into the creek. I'm sorry – there were six of them and I didn't have the strength to dig six graves – but I had to get them away from the house as far as I could – the stench was so bad."

"You had to do something," he said. "You did the right thing – once I get moving, I can try to do something else with what's left of them. I can get some lime from Draper."

"The vultures and crows have been here for a long time – they don't leave," Gracie moved one of her hands on top of his. "I'm sorrier about the barn, but I was so scared they would come back."

"What about the corporal?"

"They never came back for him – I don't know why," Gracie said. "I was going to tell them he had pity on us, and he was afraid he was going to be punished – so he took a horse and went North and set fire to the buildings. Ms. Draper told me later that they moved off upriver and past the Shot Tower – so I was able to breathe again."

"You planted the garden – the vegetables and flowers just outside my window so that's all I would see?"

"To be honest, it was the best place to get sun, and it was close to the well so I could get to water easily. It just worked out that way – it also helps that I can see it from the window and run the critters away when I see them," Gracie laughed a little. "It's God's plan I guess…but I was glad you didn't see this mess before now."

"I'll work on rebuilding the barn when I get to where I can move around better." Thomas ran his thumb across the top of her hand and noticed how soft her skin was. "My mother's hands were as rough as a porcupine, and she had folks like you who did most of her work for her. Your hands are so soft – and you do everything around here."

"I have a little jar that I keep filled with clay I dig from the riverbank – I cover my hands with that and then pour some milk over them to wash it in," Gracie felt she was saying too much. "Then I wash with water – it seems to keep the callouses down – and keeps my fingers from getting dry and bleeding. I'm sorry – you don't need to know all this."

"I told you to stop apologizing," Thomas smiled at her – lost in the golden flakes in her shimmering eyes.

Gracie stared back at him, "Miss Draper was telling me about this doctor in Richmond that is making false limbs for folks. She thinks she can get you fitted for something to help you walk – she called it an American Leg invented by some man named Palmer or some such."

"I feel like I might be better off with the crutches – it will at least make my arms stronger," Thomas shook his head. "I've seen those guys with wooden limbs – they don't really walk right, and it looks awkward."

"Miss Draper says these new ones have hinges and moveable parts – but you can stay on crutches if you want to…I think you might get tired faster though." Gracie put her hand on top of his. "She is coming up here in a couple of days…to check on you."

"It will be nice to see someone else," Thomas winked at her. "She was my schoolmarm you know - and I did fancy her when I was younger."

"I am not the jealous type, Mr. Summerlin."

"So, we are being formal now, Miss Henry?" He smiled again, and she slowly lowered her eyes. "I never implied your jealously, but it is interesting to know your immediate thought went to that."

"My mother, Mrs. Henry, always taught me beggars can't be choosers – and right now me and you seem to be the only man and woman in the entire county," Gracie laughed as his face straightened. "Relax some, Mr. Thomas, I'm teasing you…but it is so good to have someone to talk to after all of these months. I think my talking to you while you were asleep is the only thing that ever saved me from being insane."

"You have saved us both," he said. "I don't know how many times you have saved me…I think you have done it every day for months now. I just don't know why."

"I think you have it backwards, Mr. Thomas," she didn't resist his hands this time as he closed his around hers tighter. "I was left here alone – well with you – but basically alone. You gave me a reason to stay – to stay alive. I told you I have nowhere to go. I could have left with Samuel, I guess. But I couldn't leave you here by yourself – to die alone." Gracie began to tear up again.

"Don't cry, please," Thomas tried to pull her closer and this time she did resist, but just briefly. He brought her to him, and her head naturally rested on his shoulder – a human touch like none she had ever felt before. She gave into it and just relaxed -maybe for the first time in months. "You stayed with me and now I am here with you – we only have each other…nothing more." Thomas smelled the lilacs and honeysuckle in her hair and on her skin – it was perfect – it was natural. "And…that's all we need," he said.

# 24

"Rise and shine, my friend," the young man came into James' borrowed room to roust Luke. "And shine in this neighborhood you will!" He pulled down on the cloth shade and let go – it ran into a coil with a sharp snap as bright sunshine came pouring across the bed.

"Oh my God, Alvin - right?" Luke ran his fingers through tousled golden locks and tried to shake away the sleep that still held him in its' grip. "Jesus, what time is it? I need to get to my bus."

"No buses to the mountains today, buddy," Alvin stood over him now. "Blizzard came through overnight and socked in everything in the Shenandoah and westward – you are trapped in Church Hill with us colored folks for Thanksgiving – oh, and it's half past ten."

"Where's Emmaline?" Luke pushed the sheet down to his waist and started to sit up.

"Down to the church with her mama to serve some early meals to those who can't make do. She should be around by two," Alvin seemed to be in an overly excited mood this morning and Luke was just plain exhausted. "Did you bring some Keds?"

"Converse in my bag, why?"

"Get dressed and we can go for a walk – it's sunny out but a might chilly so wear what you got," Alvin headed to the door. "There's some juice and toast in the kitchen -come on out when you get ready – bathroom is across the hall."

"I need to check in on my mom." Luke got up from the bed. "I called her from the station last night, but she was expecting me this morning."

"Phone is in the kitchen – better call collect or Foster will shake you upside down 'til change falls out," Alvin laughed and closed the door.

Luke glanced around James' simple bedroom for the first time in the light. A single pineapple post bed that had been handed down, a small dresser, complete with a vanity mirror that really looked like it belonged in a ten-year-old girl's room, green and rust colored worn carpeting and a metal clothes rack with a few shirts, but many loose empty hangers. On the dresser were twenty or so small trophies of varying sports, but mainly football. The room had a definite musty odor to it but was clean otherwise. Luke smiled and pulled his sweatpants over his boxer shorts, slid on the same socks from the day before, and stepped into his Converse. Spending one more day with Emmaline Foster was not going to kill him – was it? He walked out the door and crossed the hall and into the bathroom for his morning routine. A few minutes later he joined Alvin in the kitchen.

"We are gonna head up the hill to the church – it's kind of a Thanksgiving morning ritual for us. The ladies serve the less fortunate and we shoot some hoops out back and then help clean up. Then it's back down here for our family meal..." Alvin poured Luke a glass of orange juice from a cranberry-colored glass pitcher. "Want me to make you a piece of toast in the oven – there's some marmalade my mama made in the icebox.

"Who am I to pass up your mama's marmalade?" Luke laughed.

Alvin plopped two pieces of Sunbeam bread on a v-shaped toaster rack and placed it in the oven on broil. Less than two minutes later he lifted the rack out with a dishcloth and expertly dumped the toast on a yellow Fiestaware plate. "Butter?" he asked.

"Sure," said Luke.

"Why you here, Luke? Serious…" Alvin handed him a butter tray with half a stick on it and then stuck a spoon in the marmalade jar.

"What do you mean?" Luke scraped some butter onto the first piece of toast then spooned a large glob of orange marmalade on top. He took too big of a bite to avoid saying anything more.

"Come on, man – I ain't born yesterday. You got a thing for Em, right?"

"I promise we are just friends," Luke swallowed uncomfortably and took a slug of the juice. "She had a rough week and needed a friend."

"I'll 'cept that for now, but I'm a tell you her daddy has his eye on you," Alvin laughed. "Call your mother, so we can head out."

Luke's mother answered the phone on a half ring and when she heard the operator ask about collect charges he could hear her screaming "Yes! Yes!" The phone call was quick and ended with his mother telling him what a great man he was for escorting a young lady home in her time of need. He promised to see her in a couple of days without telling her any vital information about Emmaline, her family, or what part of Richmond he was in. After he hung up, he joined Alvin on the front porch, and they headed up the street.

"People gonna stare at you – just like they would me if I was in your neighborhood – don't sweat it," Alvin clapped him on the back as they walked.

"Nobody would stare at you in my neighborhood," Luke just smiled.

"Sure thing - you know it."

The African Methodist Episcopal Church in that part of Richmond used to belong to a white congregation, but as the Church Hill area turned over so did the establishments. The new congregation treated their new place of worship with the tender loving care that it was never given by its' previous tenants – not because they didn't care, but because they just threw money at problems without rolling up their sleeves and treating the church like their own. The church itself rose proudly from the curb and stretched out over a small sloping hill just large enough for a fellowship hall to be built underneath it in the back. The parking lot was teeming with people when Alvin and Luke walked down the steps beside the church and made their way to the hall. There was a line of people extending from the back of the building – both colored and white.

"I thought you said people were going to stare at me," Luke pointed out the obvious.

"You are a six-foot something semi-famous basketball player from UVA – what did you think I meant? Alvin laughed harder this time as they went through the side door and into the back of the kitchen.

"There are sure a lot of white folks in here," Luke walked closely beside Alvin.

"Son, we ain't the only poor people up in this town," Alvin laughed. "There's a lot of good hard-working families on both sides living in this area and we love to help each other out when we can. Not everybody can throw a turkey on the table every year."

Emmaline Foster was standing behind a serving line doling out sweet potato pie, which had a one-inch layer of melted marshmallow spread across the top of it. She had a cloth net with a drawstring tightened around the bun of her beautiful black hair and gloves on her hands – one of which held a large metal spoon covered in potatoes. She melted each person with a friendly greeting and warm smile as they thrust their plates toward her for a spoonful or two. She didn't notice Luke's arrival. She was right where she belonged.

"You need a camera? Or you just burning an image into your big soft brain?" Alvin laughed and pushed Luke toward the back of the serving line.

"Good morning, Emmie," Luke said from behind her.

She turned slowly, surprised at his presence, "Wait – why are you here? I thought you were on a bus headed west." She turned back to her audience.

"Uh – I'm guessing your father didn't tell you about the snowstorm that halted buses going that way?" Luke felt out of sorts for a moment until Alvin nudged him to bring him back into his right mind.

"Snowstorm? Really?" she laughed without turning around. "My father, the weatherman."

"Can I do anything to help out?" Luke asked and another voice quickly came in from behind him – it was Emmaline's mother.

"Ever carved a turkey? We got six needing cut up back here," she motioned for him to follow.

"We have a yard full of chickens that feed us back home – can't be much difference," he responded and felt thankful to be following her away from Emmie -because he had no idea what he was going to say to her next.

Luke set to carving up turkeys as Alvin stacked the slices into a serving tray. They worked without speaking for a couple of minutes until Alvin broke the silence.

"Her daddy don't care much for any boy she ever brought around," Alvin smiled.

"That Wesley doesn't seem like a bad guy," Luke kept slicing without looking over at him. "And…we are just friends."

"Wesley? I ain't got no friends looks at me the way you look at her – or her at you when you ain't watching."

"I like you, Alvin, but you aren't as smart as you think," Luke tossed a whole turkey leg in his direction – it landed in the huge metal tray, but his mind was stuck on what Alvin had just said. Emmie was very guarded when it came to their friendship – and Luke was convinced it was just always going to be what it was – a friendship. Still, he smiled.

After an hour and six turkeys later, Luke and Alvin emerged from the back of the kitchen into the main serving area. Emmie was nowhere to be seen and neither was her mother. An older colored lady eyed Luke up and down before telling him they had gone back up the hill to their house to prepare the family meal that was to be served later that afternoon. She also told the boys that there was a "mess of cleanin' up yet to do and they was gonna pitch in", which they reluctantly set about to accomplish, but with a smile.

Around two o'clock Alvin and Luke emerged from the church and tiredly made their way across the black top parking lot in the rear. At the back of the lot there was a dilapidated tennis court with a net rolled up to one side. At either end was a basketball goal – one had a chain net – the other was just a steel hoop with a steel backboard. A ten-foot chain link fence covered the sides and back of the court. The fence behind was covered in brown dead vines that had succumbed to the harsh winter. A cliff ran up behind the fence and disappeared into a row of houses some fifty feet above. The side with the goal and net was occupied by a group of young men heavily involved in a three-on-three game to twenty. The other side was swarming with children who were mostly under ten. The boys tossed around a red rubber ball while a few girls were practicing Double Dutch with two dirty ropes. One of the basketball players motioned Alvin to come over.

"What's up G?" Alvin asked.

"You and your new friend want in?" G turned and tossed the ball back toward his teammates and Luke saw the name George sprawled across the back of his grey sweatshirt. He thought that would save him a question which he probably didn't need to ask anyway. Alvin looked over at Luke and nodded.

"I think my coach would not be happy about this," Luke tried to make an excuse to avoid getting on the court.

The recognition showed up in George's face as Luke spoke, "Lordy boys, it's Luke Montgomery himself – all the way from Charlottesville. You probably should sit this one out – you ain't never played against many of us negroes – has you?"

Alvin started, "Come on G-"

Luke finished for him, "Unfortunately not…let's see what you boys got cookin." He took off his heavy jacket and tossed it on the ground.

George looked at him, grinned, and pointed, "We hang our coats on the fence over yonder – 'cause our mamas taught us to take care of everything we got."

Luke hung up his jacket and joined the group of three facing George's foursome – which had picked up Alvin. A few quick introductions later and the ball hit the court as George dribbled to the top of the inaccurately hand painted key. Quick sharp passes moved around in a circle as Luke's team covered man-to-man with Luke on George. Alvin threw up a fifteen-footer that banged metallically off the rim as Luke turned and pulled down the rebound. Both teams traded short jumpers back and forth with Luke finding nothing but chain net from twenty-five feet out a few times. Nobody had attempted to drive to the basket at this point when Luke decided to add some dialogue.

"You guys holding back on me?" he asked in George's general direction.

"We ain't gon' be the reason Mister Point Guard gets hurt," George said.

Luke reached in and stole the ball from Alvin and made a quick behind the back bounce pass to one of his guys underneath who rose easily to slam the basketball through the steel rim.

"Okay, you're on!" George took the ball back to the half court line and turned to come back. Luke set up in his stance to provide defense on his return. George made a quick pass to Alvin and rolled past Luke on his left – streaking through the lane. Alvin launched the ball toward the basket as George went up high over the rim to slam it home with one hand as Luke stumbled backward through the lane in a vain attempt to defend.

"Very nice," Luke said. He brought the ball back to the top of the key and passed to one of his teammates who missed a short jumper. George swooped in and pulled the rebound right off the backboard and made a quick outlet pass to Alvin who took it back. Alvin dribbled straight at Luke and then made a no-look pass to George who nailed a twenty-five footer. Luke was left flat-footed this time.

Another quick exchange saw Luke missing an easy jumper which George quickly returned. This time he approached Luke at the top of the key and looked hard at Alvin – Luke shifted his weight in that direction as George brought the ball behind his back then through his legs. He went past Luke like a lightning bolt and made an easy layup through two other defenders. Luke lost his balance and banged off the cold hard tarmac with a thud. He sat there for a minute – then laughed. George walked back to his side with the ball under his arm.

"Been schooled enough yet?" George reached out and pulled Luke to his feet. "I hope you ain't mad."

"I'll say this George – er G – You just schooled me, and I ain't mad – I just want you to teach me everything you know."

# 25

Thomas's new lower leg was not much short of a miracle. When the Draper's arrived at Waverly with the limb on their buckboard Thomas was about as skeptical as he could possibly be. He was certain his new existence involved crutches, and limping, and his newfound passion – hopping. His strength was somehow returning but his anger and depression over the loss of his lower left leg were not something he could fully grasp. He had not yet found the will to come off the front porch of the house for fear he would fall face first into the mud. But the new mahogany leg was hope. He sat on the edge of the bed with his stump sticking straight out as Dr. Draper fitted the Palmer leg for the first time. It slid onto his stump and had soft but firm padding where the support would be. A stiff, laced leather sleeve pulled upward to about mid-thigh was fastened tight but breathable to keep the leg in place. Gracie smiled at him with all the encouragement he could ever expect.

"Ready?" Dr. Draper locked his hand and forearm with Thomas'.

"This feels strange," Thomas didn't feel ready.

"I know you want to ride a horse again. I've known you since I helped your mama birth you in the middle of the night," Ms. Draper offered her support as well.

He did long for the feel of a saddle again – that was sure. "What the hell – won't be the first time I've hit the floor."

The doctor didn't allow him to second guess as he pulled him upright from the bed and steadied him with his shoulders in a bearhug. "I have your weight - now you see if you can ease into the support on your own."

Thomas started to let go of Dr. Draper's shoulders three times before he finally moved his arms out like wings and rotated them to provide balance. He stood there briefly and smiled in Gracie's direction before his body tried to collapse back onto the bed. The doctor caught him under his shoulders and propped him back up. This was how the next hour went. Thomas would gain balance for a longer period and Dr. Draper would support him every time he started to fall back onto the bed – well most times anyway. Thomas was growing increasingly frustrated and losing his patience with the situation. Gracie recognized his growing unease.

"Should I fetch the whiskey?" she grinned. "Mr. Thomas likes to have a sip while he's practicing getting out of bed."

Ms. Draper fixed her good, "Some of that nice sassafras tea you are always bragging on might do the trick." Gracie stared at her, "hurry off now child – and bring some honey and biscuits if you have them."

Gracie hurried out the door toward the kitchen as Thomas slumped back down onto the bed. "I need a moment, please," he took some deep breaths and felt the pain from the pit of his stomach down through his thighs. He felt as though he had ripped the muscles away from his ribs -this was real pain.

"Thomas, you will need to take this slow," Dr. Draper sat beside him on the bed. "I need to speak with you while Gracie isn't within earshot anyway."

Thomas looked at him with regret, "You're going to tell me I slept for over a year just so I could wake up and die – is that it?"

"To be honest, I never thought you were going to wake up at all."

"That's some great bedside manner you have there, doc," Thomas tried to joke but really didn't feel it right now.

"You need to know as much as I can tell you, Thomas" the doctor turned to look him in the eye. "You were in bad shape when you were brought back here. Your leg had been cut off on the battlefield and the infection was close to gangrene when you arrived. We soaked it and wrapped it, and I cauterized much of the flesh – but it wasn't your worst injury. Your stomach was sliced open from side to side and your organs had been exposed to God knows what for days. The ladies that pulled you from the field packed your incision with saline towels and poured alcohol over everything before brining you here. They gave you morphine whenever they thought you would come out of consciousness – and I think they gave you too much. I believe this may be one reason you never woke up – but more likely it is because your body needed to heal from the inside out. I sewed you up and cauterized the area, but your intestine had to be put back in – and I'm certain your liver was badly damaged. The piece of metal that scraped your head just left a bad scar."

"Okay, so I'm back together then – well except for this," Thomas pointed to the stump with the new leg attached.

"Thomas, I don't know how well – or how long – your body will hold up."

"You're saying I'm dying?"

"I'm saying that if you eat the right things and live the right way – you will live longer," Dr. Draper put his hand on Thomas' shoulder. "Fish, chicken, and vegetables would be my recommendation – stay away from beef and wild game and probably nuts and too much grain – and watch how much milk you drink."

"You don't know for sure that I'm like this – you are guessing."

"It's what we usually see in injuries similar to yours – every case may be different."

"Mine's different," Thomas moved closer to the edge of the bed. "I'm ready to try again."

"There's one more thing and it may or may not persuade you," Ms. Draper moved from across the room. "It's about Gracie."

Thomas slouched back onto his bed a little, "What about – my Gracie?"

"Your mother told me how you felt about slavery and the plight of these poor people – about how you were always questioning the rights of man to own man," she took a deep breath. "President Lincoln has declared all slaves in the South are free – including Gracie. Now the South doesn't listen to a word the man says, but I thought you should at least know that – because I know your heart." She put her hand on his, "We can help get her out of Virginia and into the North. And we can find someone to come here and help while you recover."

Thomas lowered his eyes, "I think that would be fine and fitting for Gracie – but please allow me to tell her after you've gone. I will send for you when she is ready to go." Thomas felt tears coming back and he did his best to hold them back. Gracie was all he lived for now – he knew that in his heart. He had nothing else. She was the reason he woke up now…the reason he was trying this silly leg. He would die here – alone.

Gracie came back into the room carrying a tray with a teapot, cups, spoons, biscuits, and a small bowl of honey – she placed it on the small table and looked up at the sullen faces.

"Lordy, Lordy – who done died whilst I was away?" she said, and smiled a smile that broke the anguish of the room into a thousand pieces of sunshine.

# 26

When Luke and Alvin limped back into Emmaline's house there was a crowd waiting for them – and they were impatient. Emmie looked especially upset and she started toward Alvin, but Grandma Bea stepped in first.

"Lawd sakes, boy – why you carry this young man out and get him distracted from the importance of the day?" Bea tugged at Alvin's ear and he half-winced in pain.

"You two get washed up real quick like – we got to thank the Lord so we can eat."

Luke and Alvin shared the tiny bathroom sink and dried their hands off on their pants as they quickly returned to the kitchen. There were three tables elaborately set with plates, glasses, cloth napkins, and silverware. Varieties of food dishes adorned the table centers – rice and black-eyed peas, sliced ham and turkey, fried chicken, potato salad, collards, green beans, something Luke would later learn was called spoon bread, ambrosia, cornbread, butter beans, and macaroni and cheese. A small table to the side held banana pudding, red velvet cake, and sweet potato pie. Several adults stood around the larger dining room table. Emmie approached Luke and led him to a smaller table occupied by four children ranging from four to eight years in age. There were three empty seats.

"We haven't graduated to the adult's table yet," she laughed, and smiled at Luke then turned back to the others as everyone began to hold hands in a circle. Emmie reached out and took his hand on one side and her little cousin's hand on the other.

Anthony Foster began to speak slowly, “Firstly Father, we would like to thank you for this bountiful meal prepared by the gracious hands of some truly wonderful women who make our lives better with each passing day. We thank you for the freedoms we share in this great country in which we live – and we thank you for our Brother, Dr. Martin Luther King, who fights for us to keep these freedoms, as he fights for the new freedoms which we all dream of and pray for. And today I am especially thankful for our Emmaline’s friend Luke who saw her safely home during her time of distress and sadness.”

Emmie squeezed a little harder on Luke’s hand when her father said these words. Luke smiled but felt a little selfish for having followed her home like he did. But he was so glad he was here with her now. He glanced sideways at her and saw her smile when she sensed his gaze – she kept her eyes on her father. So it went, around the circle as people said what they were thankful for, and in some cases made confessions to having not been on their best behavior over the last year – this brought laughs and a few parental sighs. Then the circle came to Luke, and he was silent for a few seconds – but then he spoke.

“I’m so thankful to be welcomed into this loving home with this beautiful family – I don’t have so many relatives back up home. I’m thankful for school and my friends and teammates,” then he said what they all seemed to be waiting on for some reason, “I’m thankful for having met such a good friend as Emmaline – she brings me joy when we spend time together.” He shuddered when he said this – was it weird? Thank God Emmie started speaking.

“I’m thankful for this family and I’m thankful for the hard work Wesley and I are doing to bring the message of Dr.

King to the campus in Charlottesville," she paused briefly. "And I am thankful for my wonderful Grandma Bea who is my light in the sky."

"I ain't dead yet, Sweetie, so don't try and make a star outta me yet please," Beatrice laughed, and the rest of the room joined in. Emmie felt relieved when Alvin started to speak, and her time was seemingly cut short.

After everyone spoke, plates were passed around and filled with a little of everything – every plate got a taste of every dish. Luke sat down in a chair that was fit for a six-year-old and he stretched his legs way out into the hallway away from the table. Emmie sat side saddled in her little chair across from him. Luke made great friends with all the other kids at the table including four-year-old Terrence who shared a big bowl of peach cobbler and whipped topping with him. He avoided eye contact with Emmie as much as he could after her comment about Wesley – but he still couldn't resist looking at her when he got the chance. Her beauty was deafening to him.

Slowly the family began to emerge from their seats and carry dishes toward the kitchen where Grandma Bea, Auntie Sophia, Mathilde, and Emmie were slipping into aprons for the cleanup.

"Need some help, ladies?" asked Luke.

A voice came in from behind him – it was Anthony's, "If you value your life, you will put down that plate and join the other men of this family in the den."

Luke did as he was instructed, and followed Anthony into the small den where the rest of the group was starting a game of cards on the coffee table. Anthony fell into his recliner and Luke sat next to him on the plastic covered green sofa. A small black and white television broadcast an AFL football game through snow and hissing.

"Sorry about Emmie – that's a defense thing for her," Anthony leaned closer to Luke. "She - what's the word – deflects when things are uncomfortable."

"You folks have been so welcoming to me – it's been unbelievable."

"Despite the rumors, we are good people," Anthony smiled.

"That's not what I meant, really."

"We all in this mess together – everyday. We will get it sorted out." Anthony leaned back in his recliner.

"What you said about America---"

"This is our country too, son. None of us have ever known any other place. We were all born here just like you. We been here building this place since the first white men stepped foot on shore. I guess you can say we have a vested interest in seeing this country succeed just as much as you." Anthony leaned closer to him again. "I am proud to call myself an American, Luke. If you ask me – I'd say the Indians have as big a gripe as us – and they are still enslaved on their reservations."

Luke sat back on the couch and watched in amusement the younger kids playing Slapjack with a well-used deck of Bicycle cards. Terrence slapped another little boy they called Shelley so hard on the back of his hand that it turned into a brief comical melee and magazines flew across the room – followed by the whole deck of cards as Terrence yelled "fifty-two card pick-up!" Alvin scooped one boy up under each arm and marched around the room like a Grizzly, roaring and growling as the two boys giggled wildly.

"This is so fun," Luke said to Anthony.

"What is? Watching my house get destroyed by two young'uns that don't even live here?" He laughed and glanced toward the kitchen to make sure Mathilde wasn't watching. "Boys are boys – you know."

"I don't have a big family back home," Luke said. "It's just my mom and dad and me. My older brother died when I was five."

"I'm sorry, son – was he sick?"

"It was a couple of years after the war. We didn't have a whole lot to eat, and it was a very cold winter. He took sick and there wasn't anything that could be done. I remember him sometimes – I remember us laughing and throwing snowballs at the chicken coop from the back porch while my mom was hollering at us from the kitchen." Luke gave Anthony a little smile.

"It was tough for everybody after the war – I'm sorry for you."

Emmie walked up behind her dad's recliner and put her arms around his neck and squeezed. "Love you, Daddy," she said and kissed the top of his head. "Want to go for a walk?"

"Honey, I am in this chair for the night," he laughed.

"I meant your friend there," she smiled at Luke and blinked her beautiful brown eyes.

"I knew that – I swear," Anthony squeezed her arms.

"Of course," said Luke. "Can I get your coat and scarf?"

"Sure – they are laying on my bed," Luke gave her an inquisitive look. "Last room at the end of the hall."

"I am silently rejoicing that he didn't know where that was," said Anthony.

"Daddy, please." Emmie let go of his neck and went back into the kitchen to wait by the door.

Luke met her at the door with her wool coat which he placed over her shoulders as she slid her arms into the sleeves. She reached inside the pockets and pulled out a pair of gloves, a scarf, and a hat and quickly finished dressing for the cold. Luke put on his windbreaker, pulled up the collar, and thrust his hands in his pockets. "Ready?" he said.

"You ain't," Mathilde said from behind him. "Wait here."

A few minutes later she returned with earmuffs, a hat, mittens, and a multi-colored woolen scarf. "These are James' things – you can borrow them. Can't have you catchin' a death of cold on my watch."

"Thank you, Mrs. Foster," Luke said.

"Don't stay gone too long – sun's going down," Mathilde wrapped Emmie's scarf a little tighter while Grandma Bea stood observantly by the kitchen sink with a dish towel slung over her arm – she had a small, barely discernible, sheepish grin on her face. Emmie turned and went out the kitchen door, and Luke quickly followed and closed it securely behind them. When he turned, he saw that Emmie was already outside the gate and onto the bumpy sidewalk. He caught up with her as quickly as he could, and she turned to look him in the eye.

"What are you doing, Luke Montgomery? Why are you still at my house?" Emmie turned and walked up the hill – Luke followed.

"I wanted to make sure you got home - and then your parents and the storm – and-"

"There is no storm – don't you listen to the news or at least the weather."

"I've been distracted – and what do you mean?" Luke walked three feet behind her.

"Didn't you call your mother? What did she say to you?" Emmie turned to look at him as she spoke and then turned around again.

"It was brief – Alvin told me not to talk long and I told her I would be home tomorrow." Luke reached out and gently grabbed her shoulder and turned her around. "Emmie, why are you so upset?" The steam from their breath mingled in the cold early evening air between them. Emmie looked in his eyes and then quickly glanced away. "I can go to the bus station tonight, Emmie. I'm so sorry I intruded on you and your family." Luke took his hand off her shoulder and noticed a tear on her cheek. He wiped it away with James' big mitten.

She giggled softly, "Wow, that mitten smells so bad."

"Emmie, I like you. A lot. I would never do anything to purposely upset you. I promise."

"You can't do that," she pounded softly on his chest with her glove covered hands. "Please – you just can't." Another tear dripped from her beautiful onyx eyelash and clung to her cheek.

Luke covered her hands with the giant smelly mittens and held them in front of him. "I feel like I may never see you again once I leave here."

"I talked to my parents this morning – and I'll be going back to school." Emmie pulled her hands back and pushed them into her pockets. "And I like you too, Luke – I do, but it's nothing more than a friendship. I need you to understand that or I can't see you anymore."

"I understand," Luke said, but he knew he was lying. "Can your dad take me to the bus station in the morning so I can go see my folks?"

"I'm certain of it, Luke," Emmie finally looked into his eyes and he held her gaze for an impossible moment – she felt it too – he could see it in her.

"You can come with me if you want to – shouldn't be much more of a fare for two legs," Luke wasn't expecting what he heard in return.

"That sounds almost fun. Will you be back at UVA by Sunday?" She sounded serious about coming along. "As friends…"

"As friends…"

"I'll have to make sure it's okay with my father," Emmie said.

"Okay."

They walked around the block as the sun finished setting behind the western side of Church Hill. They talked about school and basketball and Emmie's job at the diner. They were comfortable talking to each other and they didn't notice how reliant they had already become on each other's advice and each other's support. "We are friends" thought Luke – maybe best friends.

That evening the Foster's house was filled with games, and stories, and laughter, and togetherness – and Luke loved every minute of it. He looked at Emmie and she looked at him – and they smiled at each other. They were good friends.

To Luke's great surprise, Emmie's parents agreed to let her tag along with him for the next couple of days. They both got a stern talking to about what it meant for a colored girl and a white boy to be travelling together – and the precautions they must take – and the words they would be subjected to – and the anger. Luke promised to always stay by her side and protect her if need be. His parents would pick them up from the bus station and they would stay around his house for the two days they would be there. Emmie would have her own room. Then a direct bus back to UVA for the both of them.

"Your parents gonna be okay with all this – with you bringing a colored girl home?" Anthony asked.

"They will be more concerned about me bringing home a girl than they will be about what she looks like." Luke laughed.

Anthony and Mathilde would drive them to the bus station at six the next morning and see them off. "Where is it you live again?"

"Cranberry, West Virginia, sir."

"Never heard of it."

"Not too many people who don't live there have."

Luke was asleep as soon as he hit the pillow in James' room.

Emmie lay her head down on her pillow and stared at the moonlight creeping around her window shade. She thought of Luke for a while – and then she put her pillow over her head and cried herself softly to sleep.

# 27

Thomas Summerlin never adhered to the contrarian belief that time could be "saved". He knew time could never be anything but "spent". It could be spent in many ways, and he never aspired as one to spend his time on "waste". To Thomas time "well spent" was used to simply make things better, or to do the right thing for the right purpose. Even if he did not find success in his endeavors, he believed it was time "well spent" for the lessons he learned. Such it was, he spent the next two weeks re-learning to walk. This morning was no different as he rose from the bed before the sun and immediately attached his leg – the more he wore it, the more it was part of him. Today he had big plans – today would be time "well spent".

No matter how he tried he could not be the first one in the kitchen, Gracie was standing over a frying pan as he darkened the doorway.

"Can I fix us some coffee?" Thomas already knew the answer.

"It's on the stove already," Gracie didn't turn around. "Good morning, Mr. Thomas.

"Good morning, Sunshine."

"Big plans today?"

"Only the biggest."

"Gonna share"

"Reckon not." Thomas poured out two tin cups of steaming coffee and put the pot back on the wood stove to simmer.

The aroma of the brew woke him even more. "Today," he said, "will be life changing."

Gracie turned, and holding the cast iron skillet with her apron, she plopped a hard fried egg on each of the two tin plates. Two crusty pieces of toast from the stove, and a pinch of salt later, she plopped herself down in one chair as Thomas slid into the other.

"So today, is going to be more life changing than the last two life changing days?" she laughed and took a sip of the hot coffee. "Ouch," she said.

"Can't say as though you d'int deserve that one."

"I hope you are right," Gracie looked concerned, "I know how hard you are trying."

"I have a new plan today."

"Good, cause I gots to tell you – sittin' on the porch and hollerin' ain't workin'.

"That's just the first two steps," Thomas laughed. "Today is the culminatin' step."

"I'll fix us a picnic – it's to be a long one."

Gracie took her time tidying up inside as Thomas made his way out the kitchen door and onto the side porch. The sun was rising over the fence line now and the early May morning was warming nicely. There was the smell of a distant fire in the air, but Thomas didn't pay much mind. The hostilities had moved somewhat South and West of them toward Mount Airy and Pilot Mountain, and they hadn't heard a cannon in weeks - let alone set sight on another human being. Thomas stumbled down the two steps leading into the courtyard and made his way toward the shell of the burned barn with the aid of the walking stick Gracie had fashioned for him out of a piece of ash. He side-stepped the charred mass and found his way back to the three-rail fence which protected the yard from the sprawling five-hundred-acre pasture rising upward to a distant ridge, before falling back toward an unseen tree line. He propped his stick on the fence and leaned into the pasture with both hands on the top rail. There was no sign of them – in fact the grass before him had begun to grow tall and green with the warm and wet Spring days. He raised his right hand to his mouth and thrust in two fingers – the exhaling result was a piercing whistle that lasted about five seconds and echoed through the valley, thudding into, and over the distant ridge.

"Mr. Thomas! What in God's name are you doing way up yonder?" Gracie approached him from behind with a towel in her hand.

"They ain't come to me yet – I come to them today," Thomas turned and smiled. "Be a dear and fetch me a chair from the porch, will you?"

"I should fetch you a right good switchin' is what I should fetch you," Gracie's vocabulary had steadily dropped off some in recent weeks as her vernacular had taken the forefront, but she thought it kept Mr. Thomas amused – so she didn't mind it too much.

Gracie brought a chair and some cold water to Thomas, and he sat right down. She watched him for a few minutes as he alternated from his shrill whistling, to chewing on a piece of sour grass, to fidgeting with a piece of wood he had picked up, to blowing dandelion seeds around. "Okay, I believe I have now seen enough for today. I will be in the garden tending to some things that might provide us with supper tonight." She sauntered away and Thomas stopped everything he was doing to watch her go. He felt the sadness rising in his heart, and he knew he had to tell her soon. His selfishness on the matter was so persistent that it made him hate himself at times. He replayed the conversation in his mind over and over, but could not bring himself to start it.

Around one, Gracie brought out some cold cheese sandwiches and some apples and a few small carrots from her garden. "How's the fishing?" she asked sarcastically.

"No bites – but gotta keep the bait out there." Thomas graciously gobbled a sandwich as Gracie re-filled his water tin. Gracie smiled.

"I've been thinking that I can get some good rope from the cellar and start dragging these burned timbers into a pile down into the holler and we can burn up what's left of those boys down there at the same time…the parts the lime left behind." Thomas splashed some of the water on his face and rubbed his wet hand through his long blonde hair. His blue eyes shone like diamonds in the bright sunshine.

Gracie had to concentrate so she looked at her apple, "How are you going to drag those heavy, filthy, timbers down that hill?"

"We have a cow."

"You ain't killing our dairy cow."

"I just need to get them to the edge – and then I can use the can hook to roll them down."

"You up for that sort of work?" Gracie handed him a carrot, "Best to not overdo it just yet."

"Maybe I will have more help later today."

Gracie glanced out over the pasture. "I haven't seen them in months, Mr. Thomas." She lowered her eyes, "I think they are gone."

Thomas looked away and put his head in his hands. "Not ready to accept that yet." He looked back at Gracie and the sun glared in a bright stream of white light off her raven hair, and he had to cover his eyes to avoid going blind. She was beautifully silhouetted by the hills rising behind her – her grey smock spread out on the grass in front of her.

"How come you never told me about the upstairs fire?" Thomas pointed back toward the house at the black streaks running from each window toward the green metal roof.

"Really nothing to tell, Mr. Thomas." she smiled.

"It's funny?" Thomas wasn't smiling.

"If you saw me hanging with a rope out those windows with a whitewash brush and a bucket of ashes painting the walls you would have laughed." Gracie giggled. "From the road it sure looks like the house is burnt. We can scrub it off later."

"Gracie, if I wasn't sure before, I am now – you are the smartest woman I've ever known." Thomas smiled a broad grin.

"You don't know the half of it, Mr. Thomas," she gave him a sheepish grin and winked. "We will need some help to rebuild this place," Gracie put her hand on his knee.

Thomas laughed, "Who is out there left to help? That doesn't have their own calamities?"

"We can make do while we work on things – slowly," Gracie spoke as if she was never going to leave this place. Thomas knew better – he turned and let out yet another shrill whistle.

"I hid some of your father's guns in the cellar," Gracie looked into Thomas' eyes. "We can shoot a deer – maybe some wildfowl and rabbits. We will be Okay."

"We can," he said. "In the early evening so nobody can track the sound for long."

"Yes."

"Gracie, there is so much wrong out there…we need to keep it away from us as long as we can."

"I know." Gracie rubbed his leg. "Every time I hear that sorrowful train coming through the pass – I pray to the Lord it won't stop – and those boys come up the hill. I've seen a few go limping through way out in the fields – I think they are running away. They don't dare come up here for fear of being caught…or shot."

"God help us where all this ends. What will be left?"

"It's best to think about just us right now – and one day at the time, Mr. Thomas…one day at the time." Gracie got up and went back to her gardening as Thomas began to doze in the Spring sunshine. He started to dream of the war but was somehow able to shift his dream to Gracie and her dance with the mayflies. It brought him some peace at least.

Just before dusk he was awakened by Gracie. The evening air had begun to cool, and it was time for them to get inside.

"We can try again tomorrow, Mr. Thomas – it's going to be the greatest day ever."

"Life changing," he reminded her.

Gracie picked up the chair by the top of the ladder back and they started back toward the house.

"What was that sound?" Gracie froze.

Thomas looked at her.

"There it is again – a deer snorting maybe…"

Thomas looked back at the pasture where the sun was now well into setting. A barely pale-yellow line filled the western sky.

"Oh my God," Thomas put his hand on the fence rail again.

"What is it?"

Thomas squinted and covered his eyes. "Sunshine," he said.

Gracie reached out and touched his arm. "We should go in – I'm a little frightened."

"No," Thomas said. "Look…it's *Sunshine* – well *Sunshine 'Til Midnight* is her real name."

Gracie covered her eyes with her hand and stared up hill, "Lord have mercy, you did it."

Gracie threw her arm around Thomas' neck, and they watched as *Sunshine* slowly came twenty feet further down the hill and then stopped to look back at the ridge. Another mare stuck her head up over the rise before coming cautiously down toward them to join *Sunshine* . Then they both stopped as a large black shape slowly made its' grand entrance and created a magnificent silhouette against the young night's sky – *Lightening!*

"He's alive, Gracie!" Thomas kissed her hard on the cheek. "I knew it – they are alive!" Thomas whistled again and the horses began to move slowly down the hill before stopping and looking back at the ridge again. *Lightening* let out a loud whinny and then snorted sharply. Two small jet-black foals breached the top of the ridge and joined the small group as they moved back down into the valley…to where Thomas…and home… were waiting to welcome them.

# 28

Emmaline Foster was nowhere near prepared for her trip to Prosperity, West Virginia. If Charlottesville was the Wall Street of Appalachia, then Prosperity was the Bowery. Lucas and Adrienne Montgomery had picked up the pair at the bus station in Beckley in their rusted 1950 Ford two-door pickup, thrown their bags into the bed, and crammed the two between them on the only seat. They had started back up out of the valley toward the mining town of Cranberry through thick fog and smoke, and light sleet that pinged off the cracked front windshield. The roads appeared paved somewhat to Emmie, but they were still covered in slimy wet brown mucky mud that splattered around the outside of the truck as they drove. She knew they were in the mountains, but she couldn't see more than fifty feet in any direction to verify it.

"Oh, Sweetie, we are so glad you could come for a visit," was what Adrienne said to Emmie the first time they met – and she meant it. She seldom, if ever had a house guest to dote over. Now she leaned over Emmie and told Lucas to make sure he stopped at the store so she could pick up a few items for supper, since they were having company. Lucas just nodded and kept his eyes on the gravel in front of him.

The Cranberry Mines company store sat in the crook of a sharp bend in the road coming from Prosperity into Cranberry. There were well used trucks and cars lining both sides of the road as they came around the curve – and Emmie could see a straggling line of rather "dirty" looking people filing from the store down the edge of the road.

"Land sakes, Lucas – I forgot it was payday what with the holiday and all," said Adrienne – or Addie, as most people knew her. "I can have Luke and Ms. Emmaline walk back up here a little later this afternoon."

"Why are all of these people in line?" Emmie whispered to Luke quietly.

Luke didn't answer in the same tone, "Payday, so the folks have to hit the store before everything runs out. What do you need, Mama? Just drop me here and I'll walk on up after I get the things."

"I can help you," Emmie offered, but she was relieved when Luke turned her down – this was a madhouse.

Addie handed Luke a piece of paper with some scribbled items listed on it. "Just put it on account, Honey."

Lucas grumbled as he reached into his shirt pocket and handed Luke a folded ten-dollar bill. "Use this, son. We were better off when we had scrip."

Lucas was a tall wiry man, and his face was crushed by dark, heavy razor stubble so thick that Emmie couldn't tell if it was really that dark – or he was just that dirty. She felt as though he looked much older than he was. He wore faded and torn overalls over a heavy grey flannel shirt, and his head, except for a few tufts of dirty blonde hair, was mostly hidden by a ballcap that said "Standard Oil" on it. He hadn't said much during the ride and Emmie remembered Addie mentioning earlier that he had just "come off shift".

"Emmie, we can get on up to the house and get some supper started," Addie climbed back into the truck after Luke jumped out.

"I promise, I'll be up there soon…" he said to Emmaline, but she saw a mob of people coming across the road to greet him as he made his way to the store.

"Our Luke – he's a bit of a celebrity around here. Not too many make it out of here with much success," Adrienne smiled at Emmie and patted her on the knee.

"It's the same at school," she grinned.

Then it was Lucas' turn to ask something that had clearly been on his mind since picking them up, "So, you guys an item back in Virginny?"

Emmaline was mortified but stayed calm, "Oh no, sir – we are just friends, and we study together sometimes – he's just a very nice boy, and he treats me with so much respect and kindness…"

"That's our Luke," said Addie. "Here we are."

They had only come maybe a mile from the store before Lucas turned the truck onto a steep muddy drive that had the remnants of the latest snowfall clinging to shallow ditches on either side. He gunned the engine to get to the top and parked right next to a small square-framed single-story home that had a dying plume of smoke exiting the chimney on the side of the house where they parked. Three sides of the house were stacked almost to the eaves with firewood – their only source of heat and cooking.

"Lucas, get that fire stoked up and go out back and bring me a hen" Addie climbed down from the truck, "I'll help Ms. Emmie with these bags."

"Another hen? We took one Wednesday."

"We have a guest, Lucas Montgomery."

"Please don't go to any trouble Mrs. Montgomery," Emmie had genuine concern.

"Nonsense, Sweetie – you make yourself at home. I'm putting Luke on the couch in the front room, and I made his bed up just for you – I don't have a great deal of feminine and lacy things, but I think we can make do."

Emmaline followed Luke's mother up the two steps into the house with both of her large cases in tow. The interior was just as modest as it could be. Pale green paint was peeling near the ceilings and there were a few small, ragged rugs laying over the oak flooring between a worn couch covered in a quilt, and a scratched coffee table with a couple of issues of *Harpers* placed just so. A floor lamp with no shade sat at the far end of the couch with a single 60-watt bulb burning in it. Lucas was stuffing the fireplace with new logs and the house already smelled heavily of smoke. Emmie assumed the fire was never extinguished during the cold months. She followed Addie past the kitchen and into a small bedroom with two single beds with brown bedspreads not three feet apart taking up most of the square footage. There was a small desk next to the only window, and it was littered with basketball trophies and awards. An old Brooklyn Dodgers pennant hung down from the ceiling over one bed which was also adorned with a football pillow, and covered in what looked to be a lace tablecloth. There was a folded towel and wash cloth at the foot. The other bed was covered in stuffed animals and didn't look like it had been slept in for years.

"This is Luke's," she pointed to the bed with the football on it. "That's Johnny's, we don't use that one. I mean you can sit there if you want to – but not for sleeping."

Emmie really noticed Luke's mother for the first time in the bedroom. Her hair was blonde but greying from the top, she had on makeup but clearly didn't wear it often. She wore what appeared to be a handmade frock and she still wore her apron – either because she forgot to remove it, or it was covering up a blemish on her dress – or it kept her warmer. Emmie put one of her bags on the floor and the other on the edge of Luke's bed.

"It's Okay, Mrs. Montgomery. I promise I will be fine – I have a brother at home and his room is just like this one." She smiled and it helped break the ice a little faster.

"I'm sorry, Ms. Emmaline. Luke had his little girlfriends around town here growing up, but he never brought them around – oh, they weren't nothing serious, or nothing like that," Addie sat on the bed next to her and their weight collectively pushed down the side of the mattress.

"Luke and I are just good friends, Ms. Montgomery," Emmie smiled and put her hand on top of hers.

"I wouldn't mind if you was more than that you know," Addie looked closely at her. "I ain't so much like other people with their hatefulness and what-not. And you are so beautiful."

"I know you aren't," Emmie smiled, "it's really just not like that for us."

"Well, I'm going to let you get settled in some. The bathroom is right outside in the hall – we only got the one, but I stay on the boys to keep it tidy." Addie started out the door then looked back. "I'll be in the kitchen if you want to visit – I can make us some tea. I've got some of that English tea – Earl Grey."

"That would be lovely, Ms. Montgomery."

"Addie, please, Sweetie," she closed the door and was gone.

Emmie leaned back on the bed and put her hands behind her for support. It was the first time she had been alone all day, and she took the time to breathe in the musky West Virginia mountain air and really look around Luke's room. Literally everything she had formulated in her mind about him was wrong...completely wrong. She felt bad about calling him a privileged boy from Northern Virginia. She quickly realized that Luke's life growing up had been one of hard times and hard work – not bright shiny automobiles and soda shops with girls in poodle skirts and bobby socks. She closed her eyes for a few minutes until there was a light tap on the door then she got herself back together.

"I'm sorry, yes come in."

It was Luke.

"Hey, my mom has made you some tea, and she has some crumb cake my dad brought back from the mine – it's really good – not as bad as it sounds. I used to take it in my lunch tin to school."

Emmie got up and went to him and wrapped her arms around him tightly, placing her head on his shoulder. "I'm so sorry," she whispered.

Luke reluctantly pulled away from her, "For what."

"For this...for being insensitive...for being stupid."

"Oh, Emmaline," Luke said. "Don't you ever feel sorry for me. I love my parents and I had a great life growing up here. Tomorrow, I'll show you around – I think the weather should be better."

A tear rolled down Emmie's cheek and Luke wiped it away with his thumb. "Please don't."

Emmie looked at him and smiled. "I'm Okay."

"My mom is so proud to have you here. She's roasting a chicken, and she's made mashed potatoes with cabbage and rutabagas, pinto beans, and some pan-fried bread. Basically, another Thanksgiving meal – just for us."

"I'll be out in just a minute," she said as she sat back on the edge of the bed.

"I'm going to get cleaned up and see if I can help my dad with the chicken – he has a hell of a time getting the things plucked." Luke winked at her. "Besides I'm a bit tired from my hike up the hill from the store."

"A big strong athlete like you?"

"Yeah, well my mother didn't bother telling me she had to make pepperoni rolls for the miner's lunch tomorrow. I just carried two fifty-pound bags of flour up this damn mountain for almost a mile." Luke laughed and closed the door.

# 29

"Get up, Mr. Thomas!" Gracie pulled the flannel cover off the bed and dropped it in a clump on the floor. "There's two more this morning! A big brown one and another little foal! *Midnight's* been busy out there in the wild." She flung open the curtain on the window but only a pale light came into the room.

"Lord Almighty, girl!" Thomas put the chicken feather pillow over his face. "Sun ain't rose a tad yet."

"This is a working farm, sir," Gracie was full of vim and vinegar this morning. "There's always work to do. Remember? We got us a barn to rebuild."

"I really need your young energy," Thomas said as he sat up on the side of the bed. "That was my first full day outside – let me take a breath, lady."

"Coffee on the stove. I'm heading outside to get them some turnips and potatoes out of the cellar. The grass is growing good – and we can harvest some hay from the North pasture by mid-June." Thomas strapped on his leg as Gracie disappeared out the door.

"Lord Jesus," he said.

The horses looked to be in fairly good shape for the most part. Their winter coats were very long, and their feet looked horrible, but they looked like they had found enough to eat to survive the season. Thomas climbed through the bottom two slats of the fence and slowly walked into the center of the group. The three foals immediately started back up the hill and stopped about a hundred feet away to watch. Thomas stood completely still as Gracie sat on the ground outside the fence.

"What are you doing?" she said softly.

"Shhh..."

Thomas stood for what seemed like half an hour before *Midnight* moved slowly to him and rubbed his muzzle up and down Thomas' back. *Sunshine* came to the front and Thomas slowly began to rub her muzzle...then he worked his hand up between her ears and rubbed her withers and straightened her forelock with his fingers. She whinnied softly and pushed the other nosy mare gently away.

"This one we call *May* – it's short for *Mayflower's Pride,"* Thomas began to rub the muzzle of the second mare. Then he turned to an obviously jealous *Midnight.* "Hello, my friend," he said softly and kissed him on the nose. *Midnight* put his head down over Thomas' shoulder and looked to be giving him a hug. Thomas put his arms around the horse's neck and pulled him closer. "I'm so very, very glad to see you too."

Gracie sat on the grass in her grey smock and apron and just seemed amazed as she took all of it in. "They are so beautiful."

"This one here is called *Whinny* – not short for anything, just because she came out of *Sunshine* talking like a crazed woman."

Gracie laughed at that. "Watch it," she said.

"Hopefully my Smith tools are in the cellar. I need to trim up these hooves." Thomas picked up *Midnight's* front foot and worked on it with a stick for a few minutes. "He's got rocks and hard mud jammed up in here deep and I'm pretty sure he has an infection that's going to break through here. His foreleg is very warm." Thomas walked around to each of the horses in turn and looked at their feet and then spent the better part of the morning going over every inch of them. "I think the best thing for them is a good soaking with salted water first."

"What about the babies?" Gracie asked.

"They will come to me in their own time." Thomas climbed back through the fence. "I'm going to hook *Whinny* to the buckboard, and we can go up to Draper's this afternoon to get what we need."

"What about the fighting and such?"

"It's been strangely quiet around here for a few weeks. We will be Okay – I'll bring the shotgun." Thomas started digging through the pile of leather straps and harnesses Gracie had brought up from the cellar earlier. "Why don't you grab us some lunch and I'll get us ready to roll out?"

Gracie went back into the house and got some bread and cheese together and a couple of Bradford pears that she had cooked the night before and placed them in a cheese cloth and wrapped them up. She then filled up a mason jar with water and dropped in two sprigs of mint. She then went about her inside business – tidying the kitchen and sweeping the floors. Then she heard the dinner bell ring once outside and ducked her head out the kitchen side door.

"Your chariot, m'lady."

"How in tarnation did you do that so fast? I figured we'd be going tomorrow." She bounded down the steps toward him.

"This is what I know…pretty much all I know," Thomas laughed and hoisted Gracie up on the seat with her picnic. He climbed up after her with surprising ease.

"You sure are getting the hang of that leg, ain't you?"

"Forgot it was there until you reminded me...thanks."

The ride over to Draper's Mercantile was very quiet – in fact they didn't see one other soul on the road, and when they arrived in town their's was the only wagon at the shop. They climbed down and went inside to find Mrs. Draper sipping some tea and leafing through an old almanac with a shotgun across her knees.

"Well..look what that old grey cat done dragged in here this afternoon," she stood up from her rest. "Ms. Gracie, you get just more perfect every time I see you."

"Good afternoon. We need some mineral oil, and some foot bath salts. Some flour, some bales of straw if you have them. Maybe some potatoes and turnips or rutabagas...some sugar," Thomas was acting in a nervous hurry.

"Slow down, Mr. Summerlin," Mrs. Draper came around the counter and looked him up and down. "I told you I would tell her if you didn't." she looked at Gracie.

"What is she talking about, Mr. Thomas?"

Mrs. Draper started to open her mouth when Thomas interjected. "I'll tell her on the way back to Waverly – I swear on my Grandma's grave."

"You do that," she shook her head. "And I'll come up there in a few days to help get her ready."

"Mr. Thomas?" Gracie sounded pitifully sad – like a schoolgirl who had her candy taken away by the marm.

"Gracie, please just help me get loaded up." Thomas started behind the counter to get a sack of flour.

It didn't take long to get what they needed, and the pair quickly got back on the road, and headed toward home. The warm sun was alternating between being directly in their eyes and behind a knoll or some thick trees. When it bobbed out of sight, they could feel the air temperature drop fifteen degrees as Spring still struggled toward Summer.

"It's nice of Mrs. Draper to extend us some credit right now," Gracie tried to make small talk.

"I'm good for it," Thomas was short.

"Are you angry with me Mr. Thomas? Did I do something wrong?" she started to feel tears welling up.

Thomas shook his head and just kept *Whinny* moving toward the farm.

"I try my best you know - to make things easier for you." Gracie lowered her eyes and pulled her apron up over her hands which sat quietly in her lap.

The wagon came around a curve in the road and Thomas pulled up near an old, abandoned farmhouse with a red metal roof that stood back in the woods about a hundred feet behind a three-hundred-year-old oak. There was no sign that anyone had been there in years.

"My grandfather built this house for the preacher about fifty years ago," Thomas looked at Gracie. "I don't ever remember anyone living in there. My brothers and I used to say it was haunted and we were scared to go inside. I think my mother made that up so we would stay away."

"Mr. Thomas, please just tell me what you been holding onto."

Thomas turned to Gracie and took her hands in his. He looked into her eyes and did the hardest thing he had ever done in his life. He told her the truth. He told her about Lincoln and his Proclamation, and about the Underground Railroad and how Mrs. Draper was going to get her moved up North where she would be safe from the hatred of slavery. She had to go. She was young and didn't need to stay down here and take care of a crippled man who fought for the very thing they both hated the most. She was free. She should go and meet someone and get married and have a family – and live a free uncluttered life. He would be fine on his own – he had plenty to keep busy with at Waverly. He would…make do.

Gracie sobbed the rest of the way back to the house and when Thomas pulled up in the courtyard she climbed down and walked about ten feet toward the kitchen door before she stopped and turned.

"Mr. Thomas, I ain't nary said one cross word to you, but you got this coming," Gracie snatched the bow out of her hair and threw it on the ground. "I never had any problem saying what I mean and I ain't gonna start now," she took a deep breath as the tears rolled down her cheeks. "I been taking care of this place by myself for the better part of two years now. This is my home!" she pointed a finger at him, "and the crippled likes of you ain't gonna make me leave – not now… not never!"

Gracie stormed up the steps and into the house, slamming the door hard enough to make every window in the house rattle.

Thomas sat back on the buckboard and watched the scene unfold. Then he dropped the reins, and what began as a smile, turned into a painful, rolling laughter filled with joy.

# 30

"Good morning, Ms. Addie."

"Oh, Sweetie, the sun ain't even up yet. You go on back to bed."

"I was just lying in there listening to you work in here, so I thought I'd see if I can lend a hand." Emmaline was wrapped up tight in a pair of flannel pajamas and a sweater. The house had a biting chill to it this morning.

"If you'd like you can throw a couple of logs on the fire in there, and a few in the stove," Addie was busy mixing dough in a large bowl. "There's a pair of gloves on the wood pile there. Try not to wake Luke up ... so it can be just us gals for a while yet."

The night before they had had quite the meal, and it was still weighing heavily on Emmaline's stomach. The miner's cake was delicious, but it was probably what did her in. The talk around the table was fairly mild and mostly consisted of what they were studying in school, and of course basketball. Emmie had drunk three cups of the Earl Grey tea – it was so nice and hot, and Ms. Addie put in real cream and sugar. She enjoyed it so much she made a mental plan to make it her morning go to instead of coffee when she got back to school. It had been an exhausting day for Luke and Emmie, so they were quick to turn in...and it helped to avoid awkward conversation.

"There's a meat slicing knife right in that top drawer and you can slice up those two pepperonis right there on the countertop – just throw the slices in the bowl," Addie had both of her hands deep into the bowl of dough kneading it over and over. "Slice them thin."

Emmie and Addie worked like a well-oiled machine in the kitchen and together they hand rolled, baked, and wrapped over a hundred pepperoni rolls in a little over two hours. When they were done Mrs. Montgomery made them both a cup of tea and they sat down next to the wood stove just as Luke was starting to stir.

"Well, Lukey, you missed all the fun this morning, but you can ride up to the mine with us to carry lunch in about an hour," Addie looked at Emmie and smiled. "I sure am glad you are here, Ms. Emmaline."

"You know what? Me too."

Lucas Montgomery had worked in the Southern West Virginia coal mines since returning from the war in 1945. He had worked in places called Pocahontas, Sewell, and Fire Creek. His days were hard and most of his nights were sleepless. He worried about his wife and son if anything was to ever happen to him – and he worried a lot. This was his main reason for sending Luke to work for his Army buddy James Connally on the horse farm in Pulaski County every summer. He had to get Luke away from the nightmare of the mines. Most kids in their teens in Cranberry went to work alongside their fathers in the mines without ever finishing school. Many died in the mines or left there crippled. Most of the men developed Black Lung later in life. He wouldn't let his son be a part of this. That's why he pushed him so hard in sports and in his books – and kept him away from the mines as much as he possibly could. This morning he had gotten a ride in for his shift and left the truck for Luke to use. This was also the reason Addie was up making pepperoni rolls at 5am and not 3am. She woke up long enough to thank the Lord for two extra hours of sleep.

Addie and Emmaline each held two large peach baskets full of wax paper wrapped pepperoni rolls in their laps as Luke wheeled the family's Ford pickup into a branch of what they called the Beckley Seam Mine. Dust covered men in green overalls with hardhats and goggles streamed out of basket lifts as they came to the surface for fresh air and food. Steam poured from holes in the ground into the bright late morning sunshine that had warmed the day into the upper twenties. Snow lay in slowly melting dirty piles here and there under leafless sycamores struggling out of the rocky soil. The men's expressions of exhaustion and worry turned to joy when they saw Luke Montgomery climb out of the truck.

"Here we go," mumbled Luke to Emmaline.

"Some of those men are awful short," said Emmie.

"Those short men would be children," he smiled at her, and his mother laughed.

Emmie must have heard the name Luke Montgomery fifty times as the crowd of men came up the hill. Other women were standing ready to deliver a lunch that included cooked cabbage and onions mixed with potatoes, cakes and tarts, and hot coffee, but the most coveted item that morning was the pepperoni rolls. The men commented about how great Mrs. Montgomery's rolls were because she put a little cheese in them and brushed them with melted butter and ground salt before she baked them. She was a star at this gathering in her own right. The men in turn lined up to get their lunch and then stopped to speak with Luke and shake his hand as they came through the line.

"I remember the night you scored forty-five against Wytheville! Man, what a game!" said one man who was greying at the temples.

"We never missed a game at Wilson on Friday night," said another.

The younger boys just stared at Luke in awe and shook his hand as they went by. Luke smiled back at each one of them – calling most of them by name.

The men's short lunch break ended with the sound of a steam whistle, and the men headed back toward the basket for the dark ride back into the depths of the earth. Luke's father lingered until the last group was ready to go.

"Son, I need to talk to you tonight about a few things… nothing bad," Lucas said as he put the hard hat and light back on his head. "God willin' the canary keeps singing I'll be home by six."

"You need me to come get you?" asked Luke.

"No, I caught a ride with the Toney boys. They can drop me back off," he turned and started for the basket. "I hope you hid some of those pep rolls back at the house," he winked at Addie and walked away.

Luke dropped his mother off back at the house in Cranberry and announced he was taking Emmie on a "whirlwind" tour of the paradise that was the valley. They drove into Beckley, and he showed her Woodrow Wilson High and the outdoor Beckley city courts where everything started for him. He apologized for the sign at the high school that said "Go Luke! We love you!" They drove past the Veteran's Hospital and down to the lake where he caught "the world's biggest Walleye", and he finally took her into town for what he claimed was the best milkshake east of the Mississippi at King Tut's Drive-In.

As they pulled in and parked a brunette in pigtails came rolling up on skates to his window with a couple of menus. He cranked down the glass and the girl leaned in and kissed him on the cheek so hard she smeared lipstick on his face and almost fell off her skates.

"Luke Montgomery! The one and only!" she said somewhat sarcastically.

"Hello, Amanda." Luke glanced at Emmie who was grinning from ear to ear.

"Friend of yours, Luke?" Emmie laughed.

"I guess you could say that," he looked back at Amanda.

"Two proms and the King and Queen of Homecoming for two years. I'll be back in a minute," she skated away leaving Luke speechless.

"Don't worry, lover boy, I'm not jealous."

"Not even a smidge?"

"Maybe just a tiny smidge."

Another girl rolled up to the window and stuck her head inside, but not to kiss Luke.

"Hello, Lisa," Luke said.

Lisa looked inside and got a close gander at Emmaline, "Yep, she's right! Most beautiful girl I've ever seen in West Virginia," and off she went.

Luke smiled at Emmie and the cab of the truck got quiet for a few minutes until their order of two butterscotch milkshakes and some fries arrived.

"I'm sorry, my dad doesn't have a radio in this old thing." Luke squirted some catsup next to the fries and placed the paper container on the seat between them.

"You know I make my own music," Emmie sipped on her milkshake. "This is very good."

"The best?"

"My diner is the best," she laughed, and he caught himself staring into her eyes again and quickly diverted his attention.

"You need to eat some supper when we get home, or my mom will scold me for ruining our appetites with junk food." Luke started the truck, and they rolled out onto Eisenhower drive heading back up to Prosperity. "I'm glad you were at least a tiny smidge jealous."

Emmie looked out the window as they passed a row of big houses on Woodlawn Avenue. "These are nice," she said.

"These houses are for the mine owners and executives... most of them have never been underground and some of them have never even been to a mine." Luke sounded resentful. "Slave drivers is what they are," as soon as the words were out of his mouth he was apologizing to her.

"See, right there is something I don't want or need," Emmie continued to look out the window as they rolled past rows of smaller houses. "I don't want someone to be guarded against saying something they think may be inappropriate or in some way offends me. I'm comfortable with who I am, and I don't need to be validated."

"You are the smartest, most beautiful woman I've ever known," Luke was reaching now.

"Don't you patronize me, Luke Montgomery."

"I'm sorry."

"Just keep being my friend. Okay?"

"Okay," Luke turned the truck into the gravel drive and pulled up next to the house. "You can go on in – I'm going to bring in a load of wood for Mom."

Supper that evening was pepperoni rolls and Irish potatoes boiled with heavy cream and onion. It was an overly hearty meal that made Emmie even more tired after her adventurous day. She apologized and found her way to bed a little after eight thirty. Luke's mother quickly followed Emmie's lead, and Luke found himself sitting on the old brown couch with his father watching the embers in the fireplace smolder and pop.

"You know, son, we went ahead and moved your Grandma's old Chevy Fleetline here to the house. I have it in the garage out back covered up," Lucas crossed his legs.

"That old hunk of junk is gonna be quite the project," Luke laughed. "Maybe I can help you with it this summer before I head down to the farm."

"Well, funny thing is Dave Pritchard has been helping me on Sundays and we have it running pretty well," Lucas stood up and tossed a couple of logs on the fire.

"That's great, Dad. It's a beautiful auto. You and Mom can go on Sunday picnics out to the lake in it." Luke pulled the blanket over his legs and was feeling sleep coming on as his father sat back down on the couch that was his son's bed for the weekend.

"Your mother and I want you to have it…and drive it back to school."

"Dad, that car is worth something. Why don't you guys sell it?"

"Luke, we want to do this for you," Lucas put his hand on his son's blanket covered knee. "This means a lot to us – to do this for you."

"Dad, I don't-"

"Not up for discussion, my friend." Lucas smiled. "You've worked so hard, and we love you so much."

"I love you guys too…you know that."

They sat quietly for a few minutes staring at the new logs which were quickly ablaze in the hot fireplace. There was a light snow flurry blowing powder against the window as the fire worked hard to keep the cold outside.

Finally, Lucas spoke again. "We really like your friend Emmie. You guys seem to be good for each other."

"We are just really good friends, Pop." Luke smiled at his father. "I'm glad you like her – she is a special person that is for sure."

"I know how other people judge, son. Your mother and I have never been like that. Your happiness is all that matters."

"There's no reason to judge a friendship if that's what you mean," Luke laid his head back on the pillow trying to give his dad a hint. "I need to get some rest, Dad – got a long day tomorrow. I can't wait to drive the Fleetline."

"I can tell you don't want to talk about it anymore."

"It's just that – "

"It's just this – Your mother and I see how you look at her when she's not looking," Lucas stood up and started toward his bedroom then turned and smiled at his son. "We also see how Emmie looks at you when you aren't looking."

Luke's father winked at him and switched off the light.

# 31

Thomas had stayed outside with the horses well into the evening, and thought it best to let Gracie cool down with the night air after her amusing outburst. She didn't know just how happy her words had made him. The idea of losing her along with everything else was simply unbearable to him. He had glanced up at the house and seen a figure holding an oil lamp looking in his direction on a few occasions and he knew she was checking on him. He made a fire and heated up some salted water in a small cast iron kettle which he presented to *Midnight* while running his fingers through the horse's mane and forelock, and scratching his nose. After a few minutes he put the kettle on the ground and lifted *Midnight's* right front foot and gently lowered it into the warm water. The horse hesitated at first and then relaxed as the salt began to work on his abscess. Thomas knew the infection was going to break through just above the hoof, so he made sure to completely immerse the hoof up into the hair line. He stood and brushed the horse for a long while in the cool night air before switching the kettle to the other foot and repeating the process. After the second soaking he used a hoof pick to clean out both of *Midnight's* front feet. The process of bringing his horses back into health was going to take time and patience, and he knew it. It was close to midnight when he finally made his way to bed, and it felt good to take that leg off – he was asleep in no time.

The next morning Thomas walked into the kitchen just after daybreak. Gracie moved about and dropped him a cup of coffee on the table along with two hard boiled eggs. She kept her back to him and didn't say anything while he ate. She couldn't see that he was grinning at her the whole time.

"Let's go, girl!" he got up from his chair. "We have got a lot of work to do if we are going to turn this place into a working farm again."

Gracie turned and looked him in the eyes. "Really?" she said.

"Yes, really."

"You won't send me away?"

"I won't force you to stay here…ever," Thomas stepped toward her and gently took her hand. "But I don't ever want to see you go."

Gracie threw her arms around Thomas' neck, and she just about squeezed out any life he had left in him.

"I'm not going anywhere, Mr. Thomas!" she battled back tears.

"I'm very glad," he said. "I'd be for sure lonely without you around calling me Mr. Thomas."

"I won't leave you here by yourself."

Thomas held both of her hands in front of him, "You just have to make me one promise."

"Anything."

"We are in this together – as equals. What's mine is yours. This is your home as much as it is mine."

"I'd like that very much, Mr. Thomas," Gracie was crying now, but her smile overwhelmed the tears.

"I'll see you outside once you are done in here?"

"Oh yes – yes, of course." Gracie turned to clean up the breakfast dishes and Thomas grabbed a handful of sugar cubes and strode out the kitchen door whistling as he went.

The horses were waiting for him as he stooped down to pass through the fence boards. Droplets of icy dew clinging to the bottom of the board dripped into the collar of his cotton shirt, giving him a chill down his spine as he stood back up. He pulled a few sugar cubes from his pocket and gave one each to the stallion and the three mares as the foals continued to keep their distance. He leaned over and lifted one of *Midnight's* front feet and picked it clean with a hoof pick, then he did the same on the other three.

"Better this morning, right?"

*Midnight* let out a soft whinny and pranced around the mares and back to Thomas. Thomas pulled the stallion's head down and laid his cheek on top of his warm muzzle. He kept his head completely still for almost a minute while the horse seemed to find a happy state of relaxation. Thomas then fashioned a halter out of a piece of hemp rope and looped it over the horse's head and tied it up under his neck loosely. He tied a longer piece into a loop below *Midnight's* chin which had grown some long whiskers.

"Okay, boy, let's see what you remember," Thomas stood away and held the end of the rope as the stallion began to run slow loping circles around him as the mares moved off up the hill with the foals in tow. Thomas allowed the horse to circle him for twenty minutes, stopping periodically and allowing the stallion to come to him and get his muzzle rubbed. "Good boy," said Thomas. He was so involved with his horses that he hadn't noticed Gracie sitting on the top rail of the fence. The rising sun enveloped her shiny hair in an almost angelic, warm orange glow.

"I might need to start calling you Cowboy Thomas," she called.

"The two of us were raised together, so he's the easiest one – besides that tub of love *Whinny.*" Thomas called the stallion in again and removed the rope and halter. As he walked toward Gracie the horse followed close behind. "It may take longer to rein in the foals. They don't know we mean them no harm."

Gracie jumped off the fence to the outside and almost fell into a heap on the ground.

"You – are scared of horses." Thomas smiled.

"Not scared just don't like 'em."

"Come give him a sugar cube…he won't bite. Just hold it in your palm and open your hand flat," Thomas handed her some sugar from his pocket.

She stayed three feet from the fence and held out her hand. *Midnight* leaned across and turned his head sideways to get the cube with his tongue. Gracie giggled as the horse plucked the cube cleanly from her hand.

"See, not so bad," Thomas rubbed the stallion's mane and forelock once again as he climbed out of the pasture.

"What should we work on today, my dear?" Thomas hung the rope over the fence.

"Why don't we start rolling some of this black wood down into the ravine like you said? The heating of the sun is starting to make the smell worse down there." Gracie held her nose with two fingers. "I wonder how much longer these boys gonna keep killing each other – maybe until there ain't none of them left I guess."

"It's bad, Gracie. War is horror. I don't need to see any more of it." He ran his hand through his long blonde hair, and it fell back right into the same mess it was already in. Stray bangs covered his blue eyes, and he swept them out of his field of vision.

"I can cut that for you tonight…if you'd like," Gracie reached up and brushed his hair out of his eyes.

"I'd like that," he said. "I'd like that very much."

"You stay here and drink some water. I'll go to the cellar and get some tools and such. What do you need brought up?" Gracie smoothed out her grey smock and turned to go.

"Wheelbarrow – the one with the steel wheel that ain't rusted through, pitchfork, and the can hook – it's a pole with a giant hook at one end. It sort of looks like a harpoon of sorts."

"I'll see what I can scrounge up. There are some gloves down there too."

Thomas watched as Gracie walked back up toward the house. He loved to watch her walk - her dark shimmering hair floating back and forth as she went. It made him smile. The leaves were growing back nicely on the sycamores, hickories, and birch trees, and the sound of the light breeze blowing through the farm was very settling to Thomas. He sat down in the grass to rest and wait for Gracie to return. He was keenly aware of everything he had missed the last year and a half. It wasn't just the loss of his family and the destruction of his home. It was little things like the tiny yellow butterflies floating above his head and the bees buzzing in and out of the clover and dandelions at his feet. It was the sweet smell of the wet leaves and the smoke coming from the wood stove. Then his eyes went back to the ruins of his barn and a shift in the wind brought the renewed stench of death in the ravine. Reality really is a double-edged sword he thought.

Gracie returned with everything he asked for and more – including an axe with a slightly charred handle.

"I missed this when I moved the tools and horse tack from the barn – sorry." Gracie stopped the wheelbarrow by his feet and stood over him with her hands on her hips. "We building a farm, or taking a nap."

Thomas laughed and pulled himself back onto his feet with the help of the blackened axe handle. He pushed the wheelbarrow over to the pile of charred rubble that had been the barn.

"If we clean all of this out then we can build back on the same rock foundation," Thomas handed the pitchfork to Gracie. "You fill the barrow, and I will start rolling some of these smaller logs to the fence and push them into the ravine with this." He picked up the can hook and clamped it down around a twelve inch log about eight feet long and started to roll it away. "Take your time – we ain't in no huge hurry."

Gracie smiled at him and lifted the first scoop of charred debris into the wheelbarrow. When it was full, Thomas wheeled it over to the fence line where he stopped.

"Now what?" asked Gracie.

"Now this," said Thomas as he picked up the axe and hammered three boards off the fence into a pile that he promptly dragged out of the way. "We have to be careful with this because it could pull us down there with it."

Gracie picked up a rope and handed Thomas the other end. "Tie it," she said.

Thomas tied the handle and then dumped the wheelbarrow as Gracie gave the rope a little slack and then pulled back on it when it was empty.

"Like I said – smartest woman in the world."

"I thought you said most beautiful woman in the world."

"My recollection is a bit foggy on that one," Thomas laughed and brought the wheelbarrow back to the barn.

The pair worked together for most of the day, and they made an excellent dent in cleaning up the pile of rubble. As they dug through the piles of soot and debris their clothes got covered in black and the smell was all over them. Besides a brief stop for lunch, they worked until the sun began to fade behind the mountains in the west. That was when Thomas decided to fall back into the grass and put his hands behind his head. Gracie lay down next to him and did the same.

"Ready for a break," he said.

"Ready for a bath," Gracie giggled.

"We should ride Whinny down to the river every afternoon and get cleaned up – that's what my mother used to do to us boys. "Go to the river!" she would yell when we came home filthy." Thomas picked a piece of sour grass and started chewing it.

"I'd like that, I think, but I a'int the greatest at swimming, " said Gracie. "Tell me more about your childhood and growing up here."

"For me it was mostly about working the farm, but I found my love in the barn with the horses. I think that's the only thing that ever really made me happy."

"What about schooling?"

"My mother taught us mostly at home when we couldn't make it to school, and my father dragged us away from any studies we ever had more often than not." Thomas took a deep breath and felt sharp pains running through him just beneath his ribs. He winced and said, "I may have overdone it today."

"We should get you inside," Gracie started to sit up and he pulled her back.

"What about you and that Henry girl? What did you guys like to do together?"

"Our was mostly studies – books and piano and etiquette – don't forget your etiquette." Gracie laughed.

"Surely y'all did something more fun than that."

"We did," Gracie paused as if in deep thought. "What I recollect as being the best part of any of my days was just swinging with her under the oak. Her father had one of his men build a double wide swing with big, long ropes leading up into the branches, and we'd sit next to each other and hold hands and pretend we were birds flying up into the treetops and then far away," she started to tear up and then wiped her face. "After she was gone, that swing was the only place I found peace – I would sit there and just rock back and forth well into the dark sometimes. I missed her and our times together, and I felt her near me when I gripped those old ropes. That's what I miss."

Thomas reached down to his side and held her hand in his for a little while. They didn't say much more – they didn't need too. Finally, Gracie stood up and grabbed both of Thomas' hands and pulled him up.

"Let's get cleaned up and put some food in our stomachs," she said.

Thomas followed her into the house and they each went to their rooms to get washed. When Thomas came back out, he found Gracie asleep in one of the ladder-back chairs in the kitchen. He put a cotton blanket over her, and she barely moved. Thomas smiled, put his boots back on, and went outside in his long underwear. He stopped on the porch and picked up his long bow and quiver before going on into the courtyard and walking to the barn. He picked out a nice sturdy piece of rough sawn 2 by 6 that wasn't burned, and cut it about three feet long with his hand saw. Then he used the hand drill to put two holes in either end. A quick gander at his pile of rope and he picked out just the right pieces he needed. Back to the oak in front of the house where he tied one end of rope around an arrow and fired it high up over a branch. Then a second rope. Then it was just slip knots and hard knots under the seat and he was done. He tied purple lilacs on each rope where her hands would go.

Gracie stood in the kitchen and watched him out the window with tears streaming down her face. Then she went into her little bedroom behind the kitchen and lay down on her pillow.

"Oh, my Mr. Thomas. My Mr. Thomas. Thank you, Lord above…for my Mr. Thomas," she closed her eyes and dreamed of smoke and ash…and golden hair…and blue eyes…

# 32

Luke's grandmother's 1948 Chevy Fleetline was an immaculate art of engineering for its' time. It had a long sleek body with raised front fenders, two doors, but rear seats, four cranking windows, and white-wall tires. Her particular model had a teal-colored body and a hard white top, and extremely low mileage. Luke's grandfather bought the car less than a year before he passed away and his wife was scared to drive it. The repairs that were done by Luke and Mr. Pritchaird were simply required from lack of use.

Addie had the auto all loaded up with snacks and clean clothes for Luke. Lucas put Emmie's bags in the trunk and closed it down and then met his son on the driver's side and slipped him a ten-dollar bill. The morning air was still frightfully cold, but the day promised to be bright and sunny as the light clouds began to burn away.

"I still don't know what to say about this, Dad," Luke put his arm around his father's shoulder. "I honestly think you and Mom should sell this – or keep it and sell the truck."

"Can you see me driving up to the mine in this thing?" Lucas laughed. "Good Lord."

"Thank you, Dad. I love you guys."

Luke climbed into the driver's seat as his mother said her goodbyes to Emmaline on the other side. Addie clasped both of Emmie's hands in hers and looked straight into her eyes.

"I cannot tell you how much I enjoyed you being here with us," Luke thought his mother was about to cry. "You can come back to see me anytime...with or without that boy of mine."

"You have been so kind to me...and I learned so many things I never knew before," Emmie sighed and looked across the car at Luke's father. "Thank you both for everything you do for all of us. Every single time I switch on a light or turn on the heat I will think of you."

"You take care of my baby, okay?" Addie held the car door open as Emmaline slid into the front seat.

"Goodbye, Mother," Luke started the car and was ready to roll out before anything else embarrassing was said. They quickly hit the end of the driveway and turned left to head out through Cranberry. "It's such a beautiful day...and we have this new car...I'd like to show you something on the way back to school." Luke glanced over at Emmie. "Would that be okay?"

"I won't say no. I've never been in a car like this one."

At the mine store Luke turned right, pulled the Chevy out of Prosperity, and headed west through the mountains. Leafless trees rose on both sides of them creating a barren tunnel of winter. Emmie tucked a blanket around her legs and settled back to take in the scenery.

"I am horrible with direction, but I'm pretty certain Charlottesville is east of here."

"We are going west to go south to go east."

"I'll take your word for it – I don't have a compass." Emmie smiled at him, and his heart fluttered again, but he didn't let on about it.

Luke turned on the radio and put Emmie in charge of spinning the AM tuner switch in a search for music – or anything they could pick up in the mountains. She wasn't very successful so they mostly listened to static or to a station that they could pick up every fourth word or note on.

"I can sing for you," she said. "But you may want to pull your ears off."

"I bet you sing like a nightingale."

"You won't find out today, my friend," she smiled at him again...and he melted again.

Luke drove them to Wytheville before turning South and then East below Big Walker Mountain. Several winding roads led them into Pulaski, Virginia and then into Draper just beyond.

"Oh my God," said Emmie. "My Grandma Bea lives here – how did you know that?"

"Wow - I'd love to be surprising you with a visit to your Grandma, but I was going to show you the Connally farm and my horses."

"Oh."

"Is your Grandma back home yet?"

"My Mom and Dad were supposed to bring her back yesterday – she never misses her church for any reason." Emmie said.

"It's half past ten, so let's go up to the farm...and then we can see your Grandma," Luke turned onto the blacktop that went past Draper Mercantile then he made a right onto a dirt road running parallel to the New River. "Just about a mile and a half or so."

"This will be easy for you," Emmie grinned, "because my Grandma lives right...there," she pointed to a white colonial style home with a faded and rusted red metal roof sitting back in the trees. A swing with long ropes hung from the upper branches of a grand oak in the front yard.

"Your Grandma lives in the Summer Place?"

"I've never heard it called that, but that's where she lives."

"The Connally's call that the Summer Place." Luke had his right hand on the seat close to Emmie's hoping she would try to hold his hand at some point on their road trip – or maybe their hands would at least brush each other's.

Then Emmie said something that caught Luke off guard. "My Grandma Bea told us never to come up the road this way because it might make the rich folks uncomfortable."

"The Connally's are good people, Emmie, I promise you."

A mile further up Luke spun the car onto a yellow dirt drive that had recently been graded and drove under an arched crossbar that said ***Connally Farms***. The enormous hay fields on either side of the road had been cut and baled, and now the Timothy grass lay dormant, awaiting Spring rains to work its way back to life for the first cutting of the season. Tall leafless sycamores flanked by evergreens dotted the landscaping at the top of the hill. Luke followed the drive around to the left and pulled up in front of the huge white four column fronted house. A huge state-of-the-art barn stood to the left at the top of a second hill. A large pasture surrounded by a black three-rail fence rose toward a bluff behind the barn. Emmie could see no less than twenty horses up on the ridge. Four smaller buildings with black doors and black metal roofing lined the other side of the drive. Emmie knew what these houses were, and she looked away just as Luke put the Chevy in park. Two black labs ran toward the Fleetline as Luke stepped out of the car. He looked back in at Emmaline. "These guys are harmless," Luke started scratching heads and fending off flying tongues. "This is Commander…and this is Daisy-May." He walked around to Emmie's side of the car and opened the door.

"Okay," she said. "Not real great with dogs...or most animals."

"Take my hand – I promise you they are harmless," Luke gave her time to gather the courage she needed, and finally she stepped out onto the gravel drive just as he heard the screen door bang shut on the front porch of the great house.

"My, my – it's Luke Montgomery!" a middle-aged woman with speckled black hair came down the two front steps and strode toward the pair. "Where did you get this car...and more importantly, who might this lovely creature be?"

Luke leaned in and gave the woman a firm hug. "Emmaline Foster, this is Mrs. Evangeline Connally. Emmie is studying to become a nurse at UVA."

"Well, that is a noble profession helping others in their time of need. God Bless you sweetheart."

"Thank you, ma'am," Emmie said. "And it is certainly my pleasure to meet you. You have such a lovely farm and home."

Evangeline laughed, "We make do, Sweetie. Would you all like to come in for some tea? I just put on the pot. There might be a little breakfast left over as well. I'll see if Macie can scrounge up something from the kitchen." She turned and headed back toward the house.

"Macie?" Emmie whispered.

"Housekeeper, cook, and nanny," Luke answered. "Very sweet colored lady."

Emmie quietly looked around the house as they walked. It was magnificent to say the least, but it made her eerily uncomfortable. Luke caught up with Mrs. Connally and told her that he was going to show Emmaline the barn before coming up to the house.

"It's always all about those horses with you, is it not?" she laughed and banged back through the screen door. "I'll see you in a few minutes...James is down there...don't scare him."

"She's a little eccentric, that one," said Luke. Emmie smiled and pulled her coat tighter around herself.

They walked up the hill toward the barn and Luke found himself slowing down a bit as Emmaline didn't appear to be even trying to keep up with him at all.

"What are those little crosses over there by the fence?" she asked – hoping it was a pet cemetery.

"Emmie..." he hesitated, "those are the graves of people who used to work here a long time back."

"You mean slaves."

"Unfortunately...I'm sorry. Luke turned to wait for her. "I probably shouldn't have brought you here."

"No, I'm okay," she fought off a cold shiver. "It's important to remember...can we go closer?"

"Sure," Luke reached for her hand, and she let him lead her over to the graves. The earth around them hadn't been disturbed in decades and the grass was winter brown. A vine hung on the fence behind them – probably honeysuckle.

"They don't even have names on them...very sad." she said.

"I have stared at these for years," Luke said. "You have to look closer at the wood – and use your finger to trace where the names were written. I think they were marked with a rock or a piece of coal."

Emmie walked closer to the first grave and Luke placed her finger on the wood. She traced the indention slowly and said, “God Bless you, Samuel”. She went down each of the six graves and traced each one, saying their names aloud until she got to “Gunther”. “That’s a strange name for a slave – I think it is German or Austrian.”

“The Connally’s don’t know the story of them – I’ve asked before.”

“Their names should be read aloud sometimes…so they aren’t forgotten.”

“The family cemetery is up there,” Luke pointed across the fence and up toward the bluff where a large ancient oak stood sentinel over several small headstones.

“You should read their names too – sometimes,” Emmie lowered her head and walked back down the little bluff toward the barn. Luke took a deep breath and caught up with her.

“Emmaline Foster, you are an amazing person.”

“We have some Native American blood in our past somewhere, and that is what my grandmother always taught me… to say the names of the taken out loud – so that they live on in our hearts.” Emmie smiled at Luke, and he wanted to hold her hand again, but a large figure of a man greeted them at the barn entrance.

“Lucas Junior!” he said. “I hope you are here to work. We got a newcomer this morning in the Birthing Stall.”

“A newcomer?” Emmie asked.

“A foal…come on,” Luke grinned ear to ear. “You will love this – Mr C., this is my friend Emmaline from UVA.”

“A pleasure to make your acquaintance, ma’am.” James Connally led them through the barn. Most of the stalls were empty from the morning turnout, but a few had large standing thoroughbreds in them that snorted and paced as they moved down the aisle.

"I've never seen horses this big," said Emmie.

"Racehorses," said Luke. "Only thing taller is a Clydesdale – only thing wider is a Draft horse."

"You almost sound knowledgeable," she poked him in the ribs.

"Or I'm faking it, because you wouldn't know the difference," Luke laughed.

They arrived at the Birthing Stall and peered over the door into the straw lined bed below. An exhausted wide-eyed black mare lay on her side breathing heavily and foaming at the mouth slightly. Standing uneasily over her was a still wet four-foot-tall jet-black colt. His dark eyes were wide and bright, and he seemed to catch Emmie's gaze almost immediately. The colt took a few wobbly steps toward the door before he fell over on his side - but he quickly used his front legs to pop back up. He stayed a few feet from the door…near his mother.

"This is amazing…" said Emmie quietly.

"No need to whisper, Honey," James Connally said. "This ain't a human baby…he's fully capable to get around on his own…and we want him to be used to noise early – to get the skittish out of him. He's a beauty, ain't he?"

"I can't wait to get ahold of this one," said Luke.

"Late Spring you can start some groundwork with him." James clapped Luke on the back. "I missed my breakfast so my blood sugar ain't happy with me. Meet you guys at the house? I'm sure you want to show Emmaline around some."

"Sure thing. We will be up in a bit…can't stay long… gotta get back to school – and I've got practice at six." Luke smiled.

"We've been following you. You guys need more defense." James headed down the aisle toward the house.

"True."

"Oh my gosh, Luke – look he's trying to nurse," Emmie put her arms up on the door. "What a beautiful little thing. What will they do with him here?"

"He's bred to race," Luke said. "We will have him ready to hit the track when he's a little over two…or he will be sold. Mr. Connally and the trainer will make that call."

"He's so fragile looking,"

"He will be running through the pasture in a couple of days." Luke said. "It's good he's nursing…sometimes we have to bottle feed – it's really up to the mare."

Luke walked Emmie around the barn and training facility. They walked past all thirty-six stalls and out the back to the racing half-track.

"They spent some time leveling this area and putting it in. We run the horses out here with jockeys and get time trials done. If we go to sell one, we have to get a third-party timer out here with the prospective buyer – and most times they bring their own jockey. A lot of companies and partnerships buy racehorses without ever laying eyes on them. It's a big business." Luke was proud of where he spent his summers even though it was clearly hard work.

He showed her the indoor training area where they had an indoor round pen and automatic lungeing machine. Then he showed her the horse "spa' where the animals were treated like kings and queens. One of the trainers had a young filly running on a giant treadmill and Luke spoke with him for a few moments – mostly about basketball and Charlottesville.

"Let's head up to the house and say goodbye…we should head to your grandma's and then get on the road," Luke led Emmie back down toward the house.

"What do they do with those slave houses now?" Emmie gestured toward the four small buildings on the opposite side of the drive.

"Honestly?" he said. "They fixed them up for guests and potential buyers…even put in running water and heat…" Luke trailed off when he realized what his words must sound like to her.

But she laughed instead. "Beats an outhouse and keeping a fire burning all night, doesn't it?"

Luke thought, "Was that last comment a dig at my family?" Then he laughed with her.

Evangeline Connally was awaiting them at the front door and rushed them into the parlor where they found a spread of tea and lady fingers. The room itself had been redone with new striped wallpaper in red and gold and a waist high wainscoting running around the entire room. It was perfectly gaudy – but a nice fire was roaring in the six-foot-high fireplace.

"Please sit down," Evangeline begged. So, they did.

They spoke of the pleasantries of the day, and she asked about Luke's mother whom she had never met, but must "lead a really hard life with little joy". James joined them and asked how Luke's father was doing in the mines and wasn't he ready to quit that and get a real job making a real living. Luke was quickly remembering why he tried to avoid conversations like this with the Connallys. Every time there was another dig Emmie would glance at Luke and give him the "can we leave now" look. She wished they had a code-word to tell each other they were uncomfortable. Finally, she mercifully put an end to the unconscious beratement that Luke was suffering.

"Luke, I hate to do this, but I really need to get back to school," she put her cup back on the table. "And I need to stop by my grandmother's house and check on her."

"Oh, does your grandma live between here and Charlottesville?" Evangeline asked.

"Funny coincidence, she lives in that little white house with the red roof just up the road," Emmie stood up. "I had no idea when Luke said he wanted to show me where he was forced to work so hard every summer," she tried to add her own dig, but it just glanced off of them...they were too busy looking at each other with blank expressions.

"Your grandmother is Beatrice Johnson?" James asked as he looked at his wife again.

"Yes, sir."

"Oh...that's no good...that's no good at all," Evangeline said.

"Watch what you say..." James grabbed her by the arm.

"What's going on?" asked Luke.

James walked toward Luke, and acted as if he was going to bump up against his chest despite the fact that Luke had him by six inches and forty pounds.

"What are you doing, Mr. Connally?" Luke took a half step back and pulled Emmie behind him.

"Listen to me good, boy...you take your negro girlfriend off this property...and you never – and I mean never – bring her here again!" James Connally looked like he was going to pop a vein in his forehead.

Luke could feel Emmie crying behind him before he heard her first sob.

"You apologize!" said Luke.

"Not in this lifetime," James said. "You heard me...leave!"

"What the hell is wrong with you?" Luke was ready to raise his fists when Emmie clutched his arm.

"Please, Luke…let's just go," Emmie was tugging his sleeve trying to move him toward the door. He followed her in a state of confusion and dismay.

Emmie pushed open the screen door and it banged hard against the wall. One of the dogs began to bark as they walked to the car, and they each climbed into their respective seats quickly. Luke was about to start the car when James Connally called after them from the porch.

"Oh – and Luke, you're fired!"

Luke started to get out of the car again and almost made it before Emmie pulled him back in. He started the car and pushed hard on the pedal throwing rocks away from the gravel drive and into the yard and the tiny slave houses.

"I'll send your parents a bill for that, you little shit."

Luke stopped long enough to yell, "And you can go straight to hell!"

Luke flew down the driveway and would have left an enormous cloud of dust if the dirt drive wasn't still wet from the melting snow. When he came out under the arched gate, he stopped the car and pushed the shifter into neutral, and took his foot off the clutch.

"Emmie – I…"

"Don't, okay," she put a finger on his lips.

They sat there just looking at each other for several minutes. Emmie was sad, and Luke was confused and angry.

"They were being nice in their own way…and then they just…lost control." Luke put his hand on Emmaline's. "I don't get it."

"Come on, Luke," Emmie held his hand briefly. "It's not you…and it's not me…it's something about my grandmother. The minute I mentioned the house they changed." She sat back and put her hands in her lap, and looked out the back window as if to make sure they weren't followed. "Please drive to her house now."

"Sure…sure." Luke shifted down in to first and eased out of the Connally's driveway. It was a short run down to Bea Johnson's house, and they pulled in under the oak tree with the swing hanging from it within a minute. Emmie climbed out of the car before Luke could cut off the engine. Mrs. Johnson had heard the automobile roll up and she came out on the porch very quickly. She saw Emmie immediately.

"Oh my, child. What you doing up in here?" She was wiping her hands on an old yellow apron hanging in front of her dress. She wore no shoes. "I thought you was your daddy comin' back – he ain't long gone now." She ran her fingers through her grey hair like she was getting ready for company. "Ya'll come on inside here - I just got the fire going." She went back inside the small house.

Luke followed Emmie up the single step onto the porch, and through the front door. A screen door hung off to one side with the screen missing from the bottom and torn on the top. White paint was chipping and peeling from the entire exterior, and termites had chewed through several of the porch boards. The inside was not much better. The floors were worn, ragged, and splintered in some areas. The kitchen and sitting area were all one room with a small kitchen table and a green vinyl couch covered in plastic. There was a small table with a reading lamp burning on it and Luke saw an open bible laying there. A fire burned in a very small fireplace only big enough for two or three logs.

"Get ya'll some refreshments?" Bea asked.

"Oh no, Grandma…we just had tea up at the horse farm just up the way here." Emmie had wasted no time as Luke stood awkwardly by the kitchen table.

Beatrice lifted the glasses up that were hanging on her neck and poised them on the end of her nose. "Now, do tell why you would be up that way." She sat down at the metal kitchen table in a metal chair and let out a sigh. "Sit down," she said. "The both of you."

Emmie spent the next few minutes recounting what had just occurred at the Connally Farm. Luke sat quietly at the table and altered his look from Emmie to Bea as their expressions changed. "How could they go from being hospitable to us…to outright hatred like that." Emmie was starting to tear up again.

Beatrice reached over and lit up a hurricane lamp in the middle of the table with a kitchen match that must have been in the pocket of her apron. "You sit right here, baby," she started up the steps to her bedroom. "I be right back."

Emmie looked at Luke across the table, but she didn't speak to him while her grandmother was gone. In less than three minutes Beatrice returned with a tattered brown leather book in her hand and placed it on the table between her and Emmaline.

"You have every right to know all of it," she said. "Your mother…she read this when she was about fourteen."

"I don't understand," said Emmie.

"This book…this is why your mama left here when she was eighteen…and why she ain't never comin' back here again." Bea pushed the book across the table toward Emmie.

"What is this?" she asked.

"You have to read this to un'erstand eve'thing," Bea tapped her finger on the book. "I can't tell it with any justice…it has to be read…in her words."

"Who? My Mother?"

"I want you to take this wit you," she touched Emmaline's hand now and rubbed it with her worn and bony fingers. "I'm trustin' you wit it as family – and you bring it back – 'cause it belong in dis house - it does."

"Grandma…please?" Emmie felt a cold chill sweep through her.

"Dis book here," she tapped on it again. "Was written by a slave what lived on Waverly Plantation."

"Waverly?"

"The Connally Farm."

"Who wrote it?"

"My mother…your great grandmother, God rest her soul," Beatrice Johnson seemed to be so sad when speaking about her mother.

"My great grandmother?" Emmie looked at Luke then back at Bea. She gripped her hands tightly and Bea gave her a little shake.

"Grace Henry Johnson…they called her Gracie."

# 33

Gracie pointed her bare feet straight up at the single wispy cloud that was floating across the bluest sky Virginia had to offer, and she giggled each time Thomas pushed her higher. She was a child again…not a care in the world. Butterflies flitted all around her and darting chickadees dodged her as she flew. She had never in her life felt as free as she did at this moment. Summer would be arriving soon, and the sun warmed every part of her that had been left cold from the long snowy winter. To Thomas she smelled of lilacs and honeysuckle, and his senses were overwhelmed each time she returned to him from her flight.

"I need to get back to the plow," said Thomas. He could see clouds building over the distant mountaintops and he knew rain was coming soon. It was easier to plow moist soil than mud.

"Just a couple more…please?" Gracie leaned back and looked at him with doleful eyes as she went higher, but her huge grin and streaming black hair showed her deception. Still Thomas continued to push her from the awkward stance he had discovered that gave him the leverage he needed to do so. He basically had his prosthetic leg planted in the ground behind him, but it kept him from falling over.

"Are you ready to jump?" He slowed her down just a little on the next pass and then she leapt out into the tall grass and rolled away laughing. She came up with brown leaves strewn through her hair and she quickly stood up and shook them out. Then she pulled her hair back and tied a scarf around it.

"Back to work, Mr. Thomas," Gracie made a salute with her right hand and smiled.

Poor *Whinny* had been left tied to the plow and standing in the field as they had lunch and played in the yard. She looked relieved as they returned to the field in front of the house to continue the plowing. Thomas checked the yoke and then draped two leather reins over his shoulders and grabbed both handles of the plow. "Let's go, girl," he said softly, and *Whinny* started forward with small trudging steps. "We'll be done soon…I promise.

Gracie followed behind them, seeding the freshly turned soil with kernels for feed corn. She used her foot to cover the seed as she went. The single wispy cloud she had reached for earlier was quickly being joined by others, and within an hour of resuming the plowing a light rain was falling.

"Perfect timing," said Thomas as they finished up one last row. "If it doesn't rain too hard, we will skip over to the next field and plant some Silver Queen tomorrow."

"I'm not walking barefoot in the mud," Gracie caught up with Thomas and *Whinny.*

"Where are your shoes, young lady," Thomas smiled.

"Never put 'em back on after swingin'…the ground feels so good on my feet," she reached out and gave the horse a good pat on her neck. "Good job, girl – extra mash for you tonight."

The pair removed the reins and bit from around the mare's neck and mouth and untied the knots that held the leather to the wooden plow. Thomas had just about worn a hole in the left-hand shoulder of his wool shirt.

"I might try to hook up a team tomorrow – maybe add *Mayflower* to the mix here," Thomas took off his shirt and wiped his brow, which was covered in wet caked-on dust. "Poor *Whinny* and me are plum tuckered."

"And filthy," Gracie laughed and ran her hand down his arm pulling away caked dust and mud. She slung it on the ground at his feet.

"I have a solution," he said. "Let's get this poor girl turned out first."

Thomas moved the plow to the side and disconnected all the leathers and carried them toward the house, while Gracie reluctantly led the mare back to the pasture gate with a single rope thrown around her neck. *Whinny* didn't fuss at all...she was more than ready to call it a day. The rain was coming down a little harder now as Thomas got back to the fence.

"Do you trust me?" he asked.

"That sounds like a loaded question, my friend," she smiled at him.

"Sit on the fence right here," he patted the top rail.

Thomas opened the pasture gate and threw a loose lead rope around *Mayflower's* neck, and led her out to where Gracie was waiting. He took a short bridle that was hanging from the fence post and easily put the bit in the mare's mouth and threw the reins back over her neck. He put his left foot up on the bottom rail and propelled his bad leg up and over the mare's bare back. He walked about twenty feet then turned to come back to where Gracie was seated patiently.

"Grab my hand," he said.

"I don't know how to ride very well," she moaned.

"You just need to hold on and let me do all the work."

Gracie shook her head before she reluctantly allowed herself to be pulled up on the horse's back, where she landed with a thump. She promptly threw her arms around Thomas' neck.

Thomas moved her hands down to his waist and turned the mare back toward the house and the dirt road leading toward town. The rain was still falling just enough to keep their hair damp, but the warm late spring day kept them from getting too cold. Still, Gracie kept her arms wrapped tightly around Thomas and turned her cheek to put her head on his back as they rode. Thomas turned *May* through a broken gate and into the bottom field that had become overgrown after years of non-use and was still brown from the winter. Taller dead grasses brushed the bottoms of their feet as they made their way down into a shallow ravine on the far side of the field.

"Where are you taking me?" Gracie really didn't care.

"My favorite spot on the farm."

"When did I become special enough to warrant this?" she laughed.

"This afternoon, when I saw you turning seeds with your bare feet."

The bottom of the ravine was shaped by a small, running, rocky creek that meandered downhill away from them. Thomas turned the horse into the stream, and they slowly worked their way down toward the river. The horse's feet clattered and kicked rocks as they went. Gracie stared up into the sycamores and wondered about the birds and squirrels that lived in the treetops, away from the horror of men. Then she looked down at her feet and saw just how dirty she was. She smirked and clutched Thomas tighter.

"Thank you," she whispered.

"You're so welcome." Thomas led them around a huge rocky outcropping that had to be ten times larger than the house. There were large trees at the base of the rock and small scraggly ones at the top, but as the formation grew from the ground it became a large elevated flat surface that was mostly barren, with a few small lichen patches here and there. They meandered around the rock and slowly worked their way down a leaf covered embankment until they reached the railroad tracks.

"My brothers and I played at this place for hours – on the top and inside…there is a cave that opens up on the other side and goes in for about fifty feet or so," Thomas moved Gracie's arm from around his waist. "We have to get down and walk her from here."

Thomas held Gracie's arm at the elbow as she slid down the side of the mare…then he dismounted onto his good leg with a quick hop before placing both feet on the ground. His confidence in the Palmer Leg was increasing daily it seemed. He led *Mayflower* across the tracks and between some overgrown Mulberry bushes where a trail of sorts seemed to open. Gracie followed closely behind as they reached one last large clump of bushes and Thomas pushed through. The New River rushed before them in a wide expanse of its' cold, green glory as it thundered Eastward. The far side was very rocky, and rapids pounded water and debris through small openings in the boulders that lined the river bed. Thomas glanced up and down the river for any other signs of activity, then he dropped the reins from around *May's* neck and looped them around a small pine growing from the rocks along the river's edge. The horse lowered her head and began to drink, then paused to nibble at a blueberry bush. The river made a hard bend at this point and boulders created an eddy on the Waverly side. It was a perfect swimming hole.

"Sit down, and put your feet in, Gracie," Thomas pulled down the suspenders that were holding up the pants that had become too big for him over the last year and a half.

"Looks like you are planning for more than your feet," she laughed.

"I'm going for a swim," he smiled at her.

"Oh...and you think I can't swim – because most of us can't, is that it."

"Can you?"

"Enough to not drown myself – and maybe drown you if the need presents," Gracie removed the scarf from her head with a giggle, then dropped her grey smock on the ground at her feet...she wore a long white slip underneath. She stepped into the water then turned to face Thomas. "It is very cold – but feels so good." She lowered herself into the shallow water and sat down on the gravelly mud at the bottom – supporting herself with her hands behind her.

Thomas took off his boots and removed his right leg at the knee, then he dropped his trousers on the bank and sat down in his long johns in the edge of the river. He walked backwards using his arms and sat next to Gracie in the shallows.

"You are right – this is freezing."

"You've done so much for me, Mr. Thomas," Gracie waved her arms over the surface of the water. "Thank you."

"I have done nothing for you," Thomas crossed his legs on the bottom and sat up taller. "I wouldn't be alive without you."

"The swing...nobody has ever done anything like that for me."

"I knew it would make you happy," he put some water on his cheeks. "I could use another shave soon." Thomas knew he could handle it himself, but he loved that attention from Gracie.

"When we get back...after supper."

They sat quietly in the shallows for a while, nursing the sore muscles they both had from a long day of planting. If they were lucky, they could grow enough to not have to ration much over the winter. Gracie plunged her head back into the water and then used her hands to wring out her hair as she looped it over her right shoulder and dropped it across her chest. Thomas noticed how sheer her slip was as the water made it cling to her body. He tried his best not to look, but there was nothing easy about it.

"Your arms are getting stronger from working," she reached out and squeezed his forearm as he floated it on the surface. Gracie flipped a handful of water up onto his blonde hair and he shuddered. "Next time we bring soap...and a towel." She admired the way his blonde curls came down around his ears and over his forehead, but she wasn't sure why his brows and beard came in darker. The contrast with his deep blue eyes was something she couldn't look away from at times – and this was one of those times.

"I'm going to get out and sit in the sunshine," she said as she stood up and flung water towards him with her fingers. "You need to stay in here and cool down some." She crossed her arms over her breasts, walked to the rocky shore and sat down without moving her arms. She used one hand to pull her slip down over her bare feet, then quickly put her arm back over her heart. Beads of water glistened on her skin in the afternoon sun as the clouds began to pull away with the quick storm.

"You...are very beautiful Ms. Grace," Thomas put his head completely under the water after he said this but arose quickly in anticipation of her response. What followed was typical Gracie.

"Not much stock to compare me to around these parts lately, is there?" she smiled and squeezed the water from her hair onto the ground beside her.

"There could be nigh on a hunert lasses round these parts and me thoughts be the same," Thomas laughed.

"So, you think acting Irish will woo me then? Or was that Scottish – hard to tell when something comes out so poorly," her smile lit up the afternoon much more than the sunlight streaking through in waves from the sycamores on the hill behind them.

Thomas used his arms to pull himself back up out of the river and onto the bank where he sat down with a crunch in the river pebbles. He wiped the mud from his hands on his white long johns. Gracie frowned at him.

"That's some extra scrubbing on the washboard."

"I'm sorry...my body doesn't seem to be much use these days," Thomas sighed.

"Don't go feeling sorry for yourself around me, Mr. Thomas," Gracie rocked back and forth trying to warm up. "Being one-legged don't make you wipe your dirt on your pants...it's stupidity what done that, sir."

"How about I do the wash tomorrow while you work in your garden... and ride on your swing?" Thomas looked at her with his sincerest blue eyes.

"Deal," she said without hesitation.

They turned their backs on one another in a symbolic presentation of modesty as they got re-dressed. Then they walked back up the path with *Mayflower* in tow and crossed the railroad tracks. Thomas stopped for a moment then reached down and placed his hand on the rail.

"Train's coming...let's get scarce."

He climbed up onto the mare's back and pulled Gracie up behind him – and with a sharp but gentle kick the horse lurched up the creek bed and they disappeared from sight. When they reached the lower field and started across Gracie could hear the chugging and clacking of the locomotive as the train rolled through below them – it was always such a lonely sound. She pulled herself closer to Thomas – and he didn't seem to mind.

As they rounded the bend in the road leading back to the house Thomas pulled *May* to an abrupt stop that woke Gracie from her brief rest against his back.

"What is it?" she said.

"Wagon up by the house…shhhh.." Thomas walked the horse a little closer until he could make out a female figure standing on the porch.

"It's the Drapers," he said as he pushed the mare up into the courtyard.

Thomas dismounted and helped Gracie down as Mrs. Draper approached.

"She ready?"

Gracie glanced at Thomas, "Ready for what?" she said.

"Your flight to freedom with the others," Ms. Draper slowly pulled back a flap on the covered wagon to expose a young negro woman and two small children. They huddled frightened in the corner when they saw Thomas in his grey flannel shirt. The youngest, a girl of about five, started whimpering.

"Oh, I'm not going to hurt you," said Thomas. "Would you like some sugar cubes with a drop of lemon juice?"

"We have to go, Mr. Summerlin…Gracie, get your things quickly," Mrs. Draper put her hand on Gracie's shoulder.

"Mr. Thomas," Gracie looked at him with the dark sullen eyes that drove him mad. "Y-You want me to go?"

"You know how I feel about all of this," Thomas took a step back.

"This is your chance to be free from all of this, Gracie," Mrs. Draper said. "There's fighting going on up near Cloyd's Mountain again, and they say the Yankees mean to destroy the railroad down by the river. This may be your only chance for freedom."

"What do you know of freedom?" Gracie said.

"Gracie, get your things…we have to hurry."

"What do you know of freedom?" she asked again.

"What do you mean, child?"

"Freedom is being where you want to be, when you want to be there, doing what you want to do…with a person you want to do those things with," Gracie started toward the house.

"Gracie – you can have freedom on your terms now." Mrs. Draper followed her a few steps. "You can leave all of this."

"Mrs. Katherine, with all due respect, this is my home, this is my life…this is my freedom…and I would thank you to leave now," Gracie went inside the house again, but this time she did not slam the door behind her…

Mrs. Draper turned to Thomas and walked closer to him, "She's a great person and she has never left your side - ever… you do the same for her."

"I can't imagine how this place would run without her," Thomas lowered his eyes.

"She is more than that…and deserves to be more than that."

"I will never treat her otherwise."

"Thomas," she reached out and put her hand on his arm. "There's something else I need to tell you…it's not especially easy for me and it won't be for you. It's about your mother."

"I've been expecting it…I felt it," Thomas put his hand on hers. "When?"

"She passed on ten days ago in Richmond," Katherine put her hand on his cheek. "We just got the word last night – I'm so sorry."

Thomas removed her hand with his and placed a light kiss near her wrist as he released it back to her.

"Thank you…and God Bless you," he said as he turned and followed Gracie inside.

# 34

Luke eased the Fleetliner into first gear and slowly pulled out onto the road heading east back toward Roanoke, and away from Emmaline's grandmother's house... and the Connally Farm. As they rounded the bend in front of Draper Mercantile, James Connally stood leaning against a blue Ford pickup talking to another man in a wide brimmed hat. They both stopped talking and stared at the Fleetliner as it rolled past. Luke started to slow the auto down, and he looked over at Emmie who was already staring back at him. She shook her head, and he gunned the engine past Connally and the other man, and rolled out onto Highway 29 headed Northeast for the three-hour journey back to school through Roanoke and Lynchburg.

"The devil with that man," Emmie pulled her knees up onto the seat in front of her and clutched her great grandmother's journal in her arms.

Luke kept his right hand on the top of the wood grained steering wheel and alternated between looking out to his left and checking the road in front of him. He didn't have any words for this situation, and quite frankly he was bewildered by the entire morning and early afternoon. They drove in silence all the way to Roanoke before he decided to speak up.

"I have to get gasoline...do you want some pop?"

"RC if they have one," Emmie stared out the window as the hills and farms rolled by them.

Luke pulled into an Esso station and asked the attendant to pump in five dollars' worth of gas as he walked into the station and grabbed two Royal Crowns and two Moon pies. He placed a dollar on the counter, got his change, popped the bottles open under the counter, and walked back outside.

"Want to pop the hood for me, sport," said the attendant.

"Not necessary," Luke replied.

"Got you a ripe one there I see," the attendant chuckled and walked toward Luke looking for a tip.

"Not a chance," said Luke and opened his door to get back inside.

"That shit's illegal, boy,"

Luke stopped and started to close the door when he heard Emmaline's voice from inside the auto, "Luke Montgomery, you are going to be late for practice!"

"Oh shit -you are – Luke Montgomery..hey," the attendant went silent as Luke slammed the door shut and started the Fleetliner. He handed both bottles of pop to Emmie and threw the Moon pies on the seat between them. He quickly had them heading back toward Lynchburg.

"You see how hard it is – for us to even be friends?" Emmie handed him his RC and then took a small sip of hers. "This has been a day…that's for sure."

They rode on in silence all the way to Lynchburg. Luke thought about getting to practice on time, and about his schedule leading into the Christmas break. Emmaline sat thinking about everything her Grandma Bea had told her about Grace. Beatrice wanted Emmie to read her great-grandmother's words for herself, but she did tell her how much Grace had loved living at Waverly - which they now called the Connally Farm. Bea told her how Grace's life had changed following the death of the last family member, and how she came to live in Summer House where Beatrice was born in 1879. She told her about how Emmie's mother, Mathilde, had read a quarter of the way through the journal at age fourteen, and vowed never to read another word... and of how Emmaline's mother left at age eighteen and told her mother she would "never again live next to the people up on the hill." Beatrice told Emmaline how she had come to discover the journal in the bottom of a hollowed-out cedar blanket chest after her mother passed away...and how she was left with more questions than answers after reading it. "Much of it seems to be a mystery – most filled with riddles," she told Emmie. Emmaline promised to read it from end to end and discuss it with Grandma Bea when she saw her at Christmas – outside of her mother's earshot of course.

"Em – you know I don't care what other people think of me...or us... when we are together,' Luke glanced over at her. "You know I mean it...don't you?"

"It bothers me though," she said. "I'm used to being passed over and not given a second or even a third chance. Your approximation to me does the same thing to you, and I don't think you are ready for that...because you don't know what it is like to be looked at a different way...every day."

"Why do you think I hide my coal-mine upbringing?"

"See that's my point again," Emmie touched his arm then picked up one of the Moon pies to peal the wax paper from around it. "You can hide from yours...I can't hide from mine."

"It can't change the way I feel about you," Luke looked at her and his blue eyes almost...almost caught her off guard and pushed her off track.

"You are a very special person, and I have never known someone with your compassion," she took another sip of her cola. "But…I can't be the reason that your life changes for the worse. I would never let that happen to you…or to me."

"I don't know if I can just be friends with you," Luke drank down a quarter of his drink and stuck the bottle between his legs to hold it.

"That's a decision you have to make on your own."

The ride went silent again after this, and around five-thirty in the afternoon Luke pulled into TP's parking lot and rolled around back to Emmie's cottage. Emmaline's father and Mr. Richard were standing out front with Natalie as he pulled up.

"Mr. Montgomery," Anthony stuck out his big paw to shake Luke's hand as he pulled Emmie's bags from the trunk. "Thank you for seeing my little girl home safely."

Emmie went straight to Natalie and put her arms around her, then walked her inside the little house.

"Uneventful trip I hope," said Mr. Richard.

"No major problems or issues," Luke lied. "I hate to run, but I'm late for practice." He got back in the Fleetliner and headed back up the hill to his dorm.

After a three-hour practice, Dom and Luke got back to their room and Luke collapsed on his pillow with a deep exhale. "Want to kill the light," he said in Dom's general direction.

Dom cut the light and laid down on his bunk, "How was break? How's your folks?"

"All good, can we get some sleep,"

"Nothing weird happened?"

"Nope."

"Nothing at all?"

"Nope."

"Come on, man…the whole campus is talking about your little road trip with the diner girl," Dom switched the light back on.

"Turn off the damned light," Luke turned to face the wall.

"Trouble in forbidden paradise?" Dom sat up on his bed.

"Are you my friend, Dom?"

"Of course."

"Then turn off the damned light."

A couple of cold weeks passed, and exams came and went. The UVA men's team lost a game at home against North Carolina State, and then won a game at James Madison University. As Dom and Luke arrived back at the dorm following the late-night return from the road trip to JMU, Joe Millstone popped his head out from his dorm room.

"Luke," Joe waited for Luke to turn around. "That girl from TPs has called here three times looking for you on the hall phone – said it was important the one time I actually answered it myself – here's a note."

"Thanks, buddy," Luke took the note and walked to the phone sitting on a small table halfway down the hall. He asked for an outside operator then read out the five-digit number. Emmaline answered on the second ring.

"Look, I know it is late, but I need to see you – tonight if possible."

"It's good to hear your voice. Let me dump off my stuff and I can ride down there real quick." Luke threw his bag in the room, grabbed his key, and headed out the door. "I'll be back in a few," he said to nobody in particular.

The drive to TPs was less than two minutes and thoughts raced through his head the whole way. Had she changed her mind? Did she have feelings for him? Was she okay? Was Natalie okay? Was it her Grandma Bea? He pulled around back to her house and climbed from the car. Emmie was waiting at the door in a cotton nightgown with a cloth shower cap on her head.

"Hey, Beautiful," he said. "Are you alright?"

"Yes…yes," Emmie pulled her nightgown close from the cold wind hitting her in the face.

"You want me to come in?"

Emmie closed the door behind her with a click.

"It's freezing out here," Luke said. "Let's go inside."

"Can we sit in your auto?"

"Not much warmer, but sure."

Luke opened the door for Emmaline, and after closing it he hurried back around to his side, got in, and started the engine.

"Takes a while to heat up," he said.

"This won't take but a minute…but I need you to know something."

"You already let me down…a few times actually – so if this is about tha-"

"Jesus, just be quiet so I can get this out," Emmie was serious, and Luke was beginning to realize it.

"I'm sorry, go on."

"I've read some of my great-grandmother's journal and it is as terrible as my mother said," Emmie grabbed Luke's hand and clutched it hard.

"I'm so sorry," he said. "What can I do?

"That's just it," she sighed. "I don't think either of us can do anything."

"What does that mean?"

"God, I'm just going to have to say it."

"Just say it then."

She clutched Luke's hand harder and then leaned in and put her head on his shoulder. She spoke very softly...so softly that Luke had to ask her to repeat what she had said twice. The first time because he didn't hear it...the second time because he couldn't believe it.

Luke was almost positive Emmaline had said, "There's so much to tell you. But I guess I can start with this – I think James Connally is your father's cousin."

## September 17, 1862 near Sharpsburg, Maryland

John Summerlin was hurt...he was hurt bad...and he knew it. All three of his brothers lay motionless on the bank of Antietam Creek near Burnside Bridge. Around them lay at least a hundred men in various stages of death. The water was running red with the blood of young men past the little church on the far side. He could lay here and die with them, or he could try to save himself. As the fighting moved across the bridge and toward the southwest, he decided to crawl away from the sounds of gun fire and screams along the bank toward the north. John pulled his leg along with both arms as he slid through the wet sand and stone. A large, jagged piece of metal protruded from just above his knee almost up to his hip. Its weight pulled at the skin as he moved. The agony was unbearable and many times he almost gave up and just laid down to await his ending. But he kept moving, and eventually crossed the shallow creek toward a small white house on the far side. The chilly water provided him with some relief from the pain but the trail of blood running downstream out of his body was hard to watch. He knew he was going to bleed to death very soon.

John dragged himself up the little hill to the front of the house, leaving a red trail following him through the grass and leaves. There was a tall grey gelding with a black saddle and matching tack being held by a young boy in a dark grey Confederate uniform. The boy stood staring away into the tree line almost a hundred yards away, doubtless longing for home. John heard indiscernible arguing coming from inside the house, and a woman screaming incessantly. Somehow, he was able to find the will to climb up the three front steps after pulling himself through the sparse shrubs in front of the house. He collapsed under a cracked window that had two or three bullet holes through several panes. A thin white curtain swayed back and forth inside the house. John pulled himself up on the sill and peered through the cracked glass. A bearded man was pulling a pair of grey pants back up around his waist and fastening them with a pair of suspenders. A dark-haired woman was leaning over a young girl who was curled up in a ball on the floor...the girl's clothes had been torn from her body and laid in tatters on the floor around her. John pulled the Colt from his waistband and buried it under his torn grey shirt. He propped himself up under the windowsill and waited. What he waited for was perplexing to him...because he was probably just waiting to die at this point. He closed his eyes and thought of his mother.

The door opened with a bang and the soldier dressed in grey stepped outside. He immediately laid his eyes on John Summerlin.

"Damn, boy," he said. "that's one hell of a hunk of shrapnel you're carrying 'round."

"Hurts like hell too," John winced and tried to straighten his leg...it was no use.

"Maybe some help will come to you eventually."

"You ain't gonna help me, Captain?"

"Got a war to fight, son."

"A war against ten-year-old girls?" John stiffened and tightened his grip around the revolver.

"You won't live to tell no tales." The captain stood at the edge of the steps and whistled. The young boy came in a hurry with his horse and stopped ten feet from the porch.

John noticed movement in the window and looked up to see the woman holding her daughter in her arms and staring out in disbelief…her right eye was swollen closed and red as a beet.

"Where's the husband?" John asked.

"In the bushes fifteen feet that way'" the captain pointed at the far end of the house. "He may have had a gun but it don't matter. War is war."

"And Americans are Americans."

"Are they now?" The captain moved closer. "What's your name boy?"

"John Summerlin."

"I'll alert your mother that you fought valiantly, but your wounds were grave," the man pulled a shining silver sword out of a black sheath at his side and raised it above his head.

"Say, Captain?" John asked.

"Got some last words I guess?"

"I'm going to die today…but not before you," John uncovered the Colt and fired a single shot which struck the captain just below his heart and to the left of his suspender. Blood splattered behind him, and a thick red patch clouded his shirt as he collapsed in a pile on the porch, and his sword clattered five feet away.

The boy came running up the steps as the horse lowered its head to graze without a care.

"Y-you killed the captain!"

"Had it coming if you ask me," John rolled on his side… the pain was blinding him now and the kick of the revolver didn't help.

"You know you will hang for this!" the boy took a step back as John cocked the pistol again.

"Boy, my suggestion is you get on that horse and ride South back to your momma…and forget all of this nonsense."

The boy did as he was told and climbed upon the grey gelding. He stuck his heels sharply into the horse's belly and cantered back across the bridge…dodging or leaping bodies and wailing men as he went. John was fading in and out of consciousness now. When he closed his eyes, he saw his mother. When he opened them, he saw two beautiful angels tending to his wounds. By the time he was fully awake the battlefield had been cleared and his brother's bodies were gone. Two weeks later he would be walking again…another two weeks saw him load up Patrice and her daughters, Emily and Lula Harris, and take them south in their buckboard toward the Virginia line with their only remaining horse – a twenty-year-old mare with bad feet. Poor little Emily had bad wagon sickness all the way to Lynchburg. John made Patrice promise to tell anyone they encountered that they were married and heading south with their daughters to get some provisions for the winter. He declared that they would, from that day forward, be called John, Patrice, Emily, and Lula Montgomery to any and all they encountered.

Meanwhile, the boy had worked his way past the advancing Union troops and headed southwest up the Potomac River until he met up with a mass of Confederate troops led by General Robert E. Lee. Upon dismounting he begged for water and food, and then he declared he had a message for the General. He wasn't granted an audience, but he offered his information to Major-General A.P. Hill.

"One of our own, John Summerlin," he declared, "murdered Captain Tallridge at the creek in cold blood...after the battle had ended...as God is my witness."

Hill carried the message to General Lee who ordered that Summerlin be tracked down, tried, and, if found guilty... hung....

# 35

"You are planning to work today, right?" Thomas stood in front of Gracie and stopped the swing as it came toward him slowly.

"It's May, is it not?" Gracie laughed.

"It is."

"It's my birthday month."

"You get a whole month?"

"The Henry's never knew the exact date – because my mother died in town at a midwife's place, and it wasn't ever recorded properly." Gracie stood up and started walking toward the barn, which was under construction, but still a long way from being anything that actually resembled a barn.

Thomas grabbed her by the wrist and swung her around to face him…she gave him a sly smile.

"Anything at all…that you want to do today," Thomas looked into her beautiful brown eyes. "Anything."

"That question brings about so many thoughts, Mr.Thomas," she grabbed his hand with her free one. "I will make us a picnic and we will ride *Midnight* down the gorge to the river - to our spot."

"You think we are ready for *Midnight?*"Thomas laughed. "That's funny."

"Where is your sense of adventure? I'll make lunch…you tack up the stallion."

"It's our funeral," he said.

The horse took to the bit easier than Thomas had anticipated, and the trio was headed out through the front pasture well before the sun was straight up in the sky. The day was warming nicely, and there were only a few small inconsequential clouds floating past them in the bright blue sky. Before long they were enjoying a beautiful day at the river, and snacking on scuppernong grapes and light honey sandwiches and cold tea. Gracie drew pictures in the sand with her fingers, asked Thomas to guess what they were, and then rubbed them out quickly without telling him if he guessed right or wrong.

"There's something coming down the river," Thomas pushed himself up and started to put his leg back in place. "We need to go – get dressed."

"What is it?" Gracie stood up and started to turn.

"Don't," he grabbed her by the hand. "Just…don't."

Gracie looked at him bewildered as Thomas watched the bodies of five negroes float by on the river with a trail of red behind them. There was a man, a woman, and three children. Probably killed by the Confederates as they tried to escape north. Gracie tried to turn again, and Thomas pulled her in and surrounded her with his strong arms – she didn't resist… and didn't try to turn again.

"Let's get back to the house," Thomas let her go when the bodies had floated around the bend. "It's not safe here right now."

The pair put their clothes back on, and Thomas untied *Midnight* from the small elm where he was loosely tied. He was leading the stallion back up the path toward the huge rock outcropping when the first cannonball exploded in the trees on the opposite side of the New River. Splintered wood flew in all directions and briefly littered the fast-flowing water until the current ran clean again. There were the shouts of men in the trees above them, and Thomas heard the clacking of the Tennessee – Virginia railroad locomotive powering toward them at an ungodly clip – he could already smell the coal burning. He reached into the saddle bag and pulled out his Bowie Knife, his father's Colt, and a blanket he had stowed there in case they got too cold. He pulled back his left arm and swatted the horse sharply in his hindquarters and yelled "Home!" *Midnight* disappeared into the craggy brush and trees and thundered around the rock outcropping. He was out of sight in mere seconds.

Thomas grabbed Gracie's hand, gave her the blanket, and pulled her toward the rocks, "We have to go! – Now!"

A bearded Union soldier appeared high above on the rocks and pointed his rifle straight down at them as they ran. Thomas saw him and started to raise the pistol when the locomotive came thundering around the bend, and what seemed to Gracie to be hundreds of shots rang out at once. The air was filled with the sweet but putrid smell of gunpowder mixed with the black smoke barreling out of the train. The soldier on the rocks fell dead in a heap at their feet…with a bullet hole in his forehead. Visibility went to ten feet. Thomas and Gracie were trapped in the middle of the war.

"Keep coming!" Thomas yelled at her over the din of gun and cannon fire. The smell of the Confederate dead train slammed their nostrils, and almost brought them to their knees as they reached a small group of bushes and Thomas pulled Gracie in on top of him. They slipped down through a thick carpeting of wet leaves and rolled into an opening in the rock face taking spiders and webs with them. Then they quickly crawled down a steep slope for ten feet into pitch black darkness below. Outside the battle raged with tremendous fury as they both took a deep breath and held onto each other for dear life.

Thomas could feel Gracie breathing deeply next to him… more from fear than exhaustion. She clutched his arm with both hands as the sharp rattle of gunfire and dull thuds near and far shook the walls of the tiny cavern. There was a little light filtering down through the entrance, but they couldn't see each other's faces.

"How high is the ceiling?" Gracie asked.

"High here but it lowers as you go further in," Thomas put his hand on hers where she held his arm. "It's jagged here and there – we used to walk with one hand in front and one hand above."

"An oil lamp would be handy about now," Gracie said softly…and it disturbed something in the darkness.

It was soft at first like coins jingling in someone's pocket as they passed you on the street. Then it was clear and sharp like two sticks being beaten together over your head in rapid succession. The sound echoed throughout the cavern like a Gatling gun.

"Get behind me…it's in the far corner in front of us," Thomas turned to face away from the opening and out into the darkness as they rose to their feet. "Stand here and don't move." He pulled the Bowie knife from the sheath around his waist and slowly moved away from Gracie and into the darkness…shuffling his Palmer leg in front of him. The rattling got louder and closer. Thomas prayed the Eastern Diamondback didn't aim too high. He shuffled again and he could almost feel the snake coiled in front of him as he pushed it into a corner. Then it struck. It hit him hard in the leg and almost knocked him down…but it worked. The snake's fangs stuck into the wooden leg just inches below the flesh of his thigh. With one swoop of his left hand, he cut through the rattler ten inches behind its' head just as it was about to wriggle loose. The cavern became silent again… for just a moment…then the sounds of gunfire brought back the realization that another nightmare was going on above and below them.

# 36

"What in that book of yours makes you think any of this nonsense?" Luke pushed Emmie back up off his shoulder.

"There's so much in there – and a lot of it doesn't make any sense...it's like riddles." Emmie placed her hands in her lap and looked at him again.

"Mr. Connally is just a friend of my dad's from the Army...nothing more than that."

"I don't know how to tell you this...your grandfather's name is Lucas Montgomery?"

"Good guess – same as my father – same as me."

"Your great-grandfather's name was John Montgomery."

"Yes...go on," Luke didn't know how she knew that – maybe his mother told her. It made him listen closer for a moment.

"John Montgomery was previously called John Summerlin."

"This is in the journal?"

"Yes...John Summerlin lived at Waverly Plantation before the Civil War."

Luke just stared at her...waiting.

"Something happened during the war, and he never returned – he must have gone to West Virginia...maybe he ran."

"You're saying my great-grandfather was a deserter?"

"I don't know," Emmaline shook her head and grasped Luke's hands. "I don't know why he changed his name – or why he left Virginia."

"What does this have to do with Connally?"

"James Connally's grandfather was John Summerlin's cousin - he lived in Roanoke and somehow he came to be in control of Waverly…er – Connally Farm."

"This has to all be coincidence – I don't see how you came up with this conclusion," Luke ran his hand through his blonde hair and looked out into the night sky. Tiny snowflakes were meandering to the ground from unseen clouds.

"This was written down by my Great-Grandmother… but she's hiding something – something bad. I need to go see my Grandma Bea – will you take me next weekend?"

"I have to look at my basketball schedule – we have a busy month coming up."

"There was another man at Waverly…John's brother Thomas. Gracie Henry was there with him during and after the war. I think she cared for him very much from the way she writes about him."

"So, you think I'm related to this John and Thomas Summerlin?"

"The names and places match – but there is something else," Emmie gripped Luke's hand just a little tighter. "James Connally's grandfather owned Gracie for a short period of time – then he traded her to his cousin Dewey Summerlin at Waverly for a cow, some seeds, and other provisions while Dewey's boys were off fighting for the South."

"That's horrible…I'm so sorry," Luke leaned closer to Emmaline until their faces were just inches apart. In any instance other than this one he would have leaned in and kissed her.

"I have much more to read…and questions for Beatrice… and I think I have questions for your father..." she put the back of her hand on his face, and he leaned into the warmth and softness of it. "Will you please help me?"

Luke turned into her hand and kissed it softly. Emmie smiled at him...and he just knew...he knew everything he needed to know.

"I would do anything...for you, Emmaline," he took a short breath. "I love you."

# 37

Besides the illumination around the entrance to the cavern, there was a small sliver of light working its way down through a crack in the rocky ceiling. Thomas and Gracie's eyes had begun to adjust to the darkness and eventually they could make out the outline of their hands in front of their faces. Thomas told Gracie to stand still as he moved around the circumference of the chamber to draw out any other snakes that may be lurking. Much to their relief – nothing else stirred. Thomas went behind himself and picked up the rattler by the tail. Then he found the head and drove his knife through it. Going back to the entrance he placed the pieces just outside near a small pile of rocks.

"Remember that's there when we leave – We can't have you stepping on that in the darkness with your bare feet." Thomas found the blanket on the floor and wrapped it around her – he rubbed his hands up and down her arms to warm her up. "You are shivering," he said.

"Not cold really…scared is all," Gracie moved closer to his shadow in the darkness.

The gunfire had begun to subside, but now they were hearing muffled voices outside around the rocks. Thomas slowly led Gracie to the back wall of the cavern, and they sat down on the rock floor. She opened the blanket around her and wrapped it around Thomas as well. They each held onto a side and huddled together in silence as the shadows began to move across the cave entrance, and night began to fall. It wasn't long before they saw no light at all. They sat in pitch blackness and Gracie's cheek found a home on Thomas' shoulder. She began to doze, and he held her tightly and stared in the direction he believed was the exit. He could still hear voices close by – probably down by the river. He assumed the Yanks had set up camp there for the night. Thomas closed his eyes and enjoyed the warmth of Gracie even though he knew it was going to be a long night.

The next morning, they were awakened by voices close to the cave entrance. There was a small beam of light trying to burn through the haze at the crack above their heads and the cave entrance was growing brighter by the minute.

"See what those crows are getting at in the brush there, Corporal," Thomas heard a commanding voice outside. "We still have some unaccounted for."

"Shoo! Shoo!" They heard a voice and saw a shadow outside the entrance. "Just a dead diamondback, sir…in a couple of pieces – still bloody."

"Come on back out of there…we need to rejoin the others down river."

The corporal rejoined his captain at the top of the ridge. "Funny, something sliced that eight-footer clean just below the neck."

Thomas immediately regretted putting the snake outside the cave as Gracie started to rustle around. She opened her eyes and he put two fingers to her lips in the darkness.

"Stay here," Thomas heard the captain say.

There was a loud rustling of leaves as the captain slid down through the bushes to the entrance to the cavern. "What have we here? he asked nobody.

"Corporal, light the lantern and bring it to me."

A moment later the corporal stumbled down the slope and almost bowled the captain over. "Jesus, be careful boy!"

He reached out and boxed the corporal on the ear. The boy didn't flinch - as though he was used to it.

"Just to let you know, I'm coming in there," the captain spoke into the entrance. "If you know what's good for you then make yourself known." The captain pulled his revolver and started into the cave…then he stopped. "Better yet – I'm going to empty this Widow Maker into the darkness in all directions. If you are lucky, I won't hit you…but then I'm going to load up and do it again."

Thomas kept two fingers over Gracie's lips as they heard the pistol hammer pull back. The first shot roared inside the entrance and almost deafened the both of them. The bullet whizzed and pinged twice before running out of steam somewhere near Thomas' head. He pulled her closer and started to tuck her head under his arm…when she pushed the blanket from around her shoulder and crawled away.

"He' I iss, Masshah…pease don't shoot me…pease I's beggin' ya!" Gracie moved toward the entrance as the captain stepped inside with his lantern. Just the front of the cavern was illuminated, and Thomas stayed easily in the shadows. She appeared before the captain in her torn and tattered smock with moisture making her skin sparkle like silver.

"My, my…a runaway. Not what I was expecting." The man looked her up and down and she began to feel as though she might vomit at the smell of him. It was as though he hadn't seen water and soap in months. He smelled of blood, gunpowder, and urine.

"Pease don't sen' me back, sir," Gracie lowered her eyes like a fragile schoolgirl.

"I won't send you back," he walked around her in a circle and lifted the back of her dress to get a better look. When he got back to the front of her he said, "I do you a favor...you do one for me."

Thomas felt around frantically on the floor for the Bowie Knife...or the revolver...but he couldn't feel either one. He slowly and methodically attempted to re-attach his prosthetic, but he was having problems with the buckles in the darkness. He was beginning to panic and knew he must keep his composure. He felt around again...still no knife. He pushed his way up onto his good leg and leaned against the wall holding the Palmer in his right hand.

"Strip them clothes down, girl," the captain said. "We have to ride and I a'int got time to waste here."

"Yes, sah...as you want sah," Gracie started to lift her dress then stopped. "I's some shy, sah...could you turn?"

"Damn, girl, it's dark in here - make it quick!"

The captain turned his back and faced the daylight. Gracie lifted her dress and removed the Bowie Knife from beneath her undergarment. She raised the knife high over her head with both hands and plunged it down into the man's neck as hard as she could. It wasn't enough. He turned toward her as the knife clattered across the floor. He lurched toward her - grabbing the front of her smock and ripping it toward the floor. He forced her to her knees as he twisted her hair in his left hand while pulling the pistol from its holster with his right.

"You dirty little whore!" he yelled and began to pull the trigger on the revolver.

Thomas swung hard. He swung with everything he had...and he connected. He felt the crush of the captain's skull as he drove the Palmer Leg into the side of his face with enough force to send him crashing into the cavern wall...

where he slowly sank onto the floor with his left eye gone and lost in the darkness. The pistol rolled from his fingers and Gracie picked it up – firing one shot into his ear to make certain he was dead. The unfortunate corporal appeared at the entrance to the cave and Gracie dropped him where he stood with one point blank shot just above the fourth button on his dark blue uniform. He fell to his knees and curled into a ball…quickly taking his last breath after calling out for his mother like so many others that day.

Thomas fell to Gracie's side and put his arm around her. She dropped the Model 1 to the floor and fell into him as the tears began to flow like the river outside.

"We have to be quick," he turned her face so she could look at him. "Go outside and clear away all evidence of them. Brush the trail leading to here. Send their horses away – hit them with a log or a rock if you need to. Then get back in here fast. My leg is broken…I won't be walking out of here and we can't get away with me hopping. When you get back, we will drag them to the back of the cave and out of sight."

"We can take one of their horses," said Gracie.

"Gracie – they will kill us both if they catch us…do you understand?"

"I do."

"Then go…we will hide here another night…then we are going to make it back home before dawn." Thomas collapsed on the ground with his broken leg in his lap. Gracie scrambled out the cave entrance and up the hill…

# 38

She didn't say it back. She looked at him for a few seconds then kissed him on the cheek and said, "You're sweet." Then she got out of the car.

Sweet? What the hell does that mean? Luke stared at the ceiling of his dorm for at least an hour before getting up and switching on his desk lamp to crack some books for exams. He heard Dom rustling around behind him.

"What are you doing up, man?" Dom rubbed his head and looked at his West Bend alarm clock thinking he had forgotten to wind it – but it was ticking. "It's two a.m."

"Sorry, can't sleep," Luke turned in his chair to look at his roommate. "Might as well get as ready as possible for my Calc exam. I'll be quiet."

"Not a problem," Dom laid his head back down and started to drift off, but then he sat back up. "I've got to tell you something, Luke."

"Spill it."

"There's a lot of chatter about you and that Emmie girl." Dom said.

"Chatter or rumor?" Luke didn't care.

"Caroline was asking about you last night at the Union," Dom switched gears. "She thought you were coming back yesterday."

"That's nice for her," Luke couldn't take his mind off the conversation he had with Emmie just a couple of hours back.

"Are you guys over with? If so, I'd like to ask her to hang out sometime."

"You don't need my blessing…or my permission," Luke wished he would shut up and go back to bed. He was relieved when he heard Dom pound his pillow and lay back down. Within a few minutes Dom's breathing developed a rhythm, and Luke knew he was back asleep. Luke ripped a sheet of paper from his notebook and pulled a Bic from the coffee cup on his desk. He thought for a moment and then started to write:

*Dear Mom and Dad;*

*I don't even know how to write this letter and I know it would be better for us to talk at Christmas. I need you to think hard about what I am about to ask you so that when I get home, we can talk about it. I don't know that I even know all the questions – and I can't ask you any of this on the telephone. If it's true or if it's just my friend reading too much into something. Anyway, here are my questions for you:*

*Have you ever heard the name Summerlin?*

*Are we somehow related to James Connally?*

*What do you know about Waverly Plantation?*

*Do you know the name of great-grandpa's father? Was it Dewey?*

*I'm sorry – it's early here and I'm half asleep and now I'm thinking you may not know the answers to these questions either.*

*I love you both and I will see you in two weeks.*

*The Fleetliner is magnificent.*

*Love,*

*Luke*

Luke folded the letter and placed it on the desk, then he crossed his arms and laid his head down. The next thing he knew Dom's alarm clock was ringing like a five-alarm fire… his arms were asleep…and he could barely move his neck.

His school day was strange and full of dumb questions and weird stares. What kind of rumors were being spread? Better yet – who was spreading them? He was told several times that what he was doing was "not right" or "against the law" or "unnatural". He didn't care…what business was this of anyone else other than him…and Emmie?

He didn't care…until he was in the locker room that afternoon getting ready for practice and the coach yelled for him to come to his office. Luke threw on a shirt and walked in his socks. Once he was inside, the coach closed the door behind him.

"You know, Luke, I'm not one for gossip and that sort of thing," Coach McCann sat on the edge of the desk and crossed his hands in his lap.

"I'm not sure that I understand your reference, sir."

"If there is a thing with the little colored girl down at the diner," Mccann waited until Luke looked up at him. "It needs to go away. We can't have distractions like that on this team."

"Where did you gather that information, sir?"

"Let's be honest, Luke, it's ringing from the damned Charlottesville City Hall. I won't be surprised if it's in the paper by tomorrow!"

The coach is way too upset about this thought Luke. "Not that it's anyone else's business, but we are good friends, and she helps me with my schoolwork."

"So, she's your tutor?"

"Well –"

"She's your tutor…nothing more," McCann walked behind his desk and picked up a clipboard. "There are a lot of powerful people who donate their time…more importantly their money to keep our athletic programs firing on all cylinders."

"Okay," said Luke.

"Any rumor of impropriety might – well- look bad to them," the coach looked hard at Luke again. "You understand me, right?"

"Sure, coach."

"Finish getting dressed and I'll see you on the court."

Luke shook his head as he walked back into the locker room where he almost tripped over Dominick sitting next to his locker.

"Jesus, man." Luke sat down to lace up his Chucks.

"Trouble in paradise, roomie?" Dom stood up and headed toward the gym laughing. "Don't say I didn't warn you – some people here hate their kind more than they hate folks from the backwoods of West Virginia."

Luke held his tongue…and his fists…for now.

The University of Virginia Men's basketball team was getting ready to embark on a losing streak that would see them lose twenty of twenty-five games in 1963. They didn't have another winning record until 1971, after an eight-year drought…the year Al Drummond became the first Black player in school history.

# 39

Every so often there was the sound of a droplet of water hitting a small pool on the floor of the cave, otherwise there was complete silence. The air was damp and earthen and beginning to grow heavier as the small sliver of light at the entrance of the cave gave way to dusk and then darkness again. Gracie sat quietly next to Thomas, holding her dress closed in front of her after the captain had nearly torn it in two. She was shivering in the cold, dark, dampness of the cave. Thomas knew they had to try to get back up to the house soon.

"Let's give the darkness a couple of hours to set in...then we will try to climb back up the far side. Once we are in the woods we can move slower in the cover." Thomas fumbled with his leg in the darkness - tying the leather straps together in small tight knots. He used his shirt to wipe away the captain's blood and bone fragments.

"There's a full moon tonight," Gracie chattered as she spoke. "It will be bright outside with no clouds – I can see stars through the hole up there already."

Thomas could see the starlight shimmering off Gracie's silken hair from time to time, but he couldn't see her face. He knew they had to get out of this place before it became their tomb as well.

"I'm cold," she said.

Thomas pulled her closer and she wrapped her arms around her knees as they sat on the muddy floor. He felt her warmth as she leaned into his body. "Is this, okay?" he asked.

"It's quite nice, Mr. Thomas."

They sat quietly as the moon rose and created a beam of light at the entrance to the cave which slowly disappeared as it moved up over the rock.

"I hate myself for killing those men, Mr. Thomas."

"They would have killed both of us...and to be fair I am pretty sure I killed the first one."

"Maybe so, Mr. Thomas...maybe so," Gracie was growing tired, and she placed her head on Thomas' shoulder as she began to drift off.

Thomas could feel her breathing level out as she fell asleep in his arms. He pulled her close and took a deep breath through his nose – filling it with the smell of her.

"I love you."

"I love you," he said softly again.

He did love her...more than life. She moved her head slowly on his shoulder and lay silent for a long while. He held her as she slept.

"Like a sister?" she asked.

Thomas swallowed hard and felt his heart about to beat out of his chest. He didn't know how to answer that one... and he was surprised even more that she had heard hm.

"Like a sister, Mr. Thomas?" Gracie asked again. "That's what you mean, right?"

He could feel her heartbeat picking up as well and he took another deep breath of her.

"If I had a sister...I would hope that I wouldn't want to take her in my arms and kiss her as badly," Thomas responded and immediately regretted it. Did he sound crazy? It was easier to say these things in the dark.

Gracie laid in his arms quietly for a long time as the moon reached the hole in the cave's roof and began to shine on her hair from above.

"Mr. Thomas?"

"Yes."

"I don't want to think of my life without you."

Thomas put his hand down to support himself as Gracie sat up…he could see her beautiful dark brown eyes shimmering in the sliver of moonlight as she stared into his blue ones.

"Mr. Thomas…I love you too."

Thomas wiped his left hand on his pants and placed his hand on her face. She gripped it with both of hers and kissed his dirty palm.

"We need to bathe," she giggled and then quickly grew silent as their eyes met again in the moonlight.

"I love you, Gracie," Thomas pulled her closer to him until they could feel each other's breath.

"Mr. Thom-" Gracie said as he pulled her mouth into his and kissed her gently once…then longer the second time… then firmly.

Gracie sat back and stared at him for the longest moment, then she slowly began to remove her torn dress as the moonlight glowed upon her copper skin.

"Wait," said Thomas.

"Wait?" she asked.

"You have to promise me one thing," Thomas smiled at her.

"Anything."

"Never – ever…call me Mr. Thomas again."

Gracie pushed him to the ground and slowly unbuttoned his shirt and lifted his arms out of it, then she pulled off the wet shirt underneath, then she slowly untied the rope holding his pants and removed them gently...then she climbed over him and pressed her body into his. They laid in each other's arms for a long while enjoying the warmth of their love for one another. Then Gracie lifted her head from his shoulder and kissed him for a long time before she pushed herself up. Thomas watched the glistening of her beauty as she moved back and forth... in and out of the moonlight until finally she fell gently back into his arms, and he wrapped his powerful arms tightly around her bare back. Thomas had never felt anything like this in his life...and as he prayed it would last forever, she whispered softly into his ear.

"I love you."

"I love you."

Around four in the morning Gracie woke Thomas and helped him strap his leg back in place with strips from her undergarments that she had torn away. There was no sign of anyone on their journey back up to the house, and it appeared nobody had been there. *Midnight* greeted them in the courtyard where he had been nibbling on Gracie's garden for a while. Thomas removed his tack and put him back into the pasture with the others. He snorted, then trotted to the top of the hill, where he was perfectly silhouetted in the setting moonlight. "Show off," thought Thomas.

Gracie fired up the stove and heated some water. They bathed each other as they sat on the kitchen floor on a blanket, staring into each other's smiling faces. Then Thomas made love to Gracie...again. They lay on the floor in each other's arms near the warmth of the stove and began to drift off as the first of the morning's sunbeams hit the windows.

"Next time, we should pick a softer venue," Thomas laughed. "Our first two choices have been hell on my back… and my knees."

"Let's try…the wildflower meadow…the riverbank… and a haystack."

"I was thinking the bedroom…but I love your ideas much more."

"And…I love you, Mr. Thomas…" Gracie giggled and wrapped her body around his as they held each other for a well-deserved, and much-needed rest…

# 40

She didn't say it back. Was he expecting her to?

Luke threw a tennis ball against the cinderblock wall in his room and caught it on a bounce. It had been a habit of his since he was a kid and his brother had died. It calmed his nerves...and they needed calming tonight. Coach McCann had basically threatened him about his association with Emmaline. Was basketball more important than she was? His head was swimming.

"Luke, can you take a break for a few minutes?" Dom sat at his desk with a pencil stuck behind his ear flipping through a notebook. "I have an English exam in the morning."

"Sure," Luke said in a tone that was barely audible as he tossed the ball against the wall again...and then again.

"Okay," Dom turned in his chair. "What is going on?"

"McCann attacked me for just knowing Emmie," Luke caught the ball and tossed it on his bunk.

"There are a lot of people who can't stomach seeing mixed couples - especially when one of them is a star basketball player at their alma mater," Dom pulled the pencil from his ear and tossed it on the desk.

"I'm sure she won't want to see me again anyway,"

"You already told her about this?" Dom leaned forward in his chair.

"No...I just messed it up," Luke leaned back against the wall.

"How can you mess up a friendship just like that? You are just friends, right?"

"You and I are friends, right?" Luke pulled his legs up on the bed.

"For three years – you bet."

"She was very emotional the other night and I let it slip how much I cared for her," Luke looked at Dom.

"You mean…you are in love with this girl?"

"I've never known anyone like her."

"She say it back?"

"No…that's why I said I messed up."

Dom stood up and switched off the desk lamp, "You have to let that one go, my friend."

"What if I can't?"

"You know the laws in this state, right?" Dom sat down on the bunk. "As your friend…I'm telling you to let this go."

"You are probably right," Luke laid down on the bunk and stuffed two pillows under his head. "I need some sleep."

Dom stood up, climbed into his bunk, and switched off the light, "I'm telling you – if you don't drop her…they will ruin you at this place."

Exams came and went, and the campus got eerily quiet. The basketball team had a couple more practices, then they got a five-day break for Christmas before they were to leave for a tournament in Washington. Luke hadn't heard from Emmaline in almost a week, but he hadn't forgotten about their last conversation. He planned to go see her after the break when school came back into session, and he guessed she had changed her mind about seeing Grandma Bea.

The first practice on the Tuesday before Christmas was an uneventful scrimmage…until Luke took a pass at the top of the key and found himself staring straight at the 6'8" David Hoffman blocking his run to the basket. Luke faked left then dribbled. He brought the ball behind his back then back through his legs. Hoffman went to his right and Luke dribbled the ball between his legs without missing a beat to the basket where he finished with a reverse layup over two of his teammates off the backboard. Hoffman had lost his footing and hit the floor behind him. Luke walked back to give him a hand up.

"Sorry, Dave," Luke reached out as David ignored his hand and stood up on his own. He had Luke by at least six inches.

"I figured that negro of yours had taught you a lot of things late at night…but I didn't figure street ball was one of them."

Luke should have walked away…but he didn't. His closed fist connected underneath Hoffman's chin with a sharp quick uppercut. The Cavalier teammates quickly had their arms around both players pulling them apart as blood flowed from Hoffman's mouth.

"What the hell?" McCann called from the sideline. "Montgomery! My office, now! The rest of you knuckleheads hit the shower and cool off! David – go to the trainer!"

Luke followed Coach McCann to his office where the door was slammed behind him.

"What was that Montgomery?"

"He had it coming." Luke didn't take a seat.

"I told you what a distraction this was going to be," McCann slammed his clipboard on the desk and took the whistle from around his neck – it dropped to the desk and Luke heard the ball rattling inside. "I want you to go home for Christmas in the morning…and don't come back for the tournament."

"Come on, coach – really?" Luke crossed his arms defensively.

"Get your head back on straight…and start thinking about this team first and foremost. I need you one hundred percent on board when conference play starts in January."

"I'm fine, Coach McCann."

"Just go – out of my sight until January," McCann lowered his eyes and Luke got the hint. He turned and walked out of the office.

Luke went back into the locker room and threw his clothes into his duffle, and without speaking to anyone he walked out the back door of the gym in his shorts and practice jersey into the ten-degree night. He immediately ran up the hill and was back in his dorm room within three minutes. He had decided to take a shower in the hall bathroom when there was a knock at the door.

"Yeah – come in."

Joe Millstone stuck his head in the door, "Emmaline Foster – name ring a bell?"

"Yes – what's wrong."

"She has called here five times for you – and she just happens to be on the phone now."

"I need a shower."

"She says it's urgent," Joe opened the door further.

"Everything is urgent…my life is urgent." Luke threw his duffle across the room onto his bed.

"Come on, man…she's just going to call again – and I will have to get up and answer it because nobody else will do it."

"Let it ring."

"Luke…"

Luke walked down the hall and picked up the black receiver off the table.

"Em – this is not really a good ti-"

"Oh Luke – it's my grandmother...she's had a bad stroke and my parents have gone to her," Emmaline was crying and breathing through the words as she forced them out. "I need you..."

Luke closed his eyes, took a deep breath, and said, "I'll be there in twenty minutes...pack a bag."

# 41

A knock sounded on the door of Summer House just as Beatrice Johnson was about to sit down to her dinner - a bowl of okra and tomato stew – it was her specialty, and her favorite. Thinking it was one of the ladies from the AME church she pulled the door all the way open.

"Mr. James," she was taken aback. "What you need with me at this hour?"

"This won't take but a minute…" James Connally stood in the twilight with a solemn look across his face.

"…and?" Beatrice Johnson clearly wanted this minute to end quickly.

"We agreed when your daughter left, that this matter would not be further discussed." Connally held the screen door open looking down on the frail eighty-four-year-old. She stood her ground.

"That's before you decided to hand my granddaughter the business up there on the hill. Why did you attack her like that? She come down here crying like the dickens." Bea took a step back from the door because Connally towered over her.

"What did you tell her?"

"What makes you think I done told her anything?" Bea glanced back at her bowl on the table.

"Because it's gotten back to me that she has been asking questions," he put his foot across the threshold and Bea picked up a broom from beside the door.

"You ain't welcome in my house," she felt her heart rate starting to rise.

"Put a stop to it – and while you are at it keep her away from Luke Montgomery…she's a distraction," Connally stepped all the way in.

"I told you to stay out."

"You like living here?"

"This all I got."

"Put a stop to this or you can go live in Richmond with your son-in-law."

"You have no right – this my house."

"Don't forget how that came to be…" Connally looked around the room. "This place looks like a tinderbox…try to be careful with that woodstove there."

"You wouldn't…" Beatrice felt her heart beating out of her chest and her temples were throbbing. She dropped the broom to the floor.

James Connally continued to berate her but she couldn't comprehend what he was going on about so she reached out for the table and sat back down in her chair. Her mind was racing in time with her heartbeat. She put both of her hands on the table and clasped them together in front of her.

"Please leave now," she said it softly and was probably the only one who heard it.

Connally followed up his attack with more loud words that drifted through the kitchen unheard. Then she heard the door slam shut and the screen door answer from the other side. He was gone.

Beatrice Johnson knew there was something wrong now. She reached into the middle of the table for a pencil and a piece of paper. She started to write but the feeling in her left arm was fading as though it was asleep. She banged her hand on the table once…and then scribbled a few words… then she folded the paper and scribbled on the front. She creased the paper twice with her fingers. Then the note fell to the floor…then the pencil…then the bowl of stew…then Beatrice Johnson.

# 42

Gracie leapt from the oak swing in mid-flight and rolled through the dandelions and clover into Thomas' arms as he lay sprawled in the grass enjoying the warm summer evening. She was at once staring into his deep blue eyes and was as quickly lost in their wonderment. She kissed him...then looked at him...then closed her eyes and kissed him longer. It was their world, and everyone else just moved through the motions in it. While the others struggled, and starved, and fought, and killed, they lived, and they loved. Nothing else mattered to them but each other. If only it could last forever.

The war in Virginia had moved back toward the east, while the Union Army under General Sherman had taken a devastating tour to the west and south where they rampaged through cities, towns, and plantations burning everything in their path. Thousands were left homeless or dead with Atlanta taking the brunt of Sherman's hatred. Slaves were freed in droves as they were confiscated by the Union Army – many ran, but a handful fought alongside the Southern men who used to claim ownership of them – whether through loyalty or threat nobody knew for sure. Gracie and Thomas knew that the gunfire was gone from around them – which made for an easier night's sleep. The quietness and the peacefulness of Waverly solidified their relationship, and every single day was cherished even more than the one before. They were doing well for themselves – the front two field had plentiful hay and corn growing, and Gracie's garden was nothing short of a miracle. She filled the table every day and the cellar was stacked with jars for the winter months. Life could not have been better for them.

"Supper?" Gracie blew into his ear.

"Not yet," Thomas rolled her over and kissed her again as the fireflies began their nightly visit.

"We have to eat," she said.

"Do we?" Thomas laughed but instantly felt a stabbing pain in the lower part of his abdomen, so he rolled back onto his back and looked up at the fading blue sky and took a deep breath. Gracie seemed unaware – so he thought.

"Don't you go and overdo it," she smiled. "Dr. Draper says you still have a long road to recovery."

"I'm fine – just when I eat certain things."

"So – you are complaining about my cooking and we ain't even married?" Gracie tickled him and he laughed.

"You know I would ask you to marry me if I could," Thomas put his hand on her cheek.

"And…I might say yes – or no – depending on my mood that day," Gracie kissed his fingers and placed his hand on her heart. He moved it lower, and she moved it back and kissed his neck.

"Let's go up," she said.

"You go get cleaned up – I'll be along shortly," Thomas put his hands behind his head and stared at the sky as the first stars began to shine.

"Suit yourself," Gracie got up and went into the house, gently closing the screen door behind her. She walked into the kitchen and stood looking at Thomas from the window.

Thomas rolled on his side away from the house and Gracie could tell he was retching into the grass. He moved one arm to wipe his mouth on his sleeve and then slowly pushed himself up onto his feet with what seemed to be great effort. He looked out over the farm and smiled…then he said a little prayer for Gracie and turned to walk back toward the house.

Gracie turned away from the window and lifted her apron to wipe a single slow-moving tear from her cheek… then she said her own prayer for her Thomas.

# 43

Luke had thrown a quick bag together, and packed up a few of his books for the classes that would carry over into the 1963 portion of his junior year. He passed Dom and Joe on the way out of the dorm.

"Where you going?" Dom called after him.

"Home," and then he added "see you next year."

"Hey – we have to be back here on the 28th," Dom answered.

"Give 'em hell on the court! It's your big shot!" Dom started to question him more but the door to the outside slammed shut behind him.

Luke jammed the Fleetliner up into second and the engine was roaring for a move to third when he reached the drive-in where he downshifted hard enough to lose some rubber to the road. Emmaline was waiting for him in front of her house, and he quickly jumped out to grab her bag – instead she grabbed him and clung to him so tightly he almost fell over her and took both of them to the ground.

"Whoa.." he said.

"She's not good, Luke," Emmie had been crying into his sweatshirt for what looked to have been quite a while. She had it clutched to her chest as she threw an arm around his neck. "They think she was laying on the floor for over twenty-four hours before Miss Mildred found her."

"Where did they take her?" Luke broke free and picked up her suitcase.

"Burrell Memorial in Roanoke."

"Why didn't they go to Christiansburg or Blacksburg?" Luke lifted her case into the trunk then slammed it, and opened the door for her.

"You serious?" Emmie climbed in the car and placed Luke's sweatshirt in her lap. He closed the door behind her and walked to his side and jumped in.

"There's a hospital in Blacksburg – we took a guy there from the farm with a broke leg last summer," Luke turned the car up Main and headed for the highway.

"Not for us there ain't," Emmaline sighed but was glad to be heading toward her family.

"Oh shoot – really?" Luke seemed bewildered.

"See what happens in a colored family, Luke?" Emmaline turned toward him and pulled her legs up onto the seat and sat on them. "We get treated differently…and we don't have choices like you…we have one choice – or none at all."

"I'm sorry. I don't think sometimes," Luke glanced over at her apologetically.

"It's not your fault - our people got freed a hundred years ago, but we ain't found freedom yet," Emmie smiled at him. "But we will – I know it."

"We will have to go back through Lynchburg again – be nice if they would get that Interstate open," Luke tried to change the subject.

"The interstate that follows the old Confederate war trails to the North. Can't wait." Emmaline looked out the window and the ride went silent for a while before she spoke again. "I'm sorry that I'm being snappy. You will never know how much I appreciate you dropping me with my family."

"I can stay for a while if you want me to," Luke answered.

"It's not necessary...I know you need to get to your family for Christmas."

"They don't even know I left early – so they aren't expecting me." Luke rubbed the back of his neck with his left hand.

"What do you mean you left early? – oh my! I took you away from basketball, didn't I?" Emmie put her hand on his leg. "You can take me to the bus station if you want to."

"Please don't be angry with me...but I got suspended for a couple weeks."

"What? Why?"

"I got mad at practice and punched Hoffman in the nose."

Emmaline fell silent for a few moments and turned to stare out the window at the lights of the farmhouses they were passing.

"I'm sorry," she said.

"Not your fault – I lost my cool for a minute is all."

"I'm sorry because I feel like it had something to do with me."

"Nope."

"You don't think I know what people have been saying about us?" Emmie looked at him and he glanced over at her uneasily. "I get the looks and the comments – all the way to the hospital and back every day. That's why I haven't talked to you much."

"People say stupid things all the time, Em," Luke glanced back at the road. "Doesn't make one lick of it truthful."

"Remember when I told you this was going to happen? You are their basketball star...and I am nothing to them...a distraction for you."

Luke pulled the car into a closed Marathon station and parked under the only light pole. He turned off the engine.

"What are you doing, Luke."

"I'm going to tell you something and I need you to listen to me – and I need to be looking at you when I tell you this," Luke turned to face her and leaned against the door of the Fleetliner.

"Please don't…" she said.

"Just listen please – I don't expect a response…it's just something I have to say."

Emmaline investigated his face…and those eyes. "Okay."

"I meant what I said to you the other night. When I wake you are my first thought – when I go to sleep you are my last. Emmaline, you are the most wonderful, gentle, beautiful soul I have ever known. You mean everything to me – to my life."

Emmie looked down at her hands and took a deep breath before she began to speak to him in a voice that he could tell was close to breaking.

"I care for you…I do…but I need this to be about friendship right now. You have basketball and school and I need to finish my nursing program. I don't want to waiver from my goals…and I don't want to be a distraction for you in the Field House."

"Em – I-"

"Can we go to my grandma now please," Emmie turned her head toward the window and cleverly masked the tears rolling down her cheeks.

"Sure – I'm sorry."

"Can we still study together at the drive-in?" Emmie asked without looking back at him.

"I'd love that – you know I would," Luke started the Fleetliner and pulled back out onto the road as they passed a sign that said, "Roanoke 12".

"I could really use a King Tut milkshake right now," Emmie laughed.

"Me too." Luke put his hand on the seat between them and Emmie placed hers next to his until they were touching. They rode toward the hospital without moving their hands – probably because both were scared of being the first to move.

After stopping twice to ask for directions, Luke pulled into the dimly lit parking area surrounding the T-shaped brick building that was Burrell Memorial Hospital. He walked around and opened the door for Emmaline, then took her hand to walk her in.

"My bags," she said.

"We will get them later. Let's get you inside." Luke let out a short grunt that Emmie barely heard.

"What's that for?"

"I'm still fuming about that first guy that sent us up into the mountains – what a wise guy." Luke grinned.

"I told you that guy was looking at us cross-eyed. Welcome to my world." Emmie pushed the door open in front of them and they walked to the nurse's station.

"Ms. Beatrice Johnson's room please," Emmaline inquired.

"Are you family?" a large colored woman in a grey dress with a white scarf pulled up around her hair answered.

"Room 310 – stairs are right there. Elevators down the hall" she pointed to a door behind the desk. "Your friend can wait here – pretty sure he's not family."

Emmaline smiled at him, and he gave her a squeeze on the shoulder. "I'll be here when you need me."

Luke walked around in the waiting area and read a plaque dedicated to Isaac Burrell who was the namesake of the hospital. He was admiring the architecture of the building and the speckled terrazzo flooring when the nurse offered him a cup of black coffee which he gladly took with a thank you. After an hour or so he saw Emmaline and her father heading toward him from the elevator bank.

"Again…always there for my Emmaline," Anthony Foster stuck out his hand to shake Luke's. "Thank you, son."

"It's always my pleasure, sir," Luke tried to grip his hand harder, but it was in the process of almost being crushed by Emmie's dad.

"Sorry about being gone so long," Emmie had clearly been crying.

"Take all the time you need," Luke said. "I was reading about the great doctor that this facility was named after in 1915…plus the nice lady gave me some coffee."

"You know what it don't say on that plaque?" Anthony asked -and then finished his story. "The doctor was here in Roanoke in 1914 treating colored folks when he had a gallstone attack and needed surgery. Roanoke Hospital wouldn't take him in because it was for white folk only. So, his family put him on a train in a box car made for animals and he travelled all the way to Freedmen's Hospital in Washington. But…it was too late for him, and he died during the surgery. That's an important part of that story that can't ever be forgotten."

Luke shook his head, "Like Emmie says – things have to change soon…she's confident they will."

"I'm going back upstairs while you say your goodnights," Anthony turned to go. "Thank you again for watching out for my little girl." He walked up the hallway back to the elevators.

"I'm going to stay here with my parents, so I need to retrieve my things from the car," Emmie took Luke's hand in hers. "Thank you for being there for me. I know my father says it – but I don't say it enough," she stood on her toes and kissed him on the cheek.

Luke savored the kiss and said, "You know how I feel. I'll get your things – you wait here."

Luke walked out to the Fleetliner and got Emmaline's two bags and started to carry them back to the hospital when he stopped, went back, opened the passenger door, and grabbed his sweatshirt from the seat. It smelled so much like her that he almost didn't want to give it back to her. He breathed in the smell of it deeply as he walked back across the parking area.

"Ms. Oliver brought you these and said you could sleep on the couch there - if you want to wait and leave in the morning," Emmaline handed him a wool blanket and two small pillows with white cotton cases.

Luke looked over at the nurse and she winked at him, "Thank you, ma'am – I'm certainly obliged."

Luke sat on the couch and put the blanket across his legs. "Get some breakfast in the morning?"

"Sure thing," said Emmie.

She turned to go back upstairs and stopped, then turned around.

"I need to show you something," Emmie took a folded piece of paper from her pocket and handed it to Luke who read it and handed it back.

"This must have something to do with what we've been talking about…it was on the floor next to Grandma Bea," Emmie stood looking over him. The paper had only two words written down on it. "It's got to be my great-grandmother."

Luke looked up at her, "I thought her name was Henry?"

"Then who…is Gracie Summerlin?"

# 44

On the morning of April 9, 1865, Thomas Summerlin saddled up two horses – *Mayflower* for Gracie, and *Lightening* for himself. This was to be a routine ride up into the northern pasture to check the fence line after the previous night's violent spring storm that seemed determined to rip the roof right off the Waverly house. The pair had found other things to occupy their time during the long howling night, and this morning they caught themselves sheepishly sneaking in smiles and glances as they checked girths and bridles. Unbeknownst to them, the remains of General Robert E. Lee's Army of Northern Virginia were making a beeline from Richmond toward Lynchburg with plans to reunite with a Confederate regiment in North Carolina – a path which would bring 28,000 soldiers straight through Pulaski County – and straight through Waverly.

The irony that was the life of Wilmer Mclean would be one of the catalysts that stopped that westward march on this blustery Spring morning. On July 21, 1861, the First Battle of Bull Run had consumed McLean's farm in Manassas, Virginia. Following the battle McLean moved his family one hundred miles south to a small dusty Southern Virginia crossroads called Appomattox Court House, where he sold staples, including sugar, for the remainder of the war. On April 9, 1865, General Phillip Sheridan knocked at his door and asked to use his parlor as a meeting place. Having been cut off from his westward retreat, General Robert E Lee was left with no alternative but to surrender – and he did so to General Ulysses S.

Grant in McLean's parlor later that day. As the Confederates stacked up their guns outside, the attending Union soldiers ransacked McLean's house and made off with everything they could lay their hands on as souvenirs. A young Yankee Colonel made away on horseback with the very table that was used to sign the surrender, and carried it back to his wife in Maryland – his name was George Armstrong Custer.

For all intents and purposes, the war ended as Thomas and Gracie enjoyed a picnic of finger sandwiches and lemon cakes high up in the mountains on the very northwestern edge of the farm. Small areas of thick snow still clung to their last hope of an extended winter in the day long shade of mighty leaf filled sycamores. The two had a brief snowball fight which ended with them in each other's arms enjoying a long kiss as the wind blew Gracie's long black hair into a cocoon around their faces.

"I love you, Grace Henry," Thomas stopped briefly for some well-deserved oxygen.

"Of course, you do – who wouldn't?" Gracie laughed and pulled her hair back and wrapped it in a scarf. "It's so quiet up here – maybe we should build a little cabin up here where we can just hide from everything."

"That's a grand idea – it shouldn't take us long to drag everything we need up that steep mountain."

Gracie smiled at him and sat down with her legs on the blanket. She could just make out the chimneys on the Waverly House way off in the distance in the valley below – and hour-long slow ride away.

"Look at everything we've done together down there – the barn – the horses – your garden. I think we need to take the next step." Thomas slowly lowered himself to the ground and stuck the Palmer leg out in front of him. Gracie knew he was self-conscious about it, and she always pretended not to notice.

"Why fine sire – whatever are you proposing?" Gracie rubbed his shoulders.

"I think we should get some Black Angus and raise beef."

"That's your proposal?"

"You don't like it?" Thomas was grinning but she couldn't see his face.

"I'm sure it's a grand idea – more to take care of." Gracie sat back and pulled his head into her lap.

"The Draper's nephews have been helping out quite a bit."

"They are ten and twelve – you need men – cowboys – to herd cattle."

"We can start small – maybe get a few dairy cows too."

"I already have Daisy to milk every day – what's a few more?" Grace ran her fingers through his blonde hair – and knew she would go along with anything he said.

"We can sell the milk to the Drapers for the Mercantile."

Thomas felt a stabbing pain running through his back and into his abdomen near his hip. He sat in silence and held back any expression…but Gracie knew, and she instinctively rubbed the middle of his back behind his ribs, The pain was more frequent now and Thomas knew something was wrong. Gracie had stopped feeding him so much meat and she used their shortages as an excuse – but he had filled the smoke-house with venison and rabbit, and the chickens were prospering so well that Gracie had to pen them out of her garden or there would be no vegetables. She kissed him on the top of his tangled mop of blonde hair and ran the fingers of her other hand through from back to front - waiting for the pain to subside.

"I love you with all my soul, Mr. Thomas," she knew this would make him smile.

"Gracie?"

"Yes…"

"I love you too," Thomas pushed himself up with an audible grimace and turned to face her. "and…I would be honored if you would be my wife."

Gracie pulled him close and kissed his forehead, "And my answer to you will never change – yes! Yes, I will marry you – right here on this very spot!" She rocked him back and forth as a mother would her child.

They both knew the laws of the State of Virginia – it was forbidden for them to even speak of such a thing. What gives man the right to ever affect the happiness and well-being of any other man? – only God can make this decision. Gracie pondered this question until it tormented her. It kept her awake at night and it just made her profess her love for Thomas more often…she knew in her own heart that she was his wife – and he was her husband. No one could ever dispute that in the eyes of God. Their heritage and the color of their skin meant nothing to them – they were one and the same.

"Stay here," Gracie got up and wandered down into the meadow. Thomas watched her as she fell to her knees and began to search the ground in front of her. He loved to watch her – in her garden…washing the dishes…combing her hair. He thought she never noticed…but she knew then just as she knew now – that he was watching over her. It meant everything to her, and it solidified their love for each other.

Gracie returned and kneeled on the blanket in front of Thomas – then she kissed him on the cheek,

"I, Grace Henry, take you, Thomas Summerlin, to be my husband – in sickness and in health, in good times and bad, in life and death, in blood and soul, forever and ever," she held a small bouquet of dandelions and clover in front of her as she slipped a small ring she had woven from the coarse dormant Timothy grass of the meadow that was so close to springing back to vibrant green life.

Thomas sat up as straight as he could and repeated her vows – as best he could remember, and then he added, "I love you more than life itself – God has granted me everything a man could ever need."

Thomas and Gracie made the laws at Waverly…where they would go for weeks without seeing another human being. No man could define who they were – or who they were expected to be. Their life was on this farm, but their love had no boundaries. She was his everything…

Thomas pulled Gracie close and kissed her. Every time was like the first time. His heart fluttered and the pain in his stomach was replaced with roaring butterflies. The world and its' war and hatred of men evaporated away. They were all that mattered. Thomas drew her into the soft blanket in the middle of the upper meadow and made love to her… again… for the first time. Their bodies and souls were intertwined. And their world was the only world they knew or cared about. This most important of days for the rest of mankind was simply another day on the farm for them.

Two weeks later a buckboard rolled up to the Waverly House and Katherine Draper jumped down and ran to meet them. She threw her arms around Gracie and almost picked her up off the ground.

Gracie took a step back and giggled, "What in the world has come over you?"

"Oh good! You haven't heard yet," Katherine reached out and took both by the hand. "Lee surrendered the South! The war is over! You are now truly free!"

Gracie began to cry as Thomas hugged her, "God is gracious!" he said.

Katherine stood back and delighted in herself for bringing this news to the farm. Then she noticed the straw rings on their fingers.

"What do we have here?" she declared beaming.

"Thomas and I get married every couple of weeks up here," Gracie laughed and glanced at Thomas slyly.

"We can do better than that," said Katherine.

Gracie looked back at her, "It's just between Thomas and me – that's all."

"That's not what I mean," Mrs. Draper took both of her hands. "The laws of Virginia are suspended pending review by the Union. The town leadership has fallen to the Elder in our church – my husband Timothy."

"I don't understand," said Gracie.

"Oh Gracie," Katherine shook her hands up and down. "We have to act fast – this very minute he has the legal right to marry you two!"

# 45

Snow was beginning to blow in from the West as Luke and Emmaline watched the Studebaker pull out of the parking lot of Burrell Memorial Hospital with Mathilde and Anthony Foster – and Grandma Bea. Beatrice Johnson had suffered a bad stroke and would likely never walk or speak again, but she seemed to at least recognize family members, and was able to squeeze their hands. Her home would now be in Richmond with her daughter and son-in-law, where she would need around-the-clock care. Emmaline wiped her eyes as the car drove out of sight.

"Okay, let's go I guess," she climbed into the front seat of the Fleetliner.

Luke got into his side and started the engine. "You know what you are getting right?" Luke shifted into first and eased out of the space. "This storm is coming in pretty quickly."

"Yes, clothes, bathroom, and bible....got it."

While the Foster's headed east to outrun the storm, Luke and Emmaline were headed west to Draper – and right into it. Luke would take Emmie to the Summer House and collect some of Grandma Bea's things – then he would drive her to Richmond. It was mid-day but the blowing snow made for reduced visibility. Better than sleet thought Luke.

"What if we can't come back this way?" Luke said.

"You can sleep on the couch, Romeo."

"You do know Romeo and Juliette were madly in love, right?" Luke kept both hands on the wheel.

"Of course, and it got them killed." Emmie smiled.

Their talk turned to school and basketball and what the next semester would bring for them both. Emmaline continued to protest them seeing each other, and it was all she could do to push her feelings to the side. Luke had treated her better than any man she had ever known – he was sweet... and handsome...boy was he handsome. She knew he would do anything for her...but he couldn't be colored – that he could never do.

"Wesley is talking about reaching out to Dr. King to see if he will visit Charlottesville in the Spring," she said.

"Wow – that would create some talk, wouldn't it?"

"The talk has to start somewhere."

"If he does come – can I go with you?" Luke glanced over at her.

"As you white folk like to say – it's a free country,"

"Sarcasm aside – can I go?"

"I'm sorry – of course you can," Emmie looked out the window and tried to make out individual snowflakes but there were just too many. "He's a good man you know."

"I think Dr. King is fantastic."

"I meant Wesley," Emmie looked for a response.

"He seems to be," Luke wheeled the car off the highway and rolled down into Draper where he pulled into the Mercantile and parked. "Unless you have eggs on your blouse, and he thinks his posters and trousers are more important." Luke laughed and opened his door. "Want to get a pop and a snack?"

"Sure," Emmaline opened her door and got out.

The Mercantile housed guest rooms on one side and the main store held a small café, and sold staples and farm supplies to the community. The building was painted a shiny white and a faded green metal roof brushed the sky up above. Numerous vultures lined the roof to hide from the blowing snow. Luke and Emmaline started up the steps to go inside when they encountered an older colored woman coming out the door.

"Oh, child, I's so sorry about your Gramma," the woman grabbed Emmie's hand with her boney fingers. "you ha' any news on her."

"Hello, Mrs. Williams," said Emmie. "She's gone to our house in Richmond to recover – but she's not in the hospital anymore."

"It's a bad thing you know?" the woman was struggling against the cold and wind. "I done went 'round to sees her few nights back but that man be up tha'."

"What do you mean?"

"That Connally fella. You know from up on da hill."

Emmaline looked at Luke as her heart sunk deep into her stomach and she lost her breath.

"I's the one what found her nex mornin' when she don't turn up to church," Mrs. Williams pulled a thin shawl around her shoulders and shuddered.

"Can I help you to your car, ma'am" Luke reached for her bags.

"Dis boy wit you, Emmaline?"

"Yes ma'am," Emmie said slowly. "More often than he should be I'm afraid, but we are just friends."

"You younguns', – I c'aint keep up wit yalls comins' and goins'." Mrs. Williams gladly handed her bags to Luke and grasped the handrail to navigate down the slippery steps. "I only live about tree' blocks down."

Luke looked over at Emmaline and shrugged his shoulders.

"I'll wait inside where it's warm...goodbye Mrs. Williams," Emmie reached for the door handle.

"When's Beazie comin' back?" the old lady struggled down the first step.

"My mother is taking her to Richmond for a while. We came to gather some of her things."

"I'll tell the ladies," she said and shuffled off through the parking lot toward the street with Luke following closely behind.

Emmie laughed and went inside the Mercantile where she quickly noticed a sign on the wall that said "All Served Here". After a short glance around she found a small cloth covered table with two black wrought iron chairs and she sat down. A beautiful young girl wearing a Virginia Tech sweatshirt came over to welcome her, and she calmly ordered a cup of hot tea and some tea biscuits. She liked this place. The folks were mostly white, but they smiled at her, and some even wished her a good day and hoped she stayed out of the weather. When she had eaten one biscuit and finished most of her tea Luke walked back in the door, rubbed his hands together, and shook the snow off his hair. He saw Emmie at the table and quickly joined her.

"Sorry about all that," he said.

"You've done well today," Emmie grinned at him.

"She tried to give me a nickel – it was sweet really," Luke grabbed the other biscuit from her plate. "You gonna eat this?"

"Not now."

"Storm is getting worse and it's going to be dark soon – we need to get moving," Luke tossed the biscuit in his mouth and finished Emmie's tea with one swallow. "Oh, that's awful...no sugar?"

"No sugar and not yours," Emmie laughed and stood up, wrapping her scarf around her neck and placing a dollar on the table. She pulled her long black hair over the scarf and started for the door with Luke following.

When they pulled up to the Summer House the wind was beginning to pick up and blow snow in a hundred different directions at once – the visibility was dropping quickly. It didn't keep Emmaline from seeing the tall figure leaning against the pickup truck parked in front of the house.

"What the hell?" Luke spoke first. "Stay in the car."

Luke parked and quickly climbed out – and as always Emmie didn't listen.

"What can we do for you, Mr. Connally?" Emmie asked, but it wasn't really a question.

"I was told you two had arrived in town, and I wanted to stop by and offer my sympathies firsthand." Connally removed his dark broad brimmed hat as if that would assist in his words.

"You failed!" said Emmaline. "She's not dead."

"Your words are quite hurtful, young lady," he took a step toward them.

"I heard you were up here the night it happened, and I'm sure you had something to do with it…now get off of our property," Emmie walked up onto the porch.

"I assure you Ms. Johnson was fine when I left here – after our little talk."

"Why are you visiting an old colored lady's home anyway?" Emmie stood on the porch looking down on him now – she liked having the higher ground.

"We're old friends."

"Is that why we were always told to stay away from your farm?" Emmie took one step back down as Luke moved slowly around Connally to get between them.

"That's ridiculous."

"You should leave, sir,"

"Maybe you should just go, Mr. Connally," Luke decided to intervene.

"I am going to find out why she hates you so much – that's a promise!" Emmaline stepped back into the yard and walked up behind Luke, glaring into Connally's eyes.

"Please leave now," said Luke, trying to calm the situation.

"Montgomery, control your little whore," Connally said as he stepped closer to the pair.

Luke felt his right hand immediately clinch into a fist and when he unleashed it he knew it would break bone in this man's face. Emmaline knew it too and placed her soft hand on his forearm. He loosened his fingers.

"No, Luke," she said softly from behind him. "No."

Mr. Connally grinned and opened the door to his truck before he stopped and looked back at them. "It's a damned shame about that suspension mess over in Charlottesville – maybe they'll hold your spot open while you are up here on vacation with your girlfriend."

Connally drove his pickup out onto the road where he turned sharply to the right to head back up the hill. His tires found trouble gripping the road for a few seconds, before he disappeared into the storm.

"Let's get inside," said Luke.

"Get my bag please - we are staying here tonight."

"The storm is getting worse – I guess I can sleep on that plastic covered couch," Luke smiled.

Emmaline looked at him and he could have sworn the gold flakes in her eyes were glowing with angry fire in the twilight and blowing snow.

"I'll check the cupboard," she said. "We may be here a few days."

# 46

Gracie wore a ring of woven honeysuckle and lilac that began above her forehead and draped down her dark silken hair to her neckline in the back. Her gown was an old white lace coming out gown that had belonged to the late daughter of the Draper's who had died from Yellow Jack a decade before the war started. It had never been worn, but Katherine Draper had kept it in pristine condition in a cedar blanket chest in her daughter's room. The morning of May 13, 1865, saw the arrival of summertime weather in Southwest Virginia. The red- breasted robins had returned from their Winter home and they danced back and forth under the oaks in front of the Waverly House, searching for any small unfortunate insects or seeds that came across their paths. Gracie sat on the swing that Thomas built, slowly moving her bare feet through the still moist morning grass. She was loved, and her life was full, and her joy was bursting at the seams this morning. In the distance she could hear the New River as its' icy power thundered through the jagged rocks that formed the rapids just above the farm. The birds chirped and the butterflies darted around her halo of flowers. A slight cooling breeze was coming in from the west bringing in the new smells of late Spring. Today was the perfect day to marry her Thomas.

Inside the house the Drapers sat at the kitchen table with Thomas across from them. There were three coffee cups on the table, one with a half-inch of cold remnants in the bottom, and the other two empty. Katherine rose from her chair and stood behind her husband, Timothy. She wore a blue and yellow flowered smock that she had sewn herself while working behind the counter at the Mercantile. Her auburn but snow-flaked hair was tastefully put up in a bun and she wore the slightest tint of scarlet across her lips and cheeks.

"Are you absolutely certain about this Thomas?" She asked him.

"Never been more serious about anything in my life," he looked up at her. "I've never known anyone like her - and I never will again. She knows how things will be for us. "

"You've told her everything?" Timothy Draper placed his hands on the table in front of him.

"Everything."

Timothy slid a piece of paper across the table to Thomas who glanced through the document with the help of a bright beam of sunlight coming through the window.

"It looks to be in order," Thomas dipped a feathered pen into the small blotter between them and scrawled his signature across the bottom of the page. "Mr. Millstone reviewed it?"

"He has."

Thomas placed a small ball of wax made with turpentine, rosin, and shellac into a silver spoon which he placed onto the wood stove top until the wax was softened. Then he pushed it out onto the bottom of the paper and lifted his family seal and steadily pressed it into the wax. Then he folded the paper in a tri-fold and sealed it again - this time with a seal of his own that left the initials TWS stamped in red wax on the fold, thus closing the document.

"Gracie understands the importance of this. "Thomas slid the paper back across the table to Timothy.

"We will keep it safe until she needs it."

Thomas looked up and glanced from one to the other nodding in thanks.

Katherine walked over to him and leaned slightly over the table. She then reached into the pocket of her dress and removed a small folded up piece of cloth. She placed it in the table in front of Thomas.

"As you know, your mother - God rest her soul, is buried in a pauper's grave outside the hospital in Richmond because of the state of her illness," she unfolded the cloth to reveal a silver band with three tiny diamonds imbedded in it. "This arrived at the mercantile by post a couple weeks ago. Perfect timing. Your mother loved Gracie too. I know she would want her to have this."

Thomas placed his hand over Katherine's. "This means everything to me - thank you so much. "

"I had Ben, the silversmith, to do a little work on it."

Thomas picked up the little band and twirled it between his fingers until the sun glistened off the inside where could read the inscription. "Madeline" was a little worn, but "Grace" was easy to read.

"This is marvelous! How can I ever repay you folks?" Thomas was going to be so proud to place this on Gracie's finger.

"Don't be silly - it's one of our wedding gifts to the both of you." Katherine Draper was beaming. "Now...let's get you two married!"

As the trio emerged from the kitchen side door Gracie began to rise from the little swing where she had been slowly drifting back and forth with the assistance of a twist of her toes from one bare foot. She marveled at the sight of Thomas in his older brother Dewey's black suit, and she noticed as he approached that he was decked out with a crisp white linen shirt and a short black bolo. He wore black leather pull on shoes that had been shined up with lamp oil from the cellar. As Thomas reached the crest of the little hill under the old oak tree he winked at his bride and she lowered her eyes nervously and smiled.

"Please…sit back down - you were perfect there," Thomas reached out and grabbed the tips of her fingers and lowered her back down onto the oak swing. Her white dress fluttered around her ankles as the smell of the flowers in her hair reached Thomas and he breathed her in with a long breath.

"Perfect," he said.

"You look…so handsome," she looked up at him and batted her long eyelashes in the bright afternoon sunshine that filled the valley with golden strength.

The butterflies continued their dance around her head, and they were joined by an occasional mayfly drifting through. Tiny bees flitted from one yellow flower to the next, landing on Gracie's feet from time to time but not daring to sting. Nature seemed to draw its power from her soul, and Thomas loved to watch as the world revolved around her. Now, he dropped to his good knee in front of her and took both of her hands in his.

"Grace Henry," he began. "From this moment forward I shall not take further breath until I call you my wife… will you do me the honor of saying "yes"?"

"There is not any part of me who will ever refuse you, my love," a tear rolled down her cheek and Thomas kissed it away. "I am yours today… and every day - for the rest of our lives together."

Dr. Draper performed the ceremony with Katherine acting as their witness in the bright beautiful Virginia sunshine. Gracie was amazed by the silver ring with her name engraved in the band, but at first, she refused to wear it - until Thomas convinced her that she was the new lady of Waverly House and that it would honor his mother for her to have it.

The group had a fine picnic on the lawn and Katherine presented Gracie with a beautiful walnut Martha Washington sewing cabinet, and then made her promise to start weaving baby bonnets the minute she went back to town. The two laughed about that for several minutes. But Gracie's mind was somewhere else that afternoon – somewhere she didn't like to go – and she had to struggle mightily to enjoy the day and keep a smile on her face.

As Thomas had lifted her hand and slowly placed the ring on her finger, she had taken a deep breath and choked back tears. For the first time, she had noticed the yellowish tinge on his fingertips.

# 47

Emmaline Foster managed to retrieve three eggs from the ice-cold coop, where she found three of her grandmother's six chickens had died overnight from the harsh winter storm that rumbled through. She kicked herself for not thinking about them the night before. She had seen her Grandma Bea let the hens go under the house on the coldest of nights so she carried the trio of survivors to the house and put them under the steps, where they quickly ran back further under the porch to get under the floorboards running under the old wood stove. She thought to herself that she wouldn't be going under there to retrieve any eggs. As she re-entered the house, she found Luke sitting up on the couch and rubbing his neck with one hand.

"Not the Howard Johnsons," he said.

"Beggars can't be choosers," Emmie laughed and put a cast iron skillet on top of the old wood stove. "Got three eggs for you – scrambled or?"

"Hard fried is good," Luke walked over to where she was standing. "But you are eating half so cook them like you like them."

"Hard fried it is," she lied.

They had found half a loaf of homemade bread in a little roll-top wooden container which gave away its' contents by having the word "BREAD" marked across the door in black paint. Emmaline tossed four slices on top of the stove and toasted them – then she spread some butter on each piece and made egg sandwiches. Luke hungrily ate his down, and they both helped to finish off a half quart of milk they found in the icebox which was very close to giving up the ghost. Emmie went out the front door and put the bottle in the rack for the milkman.

"Need to write a note to the tell the man we don't need any more right now," she said.

"If we're staying for a few days, we might." Luke washed out their cups and put them in the dishrack. "I've been thinking about something."

"Please share."

"You said the diary is missing a bunch of pages, right?"

"Yes, but it's very old and yellow and the binding glue is falling apart," Emmie pulled the diary out of her carpet bag and placed it on the kitchen table between them.

Luke pulled the book over and slowly opened it up. He looked closely at the binding and lifted it up in front of his eyes and rotated it slowly.

"This binding does have glue – but it was originally stitched."

"Okay."

"So, some of the stitches look like they were cut in places," Luke put the book back down on the table. "I think your great grandmother cut those pages out so nobody would ever see them."

"Why?" Emmaline sat down in one of the rickety ladder-back chairs and pulled one of Bea's shawls around her shoulders.

"I don't know that," said Luke. "But I do know you said your great-grandma always lived here – maybe she hid the pages somewhere in this house."

The frigid morning quickly turned to a very disorganized search of Beatrice Johnson's house. Luke searched the high shelves and cabinets while Emmie searched the lower cabinets and under furniture, tapping floorboards for hollow spots as she went. Emmie even rifled through every book on the small set of shelves in the living room, carefully returning each one to its' spot. After an hour or so, they met back at the wood stove to warm up some.

"Maybe the pages were just lost over time – the book is old," Emmaline stood up and filled up the tea kettle at the sink, then placed it on the stove top to heat.

"Just seems odd that she starts talking about someone or something and then a page or two is missing – like a cliffhanger in a book," Luke spun his chair toward the stove and sat back down leaning his chest against the back. He stared at Emmaline's long black hair as she stood over the stove with her back to him. She reached down and opened the door to the stove with two cloth potholders and threw in two more small oak pieces. The stove seemed to let out a low grumble as it began to consume the logs. After a few minutes the kettle began to whistle – and then the front door flew open with a bang against the wall. Luke almost fell out of his chair onto the floor trying to get to the broom leaning against the wall for a weapon.

"Child – wha choo doin' up in here with dis young man?" Juanita Williams stumbled through the door carrying a basket and a small grocery bag. "Best not be no hanky-panky!" she laughed and put her basket and bag on the table.

"Oh. Ms. Williams – I think you know better than that," Emmaline walked over and gave her a hug.

"N'er know wha' choo younguns' is up to deez days," Juanita grabbed a chair and pulled up next to the table. "The good tea's up in tha' old Maxwell can on the top shelf there." She pointed to the cabinet. "No sugah fer me."

"Did you walk all the way here from your house, ma'am?" Luke reached the top shelf and pulled down the old coffee can.

"Walk everywhere."

"I can drive you back," said Luke.

"Can I visit some?"

"Of course," said Emmaline. "He just meant after our visit."

"Boys dis age – alway tryin' to get us gals alone," Ms. Williams laughed and had to fix her teeth when she was done.

"The storm was bad last night – so we spent the night," Emmaline placed a cup of hot tea in front of Juanita, leaving the bag in it. "I'm afraid I don't have any cookies or biscuits."

"Oh, yes – open dat basket up."

Emmaline pulled back the red checked cloth covering the basket and removed two loaves of banana bread that were still warm. She placed them on a plate on the table and retrieved a knife from the drawer.

"You know I love your 'nana bread," Emmie sliced off the end and laid it on the plate – then she sliced three warm center pieces for them. "I remember sitting and grinding up walnuts for Grandma Bea with that old hand grinder attached to that jar," she smiled at her.

"Better wit jus' a li'l butta on it." Juanita took a bite and Luke had to look away while she was chewing.

"She gave me my great-grandma's diary when I was up here after Thanksgiving," Emmie sat down. "There's pages gone from it."

"Oh do, she telled your mama she woudn't n'er do dat," Juanita shook her head. "What happen up at dat farm what's on tha' hill?"

"All I did was tell Mr. Connally that Bea Johnson was my grandmother, and he went insane on me and Luke – yelling at us to leave and not come back," Emmie looked at Luke. "Luke's been working up there every summer for years now."

"Tha' man's no good 'tall."

"He was always good to me," Luke said.

"Was' your name, boy?"

"Luke Montgomery, ma'am."

"Wha's your family?" she took another bite of the bread.

"Beckley, West Virginia."

"Prosperity." It was a statement rather than a question.

"It's strange reading Ms. Gracie's diary," Emmaline interjected. "It weirdly seems like Luke and I are somehow either connected – or even related?"

"I brung her some yarns – fer when she come back," Juanita opened the bag and handed two rolls of yarn to Emmaline. "I should be goin' now. Put dem' in her sewin' stan' right der"." She pointed at the walnut stand sitting next to Bea's old cloth recliner.

Emmie handed the yarn to Luke who went over and placed the yarn inside and then he sat on the edge of the recliner. "I will run you back if you are ready." He flipped the lid of the Martha Washington cabinet back down and it made a funny sound. He looked at Emmaline. "Did you hear that? Sounded like a drum – not a box.

Luke opened the lid back up and pulled the yarn and knitting needles out. The cabinet wasn't as deep as he thought it was. He reached inside and tapped on the bottom. "This is hollow," he said.

Luke carefully placed the cabinet upside down on the living room rug, making sure not to damage the two doors on the top. "Hand me a butter knife," he said.

"Don't' break it…" Emmie stood over him as he gently pried four old copper nails out from around the bottom. "I'm going to turn this back over and you catch the bottom as it comes out, Em"

She nodded and got on her knees as he turned the lightweight cabinet back over. The bottom was wedged tight but as he shook the top it dropped into Emmaline's waiting hands.

"My God," she said as she held up a handful of yellowing papers before they could drift to the floor. "You were right all along, Luke!"

"I should go now," Ms. Williams rose from her chair and headed toward the door.

"Did you know about this?" Emmie asked.

"Bes' you talk ta Bea.'"

"She can't talk to anyone right now – can't even write her name," Emmaline looked at her with pleading eyes.

"Git ya' coat, Lucas," she said. "You'll catch a death."

"Only my mom calls me Lucas – and only when she's mad," Luke laughed.

"Can you tell us anything?" Emmie asked again.

Juanita stood by the door and pulled her shawl around her shoulders and covered her hair with a bonnet as if she was planning to make a quick escape.

"You both have a good listen – an' it din' come from me," she looked at both of them. "Your Gracie – I knowed her - it was said she was married to Thomas Summerlin up at tha' farm, weren't no proof of it" she looked at Emmaline. "But he ain't no blood to you."

Then she looked at Luke. "I reckon you git dat name from Summerlin. You great-granpa – he went by John Montgomery?" she sounded out every syllable of his last name.

Luke nodded but couldn't find or need words.

"He was Thomas Summerlin's brotha'," Juanita said. "Git your key."

"Is there more?" Luke asked.

"You ain't blood to none of 'em."

# 48

Thomas and Gracie got their first cows in August of 1865, a couple of two-year-old Black Angus steers and a springing heifer that gave birth to her first calf in September of that year. The winter of 1866 was especially cruel and the newly married Summerlins found themselves cutting wood daily just to stay warm in the house. Gracie had put up a good stock of canned fruits and vegetables, but the smoke house only saw one venison, and half the chickens had died in the cold. Thomas was forced to ration his hay bales between the horses and the cows, and the new cow provided some milk, but much of it was needed for the newborn calf which Gracie made the mistake of naming Gertie. Gracie spent a good part of December and January force feeding Gertie with her mother's milk because she stopped nursing in the frigid cold. Gertie soon began to follow Gracie everywhere she went – and Gracie didn't seem to mind at all.

With a new Spring beginning to unfold they made the tough decision to sell the older of the two steers to purchase seed for sewing this year's crops of corn, field peas, and tobacco. They also needed to replenish Gracie's garden, which had been decimated by the cold and the animals foraging for food. The pair was making their way to the Mercantile with one of the steers tied behind the buckboard – the ride was mostly silent… this year had been harsh so far and the despair of it all had taken its toll on the both of them. Gracie had tried to lighten the mood early on by telling him "For better, for worse,", but they really needed the "for better" part of that equation now.

Thomas dropped Gracie off at the front of the store so she could begin looking for some staples that they were in desperate need of, while he pulled around to the unloading area to turn the steer over to the Draper's stock handler. The man paid Thomas $26 - all in Seated Liberty half dollars in a small draw string bag. Thomas tucked the bag deep into his front trouser pocket and pulled the buckboard to the side of the store…a convenient place for loading the burlaps of seed they needed. Rounding the corner Thomas could hear Gracie yelling at someone so he picked up his pace as best he could.

"You will unlock these children right now!" Gracie was hollering at a bearded man wearing what looked to be an English bowler on his head.

"Look, ma'am, I'm not going to waste my time explaining the vagrants you see shackled in front of you," the man stood holding a saddled black and white horse by the reins, while a teenage boy sat mounted on a sorrel quarter horse ten feet away.

Thomas arrived on the scene to find Gracie standing over three young negro children huddled together on the ground…chained together at the ankles with shackles and balls. Their noses were all running thick with snot and the oldest one had a deep cut over his right eye, and in the middle of his lower lip. He stared blankly at Gracie with hollow brown eyes.

"There's no slavery in this country anymore, sir, remove these chains," Thomas glared at the man.

"You with this one here? She your servant?" he pointed at Gracie. "Mind her to watch her mouth."

"This is my wife – and you will unchain these boys so they can go home," Thomas was trying to hold his temper in check.

"Wife?" the man laughed and put his hand on his huge belly. "Talk about the law – you clearly don't know any law. Wife...that's rich, son."

Thomas pulled his pearl handled Colt Peacemaker from its' holster and pointed it at the man's chest. "I killed many men over the last five years and I ain't averse to one more. Now turn them loose."

"See, here's your problem, boy," the man took two steps toward Thomas and put this hand on the butt of his own gun. "Them boys are prisoners – not slaves. They are in violation of the Commonwealth of Virginia Vagrancy Law...and I have every right to return them to their overseers. Now my job used to be hunting down runaways – this is much easier though."

"You are a liar," Thomas pulled back on the hammer.

"He's not lying, Thomas." Timothy Draper's voice came from behind him.

"These are children!" screamed Gracie again.

"No matter, they are vagrants under the eyes of the law," the man climbed up on his horse and gave the chain a tug.

"Are you boys vagrants?" Gracie asked.

The older one who had been staring at her started to speak with a quivering voice, "I reckons tha' we don' now wha' tha' means, ma'am."

"What do you get out of this, mister?" Gracie approached the man.

"Five dollars a head for returning them to work."

"And where would that be?"

"Roanoke first, then Richmond most likely."

"Where did you boys start out from?" Gracie asked the children.

Again, the older boy spoke, "Tandey – he come up from Nort' Caroline', Cozy – he say he from Tennessee way, Me – I's George – from Sout' Caroline'."

"Don't sound like Roanoke to me," Gracie said to the man.

"Don't matter – they need to work for the common good."

"Again – they are children." Gracie looked at Thomas who was putting his gun back in the holster at his waist.

"We will give you four dollars each to unshackle them and give them to us – we will see that they work for their room and board," Thomas stood next to Gracie.

"I just told you I get five apiece."

"And…I'm saving you a trip to Roanoke."

"My boss ain't gonna be happy if I come back empty handed."

"I'm sure a man of your considerable skills at rounding up dangerous runaways can find a few more…don't you think?" Thomas opened the little pouch and held out twelve dollars in coins to the man.

"I hope you and your so-called wife are very happy with these vagabonds – watch the older one he likes to fight back, and he bites too…worthless little mangy dogs." The man reached down and unlocked the shackles from the children's ankles…exposing pus filled sores and scabs around each of their poor little feet.

"Can you boys walk?" Gracie asked.

"We's can manage some," said George.

"Get in the back of the buckboard" she said as she turned to look at Mr. Draper. "We need three pairs of moccasins if you please, sir."

"I'll scrounge up something, ma'am," Timothy tipped his hat to her and went back inside the store.

George helped Cozy and Tandey limp over to the wagon and then he hoisted them inside. The man and the teenager turned their horses out to the road and headed off to the west away from the little town. Thomas watched until they rounded the bend and disappeared behind the brown brush, then he went inside.

"I still need the seed, Timothy," Thomas pulled the coin bag from his pocket. "Just half as much."

"You'll get what you asked for....and pay me back later when your harvest comes in," Dr. Draper had the sacks of seed stacked on a cart and ready to wheel out to the buckboard. "You need to know something, Thomas. Your Uncle David was elected to the House of Delegates for the State. He was one of the members who presented this vagrancy law back in January."

"So...he's trying to make slavery legal again?" Thomas pulled on one end of the wooden cart as Thomas pushed and they made their way out the side door to the loading dock.

"There has always been a law compelling men to work, but this overreach with children and chains is an outrage. The governor opposed it, and the Senate overrode him. They forced him to sign off on it essentially. There are thousands of ex-slaves roaming the country looking for lost loved ones – it's sad really. Surprised you haven't seen any wander up your way." Draper handed sacks one by one down to Thomas in the back of the wagon as the boys crawled toward the front. "That man that was here – he grabs anyone small enough for him to control and drags them back to David Connally in Roanoke to sell them to him. Then, Connally rents them out to farms and factories with the assistance of the local constable."

"Gracie will be saving all of them if I'm not careful," Thomas threw his hat onto the buckboard seat and jumped down to seal up the back of the wagon.

"Be careful, Thomas – despite the fact that the military has refused to enforce this law, there are men out there who think they have unlimited power to twist it as fits their needs." Timothy Draper pulled the cart back inside the Mercantile and was gone.

Gracie had arrived back at the wagon and climbed into her seat next to Thomas with several spools of thread and some yards of cloth wrapped tightly and tied with tweed string. "The boys will need some clothes – just look at them."

"They will also need food – it's gonna be tough with three more mouths to feed."

"I won't eat then," Gracie smiled at Thomas then looked up the road.

"Still leaves two extra," he laughed.

Thomas eased *Mayflower* out onto the dusty road and rounded the western bend toward the farm. The bright sunshine darted and peeked around clouds providing warmth, then quickly taking it away. George, Tandey, and Cozy stayed quiet in the back, probably because of pain and weakness rather than just being shy and afraid. As soon as the buckboard was under the gated crossbar leading into Waverly, he saw them. Twenty yards ahead stood the bearded man and the teenager side by side. The man held a shotgun which he had pointed chest level at Thomas.

"Whoa, girl," Thomas pulled back on the reins holding his horse – and they came to a stop. "What are you doing on my property? I'd suggest you get down the road."

"Should have known you was a Summerlin – probably a deadbeat just like that awful old man of yours," the man pulled back the hammers on both barrels to draw fear from Thomas…he didn't get it.

"What the hell do you want?"

"For starters I'll take back my boys," the man looked at Gracie and said, "and I'll take your so-called wife as well – might even get a hunnert for her – she'd be great in the brothels down in Richmond."

"You will die where you stand, sir," Thomas put his hand on the pearl grip of his Colt. Gracie reached out and put her hand on his forearm.

"You'll never get off a shot before he kills us both," she whispered.

"Don't try it son!" the man took a step forward and pulled the dirty haired teen along with him. "Go get his gun belt and bring it to me, boy."

The boy obeyed him and walked over to Thomas with his hand out. Thomas hesitated until the boy said, "He'll kill you, mister…seen him do it.."

Thomas loosened his belt and slid it down to the boy who grabbed it and quickly turned around to walk back to the man. Thomas glanced at Gracie to see if she held any grand plans, but she just stared straight ahead as the scene unfolded. He thought about the shotgun that was under the blanket in the back, but realized he'd never get to it in time without a distraction – but what. He didn't have to wait long to decide.

The boy walked past the man carrying the belt and once three feet on the other side he turned in one quick motion as he pulled and fired the Colt point blank into the back of the man's head. The man dropped to his knees and then fell face first into a puddle of his own blood and brain matter. The boy dropped the gun to the hard packed drive with a clatter – then he put his hands on his head and began to walk in circles. Gracie climbed down and went to him.

"It's Okay, honey – your pa was not a good man," she tried to console him but kept looking back at Thomas.

"He warn't my pa!" The boy seemed defiant about this. "I want gonna let him hurt nobody else."

"It's going to be okay," said Gracie.

"I'm gonna hang now – I jus' know it!"

"We won't let that happen," Gracie leaned down and picked up the gun and belt slowly. "If he's not your pa, then who is he?"

"Don't know – he grabbed me from my camp in the woods by the river a few weeks back."

"Where are your folks?" Gracie moved back to the cart and handed the gun to Thomas.

"I guess I'm jus' like those boys there – I ain't got nobody left – so I guess I'm a vagrant too."

"Great news, Gracie," Thomas groaned, "Now we got four extra mouths."

## April 14, 1873

On a beautiful early Spring morning in Bland, West Virginia, John Blake Summerlin Montgomery was on his knees placing flowers on Emily Montgomery's grave in the side yard of the two-room farmhouse that he shared with his wife Patrice. Today would have been Emily's twenty-fifth birthday had she not died giving birth at the age of twelve in 1862. John and Patrice Montgomery raised young Lucas like he was their own – without showing him any regrets they may have harbored. Lucas' real father died the very day he was conceived, at the hand of the man who now raised him. This story would never be told while John Montgomery was still alive. Today was a solemn day for the Montgomery's, but one which they always celebrated with Lucas. Patrice was in the kitchen making Lemon Poppy muffins with the young blonde-haired boy whose face was presently covered in flour. The man in the long leather trench coat got to within twenty paces of the normally wary John Summerlin before John realized he was there. John spoke without looking back.

"State your business," John said.

"You John Summerlin?" The man said in a raspy voice.

"Montgomery is the name."

"I know who you are," the man said. "You are wanted for murder, desertion and dereliction of duty by the order of General Robert E. Lee."

"From an army that was disbanded almost ten years ago?" John stood up and turned now. "That seems a little far-fetched don't you think?"

"Law's the law."

"Let me get you some supper, sir, and you can be on your way." John walked toward the man who raised a double-barreled twenty gauge and pointed it at his chest. "There ain't no bounty to collect here today, sir," John immediately regretted leaving his pistol on the fireplace mantle.

"Not here for a bounty…for a debt," the man said.

"I owe no man,"

"David Connally says otherwise."

"I ain't heard that name in fifteen years," said John.

"He sends his regards…" the man leveled the shotgun and made the mistake of firing both barrels at once.

The gun roared loud enough to cause the entire hillside to tremble as the sound echoed for miles. John Summerlin was dead before he hit the ground. The barrel of the shotgun was still smoking when the front door of the little house was flung open, and Patrice Montgomery stepped onto the porch with a shotgun of her own. The man turned and fumbled for shells in the pockets of his trench coat as he went to his knees – then he looked up at Mrs. Montgomery who had a twelve-year-old Lucas standing behind her apron.

"Ma'am – you don't want to—"

But she did want to – and she did. The blast pushed her back toward the doorframe and pushed Lucas back off his feet and onto the kitchen floor where he slid to a stop against the kitchen table. The man fell backward with a thump – in nearly two pieces.

Samuel was the first to arrive and he pried the shotgun out of Patrice's clenched hands.

"I did this…" he said.

"What?"

"When they get here – I did this."

"No – no…I did." Patrice stared past Samuel without seeing him and at the group coming up the hill.

"Mr. John – he done so much for me and mine…let me take this… and you raise that young'un." Samuel put his hand on her face so she would look him in his eyes.

"I…did…this."

Patrice fainted and Samuel caught her just before she hit the floor.

# 49

"If Samuel was still alive, then who is in that grave up by the house?" Emmaline put her teacup back in the saucer with a low clink. The Draper Mercantile was crowded with folks who had ventured outside the second day after the snowstorm had rolled through. People moved from table to table talking to friends and sharing stories.

"Maybe it's a different Samuel – his father or something," Luke was finishing off a fluffy waffle loaded with more butter than maple syrup. He sipped hot chocolate on the side. He reminded Emmie of a small child while he was stuffing his face. It made her smile.

"Then what about John? She says he left with Samuel and his wife and children soon after Dewey Summerlin was killed," she said this as she glanced around the room taking in the small population of Draper, Virginia, as if she was Perry Mason.

"Can I get y'all anythin' else?" the waitress had returned and seemed eager to get her table turned over with the crowd waiting.

"I think we are finished up – but I have a question," Emmaline said.

"Sure."

"Does the Draper family still own this place?"

"Oh, heavens no. They moved over to Christiansburg years ago," the girl picked up Luke's empty plate and started to walk away – then she turned around. "But, that one over there," she pointed to a petite brunette taking an order on the other side of the restaurant. "She's named Patti Smithson – but her mother was a Draper. Probably why she works here – can't be because of her waitressing skills," she laughed and headed off to the kitchen.

Emmaline patiently waited until Patti walked by with nothing in her hands before calling her over by name.

"Yes? Do y'all need something else? I can get Diane for you?" the young girl responded.

"No, I just have a question for you is all." Emmie sat up straight and put her hands in her lap as if that would make her seem more genuine.

"Your mother was a Draper?"

"Yes ma'am – Kathy Smithson now."

"Then your great-grandmother was Katherine?"

"Yes ma'am – died before I came along."

"Did you know anything about her? Or ever heard of a colored woman named Grace Henry?"

"That's funny."

"Why?" Emmie stared up at her.

"My Mom told me they were known as Mother Katherine and Mother Gracie around here – I guess that's the Grace you mean?" Patti rocked back and forth while she was talking to them – a bad habit for a waitress to have.

"Mother Katherine?"

"They apparently worked together to reunite lost colored children with their parents or brothers and sisters – you know – back in the slave times," the girl seemed nervous when she said that and avoided eye contact with Emmaline. "There's an old plaque in the Post Office up yonder," she pointed up the street away from Emmie's Grandma's house.

"Thank you, Patti."

"You could talk to my mom, but she's way over in Christiansburg now – got to get back to work before I get in trouble." the girl walked away from them.

"I've never heard that before," Emmie looked at Luke.

"Post office?" he asked.

"Of course."

The Post Office was an old sandy colored brick building with an oversized flagpole flying an American flag in the middle of a small parking lot that had been plowed, but not very well. They ventured inside to find a bank of about one hundred post office boxes against one wall and a small service counter in front of them. An older grey-haired lady was meandering around behind the counter and didn't hardly glance up at them as they entered.

"There's the plaque," Luke pointed to a black and copper colored memorial hanging on the wall near the mailing supplies. Emmie walked over to it and began to read it.

**KATHERINE DRAPER**
**AND GRACE HENRY**

**IN THE LAST TWO DECADES OF THE 1800'S MOTHER KATE AND MOTHER GRACE AS THEY WERE AFFECTIONATELY CALLED, REUNITED OVER 300 HUNDRED MISPLACED CHILDREN OF FORMER SLAVES WITH THEIR FAMILIES FOLLOWING THE TURMOIL OF THE CIVIL WAR AND EMANCIPATION. KATE AND GRACE PROVIDED FOOD AND SHELTER AS WELL AS EDUCATION TO THE CHILDREN, WHILE**

**SEARCHES WERE PERFORMED TO LOCATE PARENTS AND SIBLINGS. THEIR KINDNESS AND LOVE MADE THIS TOWN THE VIRGINIA HUB OF REUNIFICATION AND THESE LADIES ARE OWED A GRATITUDE AND DEBT WHICH CAN NEVER BE REPAID. THE LADIES OF THE AME CHURCH OF DRAPER 1938.**

Emmaline seemed to be stunned at what she was reading. She took a step back and reached her hand out for Luke's and he took it.

"Are you okay?" he asked.

"I've never been told any of this…by my mother…my grandmother…anyone."

"Maybe there's a reason they kept this from you." Luke squeezed her hand and wished they weren't wearing gloves.

"Let's head back to the house and go through the diary pages again," Emmie let go of his hand and headed toward the door.

You ain't gonna get your grandma's mail?" a voice came from behind them, and Emmie turned around.

"I'm sorry," she said.

"You are Emmaline Foster, are you not?" the grey-haired woman looked at them through horn-rimmed glasses. "Beatrice Johnson?"

"Oh, yes ma'am I'm sorry."

"How is she? I heard she may have had a stroke of some kind."

"She's at my mother's house in Richmond trying to recover, but it's not good."

"I was your mother's English teacher in Pulaski…she was a great writer back in school," the woman smiled.

"She still is."

"Yes, I remember now…she didn't like being here – always talked of leaving and not coming back."

"She doesn't like to visit now."

"Probably for the best anyway, after all these years…you ain't moving here, are you?"

"No ma'am, I'm in school in Charlottesville," Emmie looked bewildered as she glanced at Luke.

"They are letting your people go to school up there now?" she shook her head. "Guess the times have to change."

"You have mail for her?"

"Yes. Just these two items," she handed Emmie an envelope and a Harper's magazine.

"Thank you, let's go, Luke," Emmaline turned and went out through the front door of the Post Office with Luke right behind. He had to pick up his pace to catch her.

"Your people…your people!" Emmie was mad, that was for sure.

"She's just old and you know some of those people are set in their ways."

"Maybe her attitude will die out with her generation."

"We can only hope," Luke got to the car first and opened Emmie's door.

Luke got in, started the Fleetline and eased out of the Mercantile parking lot. The snow had begun to slowly melt in the mid-day sun, but the drifts were going to hang around for at least another week. As they passed through town a few people looked and pointed at the car.

"I think they are admiring my car," said Luke.

"There's a white boy in a car with a colored girl, genius," Emmie laughed.

"I knew that," Luke said.

"There is a secret in this town…and I would sure like to know what it is," Emmie looked over at him.

"Some people do act strangely – like they don't want us here…probably because they think we are together," Luke pulled up to the Summer House and stopped as a white truck slowly rolled past on the road. "Let's get inside," he said.

Emmaline made them two cups of hot tea and they sat together at the little wooden kitchen table. Luke had brought in more firewood, and the stove was heating this part of the house nicely.

"I'm still confused by this Samuel that Grace talks about. In the original journal she makes references to the graves of Samuel and his wife and children – but the pages we found in the cabinet talk about Samuel coming to help with Elijah at the Summer House." Emmie spread the yellowed papers in front of her.

"So, who was Elijah?" Luke pondered.

"Grandma Bea once told me that my great-grandmother lost a baby boy at birth."

"But this says how much Elijah loved to run and climb," Luke said.

"So, it can't be him…can it?"

"I don't know…"

The pair sat staring at each other and then down at the pages. The house grew silent except for the occasional pop of wood in the stove and the clicking of a West Bend clock somewhere in Bea's bedroom. The sun had begun to settle down behind the trees above the house, and darkness entered the windows from all directions. Then Emmaline almost jumped out of her chair when the phone rang with a loud clanging sound that echoed through the house.

"I didn't think that thing even worked," said Luke.

Emmie picked the receiver up from its cradle and spoke.

"H-Hello." She put her hand on her head and began to pace in a small circle. "Yes, mother – I'm okay. I didn't know the phone even worked. Yes, the storm was bad. Yes, I think I can get on the road tomorrow. Yes, he's here with me now. Nothing is going on. I'll tell him to call his parents. It's cold but we have a fire. I have her things together. The roads should be cleared tomorrow. I love you too. Good night."

"Call your mother," Emmie sat back down at the table. "We should get some sleep and head out early when the sun comes up."

Luke laid on the couch under a patchwork quilt that smelled like his own grandmother used to smell. His pillow was hard and bristly, and covered in an old bedspread cloth that had been cut up and made into pillow cases. The heat coming from the stove in the kitchen made him sweat into the pillow. The plastic covering on the couch crinkled every time he shifted his weight. It was uncomfortable to say the least. But Emmaline Foster was asleep not twenty feet away – and that felt right to him. Life was good at this moment.

Until in an instant it wasn't.

Something hit the side of the house with a loud thud near where Emmie was asleep.

"Luke? What was that?"

Luke was in the bedroom in an instant, and he pulled back the curtain to look outside - two items caught his immediate attention – both were horrifying. In the distance he could see two shapes running down the road – one was holding his arm. Their shapes were easy enough to see - silhouetted in the moon light and mounds of white snow. They would have to wait…for now.

Flames were beginning to leap up the side of the house and lick the eaves of the roof above.

"Get up! Get dressed! Get Outside!" Luke barked at Emmaline, and she moved quickly. "Go get in the car." He tossed her his keys.

Luke threw on his pants and jacket and rushed out the door to the fire. He found a hose and tried to turn on the spigot, but it was frozen. He remembered seeing a shed behind the house through some thick dead underbrush and he headed that way. In the darkness he tripped over something in the yard and fell face first into a snowbank. He got up and found his footing again, and was inside the rotting building twenty steps later – in the dimness he could just make out a stack of tools with long handles leaning against the far wall. He grabbed two of them and ran back to the fire. Tossing the rake aside he began to shovel snow as quickly as he could onto the flames – but they didn't seem to be subsiding at all. The sun had melted much of the snow on this side of the house, so he was throwing snow and mud and stone at the blaze. It wasn't working.

Then he saw an opportunity.

Luke grabbed the garden rake and went back to the front of the house. He threw the rake on the roof and then climbed the trellis next to the porch, praying it wouldn't break under his weight – it creaked and protested, but it held. Then he was on the roof and feeling around in deep snow for the rake.

He found it, and worked his way to where the flames were coming up above the eaves. Using everything he had, he dug the rake into the base of the snow and plowed his weight into the handle. An entire run of snow almost a foot deep began to move…and he pushed it down onto the fire. Then he did it again…and again…and again.

The flames began to shrink and suffocate…but Luke was out of snow. So, he leapt off the roof over what was left of the fire, rolling his left ankle on the landing. He grabbed the shovel and pounded the remaining flames until they began to diminish …and finally go out. Then he threw shovel after shovel of melted muck on top of everything.

Emmie helped Luke get cleaned up in Bea's bathroom and she wrapped his ankle as tightly as she could with some gauze and tape she found in the cabinet, then she moved into the living room with him and laid on the couch while he sat on the floor in front of her. They didn't speak, and Luke didn't tell her about the shapes he saw running from the house. He also didn't tell her that he had tripped over something in the thick underbrush and that when he pushed himself up and looked down, he saw a wooden cross that had almost completely rotted away. With the glare of the flames there were shadows dancing in and out of the brush – but the shadows formed, then erased…and then formed again – one word.

"Elijah."

# 50

"We found his horse six miles down the river at an abandoned farm," Adam Rolls called himself a constable, but Thomas wasn't very convinced.

"Sir, the New River is running mad right now with all of the snowpack melting we've had," Thomas shook his head and held his hand over his eyes to soften the afternoon sun's glare. "One wrong step or slip down there and a man is gone in a blink."

"This is an experienced rider who knows the rivers and mountains," the constable cocked his hat. "I know you took possession of them from him back in town." He pointed to the three boys raking in hay from the lower field after the first cutting.

"There's a lot of underhanded folks wandering these parts since the war ended." Thomas stared the man down. "Could be he got robbed."

"Saddlebags still held the coin you traded for them."

"I wish I knew more," said Thomas, "truth be told he weren't a very nice man and there's people around here that will gun a man down for a threat."

"His boss is Delegate Connally – he ain't gonna be happy about this."

"Give my uncle – my warm regards from Waverly." Thomas began to turn to head back to the field.

"What you give for that one's on the swing there?" Rolls nodded in the general direction of Gracie who was sitting on the swing knitting socks for Cozy, who said he had never had a pair on his feet. "Looks like a right fine piece of a—"

"I'll trouble you to speak with regard if you speak of my wife," Thomas put his hand on the handle of the Colt in his belt. "Which I would prefer you did not!"

"Wife you say? There're laws again' something as unholy as that in this state."

"This state is barely a state – and is occupied by Union troops who suspended your so-called laws," Thomas was growing agitated, but he sensed the man was hoping he would lose his cool.

"Strange tool for a farmer to carry into the hayfield."

"You never know who is going to ride right in here unannounced," Thomas removed his hand from the gun. "Best you be on your way now."

"If I don't find the answers I want – I'll be back," Rolls turned his horse and headed back down the clay path leading to the road.

The Franklin Farm was six miles downriver, but near a gentle bend where Thomas could walk the horse in the water for almost a mile. Leaving the horse near the homestead was Gracie's idea – it was more likely to be found, and with the money still inside the saddle bags it would at least give some doubt as to the fate of the man. Thomas had knelt by the river's edge and made imprints with his knees near where the current began to pick back up with some force. Hopefully, whoever found the horse would assume he had fallen in and been swept away. Then, Thomas dropped two empty whiskey bottles near the site to create even more doubt. They also knew the locals would stay away from the farm for the most part. Dr. Draper had made a routine call to check on

Mrs. Franklin's condition about three years earlier, and he found her and her husband hanging from nooses in the barn. The smokehouse and store house were both empty, so it was assumed they took this route rather than starve. It wasn't unheard of in Virginia at all. Thomas left the gate to the paddock open so the horse could get out of the weather if he needed too – then he walked back upriver for six miles to the cave where he and the young man had carried the body and left it to rot with the badly decomposed bodies of the Union Captain and his hapless corporal. The captain still had the evil grin on his face even though most of the skin was gone from his cheeks.

Thomas learned as much as he could about twelve-year-old Rhett Hampton while they were covering up the boy's "misfortune" – as Thomas referred to it. Rhett's mother had died of the Consumption when he was very young, so Thomas felt an almost instant connection to the boy. His father warehoused and handled large bales of cotton that were farmed in the counties surrounding Columbia, South Carolina. The city had the unfortunate luck to be overrun by Union troops led by General William Tecumseh Sherman on February 17, 1865 – less than two months before the effective end of the Civil War in Appomattox Court House. Mr. Hampton's warehouse was overrun by a drunken mob of residents who were attempting to burn everything so the Yankees wouldn't get their "filthy hands on our things." They dragged several bales of cotton out onto Gervais Street and set them ablaze. Rhett's father had made commitments to his clients to protect their property, so he was out in the street doing his best to extinguish the blaze when he was killed by a single musket ball to the temple. Rhett never saw who fired the shot, but the blaze was put out by Union soldiers a short time later. Rhett fully believed that they thought his father was setting a fire instead of trying to put one out. In the drunken chaos Rhett had fled the city with very few belongings – and he headed north in search of his aunt near Fort Mill, South Carolina – but the Union Army was right behind him, so he took to the woods and eventually found himself at a tributary to the New River more than two months later. He didn't know it, but he was at Chestnut Creek, which ran through a beautiful meadow filled with Appalachian Galax plants – which was where he was taken by Connally's man.

Now, Rhett came out of the Waverly House ever so slowly and walked over to Thomas who put his arm around the boy.

"That man scared me," Rhett looked up at Thomas.

"He's gone," Thomas dropped down to his good knee and then he had to look up into the boy's eyes. "You saved us all that day – we are all forever in your debt. Never forget that." Thomas pulled Rhett closer and hugged him. The smell of the horses and the farm was overwhelming even to Thomas.

"Gracie?" Thomas said. "I think Sunday we should go have a picnic at the river."

"I think that is a grand idea," Gracie stood from the swing and walked to Thomas and Rhett. "I'm going to go in and start some supper – you boys look famished." Gracie walked toward the house, and her calf Gertie followed her to the steps, but she hadn't quite learned how to climb yet – so she took up her usual pouting position by the trellis.

Gracie stood by the drysink and watched Thomas and the boys finish raking the hay into a large pile. Cozy disappeared into one side of the stack and came out giggling on the other side. Tandey stood with his back to the pile and fell backwards into it. Before long all four boys and Thomas were in the middle of the pile in a full-blown tussle.

A single tear rolled down her cheek…again.

She knew this was where she belonged.

"God is good," she said and started peeling potatoes for her family's supper.

# 51

"Is he for real?" Emmaline moved to the back of the the Fleetliner and put her small bag in the trunk.

"You'd best tell your girl to watch her lip, boy." The Pulaski County police were not being very helpful in this investigation. "You want us to believe that James Connally, a man who is about to announce for the State House, set your woodpile on fire last night sometime after midnight."

"No, what I said was I saw two men running in the direction of his house that looked like some men I remember from working up there last summer." Luke had restated this several times now.

"In the dark you recognized these men. Can you give us some names?" The officer opened up his pad and pretended he was about to jot something down.

"There's a lot of men working up there on the farm."

"I think what happened is a spark come out your stove pipe and lit up that pile of wood. You really shouldn't keep it so close to the house either." The officer closed his little book. "We will go on up to Mr. Connally's and see if anybody saw anything last night – we'll come back if we get anything to go on." The second officer climbed back into the squad car and closed the door.

"You should really think twice about what company you keep, son," the officer put his pad back into his shirt pocket.

"Please explain your comment to my friend, sir," Emmaline came back around the car.

"There's rules in Virginia, ma'am." The officer stepped back on his heels.

"He told you again and again and again that we are just friends! He says it so often that I wonder why he even says it! It's like he's afraid somebody might think something else – just like you are doing right now!" Emmie was clearly upset.

"Look, ma'am – like I said there's rul-"

"You mean like the Racial Integrity Act? Afraid me and Luke might start putting forth some inbred offspring to taint the almighty one-drop rule of this fine Commonwealth we unfortunately have to call our home."

"Em – let's just go," Luke could sense a night in jail was close at hand.

"Young lady you are getting out of hand, and I would suggest you -," the other officer climbed out of his side of the squad car in case he needed to assist in any way.

"Racial integrity - keeping the young white boys off the young colored girls – what a novel approach to dealing with the human species," Emmaline moved in front of Luke then turned to face him. "I have a little racial integrity of my own, sir."

Emmie pulled hard on the front of Luke's jacket and brought his lips down to meet hers. She kissed him long and hard until he felt like he was going to collapse from it. Then she stopped – and opened her eyes – and smiled at him as if to say "that was better than I expected" – then she walked to her side of the car and pulled on the handle.

"Luke, please take me home to Richmond so I don't miss Christmas," she climbed inside and closed the door with a bang.

Luke shrugged his shoulders at the officers, got in the car, and headed toward Lynchburg – leaving the two cops laughing in the driveway.

Luke drove until he reached the Mercantile, then he pulled into the lot and stopped. He put his arm up on the back of the seat and looked at Emmaline who slowly lifted her gaze to his.

"Not going to talk about that," she looked back out the front window again.

"Let's stop by Ms. Williams house on the way out of town," Luke eased the car forward and back into the road. "She knows more than she told us – and we just let her walk out the other night."

Juanita Williams lived in a small white house with lap siding with a pale green wrought iron railing protecting a small porch made of concrete. She was sitting outside on an aluminum glider chair when they pulled into the one car drive.

"Lawd sakes, I figurin' y'all back in Richmond 'bout now!" she called from the porch as they walked up the two steps needed to get to her level.

"We are just headed back now, ma'am," Emmie walked over and gave her a hug through her thick shawl and blanket. "We stopped to say goodbye – and thank you for checking on us out at Grandma's."

"No problem 'tall," she squinted as the glare from the snow hit her eyes. Luke could see the cataracts growing there.

"Mrs. Williams, before we go can I ask you a question?" Luke went down on one knee in front of her.

"Oh, I'm too old for marryin', boy," she laughed, and her teeth moved again, "but if I weren't you'd be in for uh good run Emmaline Foster."

Luke and Emmie laughed with her before he said, "You told me that I wasn't blood to any of the Summerlins, right?"

She nodded.

"That means that you knew who I was before you came to Ms. Bea's house."

Juanita looked at Emmie and then rubbed her bony fingers together under her shawl. "Beatrice my bes' frin' in tha' world – she tol' me everthun."

Emmie took her hands, "You can tell us anything that she told you – I know she wouldn't mind."

"The blood in da' house ended wit' Thomas – when he dead," she shook her head. "Your grampa want' no Summerlin – but tha man what raised him up – he was Thomas brother – went by John."

"But, John Summerlin is buried at Waverly in the side yard," said Luke.

"Ask yo'self this? Why would dem' folk bury him 'der – an not up top tha' hill wit da res' of he family?" Juanita leaned forward and Luke could tell she liked to spin a good yarn. "John Summerlin buried up Wes' Viginny way – only he tombstone say Montgomery right 'der."

"How do you know all of this?" Emmie asked.

"I knowed yo' Grandma right near sebenty year – an you ask 'dat? Lawd child." She laughed again.

Luke looked at Emmaline with disbelief. The questions were swirling in his head now – but he would have to save them for his father.

"Was a rumor 'round these parts when we was younguns'. Might been another blood Summerlin born from Gracie Henry – yo' great-grandma. Y'all want some tea?"

"No ma'am, we need to get down the road with the daylight but thank you." Emmie put her hand on Luke's shoulder. "What happened to this child?"

"Dead before five year – some accident they say."

Luke and Emmie rolled on toward Richmond without speaking for the first half hour. Each one of them lost in their own thoughts of family long gone.

"Elijah," said Luke.

"Elijah?"

"I tripped over what must have been his old grave marker in the yard at Beatrice's house," Luke looked over at Emmie. "She must have buried him in the back yard there."

"Elijah," Emmie said his name again. The pages they found talked about Thomas, and Waverly, and her love for the "boys" which she never named – but never Elijah. Something else was missing, but what was it?

Luke dropped Emmaline off at her parent's home in Richmond on the evening of December 23, 1962. Emmie's father Anthony spent thirty minutes talking to Luke about his car before he let him leave for the long drive to Prosperity, West Virginia.

"I really like that young man," was what he threw at Emmie on his way through the kitchen as Luke drove away.

Luke Montgomery arrived home about four hours later after battling slick roads and freezing drizzle part of the way. He was so tired he barely stopped to kiss his mother and wave at his father on the way to his bedroom.

Christmas went as expected in the Foster house – plenty of great food, relatives stopping by, and gifts that were "needed" by all.

The Montgomery house also experienced a typical Christmas – a few small gifts, another chicken for dinner, and a quiet day of rest around the fire for the three of them.

Late on the afternoon of Christmas Day Luke found himself alone with his father in the living room. Lucas Montgomery was normally a man of very few words, but this afternoon he was a little bit chatty.

"What's happened at school?" he asked.

"What do you mean?"

"I follow the team you know," Luke looked over at his son. "You have a tournament starting tomorrow – shouldn't you head back?"

"I injured my ankle – Coach said to rest it before we start conference play."

"I got a telephone call from James Connally a couple of days ago," Lucas put his newspaper on the small worn walnut coffee table that was too short for the sofa. "Said you were shacked up there in Draper with a colored girl – who I can only assume was Emmaline."

"Her Grandma had a stroke, so I took her there to get some things for her – she was taken back to Richmond by Em's parents. The snowstorm caught us – and I called Mother – she didn't tell you?" Luke was tired and didn't feel like being grilled.

"James just called to remind me that Virginia law is very clear regarding such matters. He was concerned about appearances."

"Was he really?" Luke looked at his father. "Did he tell you how horribly he acted toward Emmaline when he found out who her grandmother was?"

Luke Montgomery shook his head.

"Did you know that we are related in a roundabout way to the Connallys?" Luke was growing agitated. "Is that why I have a summer job there?

"Your great grandfather was related to the Connallys, but your grandfather was not. We knew each other as boys – James and I - and to be honest it was your mother's idea that you go down there to work – to keep you from the mines." Lucas drank cold black coffee from a mug on the table.

"What's wrong with being a miner?"

"She – We want more for you," he looked up at Luke again. "Emmaline is a sweet girl."

"I think I know where you and James stand on that issue."

"He doesn't speak for me," Lucas got up from his recliner and moved onto the couch next to Luke. "Your life is your own to make of it what you will. To your mother and I your happiness is all that matters. I told you Emmaline is a sweet girl because we believe she is what makes you happy – that is all that matters – no matter what any man tells you otherwise."

Luke looked his dad straight in the eye and smiled at him – then he received a very rare moment of closeness that he had only seen a few times before from him – his father leaned in and gave him a hug.

Emmaline Foster sat with her mother on their little glass sun porch on Christmas evening, with a cup of tea held with both hands. She was perched under a large patchwork quilt. Her grandmother sat quietly on the sofa inside calmly turning the pages of a Casper comic book. She couldn't speak but she had a newfound love for the friendly ghost. Mathilde Foster sat staring out the window at the light falling snow. Emmie had been scared to ask her mother anything about Draper - and she never told her about the fire. Her mother seemed so disconnected from that place. But now it was her mother who spoke.

"Sweetie, we only get one light – and there are times in life when it shines brighter – or slips off into dimness," Mathilde Foster looked softly upon her daughter.

"No riddles please, Mom," Emmaline rocked back and forth with her teacup.

"It's not a riddle – I've never seen your light shine more brightly than when Luke Montgomery is around."

# 52

Cozy pumped water with a driven ferocity into the cow's huge trough. Tandey was using a pitchfork to throw old hay over the fence in large flakes from the small wagon as the cows pushed forward. Georgie and Rhett had two mares tied to posts in the yard and they were furiously brushing their coats and fitting them with saddles. Two other horses stood tied and ready to ride at posts not fifteen feet away. Thomas stood with the older boys providing guidance as they tacked up. Gracie finished watering her garden with the watering can and just stood and smiled at them. The three negro boys didn't really know what a birthday was, so Gracie had declared that the first Saturday of each new month would be one boy's birthday beginning with the youngest. Today was determined to be Cozy's ninth and he was over the moon with excitement. This day marked nine months that the boys had been at Waverly, and it was the first really warm day of 1867. Cozy demanded to have his "birthday" at the river even though he knew the water was too high and too cold to venture into. They had seen no snow in almost three weeks and the planting had begun in earnest – they all needed a good break.

All the boys were becoming good riders even though Rhett was the only one who had ever been on a horse. Today, Rhett and Georgie would ride alone, Grace would have ten-year-old Tandey, and Thomas would carry Cozy. Gracie had packed a picnic of smoked ham and beef, crusty bread, cheese, homemade mustard, spiced cut apples, and lemon cake squares, which were Cozy's favorite. The New River was their special place to be a family. The children swam if it was hot and the river was down, or they dipped their toes in the wintertime. Gracie loved to sit in the deep Timothy grass and tell the boys stories of her life – some of which may or may not have been true. She worked with the boys on their diction, and she was slowly teaching them to read and write and do some easy arithmetic. Rhett helped as much as he could with the teachings, having helped his father to run the cotton warehouse in Columbia. In the evenings Gracie would sit on the back porch and read to them in the lamplight from any book she could find. The boys started calling them Mother and Father at some point during the Winter. Neither of them minded it one bit.

Thomas and Cozy led the way through the lower pasture and crossed over the little creek that led down past the rock outcropping to the river, but then Thomas stopped *Lightening* and just stood there – looking up the mountain on their right and back out toward the pasture and the way back.

"What's wrong, honey," Gracie and Tandey stopped behind them on *Mayflower* – she pulled Tandey closer out of fear.

"I'm sure it's this way, Annabelle," Thomas said.

"Who's Annabelle?" asked Tandey.

"Everything all right, Thomas?" she asked.

Sunbeams streamed down through the sycamores and birch trees and glistened off the rocks and cold water of the stream. Nobody said a word. Thomas looked around again and, in an instant, seemed to regain his bearings.

"I'm sorry – it is this way," Thomas nudged the horse and he and Cozy started up the ridge toward the rocks.

Cozy laughed. "Tha' was silly!" he said.

"Yes – it was." Gracie followed him up the trail with a growing look of worry on her face.

The day went on just as Cozy had planned it. They stuck their feet in the water and built little castles out of stones away from the river's edge because Gracie worried over them too much. They caught yellow butterflies and then released them again to watch them fly away. They blew dandelions into the river to spread life downstream. They skipped stones across the glassier parts of the river. They hid behind the rocks by the river's edge when the train came by. They ate lemon cakes and Cozy ate three by himself. Then they laid down in the tall grass and napped in the warm sunshine. Cozy curled up next to Gracie and put his head on her shoulder. He sniffled and wiped his eyes on her flowered smock.

"What's wrong, Sweetie," Gracie asked him.

"I t'aint 'ner had nothin' done fer me like 'dis," Cozy wiped his nose on her shoulder.

Grace laughed and hugged him tighter, "Happy Birthday, Cozy!"

In the mid-afternoon Gracie declared it was time to get back to the house and take care of the animals and get washed up before supper. Nobody complained – this had been a good day. The ride back was filled with laughter and Tandey's silly questions.

"Why the sky green?" he asked.

"That's a silly question," said Rhett.

"Mr. Thomas say a'int no silly queshuns," Tandey laughed.

"Questions are how you learn," said Thomas.

"Then why the grass be blue?"

"Because it's Kentucky Bluegrass, son," Thomas kicked his horse and they all cantered back across the lower pasture and into the yard.

Gracie lowered Cozy to the ground and stayed in the saddle, "I'm going to ride up to the Mercantile for some coffee – we ran out this morning and I know how you tend to get."

Thomas stood on the mounting block and kissed her to the moans and groans of the boys. "I love you, Grace Henry," he said. "Want someone to ride with you?"

"No, it's still light – I'll be back long before dark," Gracie didn't like to take the boys off the farm if she didn't need to – she trusted nobody when it came to them.

Gracie cantered down the dirt road and disappeared in a cloud over the hill. It was just a few miles to the Drapers, and she needed to speak with Katherine – and Timothy if he was there. She found Mrs. Draper closing the store.

"Good afternoon, Ms. Katherine," Gracie climbed down from *Mayflower* and tied her reins lightly around the hitching post – that mare wouldn't go anywhere without her anyway.

"Gracie, Sweetheart, what do you need? Come on in." she opened the door to the Mercantile and went back inside, pausing to open the curtain covering the front window for some light.

"Give me some coffee straight away – I can't go home without it – but that's not really why I'm here," Gracie pulled a silver dollar from her pocket.

Katherine reached up on the shelf behind the counter and slid a small tin of coffee over to Gracie who placed her coin on the counter.

"Should I make us some tea?"

"No – no, I just have to tell you something about Thomas real quick like."

Gracie proceeded to tell Katherine about Thomas' confusion in the woods and how he seemed to be disoriented. She told her about him thinking he was speaking to someone named Annabelle. Katherine just listened and nodded her head slowly. She waited for Gracie to finish before she started to speak.

"First – the confusion…as we have spoken before – Timothy doesn't know the extent of the organ damage that Thomas has suffered from the cannonball that exploded in front of him. Honestly, his condition could be very grave." Katherine reached out and took Gracie's hands in hers. "The jaundice in his fingers you saw, the confusion – those are indicative of a liver situation. These are symptoms of a drunk who has – well – drunk himself to death. This doesn't mean the same outcome for Thomas – at least not right away."

"What can I do?" A tear rolled down Gracie's cheek and she tasted it in the corner of her mouth.

"Coffee is good – as well as tea. Helps with poisons in his body. Greens and nuts. It's about what he eats – and making sure he doesn't drink any whiskey."

The women talked for a while longer until Gracie said she'd best be getting home before the sun went down. Katherine walked her towards the door and then stopped her.

"Something else you need to know – it's about Georgie," Katherine grasped Gracie's hands once more.

"You did it – you found his mother?"

"Yes, Gracie, she's living on a farm in a town called Bamberg, South Carolina with Georgie's brother – we haven't sent word to them yet."

Tears rolled down both of Gracie's cheeks now, "Tha-that is such wonderful news – I'm so happy for him."

Gracie turned to go out the door and Katherine followed her out.

"I'm sorry that I had to tell you that," Mrs. Draper closed the door behind her.

"It's what I asked you to do for all of them," Gracie smiled. "You've done well by him."

Gracie climbed back up on the mare and slipped the little tin of coffee into her skirt. "By the by, do you know who Annabelle is?"

"He's never told you?" Katherine's face turned white.

"Told me?"

Katherine stepped up to the horse and put her hand on Gracie's leg.

"Annabelle was Thomas' sister. She drowned in the river when she was only eight."

# 53

"I'll just get the trainer to wrap it," Luke pulled his foot down off Coach McCann's desk with a thud.

"I think we'd be better off waiting for it to heal completely," said the coach.

"I've played through much worse than this – I'll be fine," Luke leaned over to tie his other shoe.

"Dom has filled in nicely – we will be okay for a couple more games."

"Seriously, we lost both tournament games by more than twenty points," Luke laughed and stood up from the metal chair.

"He's coming along," the coach looked up at him from behind the desk. "You took care of that other problem I hope."

"What problem would that be, sir?"

"The colored girl – what did you call her - your tutor?"

"She's not my "problem", but she is a student at the university that pays your salary," Luke started toward the door.

"She lives in a shack behind the drive-in."

"She pays her room and board by working – maybe I should ask you what your problem is with her."

"What is your obsession with this negro girl?"

"What is your obsession with being a God damned bigot?" Luke slammed the door behind him hard enough to rattle the opaque glass that said "Coach McCann" on it in black letters.

The door opened behind him almost immediately. "I'm not the only one who needs to see you end this relationship you have with her." McCann followed him out.

Luke turned around, "Or what? You gonna suspend me again?"

"Don't be a smart ass, Luke Montgomery!"

"Don't be a horse's ass, Coach McCann!"

The pair stood staring at each other for an awkward few seconds until Luke spoke up. "I'm going to get my ankle wrapped – see you on the floor in fifteen."

It was a good practice for the Cavaliers – Luke blew past Dom several times and moved easily to the basket for layups. By the time the evening practice ended the group was sweating heavily in the gym even as the temperature outside began to plunge with an arctic freeze moving into Charlottesville as the cold winter got colder. The coach had no other words of wisdom for Luke, and he and Dom headed back to the dorm before taking a shower to avoid being outside with wet hair.

"How's your break?" Dom asked.

"You should know," said Luke.

"Don't blame me for your situation."

"Somebody's giving coach the play-by-play on me and Emmaline – sure as hell a'int me – or Emmaline." Luke slammed open the door to the dormitory and they both rushed in out of the cold air.

"You seem awful angry, my friend." Dom twisted the knob to the metal door of their room and pushed it in. The room was dark and much colder than the hallway. Dom walked over and twisted the knob on their heater. "You really think I'm talking to the coach about your love life?"

"Sure is helping your playing time."

"You need to check yourself, Luke." Dom threw his jacket across the chair at his desk. "You've made somebody outside of this school mad – don't you see that?"

Luke realized at once where all of this was coming from… James Connally. "My God," he muttered to himself. "What the hell is he hiding?" he thought.

Luke got showered and dressed for bed – then he walked to the hall telephone and dialed the number for TPs. Mr. Richard picked up on two rings and told him they had closed because of the cold and the girls had gone home. He was wrapping a couple of pipes in the kitchen, and he promised to let Emmie know that Luke had called the next morning. Luke hadn't seen her – or heard from her since he had dropped her off in Richmond twenty days earlier, and he couldn't stop thinking about the kiss she had unexpectedly planted on him. He wondered if she had been thinking about it too. He laid on his bunk and found it easier to sleep than he had expected.

Mr. Richard turned to Emmaline Foster and said, "Don't you ask me to lie for you again, girl – I a'int gonna be no more part of it – you hear me?"

"Yes sir," Emmie sighed and got back to scrubbing pans in the soap filled sink at TailPipes.

Natalie loaded up another rack of serving trays and slid them into the washer while Emmie started drying the last rack and stacking the trays up on a stainless-steel shelf behind her.

"Why are you avoiding his calls?" Natalie asked.

"Because."

"What are you a four-year-old?" Natalie pulled down the door of the washer and it automatically started washing.

Emmie looked around and then leaned closer to her friend, "Because – I kissed him."

Natalie grabbed Emmaline with her wet hands and spun her around. "How long were you going to keep this from me?"

"It wasn't anything – I was mad at this idiot for saying something about us being a mixed couple," Emmie turned back to her drying. The only noise they listened to for the next several minutes was the hum of the washer and the clattering of the trays.

"Did you like it?"

"Was different – I've never kissed a white boy before."

"Was he good at it?"

"He wasn't ready for it – so he didn't have time to prepare."

"Not what I asked you…"

"Wasn't the worst thing ever happened to me," Emmie turned and gave Natalie a love tap on the arm with a tray before she put it up in the stack.

"So now you refuse to speak to him?" Natalie smiled at her. "Makes perfect sense."

"I just don't want him to take it the wrong way – you know?"

"Follow your heart."

"Not that simple – his just being around me has already caused him problems." The washer finished and Emmie pulled up the handle and pulled out the last rack of the night. "He got in trouble with his coach…and I cost him his summer job."

"You really think he wants to go back to work for that ass-"

"Natalie!"

"Besides, if he thinks you are worth it that's for him to decide."

"He has no idea what we go through – his life would be the same as ours." Emmie finished drying the last tray and took off her apron and threw it in the laundry cart.

"Is that so bad..."

"You of all people should know how bad that can be."

"That's hurtful..." Natalie tossed in her apron.

"I'm sorry, Nat – I'm just frustrated...with school, work, my Grandma."

The girls gathered at the back door and yelled simultaneously a "Good night" to Mr. Richard who yelled back "Be careful, ladies". Then they made a quick run to their little house behind the drive-in through the bitter wind and light falling snow.

The Exchange Hotel was a Gordonsville landmark built in 1860 less than one year before the beginning of the Civil War. Its owner had no idea of the importance the building would play for both sides over the next five years. As a waypoint for the Virginia Railroad, thousands of wounded from both the North and the South were sent to Gordonsville where the hotel would be turned into one of the largest Civil War hospitals in the country. By 1865 over 70,000 men had been treated there and 700 were buried in the surrounding grounds.

On this bitterly cold mid-January night one man sat at the bar sipping Scotch when another approached and sat on the stool next to him.

"Bourbon – neat," the man told the bartender.

"Good evening to you, sir," quipped the waiting man.

"No need for small talk, McCann...has our little problem been resolved?"

"There is no doubt trouble in paradise – they haven't seen each other since we came back," the coach turned to the man. "But, the boy got really fired up today when I pushed him on it."

"Maybe they haven't called it quits yet,"

"Maybe..." McCann said.

"Turn up the heat on him until he squirms then," the man swirled his bourbon and downed it in one sip.

"I can probably do that."

"Then do it," the man stood up and turned around to leave. "I'm late for dinner with the Governor."

James Connally walked through the front door of the Exchange Hotel and down the steps to the waiting black sedan in the street below...almost ninety years to the day after Gracie Henry Summerlin had walked into the hotel through the same door when the building was set up to help freed slaves. In 1867 the Exchange had housed the Bureau of Refugees, Freedmen, and Abandoned Lands and acted as a Freedman's hospital.

# 54

Gracie sat against the giant oak tree that held her swing on a warm early summer evening – with Thomas' head laying in her lap. They both had been crying from the entire evening's conversation. Georgie was going to be going home – the happiness outweighed the sadness by a longshot for this ending. It still brought tears to them both. The other part of the conversation was Thomas recanting the tale of the loss of his sister.

Annabelle Rachael Summerlin was the only girl in the Summerlin clan. A beautiful blonde freckled faced child who ran around covered in dirt with her four older brothers. She was, out of necessity, the toughest girl in the schoolhouse… and probably in the county. She idolized Thomas and went almost everywhere he went. One extremely cold winter day found the Summerlin boys, and their father being forced to lug water from the river to the livestock because the well was frozen, and the bucket couldn't be pulled up without breaking the handle...or the rope. The hand pumps were also frozen and useless even after attempting to warm them with torches.

Annabelle broke her father's cardinal rule about the river and ventured downstream while the men were working. Nobody heard her scream. Thomas saw her first waving her arms, and he yelled at his father who immediately dove into the icy river. With Dewey Summerlin swimming as hard as he could toward his daughter, they both disappeared around the bend and into the rapids below. The boys sat on the bank for three hours waiting on their father to return, and they were about to head back to the house to tell their mother – when their father appeared on the riverbank walking toward them…with Annabelle's lifeless body in his arms. By the time the boys got their father home he had almost died of hypothermia – and the doctor would later remove three of his toes and the pinky finger of his right hand. When the ground thawed that spring, Annabelle was buried under the oak above the pasture with her ancestors.

Now Gracie ran her fingers across Thomas' forehead and through his hair. There was so much she may never know about this man, but she was determined to learn everything she could. The boys came outside after cleaning up from supper, and Cozy and Tandey chased fireflies in the grass around the oak. Rhett sat on the swing trying his best to whistle. Georgie sat next to Grace and put his head on her shoulder – he had been crying too.

"I ha'int seen her in years now," Georgie said softly. "May she don' 'member me."

"A mother never forgets her child, Georgie," she kissed his forehead. "And she never, ever stops looking for him."

"Wa' if I don' wanna go wit her?"

"We will always be your family too…and you can come see us sometimes – it's just a few days trip to South Carolina. Maybe you can ride the train if they let you."

"Tha' may be fun don' you tink," Georgie smiled at her.

"I do think," she used her other hand to tickle his ribs and he rolled around on the ground laughing in front of them. "If you don't start speaking the way I've been teaching you there will be a lot more of that."

"Yes ma'am, but you must know I quite enjoy it," Georgie laughed and grabbed the ropes of the swing and began to spin Rhett around in circles. Rhett slammed his bare feet onto the ground in a futile effort to stop himself from spinning.

"Good Lord! We just ate supper!" Rhett jumped off the swing and tackled Georgie into the grass where they proceeded to wrestle. Tandey and Cozy stopped chasing bugs and joined the pile.

Gracie smiled and kissed Thomas on the cheek.

"Thank you – what was that for?" he asked.

"For loving me…that's all."

"You never have to thank me for that – that's something I just can't help – kind of like a chronic ailment," he laughed, and she pushed his head off her lap and onto the ground.

"Let's head inside and get to bed everyone," Gracie pushed herself up from the oak. "We have a long trip to start on tomorrow and we need our rest."

Georgie and Rhett helped Thomas get up off the ground by each picking up on a shoulder. Then the Summerlin family walked toward the flickering kerosene lantern in the kitchen window and went inside.

The morning came quickly, and the boys were up early. Rhett and Georgie had the buckboard ready to roll out before the sun had even hinted at showing itself over the river to the east. They proudly waltzed back into the kitchen for hotcakes, gloating about their work. Thomas told them how proud he was of what they had learned and "put to use." Gracie stood by the stove packing a picnic basket and covering it with cheesecloth for the trip. She didn't face the family – and Thomas knew she had been crying. Giving up Georgie was like giving up a son – hell it was giving up a son.

They got loaded up just as the sun started to rise and Gracie leaned in and kissed the three boys who were staying back on the farm.

"Watch each other...closely...and no going down to the river – the water is still very high. I made extra bread and there is plenty of salt pork and apples." She climbed up onto the front of the buckboard.

"We will be good here, Mama," Rhett put his arms around the younger boys.

Thomas climbed up onto the buckboard and settled in next to Gracie. "Not expecting company. Shotguns in the kitchen are loaded, Rhett. If more than one person comes up here – you hide in the woods and don't come out 'til we get back. Check the brood mares' feet – they may need filed down a bit since they foaled."

Georgie stood in front of his brothers – Tandey and Cozy were crying, and their dark faces glistened in the morning sun.

"I'll see you boys again – that I promise," Georgie was trying his best to be brave, but he was scared to death.

"We love you Georgie...and we are glad you are getting to go back home again," Rhett hugged him and then both Tandey and Cozy did the same at the same time.

Georgie climbed up on the far side of the buckboard and Thomas coaxed the horses to lead them down the road and off for the four-hour ride over to Christiansburg. The journey itself was uneventful, but it was mostly about Gracie telling Georgie how much she would miss him – and telling him how to act like a proper gentleman for the rest of his days. Thomas smiled and drove the team hard all the way to the livery beside the train station where he paid a man he knew to take good care of everything until they returned in two days.

Thomas procured three tickets for them, and they got up on the platform just as the train was pulling into the station. They stood in line to get on the second car from the front – it was painted a shiny brown and glittered with gold letters that stated "Norfolk and Western Line". The seats inside were plush with sewn pillows for a comfortable ride. But the Summerlins never got to experience it.

"Ticket please," the conductor said when it was their turn.

"We have three," Thomas held out his paper tickets to be punched.

"Three? Okay – you in here, negroes in the last car."

"This is my family."

"I don't make the rules, sir."

"I'll sit back there with them." Thomas held out the tickets again and the man punched them and leaned closer to him.

"Sit in the front of the car – and keep the window barely cracked. It's gonna be hot – when we go through a tunnel close the window to keep the coal soot out."

"Thank you," Thomas took Georgie and Gracie by the hand and led them to the last car and up the two steps. The inside of the car was covered with large wooden benches that had been bolted to the floor. The walls were covered in black soot and several of the windows were cracked.

"Let's sit in the middle," said Thomas. "Away from the windows."

The car never got completely filled, but they would pick up more passengers at stops on the way to Gordonsville,

Virginia, where Georgie's mother and little brother were waiting. As the train pulled away from the station, they found out why the windows were cracked – several rocks found their mark on the side of the train and one window sustained a heavier crack than it already had as a piece of granite bounced off. Thomas stood up and glanced out the window to see a group of white children gathering more stones. The engineer blared the whistle a few times and the train moved away from the troublemaker's onslaught. They settled in for the bumpy, dirty, four-hour ride to Gordonsville.

"You could have sat up front," said Gracie.

"My family never leaves my sight." Thomas took Gracie's hand as Georgie sat down on the floor in front of them.

Gordonsville, Virginia, was a seemingly unnatural American crossroads. Railroads crossed each other there and people were teeming all about the town. They saw negro men in suits and negro men in shackles – the same could be said for the white men. People argued in the streets with paper in hand, and wagons filled with workers streamed off into the twilight of the afternoon in all directions. Thomas told Gracie and Georgie to hold his hands and not let go as they worked their way through the crowd. "Don't let go no matter what," he said.

Katherine Draper had received word that Georgie's mother had come to the Bureau of Refugees looking for her son. It was a miracle word had spread that far from her arrival, but the Drapers were well known in these parts. Timothy Draper had worked as a surgeon during the Civil War in the hospital that had been the Exchange Hotel and was now the Bureau.

There was a long line of negroes, whites, and even Indians standing and waiting their turn. They took their place in line behind a negro man and woman.

"You've been waiting long?" Gracie spoke to them.

"Dun been hea' ten day gone now," the man spoke to her.

"You've been in line for ten days?" asked Thomas.

"Naw, sir – we comin' back e'ry day tryin' to get our fohty."

"Forty what?" asked Gracie.

"Fohty acre a land dey promus us." the man turned back around, and the woman with him looked nervously at the ground. Thomas realized he was the one making her anxious, so he stepped back behind Georgie and Grace.

The line moved at a treacherous pace, and it was well into the night when Thomas got to the desk to speak with someone. The clerk was a white-bearded man who was missing most of his left hand – what he had left was just a huge, scarred ball of flesh. After a couple minutes of descriptions from Thomas and Gracie the man realized who they were talking about.

"That woman, she drags that child around by the hand everywhere she goes. Been cleaning the latrines in the basement here for some weeks now. Sleeps on the floor or out in the livery at night – owner keeps her and that youngun' fed pretty much – so she cleans up. Go look for her downstairs or out in the back."

Harriett Smith saw them first and she came running to Georgie and fell to her knees in front of him and hugged him around the waist – holding on for dear life. A small boy of about four came behind her wailing at the top of his lungs – he tried to push Georgie away from his mother and Georgie just started to laugh. His mother stood up and he put his arms around her. Gracie stood holding Thomas' hand as tears began to well in her eyes.

On June 5, 1867, Georgie Smith became the first of almost one hundred negro slave children that Gracie Summerlin reunited with their families…all of them without one single shred of assistance from the Bureau of Refugees, Freedmen, and Abandoned Lands.

# 55

"Now he's brought you some chicken soup!" Natalie put the glass Pyrex container on the counter near the tiny one burner hot plate, which they used to heat the place more than they ever used it to cook. "Where does a college boy go to get chicken soup in the middle of winter besides his mama's house? I ain't telling him you're sick again – he's gonna have the whole hospital over here next."

"After that kiss…I don't want him getting the wrong idea." Emmaline said as she opened the container and sniffed the soup. "Smells good – want some?" She poured some soup into a small saucepan and placed it on the burner.

"Tell me, my dear, what would you think if he kissed you like that?"

"Not the same – he wants to do that."

"…and you didn't?" Natalie took two bowls from the small cupboard above the hotplate.

"Well…no…I don't think – not like that."

"You sound very confused for such a smart woman," Natalie grabbed two spoons from the dishrack and rinsed them off, then dried them on a towel. "You can't avoid him forever."

"Says you – he has three games in a row coming up on the road – two are in Florida." Emmie sat down at the table to wait for the soup to warm up.

"You know his schedule?"

"There's posters in the hospital, Smartie."

The girls sat down to eat, and the talk turned to school and their nursing program. Natalie Sharpe had come into the University of Virginia Hospital program through a program done in conjunction with Jackson P. Burley High School in Charlottesville. Emmaline Foster's path had been radically different.

Emmaline attended colored primary and secondary public schools in the Church Hill area of Richmond until 1958. Four years earlier the Supreme Court case of Brown vs. The Board of Education had ruled that segregation of public schools was unconstitutional. Virginia had flown into a frenzy of resistance in opposition to desegregating schools. When forced to integrate, Prince Edward County near Lynchburg had actually made the decision to shutter every single school in the county, a defiance which lasted for five long years. Rather than help to educate colored folks, they made the rather uneducated choice to withhold education from their own children. She had heard of a pair of siblings named Patricia and James Turner in the Norfolk district who had qualified to attend white schools in the area – in fact 151 colored children were slated to integrate the Norfolk public schools when the schools were shut down in protest. Only 17 colored kids had actually enrolled. The Turners had attended classes in the basement of their church while awaiting the outcome. They were even given handkerchiefs and taught to just wipe away the spit when it hit their faces. They were told to just think of it as "water". Later that year they joined 10,000 white students in a return to the Norfolk Public School System.

Emmaline's father didn't want any of this for his own daughter and when his friend Richard told him of the Burley High program, he did everything he could to get Emmaline ready to be included at UVA Hospital. Anthony Foster had talked to the family pastor and uncovered a connection with the St. Phillip's Hospital in Richmond where a colored nursing program had begun in 1957. In 1959 Emmaline was able to assist and learn at the hospital as part of her high school curriculum, and in 1961 the director of St. Phillip's wrote a magnificent recommendation to the director of the Burley School Program at UVA Hospital. Emmaline Foster was admitted for the next school year.

Then she had the misfortune to run into Luke Montgomery five weeks into school. Anthony Foster had unwittingly put her on a collision course with him.

Luke sat on the edge of his bunk and slammed the dirty tennis ball repeatedly into the wall until their neighbors banged back with a wooden baseball bat handle.

"You really need to relax some, my friend," Dom sat in the corner under a lamp with a history textbook open and a pencil tucked behind his ear.

"She won't even see me – I took her some soup today even though I know she isn't sick," Luke grumbled.

"How do you know that?"

"I saw her in the back of the kitchen when I got my order at the window."

"Why didn't you just do what you always do and lurk out back by the dumpster like some sick puppy looking for a scrap of food?" Dom closed his book and tossed it on the desk.

"My God, man…do you want me to seem desperate?"

"Taking her some soup is fairly desperate – don't you think?" Dom switched off his light and started to brush his teeth in the little sink they shared.

"I'm beginning to think the stupid coach got to her – or that James Connally ruffled her feathers."

"Let's go back to the kiss thing," Dom wiped his face off with a rough white washcloth. "She's probably embarrassed – or she just can't face you yet."

"Do you think so?" Luke laid his head back on his pillow and clasped his hands behind his head.

"Man, you are pathetic."

"Thanks for your support and advice my friend." Luke tossed the tennis ball at Dom, and it bounced off his chest and rolled under the bed.

"Sleepy time, Sir Lancelot," Dom turned off the overhead light and climbed into his bunk.

They talked for a few more minutes – mostly about basketball…until Dom drifted off.

The next morning Luke rolled out of bed and headed to the weight room at exactly five-thirty. He wore grey sweats and a pullover cap as he crossed the frozen expanse of lawn in the Quad toward the gym. As soon as he got in the building, he saw the light was on in Coach McCann's office, so he walked past, tapped on the glass, and waved in an awkward attempt at making up. McCann threw up two fingers and waved back before looking down at his desk. The light was off in the weight room, so he switched it on and started to stretch before his regimen. As he sat down on the floor and stuck one leg out to stretch his hamstring, he heard the door to the room open and looked up to see the coach walking in.

"Montgomery. You're up early."

"No earlier than usual," Luke said. "Just usually don't see you in here."

"You take care of your problem?"

"If you mean the ankle – then yes – it's one-hundred percent," Luke stretched out his other leg. "I'm ready for the Gators."

"You know that's not what I mean," McCann sat down on the bench next to where Luke was stretching.

"Again – her name is Emmaline Foster and she's not a problem," he sat and put his feet together to do a butterfly stretch. "I guess ya'll got to her though – because she won't even see me now."

"It's for the best – it ain't right and you know it," McCann put his hands on his knees and leaned forward.

Luke stood up and grabbed a curl bar with about ninety pounds on it. He began to hoist it and his forearms looked ready to burst after twenty reps.

"Why? Why ain't it right for me to be friends with someone that ain't like me?" Luke never used "ain't" but he needed to get down on the coach's prejudiced level. He dropped the bar on the mat with a thud and looked at McCann.

"Certain, very powerful members of the school's alumni don't like the way it makes the program look."

"You mean James Connally don't like the way it makes him look." Luke picked up the bar and started pumping again.

McCann stood up and walked to the door – and Luke knew he had struck a nerve. Then he stopped and looked back at his star athlete.

"Luke, you are in jeopardy of losing your scholarship… and there isn't a damned thing I can do to stop it," McCann closed the door behind him and felt it had been taken care of just like Connally had ordered.

The coach's words did sink in on Luke...but not in the way he had intended. Luke stayed away from Emmaline – but his heart was broken... although he never showed it. His play on the floor remained consistent through the end of the season in March. But, the team finished very poorly, and their losing record turned fans away and toward the spring sports sooner than usual.

In mid-March Luke had just cleaned out his locker in the gym and was headed back across the Quad to the dorm carrying a load of personal laundry in a drawstring bag. The weather was still cool, but the threat of snow was waning – and green shoots of grass had begun to pop here and there. Then he saw her – standing amongst a group of other colored students at the upper end of the far hill. The group seemed to be involved in a celebration – there were hugs and handshakes going in all directions.

Luke detoured and walked up the far hill until he reached the group. Several of the men and women looked at him as though he were interrupting a secret meeting. Emmaline saw him and walked about ten feet out of the crowd to meet him - she had a wide grin on her face.

"Hello, Em."

"Oh, Luke, he did it – he actually did it."

Wesley walked up behind her and put his arm around her waist and planted a kiss on her cheek followed by a glaringly triumphant stare at Luke. Emmie looked down and then looked back at Luke.

"Who – did what?" Luke asked as he felt a tinge of jealousy rising in him.

"Wesley did it!" Emmie smiled wide again. "Dr. King is coming here next week!"

# 56

Georgie's mother had arrived in Gordonsville, Virginia, in 1867, with no apparent means of supporting herself. After Gracie and Thomas procured food for a decent evening meal, Harriett Smith announced that she really wanted to go home to Bamberg, South Carolina, but she didn't really have any way to do so. Her plan was to hop on a Southbound train late one night and jump off with Georgie and the baby the minute she recognized any landmark. Thomas immediately denounced this plan, and he arranged tickets for all of them to return to Christiansburg – and then Waverly. The plan was to get everyone there and decide what to do next. To both of them it was humanitarian – though to Thomas, it worried him even more that they had extra mouths to feed.

The trip home was uneventful except for a nasty spring storm that flew in and forced them to hide under a wooden bridge for almost an hour as wind, rain, and hail pounded the earth around them. Thomas had thrown the buckboard tarp over the horses, but the hail still appeared to take its' toll and the animals were sluggish and sore the rest of the way home. The boys were overjoyed to see all of them return safely – especially Georgie – who they declared the next month's birthday. Rhett and Thomas rubbed the horses down with liniment oil and gave them extra hay and a night in the stalls on straw. Harriett didn't believe Gracie and Thomas could be betrothed and kept asking "wha' dem' younguns' at?" as if children would bring validation of their claim.

Harriett and Georgie and his brother stayed at Waverly for most of the summer of 1867. Georgie's little brother was named Francis, and he was a four-year-old ball of spitfire. Gracie found herself pulling him out of trouble at least five times a day, and she was especially upset by his desire to pick the young vegetables from her garden. Francis' propensity to throw rocks at the livestock made every animal on the farm skittish, but his cuteness was undeniable, and Gracie found herself longing to be a real mother.

Thomas spent most of eachy day with the older boys teaching them to ride, shoot, and fight – much to the chagrin of Gracie and Harriett. His drive was that "men need to be able to defend themselves and their loved ones – especially during this time of uncertainty." Virginia was indeed a lawless frontier and the U.S. Government had been forced to re-occupy the state with Union soldiers and cavalry to defend the rights of all men – not just the freed slaves. The boys were taught to ride horses and fire pistols at breakneck speeds. Their first lesson was to canter to the end of a field and retrieve an apple off a post, then return and put the apple on another post at the other end of the field. This slowly graduated to a gallop, and the apple was replaced with a target at both ends that they had to hit with a thrown rock – then eventually shoot with a Colt .45 revolver. They learned to rope cattle and to herd large groups of steers. Then they learned to fight – first in a pile of hay with fists – then in an open field with sticks they pretended were knives. They were taught the art of cunning and how to outwit their opponent. Gracie taught the boys to read, and they become avid consumers of anything they could get their hands on, especially Western periodicals. In *The Pioneer*, Rhett read about the Comanche Indians ability to fight on horseback with speed and precision. They could ride on the side of their mounts at full gallop and fire twelve arrows per minute from underneath the horse's neck. They were considered the greatest horsemen in the history of the world. Rhett and the other boys wanted to garner these abilities, so in between chores and studies, they trained. Their weapons of choice were the Colt .45 pistol and the Sharps carbine. Over the course of the next four years, they would become some of the most talented cowboys west of the Mississippi.

As August was rolling to a close, Thomas made plans to carry Georgie and his mother and brother back down to South Carolina on the buckboard. According to his calculations it was going to be a two-week trip. Once again, the boys would stay behind to tend to Waverly.

"Why do they waste so many bullets?" Gracie put her arm around Thomas who was leaning against the three-rail fence watching the boys in the upper pasture. "I'm scared they will get hurt."

"Gracie, darling, this country is a powder keg of left over hatred from the war," Thomas needed a shave…and a bath. "They need to know how to protect themselves."

"They train like they are in the military."

"No, they train to defeat the military," Thomas pushed back from the fence and stumbled – Gracie caught him. "The government is the problem – can't you see it?"

Gracie smiled at him…the war was still taking its' toll and she could see it aging him more each day. "I love you," she said.

"We need to spend most of tomorrow getting ready to take Georgie's family south," Thomas started to head toward the barn to start getting the animals fed – then he stopped and turned around. "I love you too." He never took her love for granted – it was just another thing for him to lose...so he protected it without pause.

The road south would be somewhat easy on the horses once they reached North Carolina – coming back up from there would be a different story. They would need to carry water and hay for two weeks, and rest often in the heat of the summer. Travelling at night would be better, so they planned their trip hoping to use the moon whenever they could...and the Southern afternoon thunderstorms were always a threat.

They were leaving the other boys behind to watch the farm again – and this would be for a longer period. Thomas talked to them about keeping a watchful eye on the road, the fields, and the woods. The panhandlers and junk salesmen had started to rear their heads again to peddle their wares. Thomas didn't trust them.

"You all stay together in one room while we are gone – and leave the bells hanging on all the doors," Thomas had said.

"The cat knocks at them all night," offered Rhett.

"Put the cat outside where it belongs."

Thomas made Georgie's family comfortable in the back of the buckboard and then climbed into the seat next to Gracie.

"Above all else – protect each other," Gracie said. "If you need to, you can run to the Drapers – they know we are going to be gone," She looked each of them up and down as if burning their images into her mind. "We love you boys, and we will be back in a fortnight or so."

"We love you too," said Rhett. Tandey and Cozy nodded and smiled.

"Bye, Georgie!" they hollered as the buckboard rolled down the rocky path to the main road south.

Besides a few offers to "rid the white man of his slaves", and a few jeers, and thrown rocks, the road to Bamberg, South Carolina was smoother than Thomas had anticipated, but the distance was much greater. On the eleventh day of travel, the group pulled into a small homestead surrounded by small fields of corn and beans. An old hound dog trotted out from under the porch of the small white structure that was clearly still being built. A dozen hens and one big rooster roamed the yard with two small goats. Thomas was helping Harriett down from the wagon when the screen door opened behind them.

"Oh, I find 'em George – jus' like I tol' you so!" Mrs. Smith beckoned the man to come over and he did so with a very bad limp.

He walked up to Georgie and took him by the shoulders to get a better look. Georgie was almost as tall as he was. "Ma boy 'bout done got he daddy good looks." The man drew Georgie in and held him close until Georgie pushed him away.

"Wh-who are you?" Georgie took a step back.

"Georgie – this yo' pa," Harriett put her arm around him. "He a'int seen you sin' dey sol' him off ten year back. Praise Jesus – ma' famlys back!"

"Why didn't you tell me?" Georgie walked toward the cornfield and the dog followed him.

"Just give him some time," said Gracie. "This is a lot for him to take in."

"Your leg okay?" Thomas asked George senior.

"Cut dat lil' strip back o' ma' foot – kep' me from runnin'."

"Least you a'int got this," Thomas knocked on his leg and it sounded like a rock hitting a tree. Both men laughed. "And...you a'int got to run no more."

Thomas and Gracie stayed on the Bamberg farm for a few days to allow the horses to rest and so Thomas could help George finish the house. Thomas made Georgie help, and by the time they were finished at least the two George's were friends. On the morning of the eighteenth day, the buckboard headed back north. Bad weather and steep inclines hampered their journey, and on day thirty-one Gracie had to take over for Thomas as his stomach started to constrict on him and cause him a great deal of pain. When Gracie crossed into Virginia on day thirty-four...she thought he might be dying.

At two o'clock in the morning on the twentieth day, Rhett heard the bells ring on the kitchen door of Waverly House. He whispered to the other two in the darkness. "Who let the cat back in?"

"Not me," said Tandey.

"I did," said Cozy, "he was cold."

"Okay, back to sleep then," Rhett laid back down.

"Rhett?"

"Yeah,"

"The cat's been 'sleep by ma' head all night," Cozy's voice wavered.

"Tandey – back steps – take the Colt," Rhett said. "Cozy stay here."

A board creaked downstairs.

"In tha' kitchen," said Tandey.

"I'll go down the front and we'll meet at the kitchen – don't shoot me."

Rhett carried the old Colt war revolver that didn't have a trigger guard on it – it had belonged to Dewey Summerlin. They crept down the stairs in the dark. The sounds in the kitchen grew a little louder, but clearly whoever it was was going through the cupboards looking for food. They heard a jar lid being opened and then a clunk on the table – the intruder was in their peaches. Rhett reached the doorway coming from the dining room and peered across to see Tandey standing at the base of the back stairs. He held one finger over his lips to signal silence. Rhett stepped into the lamplight of the kitchen.

"Time for you to go now, mister," Rhett said – and his voice didn't waver.

The startled man stood up and quickly pulled a pistol from his belt. The stench from him was overwhelming...he wore a tattered white shirt that was missing most of its' buttons, and he still wore his confederate greys down to a pair of boots missing the toes. He cocked his pistol.

"I wouldn't do that mister," Tandey stepped in behind him and he quickly glanced back to face this new adversary. The man started laughing.

"Couple of brats! Where's your Mom and Dad?" the man put the pistol on the table and picked up the jar of peaches again.

"I said – get out," Rhett remained calm.

"The way I see it – you children are squatting in an empty house you found – a'int nobody gonna let a scrawny slave move into the big house with 'em," the bearded man drank peaches from the jar with a horrid slurping sound.

"I a'int gonna say it again mister," Rhett cocked the hammer on his revolver.

"You die first!" screamed the man as he picked up his gun and pointed it straight at Rhett's chest. Two shots rang out – one just a split second before the other. The wood of the doorframe next to Rhett's head exploded into splinters and immediately drew blood as hundreds of chards dug into his cheek and forehead. Tandey saw the flash from the kitchen window as the glass exploded inward and the stinking man fell face first onto the table, crushing the legs and collapsing it with his weight. Peaches and glass flew in front of him and littered the far wall. Blood slowly seeped from his head and began to pool on the table and drip onto the floor.

Tandey called out to Rhett to make sure he was okay as the screen door slowly opened.

There, silhouetted against the dimly lit night, with smoke rolling around his body… and pouring from the barrel of the Sharp's… stood a defiant nine-year-old Cozy Summerlin.

# 57

The hard press that Wesley had put on a UVA professor had paid off. On the afternoon of Monday March 25, 1963, the Reverend Martin Luther King jr. arrived by car – and by himself - at his designated hotel on Emmett Street. Professor Gaston met him there and then escorted him to dinner at the cafeteria, which was the only place he was allowed to dine in the area. There were no protesters – most of the faculty as well as the president of the university had disappeared prior to King's arrival. Wes and the professor showed Dr. King around campus and then slowly made their way across the McCormick Road Bridge to Old Cabell Hall. It was a beautiful but cool spring evening in Charlottesville.

Luke's busy basketball schedule had wound down to a disappointing losing season for the Cavaliers – he was kind of glad it was over for now. Following a devastating loss to South Carolina, Luke had made comments to the *Cavalier Daily* about not having enough support from his teammates, and he told the reporter he couldn't do it all by himself. Some of the team turned on him – and he got another tongue lashing from the coach. Tonight though – his only thought was Emmaline Foster. They had talked on the phone a few days earlier and agreed to meet in front of Cabell Hall for Dr. King's speech. Luke wore a white shirt and a tie – and had debated on bringing Emmie a flower – then decided against it. He was nervous. He could feel his collar getting wet around his neck. He hadn't seen enough of her this year…and he missed her terribly. He wondered if she felt the same. Then he saw her and Natalie approaching from the road.

Emmie was magnificently dressed in a black skirt that ended below her knees and a white ruffled blouse tied around her neck by a green ribbon. Her straight black hair was pulled back into a ponytail and another green ribbon held it firmly in place, where it bobbed back and forth symmetrically as she walked. She wore bright, black, newly shined shoes and white bobby socks. Luke's nervousness shot to the boiling point, and he turned around a couple of times to regain his composure.

"Good evening, Lucas," said Natalie.

"Hello, ladies," he smiled at Natalie and turned his gaze to Emmaline.

"We should get inside if we want to get a good place to sit," Emmie held a sweater in her hand, and she gave Luke a small but noticeable enough grin as she walked past him.

Natalie brushed past Luke and caught up with Emmie, "Why do you torture that boy like you do?"

Emmaline stayed silent.

The trio was able to squeeze into the fifteenth row off the stage and they were afforded a great vantage point for Dr. King's speech. Both Luke and Emmaline were surprised at the mix of the crowd – at least a third were white. It was a far cry from a few days earlier when Emmie repeated her mother's comment to Luke that he was going to be "a single grain of rice in a bowl full of black-eyed peas." He smiled at her, and she shyly looked away.

Dr. King rose to the podium to a thunderous standing ovation and what everyone assumed was going to be a fiery sermon turned into a calm political discussion, and a rendering of the calamities facing a society that was feeling the heavy weight of inequality. Dr. King's speech addressed the injustices of wrongly accused colored people – ironically on the thirty-second anniversary of the wrongful indictment of the Scottsboro Boys in Alabama.

"We must transform the jail from a dungeon of shame to a haven of human dignity," Dr. King said.

The crowd remained silent throughout most of the speech - absorbing every word. At the conclusion they all stood again. It was a very emotional evening – Luke watched as Emmie used the sweater to wipe her eyes several times.

Afterwards, Luke offered to drive the girls back to TailPipes, but they said they wanted to walk and talk, but he could walk with them if he liked. They talked about the speech and what it meant for them to be there for it. Luke tried to add to the discussion, but he really couldn't commiserate with what they had gone through their entire lives. Sure, he had been treated differently outside of Prosperity, but it was never because of the color of his skin – just his low standing in life.

"How is you Grandma Bea' doing?" Luke asked – trying to make things more personal.

"The same – still reading her nickel comic books."

Things had gotten extremely awkward between them, and Luke was running out of things to say to her. They got back to TPs and she opened the door to the tiny apartment she shared with Natalie, who brushed past her and went inside. Emmie turned to face Luke.

"Thank you for walking us – it was very kind of you," Emmaline said.

"Kind of me?" Luke spun himself in a circle. "What's going on Em'? Why won't you see me anymore?"

"I want us to be friends...I really do."

"You don't act like it."

"I'm supposed to meet Wes for coffee in a bit – I need to go," she said.

"So - it's Wes?"

"I don't think we can just be friends, Luke," she went inside and closed the door behind her.

"You think he got the hint this time?" Natalie said coyly.

"Stay out of it, Nat."

"What did you tell him?" Natalie glanced out through the curtain. "He's walking slowly back toward the highway."

"I told him I didn't think we could just be friends."

"Did you tell him that you couldn't just be friends...because you were in love with him."

Emmaline started toward her room, "Stay out of it, Natalie!"

The first week of April saw Luke Montgomery being called into the coach's office where the Athletic Director was also waiting for him. He was informed that his distractions during the season had a detrimental effect on the team and they were terminating his scholarship. His "antics" from the previous Monday night had sealed his fate. Certain alumni had "seen enough".

He spent the next few weeks trying to figure out how to pay for his senior year – and tell his parents that he was off the team. The Coach promised not to tell the press until he went home for the summer. He thought about trying out for an NBA team, but he thought his release from UVA would taint any chance he had.

Luke made plans to go back to Prosperity after exams, and he knew his father couldn't afford for him to come back to school – so he planned to go to work in the mines...just like every other son who had failed in their attempt to escape. He sat down and wrote a letter to Emmaline – he planned to slip it under her door on his way out of town the following week...he never got the chance.

It must have been close to three a.m. on the morning of April 26,1963 when there came a loud pounding on the door that immediately stirred Luke and Dom to their feet. It was Dom that ripped the door open to find Joe Millstone standing there.

"Good Lord! What is going on? Is there a fire?" Dom rubbed his eyes.

"The hall phone has been ringing for thirty minutes and I finally walked down there and answered it," Joe looked past Dom at Luke. "It's your mom – I think you'd better come take it.

Both boys walked out into the hall. Joe and Dom stood by the door as Luke walked the thirty feet to pick up the receiver. He seemed to be mostly listening, but then he dropped the receiver back into its' cradle and slid down the wall to the floor. The end door to the dormitory hall opened with a clatter and Coach McCann appeared. He walked past the two boys in the doorway and knelt in front of Luke. He spoke to him for a while and then grasped his hand and pulled him up. Then he hugged him for a few moments, before they both walked back down the hall to Dom and Joe.

It was around eight a.m. when Dominick got to TPs and made his way back to Emmaline and Natalie's place. The morning had become very still, and the arriving cold front had settled in with the harsh reality that the next several days would be unseasonably cold. Dom knocked on the door and Natalie answered – she was dressed for school and looked like she was just about to walk out.

"Hello – is Emmaline still here?"

"Aren't you that friend of Luke's?" Natalie started to close the door. "This ain't gonna work neither."

"Please, I need to speak with her for just a minute," he grabbed the door to keep it from closing.

"You must want me to scream..."

"It's okay, Nat," Emmie emerged from the bedroom in pajama bottoms and Luke's sweatshirt. She stepped into the doorway but kept it cracked to fend off the cold. "What is it, Dom?"

"I'm horrible at this sort of thing...and I want you to know Luke didn't send me here," Dom cleared his throat and wrapped the checkered scarf around his neck tighter.

"Luke went home...he left this note on his desk...his father died last night."

## April 26, 1963

At around 10 a.m in the morning Lucas Montgomery kissed his wife Addie goodbye and drove off in their old Ford pick-up with a basket of pepperoni rolls, two apples, and a jug of cold mountain spring water. He was headed to Clarksburg, West Virginia, 133 miles away, to perform some training for the miners in the Dola Mine. He was to go down into the shaft with a group of twenty-one men to conduct explosive ordinance training that would involve setting and "detonating" several false charges.

The men entered Compass Mine number Two around 9 pm during a shift change and made their way down into the mine through the Dola shaft and crossed over to the face crosscut of No. 5 entry. At around 10:57 pm an arc from a poorly maintained loading machine ignited methane and coal dust. Lucas Montgomery was thrown fifty feet and slammed into a wall. He was killed instantly.

Luke Montgomery and fifty-eight other children lost their fathers in the blink of an eye.

# 58

Gracie Summerlin had driven the team hard ever since she passed over the New River – and she went straight to Timothy Draper. Thomas was pale as a ghost, but he was now burning with a fever. She had stopped often to fetch water from streams to keep cold compresses on his head and chest. She thanked the Lord when a cooling rain shower came through earlier in the day. She pulled up the horse at the Mercantile on the thirty-seventh day since she had left the boys behind at Waverly…and she could barely breathe from the nervousness in her chest. She fell more than jumped from the buckboard and screamed for Katherine to come quickly – then she collapsed on the ground in a heap.

When she awoke, she was lying on the porch in front of the Mercantile with a cold cloth on her forehead. She sat straight up to find Katherine sitting behind her.

"Thomas!" she yelled.

"Calm, sweetie."

"The boys – I have to get home!"

"The boys are just fine – we've been up there every day since you left." Katherine put her hand on Gracie's shoulder.

Gracie took a deep breath…" Where's my Thomas?"

"We have him inside, Gracie," she dipped the cloth in a bucket of water and wringed it out, then she put it back on Gracie's head. "You been drinking any water?"

"Some."

"Not enough."

"Take me to him, please."

Katherine helped Gracie up and walked her through the store and into the back room where Dr. Draper kept his practice. Thomas was lying on a cot with his eyes closed. His fingers were jaundiced and sweat poured from his brow. His blond hair was dirty brown and matted.

"I couldn't help him – I didn't know what else to do," Gracie wiped her eyes on the cloth that Katherine had given her.

"It's good you got him here, Gracie," Timothy Draper turned to face her.

"What's going on with him?"

"He's very sick."

"Just tell me," Gracie wiped her face again. "Is he dying."

"Gracie, he could pull out of this – I will keep him here," the doctor looked down and then back up and into her eyes. "He's very sick…and he is going to die…maybe not this time…maybe not next year…but he will."

Gracie already knew Thomas was dying. She felt it in her heart – it was being torn to pieces. How could she take even one step forward without him? She just couldn't. She sat down on the floor and curled her legs up underneath her skirt. She began to whimper and rock back and forth.

"You have to be strong for him, Gracie," Timothy walked over and put his hand on her shoulder. "He needs you now – more than ever."

She looked up at him and tried again to dry her eyes.

"You go to the boys – and leave him here with us for now."

"I'll take you up to the farm," Katherine said from behind her.

"When he comes home," Timothy helped her get to her feet, "no more meats from now on – and absolutely no whiskey."

Gracie nodded her head and walked out the door with Katherine.

Katherine led the team back to Waverly on the buckboard. Gracie sat next to her in exhaustive silence for most of the trip. The long hot summer was ending and there was just that slight smell of Fall in the air. The leaves had just sparsely begun to change to burnt orange – but none were falling yet.

"The boys did well?"

"Nothing died that I could tell," Katherine grinned just a little.

"That was a much harder trip than we imagined, Mrs. Draper," Gracie let out a sigh, "not going south again if I can help it."

"I will tell you – one morning I went up to the house and the boys were acting strangely," she looked over at Gracie. "I had them a basket with jam and cornbread, but they wouldn't let me go inside and heat it up for them. They said they had a bunch of chores and would get to eatin' it later according to Tandey."

"They probably had a mess in the kitchen," Gracie said. "You know how boys are when left to their own accord."

"Probably right – just seemed nervous the three of 'em."

"They act a little nervous sometimes – I think they may be scared we are going to find a relative to send them too. Plus, Thomas has them on their guard for pretty much anything – all the time," Gracie did manage a smile when she thought of him. "You know how he can be – very protective of us all."

"That's not a bad thing in this day and age," Katherine brought the buckboard to a halt just in front of the house. "The boys can take it from here."

"Mama!" It was Cozy…he came running up from the lower pasture where he was forking hay to the cows from the back of a pull cart.

Gracie climbed down just before he hit her like a runaway gelding.

"Where are your brothers?"

"Upper pasture, Mama," Cozy was grinning from ear to ear. "We have another foal, Mama, jet-black with a white blaze. Can I have him?"

"Well, that's going to be up for discussion – isn't it?" Gracie walked toward the barn with her arm around Cozy.

"Where's Papa?"

"He will be along soon…" she trailed off with no better explanation in her mind.

"I'm going to head back to the Mercantile, Ms. Grace," Katherine called after her. "I'll come back in the morning with any news."

Gracie turned and stared at her for a minute, as if she was thinking of the right thing to say – but she was so tired she couldn't muster anything more than, "Goodbye then, thank you," she turned and continued with Cozy. "I'ma need you boys to unhook and pasture the team while I get some tea."

"Yes, ma'am," Cozy could feel her starting to sway by his side.

Gracie took a few more steps before she went headfirst into the grass and leaves.

When Gracie came to, she was in her bed and the boys were standing over her like they were on some sort of death watch. Katherine squeezed out a cold cloth and put it back on her forehead. "I'm going to get these boys some supper after I see to it that they wash up some," Katherine walked to the window and pulled the thin curtains closed to block out any light that might creep in from the setting twilight.

"I can manage," Gracie tried to prop herself up.

"What you can manage is a well-deserved good night's sleep," Katherine gently pushed her head back to the pillow. "These boys have been just fine - one more night won't do them in."

Gracie closed her eyes and didn't hear anything until the rooster started crowing the next morning around five. She sat up and put her slippers on then strolled to the kitchen in her night-shirt to make the boys some breakfast. Around six they all wandered in and sat around a table full of eggs, salt pork, and frybread. They began to eat like they hadn't seen food for days. Gracie let them finish before she sat down at the table and placed her hands in front of her as they washed down their meal with cold milk. Then she closed her eyes and began to speak.

"Lord, please forgive these boys for not pausing to thank you for your blessings on this beautiful morning. They just must have really missed their Mama's cooking. Thank you for taking such good care of them whilst we was gone – and Lord I pray you will guide my hands to fixing this rickety kitchen table that wasn't so rickety when I left. Please give me the strength to help Thomas change out the pane of glass above the stove that wasn't broke before…and above all else please assure me that the fresh dug ground next to Samuel's grave doesn't really have a body under it. Thank you, Jesus. Amen."

"Amen," said Cozy as Tandey kicked him under the table and Rhett shot him a dagger stare.

Gracie sat staring at the boys one by one as they sat around the table. Rhett still had a napkin sticking out of his shirt. There was deathly silence as they all just kept looking around at one another. Then the rooster crowed again.

"Mama – I has to tell –"Cozy stood up and almost knocked his chair over.

Then Rhett rose to his feet and put his hand on Cozy's shoulder…and he spoke softly.

"Ms. Gracie…while you was gone…I killed a man," Rhett lowered his eyes and sat back down.

"Who?"

"Don't know him…he had a gun."

"Hide the grave better – it has to look just like it did before you dug it up."

Gracie picked up the dishes and walked to the wash sink. She gritted her teeth and did her best not to scream…

"Papa will be home soon…please get to your chores," she said.

The boys grabbed their boots and scrambled out the screen door – it slammed back with a bang."

Gracie sat back down at the table and put a dishcloth over her face – then she laid her head down on the table and began to cry.

A few weeks passed before Gracie had the boys up at the Mercantile to pick up some dry goods one afternoon. The Drapers stood on the porch talking to a man with a star on his vest who held a piece of paper out to them in one hand. As they climbed up the stairs Dr. Draper called out to her. "Gracie, haven't by chance you and the boys seen this man, have you?" Gracie glanced at the boys, and they walked over to the group. The man turned and held up a photograph. Cozy stumbled backward and fell square on his butt.

"The boy looks like he's seen a ghost ma'am," the man looked down at Cozy.

"Likely he ain't ne'r seen a pitcher like that 'un," Gracie turned and pulled Cozy up by his outstretched hand. "an' that man – he look like a monster."

"I'm Marshal Simmons from up Lynchburg way," he glanced across the boys faces. "This man – goes by Godfor or Godfrey – anyway he's gotten himself a nickname. The Ghoul of Gettysburg...robbed the dead on countless battlefields around Virginia. Followed Lee from a distance mostly. Dug up fresh graves too."

Gracie looked at the photograph again – it showed a white man with hideous facial features including an enormous nose that covered more than half of a long drawn face. He wore a white shirt and darkly stained white pants that Gracie assumed were covered with blood. He could have passed for a butcher. "That's a pret' bad spectacle of uh man."

"He may have killed a man and his wife outside Lynchburg. Since the war ended, he goes looking for abandoned homes – he may have found one occupied or been there when they come home," the man put his hand on the butt of his pistol. "We aim to hang him."

"We'll let the Draper's know if he wanders up our way," Gracie turned the boys and went inside the Mercantile.

The ride home on the buckboard was quiet until Cozy spoke up.

"I's sorry mama,"

"'Bout what?"

"That man."

"Don't worry, Sweetie.... sounds like ya'll done in the devil himself."

# 59

She didn't go to the funeral.

She didn't answer his letter.

She let a few weeks go by.

But, she read his letter ten times a day.

Now, she sat in the front seat of her brother James' Bel Air as it headed out of Charlottesville toward Richmond – and home. She looked out the window at the bright Spring sunshine and clutched Luke's letter in her right hand.

"What ya got there sis'?" James put his hand on the top of the steering wheel and settled back into his seat as he turned out onto the highway headed east.

"Nothing, really."

"Hasn't left your hands since I got here to pick you up."

"When do you go back to Lejuene?" Emmaline kept her stare out the window.

"You act like you aren't happy to see me."

"I told them I would ride the bus home."

"It's just me and you – we can take our time, you know," James smiled from behind his freshly shaven face. "We can catch up."

"Are you in a hurry to get back to Church Hill?"

"Not today I ain't."

"Ever been to West Virginia?"

"Once – by accident."

"Can you take me there?" She looked at him with the eyes that always made him stop what he was doing for her – no matter what.

"Got something to do with that letter?"

"Maybe."

"Let's stop and get a map – I ain't gonna aimlessly drive through West Virginia looking for some boy," James laughed. "You sure you got the right state? – ain't too many colored folks up that way you know." He winked at her.

"Right state – just maybe the wrong time," she sighed and gave him a small grin.

"Thanks, Jimmy."

"It's James now," he laughed again. "The Marines say I'm a man now – I have to act the part."

"OK, Flash," she used his high school football nickname because he loved being called that on Friday nights…and she knew it.

They pulled into a Marathon Oil station and James went inside for a few minutes. He came back out with a map and two pops.

"Where to next, my dear?" He slammed the door shut behind him and started to open the folded map between them.

Luke Montgomery was sitting on the front steps of the little red brick home that the mining company allowed his family to reside in as long as his father toiled in the mines. He glanced up as the Bel Air pulled to a stop and Emmaline stepped out of the passenger door. She looked as beautiful now as she ever did, but Luke didn't stand up – instead he looked at her inquisitively as she slowly walked through the loose red gravel that was his front yard. She reached the base of the steps and stood looking at him face to face – her standing, and him still seated.

"Hello, Em," he glanced past her at the car. "Why are you here?"

"You left so quickly I didn't get to see you…to tell you how sorry-"

"I'm not coming back to school."

"Dom told me about your scholarship."

"It's not even that," he looked back at her, and his eyes seemed to look right through her. "My mother can't do this alone."

"She could move to Charlottesville while you finish."

"We are coal miners – we don't just move to another town when things go bad, Emmaline. We don't have money for that."

"Doesn't the mining company help? – do they do anything?"

"Do you want to come inside, Em?" Luke stood up and she saw for the first time that he was wearing overalls covered in soot. "I'm sure my mother would like to see you again."

"What are you wearing that for?"

"I'm working in the mine – what did you think I was going to do?"

"You have to come back to school!" She reached out and took his hand.

"There is nothing back there for me…I have to stay here."

"Your parents didn't want that for you." She felt a tear coming but blinked it away.

"Sometimes life deals you a bad hand…this is my bad hand I guess."

"The scholarship thing is my fault – maybe I could talk to the coach or the chancellor."

"Don't make waves - you need to finish…" Luke tried to lead her up the steps.

"My brother is waiting, he's home on leave from the Marines, I'm sorry."

"I wondered who that was…figured you would tell me if you thought it was important," he let go of her hand.

"I – I guess I will need to say goodbye to you then – if you won't come back," she had to blink harder.

"What did you come here for? You said we couldn't even be friends."

"I'm very sorry about your father," she trailed off. "Luke, everything bad that has happened to you…school…the team…your job in Draper – I cost you all of that -even some of your friends."

"I won't ever regret knowing you, Emmaline Foster," Luke lowered his eyes. "You can't make me do that."

"And – I will never forget you," she leaned in and kissed him on the cheek. "You will always be my friend."

Luke watched as the Bel Air headed down the dirty old road where he lived in Prosperity, West Virginia until it was out of sight around a curve. Emmaline was right about one thing, he had promised his parents he would not work in the mines, and he realized he had just been handed a better idea.

Back on the highway James had them finally headed toward Richmond – and home…Emmaline for the Summer and James for another three days. He reached over and put his hand on her shoulder as she laid her head against the window with Luke's sweatshirt covering her face. James knew she was crying so he decided to just let her be for now. An hour later he decided to say what was on his mind.

"You know – dad really likes that one." James laughed. "And he don't like too many."

Emmaline removed the shirt from her face and smiled – her eyes were swollen.

"Are you sad because you broke his heart?"

"No, I'm sad because I broke my own."

# 60

August of 1871 had been as hot as anyone could remember. Gracie and her boys made almost daily trips down to the river in the afternoons to cool off. She had done her very best to keep Thomas comfortable…cold tubs seemed to be the best thing for his pain. His new diet – the only one he could tolerate – had made his weight dangerously low. In fact, twelve-year-old Cozy had grown so much that he was taller and heavier than Thomas now. Rhett and Tandey were hands down the greatest horsemen in all of Pulaski County – and maybe even in all of Virginia. They won competitions everywhere, including at the recently restarted Virginia State Fair in Doswell near the site of the Meadow Farm, which would one day produce the great racer *Secretariat*. The boys excelled at barrel racing and roping, two activities which they naturally practiced daily while running the Summerlin Angus herd which had grown to almost a hundred head. Gracie and Thomas were so very proud of them. They had tried to have children of their own, but it didn't seem to be a gift that God was going to provide them. They were at peace with it – as disappointing as it was.

This morning had a simple bite of Autumn to it, and the early mists were heavy and slow moving in the pastures and over the ridges. The great sycamores seemed to hide on the very edge of it all and in the midst was the majestic Waverly House with its grand oaks in front. Gracie went to Thomas before sunrise, and he pleaded his case to go outside in the cool morning air to sit under the oak and watch her in the swing. He mostly made it there under his own power, but Gracie helped him sit down and handed him a warm cup of sassafras tea which he held in his hands, for warmth mainly. Getting it to his lips without her help was not going to happen. He was able to unstrap the Palmer leg and toss it to the side so he could "feel the wet grass on his leg."

Gracie pulled some honeysuckle from the fence line and tied it in a crown around her face and through her long black hair. She knew he loved the smell of it on her. She simply shimmered in the early morning black and white. Slowly she went back and forth but not too high. She clung by the ropes with her arms wrapped to the elbow on both sides, and sipped at her tea as the steam rolled from it to join the morning mist. Her sheer nightgown flowed past her bare shoulders and rolled off her beautiful legs as she cut through the stillness. Thomas smiled at her and clutched his teacup. He loved her so much. He breathed as deeply as he could afford and let the smell of her drift through his body. It filled him.

Gracie watched him from the swing, and she smiled every time she rose above him. But her heart was pounding…so hard she could hear it – and feel it. The mist swirled around her as she slowly glided back and forth. Behind her the sun began to creep golden beams into the meadows over the eastern rise. The glow framed the beauty of Gracie – and to Thomas she looked like an angel. He smiled even as his breathing slowed. The teacup rolled from his hands and into the grass. Gracie was by his side at once, and she kissed him softly.

She put her head on his chest and together they took their breaths. Gracie drew hers in as Thomas lightly exhaled.

The breaths came further and further apart until she found herself having to take hers more often.

"Don't forget – lilacs and honeysuckle."

"I won't my love," Gracie had to struggle to keep her voice from wavering.

"Elijah," Thomas said.

Gracie held him tightly.

"…is a fitting name." Thomas' breathing went shallower even still.

Gracie put his hand on her belly and allowed him to breathe in the honeysuckle that framed her face. She put her head back onto his chest and felt him breathe. Then nothing. Then another shorter breath. "I love you Mr. Thomas," she felt him breathe again but just barely. "I will see you again – I promise it." She kept her head on his chest and prayed for another breath… but it never came. She lifted her head and kissed him long and hard. Then she settled into his chest again…and every ounce of strength in her body ran from her eyes into his shirt.

Gracie Summerlin's life took a cruel turn that morning – and she would never wholly recover from it.

# 61

Emmaline Foster's summer was decidedly calmer than most of the colored community in 1963. While she was leading Bible camps and Sunday School at the AME Church in Richmond, protests were exploding across the country, and especially in the South. On June 12th the movement was dealt a devastating blow when fiery Civil Rights leader Medgar Evers was murdered in front of his family in Jackson, Mississippi. Emmie's whole church was in an uproar and demanding change while planning a march on Washington for August. Twenty-one-year-old Emmaline would be in her fifties before Evers killer would be brought to justice. Her brother James had returned to Camp Lejeune and her mother and father were busy working, so Emmaline spent a great deal of time with Grandma Bea reading her comics, and hoping she would participate in piecing her great grandmother's diary back together. Beatrice wasn't any help in this at all, but she sure loved Casper the friendly ghost.

Each night when Emmaline went to bed, she would pull Luke's letter from under her pillow and read it in the low lamplight. She most certainly could recite it by now. Most nights this process ended with a long sigh or a few tears and sometimes she dreamed of him. But tonight, she fell asleep reading it and it fell from her fingers onto the pillow next to her long black hair. When her mother came in to turn out the light, Emmaline never heard her – until she sat next to her on the bed.

"Do we need to talk about this?"

Emmie opened her eyes sheepishly and saw her mother holding the letter.

"It's nothing, Mother, really," she reached for the letter, but Mathilde Foster pulled it back.

"This thing is falling apart you've handled it so much."

"Mother…"

"Emmie," Mathilde put the palm of her hand on her daughter's face. "Live your best life, my dear."

"You know it's not that easy," she rolled on her side and faced away from her mother, who folded up the note and put it next to the lamp which she clicked off.

"Good night."

"Good night." Emmaline waited for her mother to leave before she turned the lamp back on and read the letter again.

*My dearest Emmaline;*

*Since the day we ran into each other I have not been able to go five minutes without thinking of you. I won't pretend that it is anything that I can just stop from happening. You seem to worry about our differences - this is something I simply don't see when I am with you. I meant every bit of it when I told you that I love you. I only wish you felt what I did when you kissed me in Draper. I think about that moment all day every day. I guess there comes a moment in time when you feel like you are exactly where you are supposed to be - with me, that is when I am with you. If you don't feel the same way, then I will have to try and forget you, even though I know I never will. I want you to remember one thing - my arms are always open and waiting to hold you. I do love you and I surely always will. I wish you nothing but happiness wherever your life takes you.*

*All my love,*
*Luke*

"My God – that is one dopey letter," she whispered to herself. She folded up the letter and put it back under her pillow, then she turned out the light and laid her head back down – only this time she closed her eyes and smiled.

The next morning Emmaline waited for her parents to leave for work before she cleaned up after Grandma Bea and helped her go down for a nap. She sat at the kitchen table twirling an empty teacup in her fingers for at least fifteen minutes before she got the nerve to pick up the phone receiver and start to dial. Before dialing the last number, she stopped and hung up. She took a deep breath and dialed again. She heard the phone ringing…once…twice…halfway through the third she started to hang up, but then she heard a voice.

"Hello?"

"Mrs. Montgomery?"

"Yes."

"This is Emmaline Foster."

"Oh, Sweetie…it's so good to hear your voice," Addie sat down on the kitchen floor.

"I'm so sorry about Mr. Lucas."

"Thank you, dear."

"Can I maybe speak to Luke,"

"I'm sorry, Honey, he's not here."

"Can he call when he gets back from the mine…I really need to speak to him."

"No, I mean he's not here – in Prosperity...he's gone."

"I'm sorry – I don't understand." Emmie sounded confused.

"He left for Parris Island two weeks ago."

"Parris Island?" she already knew what that meant.

"Yes, Sweetie – he's joined the Marines."

# 62

It was basically no time at all before the vultures began to encircle Waverly Plantation. David Connally arrived with his despondent wife and their two boys within weeks of the passing of Thomas Summerlin. Thomas had warned Gracie that he would come if he found out...the news had somehow spread to Roanoke quickly.

Rhett, Tandey, and Cozy had joined Gracie as she sat with Thomas under the oak tree. They all lay there and stayed relatively quiet for most of the day, until Gracie announced that her boys needed to eat. As she walked Cozy back up to the house, the older boys gently moved Thomas to the barn and placed him inside the pine coffin that he had built for himself over the past year. He wanted this to be as easy as possible for all of them, and he took great strides to ensure that it was. The next day, together as a family, Gracie and the boys buried Thomas underneath the large oak just outside the pasture fence at the first ridge. This vantage overlooked the valley and the house below, and it marked where the family cemetery had resided since the early 1700's. Gracie kept her promise to her husband, and they filled his casket with Honeysuckle and Lilac...then they planted roses around his final resting place.

Knowing for all these years that her time with him was limited didn't make any of this any easier, and Gracie cried every day now – sometimes uncontrollably. Some of it was loss...some of it was fear of the unknown...most of it was intuition.

The barrister Joseph Millstone arrived an hour before the Connally party made their triumphant stroll toward the house from their buckboard which was pulled by two magnificent geldings. Joseph warned Gracie that the new State Representative was on his way…and that he planned to claim the property as his inheritance.

"He's become a very powerful man since the war, Gracie," Joseph said. "He did his best to stay on both sides of the conflict – and the Yanks are welcoming him into power here."

"Thomas assured us that this would be our home," if only Gracie could find the strength to fight.

"It's going to be okay – the Connally's want you to stay in the Summer House."

"Nobody has lived in that house for decades." Gracie sat on the steps holding her knees to her chest. "How can he just waltz up here and do this?"

"He is family…"

"So am I! I'm his wife!"

"The state has declared that to be illegal – I'm sorry Ms. Grace."

"Thomas had papers drawn up – did he not?"

"Do you have those papers?" Joseph sat down next to her.

"I have the will – is there not a duplicate in your office?"

"Gracie – I think I can help you negotiate with Mr. Connally."

"He a'int here to negotiate! He's here to steal my family's home!"

"He's white…and powerful. You won't win this."

"Because I'm a negro woman! I get it." Gracie walked toward the barn, and Cozy followed her and tried to hold her hand until she finally gave in.

Gracie sat with the boys by the barn for a long while. From the house it looked as though they were having a calm picnic in the shade of a large sycamore. She was explaining everything to her boys, and at times it appeared that Rhett and Cozy were beginning to get quite agitated, but then she would calm them back down. As the sun was just showing its first hint of giving up the day she walked back down to the house where the "negotiation" was underway without her.

"I need to talk with Dr. Draper about moving our cows to his land in the bottom," was Gracie's opening salvo.

"Honey, the herd is part of the farm – they stay," David Connally was a condescending ass just like she remembered him to be.

"I a'int your Honey...and those are my cows."

"Don't you go getting surly with me or I can just have your scrawny ass hauled away," Connally looked at the barrister. "This isn't going anywhere Millstone...I'll leave you to wrap it up and see her and those vagabond children off the property by tomorrow."

Connally walked back to the buckboard and turned the team back down the drive toward the Mercantile.

"Ms. Grace, I would advise you to be reasonable about all of this," Joseph tried to put his hand on her shoulder, and she backed up a step.

"Don't touch me! You know this is not what he wanted!"

"Nevertheless...it is going to happen," Millstone looked over at the boys who were now standing ready to defend the woman they considered their mother. "He's offered you a home to raise your boys in – and a chance to stay here at least."

Gracie looked at the boys who stood huddled twenty feet away. I can't fight this one without my Thomas, she thought. She shook her head in disgust.

"I want the boy's horses and all their tack, and the boy's guns. I want our buckboard and harness. I want my sewing cabinet that was a wedding gift. I want my cow – just the one. I want all that we have canned and smoked this season. I want the boys to have paying jobs up here on the farm if they choose. I want to be able to visit my husband's grave whenever I choose – day or night." Gracie hung her head in defeat knowing she had no chance for this to go in her favor...nobody was out there that could fight for her in a court and win...she decided to take what she could get.

"I think all of that will be acceptable to Mr. Connally," Joseph lowered his eyes. "I wish I saw any other way around any of this, but I don't think this is a fight you can win...and it could cost you everything...taking the Summer House is the right thing to do."

"I want it drawn up legal – stating that I Gracie Summerlin own the Summer House and surrounding property and have rights to leave it to who I see fit when I die."

"I'll draw up papers, but I think you should leave off the Summerlin name since the state doesn't recognize it." Millstone walked back toward his horse that was tied up near the barn.

"I want one more thing!" Gracie called after him.

"What's that?"

"I want my swing...and it's Grace Henry."

# 63

Parris Island was everything they promised in the brochure and more. June through August of 1963 in the Lowcountry of South Carolina was a monsoon and humidity plagued, mosquito and snake infested nightmare. Luke Montgomery's physicality as a former college athlete made boot camp easier for him – at first. Once his squad leader found out who he was, he was expected to move twice as fast, and go twice as far as everyone else in his platoon. As his sergeant liked to say – "Parris Island is just like your next home in Southeast Asia – we are just getting you prepared." Thankfully Luke knew he would be heading to Camp Pendleton in California when he finished his induction into the Marine Corps. As far away from Emmaline Foster as his new path could take him. He had to forget about her…so why couldn't he. Sleepless nights thinking of her made for long days on the obstacle courses. He knew his mother had told her where he was – but she hadn't tried to reach him, and he wasn't ready to be shot down for the umpteenth time again anyway. It was better this way, right?

Instead, Luke turned his energy into becoming the finest Marine he could be. He was the true embodiment of "no man gets left behind", and it showed every day on the course, on the firing range, in the woods, and in the barracks. Some of the guys that were just out of high school were quick to regret their decision and longed for the comfort of home… Luke brought encouragement to every one of them, just like he did on the basketball court to his teammates. It also helped to pass the time and make Emmaline more of just a passing thought. But when he did have one of those passing thoughts it poured over him like a wave and scrambled him back to reality.

At the end of thirteen weeks of grueling physical and mental training, recruits experience a rite of passage known as "The Crucible'. The best description for this torture in a recruit's training is a 54-hour, 40-mile, sleep deprived, forced starvation, of physical and mental anguish. When it's all over you are a Marine – a member of the Band of Brothers. Luke Montgomery dragged many of his brothers by their belts and backpacks through two nights of the driving rain of a late August tropical storm. His dedication would not go unnoticed.

Luke crossed through the hallowed gates of Camp Pendleton in Oceanside, California, three days after his mother arrived in Beaufort, South Carolina on a Greyhound bus to kiss him goodbye. They made promises to see each other whenever they could, and Luke held her as she cried. Half of his monthly pay was going to help her stay in their home back in West Virginia even though Luke wanted her to move back closer to her family in Pennsylvania. California was an eye opener for Luke, and he not only fell right into his training for combat, but he also found a love for the beach, and ultimately he ventured into the ocean. He was one paycheck away from putting money down on a surfboard when the sergeant called him into his office as he came off the gunnery range one afternoon.

Luke's sergeant explained the development of the Military Assistance Command Vietnam – Studies and Observations Group and the proposed role it would have if war were to break out in Southeast Asia. The force was to be an all-volunteer Special Operations force that would be trained in all walks of Vietnamese life and learn to fire the enemy's weapons if it became necessary. Luke thought about it for less than 24 hours, and two days after that he was on a flight back to North Carolina, and Camp Lejeune for Recon training and full immersion. He didn't tell his mother, and she never knew he was no longer in California prior to his deployment.

Luke arrived at the coastal base ten days before John Fitzgerald Kennedy was assassinated in Dallas on November 22, 1963. He told the base sentry that he was assigned to SOG and after a brief phone call was made, he was picked up and driven several miles into the base to a Quonset hut deep in the coastal pine forest. His driver dropped him and his rucksack on the curb near the door and drove away without a word. Luke threw his sack over his shoulder and ventured inside as night began to fall, and the woods around the hut grew darker. Inside there was a corporal sitting behind a pale green metal desk with a clipboard in his hand. Luke stood at attention."Private First-Class Montgomery reporting for duty, sir."

"At ease, private," the man stood up from behind the desk. "In this unit we are all one and the same – the SOG."

"Yes sir!" retorted Luke confidently.

"I am the barracks lead here, and your liaison to get you settled," the corporal wrote briefly on the clipboard. "I am Corporal James Foster."

Luke glanced down in realization and held back the smile that was trying to push its way out.

"Glad to be here, sir."

"Welcome, Luke," he said. "I'll show you to your bunk."

# 64

"Elijah is a good name," thought Gracie as she used her toes to slowly move the swing back and forth. It was hanging from a new tree...on a different hill...but it was the same rope and same boards. And it belonged to her. She rubbed her bare hand across her now obviously protruding belly, got to her feet, wrapped her sweater tightly around her shoulders, and walked the fifteen steps to the front porch of Summer House.

The boys were seated around the table and had prepared a nice quick meal for themselves. They were waiting for Gracie to come in and bless the food.

"Getting mighty chilly out – Tandey, can you bring in more wood for the stove after supper?' Gracie sat down in the hard oak chair at the head of their table.

"I'll have to chop some," said Tandey.

"Then go while it's still light out...I'll put your supper on the stove."

"Yes ma'am," Tandey grabbed a biscuit and headed out the front door.

"Get your coat," she called out behind him barely loud enough to be audible.

Gracie's life had been completely overturned with the loss of her husband, and now the home she shared with Thomas and the boys had been ripped from under them. She knew she had to go on, but it took every ounce of her strength just to get out of bed in the morning. Maybe it was the pregnancy dragging her down. She knew she had to regroup and think of something to get their lives back on track – especially with another mouth to feed coming soon. The Summer House was dank and dark when they first entered. Cobwebs, fleas, spiders, snakes, racoons, and opossums were just a few of the guests that inhabited the place where nobody had lived for decades. The worst thing they encountered though, was the large family of squirrels living in the ceiling. It took the boys days to trap or kill them all. The only good side was that everything hit the dinner table. Finally, after several weeks the family had reached a point where sleeping in the house wasn't just a little terrorizing. They had built a small corral out back and Gracie had started a new garden…and the boys had hung her swing from the big oak out front. Gracie told them it was the perfect vantage point for her to keep an eye on the demon up the hill. Gracie started to work at the Mercantile a few days a week, and she and Katherine became even better friends. The boys worked up at Waverly for not much money – mostly just grain and flour. They hated the Connallys more each day and Gracie knew the situation couldn't last, but they needed what little they got from them.

Tandey came back inside with an armful of split oak which he promptly dropped into the basket on the floor next to the stove.

"That was too fast," said Gracie.

"I cut enough for tonight," Tandey was slightly out of breath. "I'll cut a larger stack in the morning before we go up the hill." He opened the top lid to the stove with a folded flour sack over his hand and tossed several pieces inside, then he grabbed his plate and sat down.

"How much longer we need to go up dat hill?" asked Cozy.

"We need the supplies y'all are bringing."

"We can work somewhere's else and get some real money," Rhett bit a biscuit in half and looked at Tandey.

"We hate going up there – and we hate that man," Cozy said.

"He unstrapped his belt and whooped Cozy good yesterday for dropping a basket of eggs." Rhett swallowed and tossed in the other half of his biscuit. "Lucky I didn't kill him right there…we a'in't slaves."

"You'll not kill another man – do you understand...and those are my chickens too," Gracie looked at him sternly.

"That man – he gave us no choice."

"You know – that Connally is selling off the herd," Tandey took a sip of his buttermilk and winced – it wasn't his favorite.

"How do you mean?" asked Gracie.

"Some to the slaughterhouse – some to other men that come up there," Tandey said.

"How many's gone?"

"At least half…he says he's gonna raise racing horses," Rhett shook his head.

"With our brood mares? Bastard."

"Mama!" said Cozy.

"He asked Rhett if he could break a couple of two-year-olds," Tandey stood up and went to the stove for another biscuit.

"I don't want you boys getting hurt for him." Gracie folded her hands on the table. Her long black hair now had a single white streak running through it and she told the boys it would never get cut because Thomas placed it there. She caught her breath as the baby kicked her – and then smiled.

"Can you read to us tonight?" Cozy asked as he slid a Western magazine toward her.

"Let's see how you do with it first – come sit with me."

Cozy dragged his heavy chair across the old wood floor with a screech and crawled up next to Gracie. He was getting bigger by the day – and stronger…he was going to be a mountain of a man in the blink of an eye. For now, he was but twelve.

He read slowly from a page he had previously marked. "T-the Tekas Rangers fight …the..um…com…com..chi…"

"Comanche," said Gracie. "Good try – go on."

Cozy read for a while until eventually the older boys put their heads on the table and fell asleep. Gracie told Cozy it was time for bed.

"Why are they hunting the com…?"

"Comanche," Gracie put her hand on his cheek. "They want all of the land, Cozy…and they will do anything to get it."

"Seems mean."

"They call it progress," she folded up the magazine and put it on top of the Martha Washington cabinet. "That's why our freedom must endure…as little of it as we have."

The birth of Elijah Bethea Henry came just in time to free Gracie from enduring her pregnancy during the sweltering summer that was coming. He was a beautiful baby boy and loaded with energy, and he had many of the subtle features of Thomas. Mostly features that only Gracie would immediately recognize. Katherine Draper had come in the middle of the night for the birth after being summoned by a frantic Tandey on horseback. Gracie could hear the boys pacing in the other room as dawn arose, and she finally yelled for them to go outside.

"Don't be too hard on them…you need to remember they already lost Thomas, and they are scared to death of losing you too." Katherine had said.

In the middle of July Gracie sat on the front porch of Summer House rocking Elijah back and forth in a chair they had found in the cellar and Rhett had modified. It wasn't perfect, but it worked. It made a knocking noise every time Gracie rolled forward, but Elijah was accustomed to it, and it seemed to soothe him. Gracie had just buttoned her blouse back closed when she saw Katherine coming around the bend in the road with another woman. Elijah had begun to drift off, but he sprung back awake as the two ladies came up the two rickety wooden stairs onto the porch.

"Good afternoon, Gracie," Katherine didn't usually sound so formal. "I have a lady here from Richmond who has come to the Mercantile and asked for you by name…this is Lucy Brooks from Richmond."

"Hello, ma'am," Gracie offered.

"Do you mind if we sit and talk a bit?" Lucy asked.

"As you can see, I've got time on my hands," Gracie lifted the baby and cradled him in the crook of her right arm.

"Your baby is beautiful," Lucy said.

"He's not for sale," Gracie may have been letting the summer heat get to her a little.

Lucy Brooks laughed, "I heard about your efforts to place the boys you're caring for and I wanted to come and meet you – because I know you and Ms. Draper found success in getting George back to his family."

"Did you find Cozy and Tandey's mother?"

"No, unfortunately that's not why I'm here." Lucy sat sideways on the steps and looked at Gracie.

"Okay, why then?"

"I know after all you have been through you are skeptical of strangers, but I have an opportunity for you in Richmond."

"That's far away."

"I run the Friend's Asylum for Colored Orphans…we make every effort to find children's lost parents – or place them with new parents like you have done with your boys," Lucy took a paper fan from her pocket and began to wave it back and forth.

"What does that have to do with me and my boys?"

"Give her a chance, Gracie," Katherine reached for Elijah, and Gracie gladly handed him over for a few minutes.

"I'd love it if you would come to Richmond and live there…we have a house for you and your boys…and you could teach the other children to read and write – and help us place them." Lucy smiled at her.

"Thank you, ma'am, but my home is here. I don't want my boys in a city like Richmond."

"We can pay you, and your boys can go to the school."

Gracie glanced at Katherine and said, "I'm not leaving here…this is my home."

"I have forty children who could use someone like you." Lucy leaned forward.

"Why do you care so much about these children?" Gracie wiped the sweat from her brow with her sleeve.

"I was a slave just like you for most of my life…and I was forced to sell four of my children so the others could be free."

"You sold your own children?"

"The older boys were promised work in a factory, and they are free men now…my daughter I regret – she's gone now – died in slavery in Tennessee ten years back." Lucy stood up and walked toward Gracie.

"How can I believe your story?"

"Because I look white? My mother was a negro slave, and I don't know who my white father was. Sometimes when you put two ingredients in a pot you end up with one or the other," She laughed.

"I just…don't want to leave this place – my husband is buried here…and you wouldn't know it right now, but the Summers are cooler here." Gracie finally smiled at her.

"Fair enough," Lucy took Gracie by the hand. "There's a small boy's home about ten miles downriver toward Christiansburg. We help to fund them…would you be willing to help with their teaching?"

Gracie thought long and hard and then looked at Katherine.

"You can still help out at the Mercantile…and I will help you with teaching them." Katherine said as she returned Elijah to Gracie's lap.

"I would like that quite much I believe…it might give me some joy in life...okay I will." Gracie rose with Elijah and walked down the steps behind them.

Lucy turned to face her. "I know it's hard to believe I was a slave, but I promise you my mother was darker than you."

Gracie smiled at her.

"Like I said – when you mix all the ingredients in a pot you never know what you can get," Ms. Brooks held Elijah's little hand in hers. "Same reason this precious little one has the most beautiful blue eyes I've ever seen."

## May 1874

*Thomas' Nighttime Lightening* didn't eat any grain that morning or that afternoon. Just before dusk he headed way up pasture to the top of the hill where the old oak thrust her branches out over the green grass. Two old rotting pieces of rope hung from the strongest branch just outside the fence. Twenty feet away was the final resting place of his boy, Thomas Summerlin. He stopped and looked over the three-rail fence at the gravesite and gave a tiny snort and swung his head from side to side – his dark mane was still the most magnificent of any horse for "five counties around". A few minutes later, *Lightening* went to his knees and sat sentinel over Thomas' grave. The sun was sinking slowly over the upper hill leading to the back pastures and miles of rolling land.

In the barn, *Sunshine 'til Midnight* lay on her side giving birth to the pair's fifth and final foal. She was struggling mightily with this one – it was breached, and two teenage boys were doing their best to pull it free. They had a rope tied around one hoof while their father maintained pressure on the other end. *Sunshine* whinnied loudly and tried unsuccessfully to stand back up in her stall – she already knew the outcome. Her eyes were watering, but only a small tear made it down her cheek and onto her beautiful brown muzzle. The boys and their father gave one last tug on the rope and legs, and the foal was free. He immediately went to his feet and his height was astounding. Jet black with a small lightening bolt on his forehead, he was destined to become *Lightening's Sacred Son* – one of the greatest racehorses in the history of the state of Virginia. *Sunshine* seemed satisfied that she had completed her task, but at the age of twenty-two, and with her body torn by the size of the foal and his violent entry into this world, she closed her eyes for the final time.

*Thomas' Lightening* rolled off his stifles and lay on his side as the full Draper moon rose over the distant horizon to illuminate the farm. He breathed deeply – and waited for Thomas. A low cool mist quietly creeped into the valley from the upper ridge. *Lightening* lay still on the ground just beneath the envelopment – his eyes were open but not seeing. A little after midnight his boy came to him – he knew he would. He sat down beside him and gently rubbed his muzzle and underneath his neck. He leaned over and whispered into his ear, and it twitched back and forth in the early morning stillness, "It's time, my friend." *Lightening* rose to his feet, and he felt a strength he hadn't felt since he was a three-year-old, and he and his boy had galloped along the river side for hours at a time. Thomas grabbed *Lightening* by the mane and swung his body up and over the back of the mighty stallion. He leaned into his neck and whispered once more – and the pair rode defiantly into the heavens...

# 65

Luke Montgomery knew he was being asked to join an elite group of marines in preparation for covert overseas operations, but what he didn't know was that he would be preparing to infiltrate the enemy territories of Laos and North Vietnam wearing nothing that would identify him as a U.S. Marine, including his dog tag. Men in his group were even made devoid of their tattoos and even gold teeth were replaced with an early form of composite. They were required to grow their hair longer and dye it black, and consume a diet of fish and rice so their waste in the jungle would smell the same as the enemy. They learned to handle the Chinese DP Machine gun, and the Lejeune armory copied the North Vietnamese handmade pistol that was crudely like the German Luger or Mauser. They learned some Vietnamese but were expected to heavily rely on escorts from the South, and defectors to aid in their infiltration behind enemy lines. For all intents and purposes, they were going to be men who had never even existed. Theirs was a mission that would most certainly result in most of them never coming back. None of this influenced Luke – he was already a Marine through and through, and being allowed to volunteer for this project was an honor. He had nothing to lose.

Corporal James Foster was also a Marine first and foremost. His duty was to his country, and he felt compelled to volunteer for this operation. Training for these men was done in and around this heavily wooded area of the Camp, and their interaction with other Marines was minimal as they extended their cover story to whomever they encountered. Following their first three months of training, their group was finally given a name that only they would know until the Vietnam War ended in 1974. These were the first members of the Military Assistance Command, Vietnam – Studies and Observations Group or MACV-SOG later to be simply called the SOG. They had had a rather nonchalant name for a group that was so skilled in logistical and lethal operations. Their skills ranged from recon to covert ops, to psychological warfare and friendly and hostile prisoner extraction.

The small group of men became very close because their lives literally depended on each other. Luke and James got very close, and many nights they sat outside the barracks talking about sports and politics and even shared a few cigarettes from time to time, when the sergeant wasn't around to stop them. The smell of American cigarettes would get them killed in Laos according to their handlers. Luke never brought up James' sister Emmaline, and James never offered any information. On the night of February 24, 1964, the pair sat outside on a chilly evening staring up at a clear sky unencumbered by artificial light. Whenever they had a rare break, they normally stayed on base because the local community of Jacksonville was still quite combative despite the end of segregation there in 1963.

"Today's her birthday," said James.

"I'm sorry?" Luke replied with a question.

"My sister."

"Oh – Emmaline?" Luke glanced off into the darkness.

"Only one I got…"

"That's nice…I hope she is doing okay at school."

"She's about to get her certificate."

"Then what?"

"Back to Richmond or over to Roanoke to work in a colored Hospital." James pulled out a cloth and started to run it over the boots that sat on the ground in front of him.

"She will be a great nurse…very caring person your sister." Luke felt thoughts coming back that he had pushed deep down. It had been almost a year since he had spoken to Emmaline.

"I'm sorry I didn't come up and introduce myself at your house that day," James looked over at Luke. "Emmaline told me to stay in the car."

"Oh – no it's fine…didn't need any witnesses to what she told me anyway."

"My Dad asks about you every time I speak with him – for some reason he really likes you." James laughed.

"Your father is a fine man - I enjoyed our talks." Luke smiled.

"I'm calling her at 9 – if you want to say "hello".

"She probably doesn't want to hear from me," Luke tossed a rock into the woods.

"Man, look," James put his hand on Luke's shoulder, "we could be God knows where tomorrow and never ever get the chance to speak to someone we care about ever again – I'm giving you the chance."

"Thanks, Corporal." Luke stood up and followed James back into his office at the front of the Quonset hut.

James popped the black receiver off the phone and cranked out a number on the dial then looked up at Luke. The phone rang a few times and then there was a soft voice on the other end. James sat on the edge of his pale green metal desk.

"Hey, Peanut – Happy Birthday!" James listened for a minute then laughed. "I have a birthday surprise for you – hold tight." James put his hand over the mouthpiece, "Okay, Private, here she is…not one word about what we are doing here or what our mission might be – got it?"

"Yes, sir," Luke stood up straight in an attempt to be taller than he already was.

"Again – how did they pick a giraffe for this mission?" James laughed and handed him the receiver.

Luke held the phone to his ear without saying a word for a few seconds.

"Hello?" He heard Emmaline's voice – it was like a punch to the stomach and a breath of fresh air all at once.

"Em?"

"Luke?" He heard her voice. "Luke is that you?"

"Yes – yes it's me."

"Oh my God, Nat, it's Luke," he could hear her smile through the phone and his sweaty hands almost caused him to drop the receiver. She got silent for a moment, then said, "How are you?"

"I- I'm good…your brother, um, Corporal Foster is watching out for me down here." Luke smiled at James. "How's your school coming along?"

"Nicely," Emmaline said then she thought "nicely" – that sounds ridiculous. "I mean it's good, you know, I'm almost finished…how's Army life?"

"Well…it's Marine life, but it's good so far."

"How's your mother?"

"Good – still in Cranberry – they'll let her stay a little while longer – I 've been sending her some money each month."

"I'm sure she's glad you aren't in the mines anymore."

"I'm sure," he almost said, "this might be more dangerous", but he held that to the vest. "How's Natalie?"

"Sitting right here. Doing good."

"Wesley?"

"He's good – having lunch with him tomorrow to talk about him moving to DC."

The conversation began to suffer after that, and Luke could have kicked himself for bringing up Wesley.

"I'm going to give you back to your brother now – don't want to run up too much of a bill for the Sarge to hold over his head," Luke started to hand the phone back to James and then he just blurted it out – it was like he couldn't control his own mouth, "I love you, Emmie…Oh my God…I mean… Happy Birthday!" Luke handed the phone to James, and he put the receiver to his ear just in time to hear her response.

"Luke – I really do miss you."

James and Emmaline finished their conversation talking about their parents and then hung up the phone.

In Charlottesville, Emmaline Foster slowly placed the receiver back into its' cradle and turned to see Natalie's scowl.

"Again, with the Wesley garbage…and you sitting there curled up in his sweatshirt which you still ain't never washed by the way."

Emmaline brushed some tears into the sleeve – and then she brushed past Natalie and into the bedroom.

In North Carolina, Luke Montgomery started to tell his corporal good night.

"Are you okay, Private Montgomery."

"Yes, sir,"

"Are you okay, Luke?"

"It's best this way, right?" Luke looked at James. "I mean she deserves someone like Wesley – he is much more than I'll ever be for her."

"Wesley?"

"Yes, this guy at school – she hangs around with him… same cause and all. I can't compete."

"Wesley?"

"Yes – I guess she will marry him."

"My father won't approve of that."

"Why? He's very smart and he will do well in Washington."

James shook his head, "He's also our cousin."

# 66

Gracie Summerlin quietly slipped out of the Summer House and into the cool night air of May 1876. She left four-year-old Elijah and the boys asleep on mats on the floor in the main room just as the wood stove was cooling down. She wore a long black dress that had belonged to Thomas' mother Madeline. Her perfectly straight black hair was adorned with a string of lilac and wrapped honeysuckle vine. The rising moon was full and aided in her journey as she strode up the road toward Waverly, and cut through familiar fields, and finally through the upper pasture where she and her Thomas had spent so much time together. His grave was still marked with the simple wooden cross that he had built for himself. She wanted to save money for a proper headstone, but she often had the thought that this was all Thomas would have wanted and that satisfied her.

She dropped to her knees and placed the flowers from her hair on his grave then she took out a freshly made white candle and lit the wick by striking a match on a rock. She carefully placed the candle on Thomas' grave in front of her so it could not be seen from the house, then she clasped her hands in front of her and watched it burn. She mostly prayed and composed her own thoughts about why her husband had left her behind. She was mad at him for that, but she would never have traded one minute of the ten years they spent together. Today would have been his thirty-fifth birthday – the ache in her heart could never be filled. As the candle flickered and burned out, she kissed the palm of her hand and placed it on the ground in front of her for a long minute – then she stood up to start the long trek home in the early morning darkness.

"You loved him very much, didn't you?" a voice came from behind her, but she didn't want to turn.

"More than my own life," she said softly.

"I'm so sorry you lost each other so young," the voice came again.

"How long have you been standing there?"

"Not long – I have seen you out here before, but I think it's best you have your visits alone with him."

"Does your husband know I come here?"

"I won't tell him, Grace."

Gracie turned to face Rosemary Connally who stood before her in a white night gown and flowered night cap. Gracie watched as she wiped away small tears on her shoulder. Wonder why she's crying she got what she wanted thought Gracie.

"I hate him, you know," Rosemary said.

"He's your husband."

"He's a bastard," she pulled up the sleeve on her nightgown to reveal deep bruises on her forearm and wrist.

"Why don't you leave?" Gracie asked.

"I'm trapped - I have nowhere to go," She wiped away another tear. "I'll die here if he doesn't kill me first."

"I can't help you."

"I know…I just want you to know that what he did to you and your boys was wrong – and I know that."

"That doesn't help us," Gracie started to climb back through the pasture fence to head for home.

"You need to know something, Gracie."

Grace turned and looked back at her over the top rail, "What is it?"

"He knows."

"He knows what?" Gracie showed her impatience. "I need to go, Mrs. Connally."

"He knows that boy of yours belongs to Thomas…he knows it has blue eyes."

"It? Really?"

"He knows he has blue eyes."

"So what?"

"Just be careful – that's all," Rosemary walked to the fence and put her hand on Gracie's bare arm. "He doesn't like complications."

"Don't you ever threaten me or my family again," Grace pulled her arm away and disappeared across the pasture into the rising mist. Overhead the moon shone brightly with a magnificent halo around it. "Rain's coming," she thought.

It was only a month later that her boys pulled her outside and sat her in the swing. Cozy began to push her back and forth – he was every bit of six feet at age thirteen. Elijah began to climb the oak like he always did and Rhett and Tandey sat on the ground in front of her. She smelled a rat.

"Okay, I have dishes to clean," she smiled at them. "Spit it out."

Rhett stood up and grabbed her hands pulling her to a stop. "We don't want to work up there anymore."

"There's nothing else around here – can't have idle hands – and can't feed mouths with nothing coming home to eat." Gracie sighed.

"Tandey and me…we are grown men now…and Cozy might as well be," Rhett started. "We need to find our own way in life."

"So – you want to leave us – me and Elijah?"

"It's not like that," but Rhett knew it was. "We have no other prospects for work and no prospects for wives."

"Wives?"

"Not now…but you know when the time is right."

"So where will you go? Richmond? Roanoke?" Gracie felt bad news coming.

"There's a cattle drive leaving to head West – we want to be a part of it?"

"West?"

"Texas – then maybe California." Rhett offered…the other two stood silently by. "We can send back money for you and Elijah."

"And this is what all of you want?"

Cozy and Tandey both nodded.

"Absolutely not!" Gracie strode toward the house. "I forbid it."

The house was especially cold that warm summer night. Words weren't spoken and looks weren't given. The boys laid out their mats on the floor and laid down early, as Grace sat at the kitchen table pretending to darn socks and sipping at long since cold tea from a chipped China cup. As the boys dozed off, Grace watched over them – until she finally laid her head down on the table and drifted off.

The next morning saw the boys rise to a large bowl of eggs, ho-cakes, and salted country ham.

"Is it Christmas?" asked Cozy wiping the crusty sleep from the corners of his eyes. He towered over Gracie now.

"Sit down and eat," Gracie poured each of them a glass of cold milk. "We have a long day ahead of us."

"What?" Rhett was right to the point.

"We are going to the Mercantile first thing."

"Do we have to clean out those rotten grain bins again?" Tandey grumbled.

"No, sir"

"Then why?" asked Rhett again.

"Because I won't let you boys go West without every single proper supply you need – that's why."

The family hug lasted for ten minutes and brought tears to everyone except Elijah who didn't know what it was all about – he just knew he liked hugs – and Gracie knew she didn't want to keep her boys trapped in Southwest Virginia.

Summer was nearing its' end when Gracie found herself behind the house hanging laundry that she had just finished scrubbing on the washboard, and rinsing out with a bucket. There was so much less laundry to do since the boys had left – that was the only thing she was thankful for. Elijah was in the front climbing up the oak again – there was a large branch he liked to shimmy out onto, He would sit for hours looking down on the world below him while playing with bugs on the limb. He was a smart child and Gracie already had him writing his name and doing some simple math work – he could recite his ABCs flawlessly.

As she was putting her basket back on the porch she heard and felt the blood curdling scream as it crept to her ears from the front yard. Then she heard the thump. She knew right away what it was, and she rounded the corner of the house to see Elijah laying awkwardly on the ground near the huge roots of the oak – there was blood coming from the corner of his mouth and his eyes were closed tight. She screamed and fell to her knees, immediately cradling him in her arms – she quickly jumped back to her feet and began running toward the Mercantile and the Drapers, but something caught the corner of her eye as she reached the road – and she stopped to look. Two boys were running back up through the woods in the direction of Waverly…and one of them carried a slingshot. The Connally boys…

Gracie didn't waste time thinking about that – she turned and continued running up the road – with the limp body of the now five-year-old Elijah Thommkin Summerlin in her arms.

# 67

Luke never thought about the deafening sound of millions of frogs buzzing and whistling and calling all at once. It wasn't something you encountered in the mountains of West Virginia – sure they had cicadas – but nothing remotely like this. The sound was so overwhelming that the mandatory whispering communications between the men were all but impossible. This wasn't West Virginia or Charlotteville or Parris Island or Oceanside…or even North Carolina. Tonight, under planned cover of pitch-black darkness, Luke Montgomery, James Foster, and three other Marines were hidden in the deep jungles bordering the Mekong River in Laos. They had been hard at work planting listening devices in and around the communist resistance that was attempting to rise to power with the backing of the Soviet Union, five years after the death of King Sisavong Vong, the last monarch of Laos. The United States government feared a growing alliance between communist factions in the middle of the Indochinese Penninsula, and they needed information – as much as they could get.

They had made contact with very few people since they arrived in the country by crossing through Thailand a few weeks before. Though part of their mission was to make contact and attempt to win over those still loyal to the King, they had been forced to kill four of the five men they encountered who were going to attempt to expose them. The other was an older schoolteacher they encountered crossing a road in the jungle. His name was Mahasajun Park and he claimed to be a descendant of the king. The Marines took to calling him Park, which he found to be quite amusing. Park guided them to the Mekong and to the edge of the communist camp, where they had been for ten days. They were told this was a probable suicide mission in the middle of a civil war and their only real source of extraction was by unmarked Bell UH-1 Iroquois chopper. The aircraft were as unmarked as the men. Their mission had thus far been successful.

The worst part for Luke was having to lay in the mud – always in the mud. It was monsoon season, and the rain was constant. The group seldom moved during the day, preferring the cover of darkness. The consistently overcast skies kept them hidden for the most part. Painted from head to toe in camouflage and carrying Soviet made PPS-43 submachine guns – these men were ghosts. They carried no MREs, so they ate what they found. This included rice and fish as well as long beans, papaya, and water spinach. Once Park joined them the food got decidedly better.

Since their unexpected phone conversation and James' bombshell information on Wesley, Emmaline and Luke had talked a few times and had been exchanging letters. Luke put the lid on the romantic talk and instead asked her about school and her plans when she finished. This was all at the advice of her older brother. Now, Luke was laying here… shivering…wondering why he didn't get the chance to say goodbye to her. The call came during the night, and they were in the air within two hours. Nobody was allowed to contact anyone. This was what they trained for. Emmaline was left in unknowing silence about the whereabouts of Luke and her brother. He was certain he may never see her again. Their only way out was a rendezvous point ten clicks south and two days later. Luke prayed in the darkness that he would get back home to her.

Luke leaned closer to James so he could whisper in his ear, but Park reached over and put his hand on Luke's arm. The eerie silence of the frogs was all he heard. Then Park put his finger up to Luke's ear and covered his lips with the same finger. Then Luke heard it too. Mixed into the blaring frogs and almost too faint to hear was a whistle. To Luke it sounded like a basketball whistle – a sound he would recognize anywhere. Then it was louder.

"We have to move, now!" he told James and the others.

There was no gear to gather…just men on their feet headed south along the river…in the darkness. Their movements had drawn attention and the whistles increased in volume and frequency. They ran down the riverbank now as fast as they could move…until Park grabbed James by the shirt and almost pulled him to the ground despite being outweighed by a hundred and twenty-five pounds.

"Trap," said Park.

"What do you mean?" James was catching his breath.

"They- uh – use tha sound to guide you moves," Park spoke better English than they spoke Laotian.

"Which way then?" Luke asked.

"Only one way out," Park looked to the East.

"The river?" James frowned in the darkness. "That's suicide!"

"So is waiting here," Luke stepped forward as the whistles got louder behind them and to the west. "They've surrounded us, corporal."

"We are not to be taken captive – no matter..." James slid down the bank to the raging river below then he turned and grabbed Luke's arm who was right behind him.

"Let's go!" said Luke. The other three Marines stood close behind waiting for the order from James Foster.

"Don't ever quit on her," James said to Luke.

"What?"

"Emmie – don't ever quit on her...you will regret it," James clutched the machine gun in front of him and plunged feet first into the icy river, which was swollen by the monsoon rains. The rest followed without question...even Park.

They found and clung to each other in the darkness as the river boiled around them. Limbs and fruit and logs the size of cars ran hopelessly out of control south with them. James pulled a log toward the group and each man wrapped his arms around it in the desperate hope that it would somehow save their lives. They hit a steep rapid and another tree went air born behind them. When it came down it peeled away the furthest Marine on the log with the sound of crushing bone. Robert "Rooster" Cauthen, who was going to go back to his home in Olathe, Kansas and marry his high school sweetheart Millie, and grow corn "as tall as redwoods" ...and have nine boys and one girl...became one of the first casualties of what would later be called the Vietnam War.

The men grouped closer together on the log as they rolled along in the dark. Luke realized the sound of the frogs had been replaced by the sound of the roaring river and he longed for the frogs to return. What seemed like hours was actually a thirty-minute four mile run down the Mekong that resulted in a landfall not five miles from the rendezvous point. As they scrambled up into a large rice patty there was silence amongst the survivors. Each man checked his gear and nodded to the corporal.

"Let's go," whispered James as they started south again in silence.

Luke could feel the water eating away at his feet inside his boots. He knew he was covered in open sores, but he kept moving, and with each step he felt closer to escape. The sun was beginning to rise as they reached the Cambodian border where they were due to be extracted. They hit the mud again at first light and laid completely motionless throughout the heat of the day as mosquitoes tore at their flesh anywhere it was exposed. Nightfall brought the frogs and a few snakes that slithered through. Still, nobody spoke. Daybreak brought nearby voices and a few more whistles. They never moved. They drank water from the swamp where they laid. Ate nothing. Urinated in their camos. Prayed for home.

At 0200 the next morning, the Huey came roaring in low from the south and the Marines revealed themselves as they stormed toward the chopper. The first bullet from the Laotian Mosin-Nagant bolt action rifle went through the back of Charlie Grimes head and came out his forehead. He dropped without a sound into the boggy marsh. Charlie was from Omaha and was a fourth-generation soldier in his family – and the first to be killed by another human in action.

They made it to the Huey and Luke jumped inside and turned to fire his machine gun into the darkness of the jungle...his legs dangled from the open door. He fired anywhere he saw a flash. Tommy Atkins from Daytona, Florida took a bullet in the back of his leg just above the knee as he started to climb aboard. Instinctively Luke let go of his gun and grabbed Tommy's wrist and yanked upward. From below,

James Foster pushed him by the seat of his pants through the open door where he fell in a pile against the far door.

Luke reached back down for James' hand but never touched it, he also never felt the bullet that shattered the shin of his right leg…because the next one hit him square in the chest and his world went black as he fell back into the chopper.

Luke also never saw the Laotians pouring out of the jungle toward the helicopter...nor did he feel the pilot take off straight up with such force that it threw James and Park back to the ground.

He also missed the ensuing chaos on the ground caused by the rotor wash that allowed James Foster to help a limping Mahasajun Park into the Northern Cambodian jungle.

On April 28, 1964, James Foster became the first MIA of the Vietnam War – but it wasn't officially reported to his family as such for another two years, when two men showed up at the Foster home in Richmond to report him missing and presumed dead or captured.

# 68

The little white pine coffin sat on the porch at her feet.

"So, you still know how to reach him?" Gracie leaned back in the rocking chair that Rhett had built for her, as flies buzzed in droves around the porch in the simmering summer heat.

"I feel certain I can get a message to him," Katherine Draper said while sitting perched on the rotting steps of the front porch of Summer House – she shooed away flies with a small fan in one hand. "I'm just not sure I can get him to return to Virginia for any reason."

Gracie sighed and hot tears rolled down both cheeks, "Just send him a simple message – "Gracie needs you, come quickly.""

"I'll do as you ask, Gracie, but it may take a few days for any message to get up to him."

"If he doesn't come in ten days, I will have a funeral without him…then I'll have to figure out what's next for me," Gracie clutched her hands in her lap and covered them with her white apron to keep the flies from roaming all over her fingers. She looked up at Katherine, "he will come – I'm certain."

Katherine stood up and went to Gracie. She leaned over and put her hands on Gracie's cheeks, "It's gonna be OK, Sweetie…you're gonna get through this. I'm so sorry." Katherine leaned in and put her arms around Gracie who buried her grief into Katherine's stomach as they both rocked back-and-forth in the motionless humidity.

"That son-of-a-bitch up yonder's gone get his one day," said Gracie.

It took just four days for Gracie to receive the response she expected, but also desperately needed. Gracie was at the Mercantile picking up some sugar, salt, and flour when Katherine approached her. She gently reached out and took Gracie by the hand. "It's done," she said. "He's coming."

"Thank you, my dear friend, this means everything to me," Gracie hugged Katherine and then hurried up the road with her cart in tow to prepare for her guest.

Three days later, about a half hour before sunset, a small rickety buckboard pulled by a single mule arrived at Summer House. Gracie stood patiently waiting on the porch steps, but the very second her eyes locked with Margaret's she bounded down the steps and into the woman's waiting arms.

"Oh, ma little Gracie Henry," she said. "I's so, so sorry for y'all." Heavy tears rolled down both of Margaret's cheeks.

"Thank you so for coming, Margaret - I've missed you so much!"

Moments later a tall, stout man stood next to Margaret and Gracie let go and plunged herself into his powerful arms - her cheek pressing into his barrel chest, "Oh, my God, Samuel! I love you both so much! "I'm so very, very happy you are here!". "Let's get inside away from the prying eyes up on the hill - I've got a nice okra and tomato and rice stew on the stove. I'm sure you're very tired from your long trip!"

"I'll scramble dis fella on back, and I be righ' up.y'all goes inside," Samuel began to loosen the harness around the mule's neck, and the animal gave him a solemn look of gratitude after he promised him extra grass and a straw bed.

Margaret put an arm around Gracie's shoulder and led her up the steps and into the house. The joy of the reunion quickly turned into an air of sorrow as both women lowered their heads when they stepped across the threshold and saw the small white wooden coffin in the center of the room.

Early the next morning, Samuel toiled in the quickly rising summer heat as he dug a grave for Elijah underneath the oak tree standing in the front yard of Summer House. Not twenty feet away from where the old wooden swing drifted almost unnoticeably on the two ropes that hung it there. Around noon a few people began to appear in the yard including Dr. Draper and his wife along with several children from the negro school and orphanage in Christiansburg. The children had known Elijah from school even though he wasn't old enough to start real learning yet. The new young preacher from the AME Church in Blacksburg, Robert Johnson, had heard about the tragedy and made his way down on horseback to "help out if he could". Samuel asked him to lead a prayer and scripture reading for the boy. There were other unwanted visitors as well. Sitting on horseback just across the road was David Connally and his two sons. They were dressed in their Sunday finest and had removed their hats, holding them clutched to their hearts as if mocking the gathering. Both boys looked on with indifference and occasionally they smirked.

"Wha' you wan' dun ta dem' wha' sits der'?" Samuel asked Gracie.

Gracie looked up from her weeping and looked Samuel in the eye, "Let them sit right there and admire their handiwork…let God watch them gloat and remember their faces for their day of judgement. God willing it be soon."

There was no fanfare for burying one's child under a tree in the front yard. There was no procession with golden wagons and people lining the streets crying and throwing roses. This was a young boy with impure blood – born from the outrage that was the love between Gracie and Thomas...he was, simply put, a perfect example of the war – no, a perfect example of America. Now, a small white painted casket simply sat on the ground next to a hole, while a few men said some words and held bibles, and Gracie cried with Margaret and Katherine as they sat on the hard ground. The Reverend Johnson was very kind, and he said some important things about the loss of children and living on for them – but Gracie didn't hear most of it. Gracie wore a gray smock and kept her hair up under a black bonnet – the perfect wardrobe for a poor grieving mother who was once again left cruelly all alone. She hadn't worn this dress since the last day she slept in a slave quarters. Thomas wanted to burn it, but she told him she needed a stark reminder of who she really was, and where she came from. Today was that stark reminder.

"Would you like for me to open the casket and say a prayer for Elijah's swift passage to heaven – and anoint him?" Reverend Johnson asked Gracie.

"My boy's been in that box for over ten days now – in this ungodly hot summer heat. I don't think it will do anyone any good to see that box opened." Gracie shook her head.

"Yes, ma'am. I understand."

Samuel and Timothy Draper used two ropes to lift and then lower the pine coffin into the grave. Reverend Johnson said a prayer that included "ashes to ashes and dust to dust" as the box disappeared into the ground. Then the Reverend helped Samuel shovel dirt into the grave until it was filled. The Connally's stood across the road through the entire display holding their horses by the reins and sipping from water skins. Gracie refused to look in their direction. After the short ceremony, Gracie put out some bread and cheese along with some lemon tea cakes that Katherine had made. She also served a cold apple cider she had been keeping in the well for a day or so. The few guests started to meander towards home, and Reverend Johnson said his farewell and asked if he could "check in on Gracie from time to time." She had innocently consented to it.

It didn't take long for Samuel to get the mule tacked up to his buckboard in preparation for their long trip back to West Virginia. They planned to travel in the moonlight of a nice clear night to make the trip more comfortable. They would have to go slower, but the daytime heat had been oppressive.

"I'm so sorry you have to go back home so soon – I would have loved a longer visit," Gracie had her arms around Margaret as they walked out from the house.

Margaret turned to look at Gracie and put her hand on her cheek, "Ya can alway and I mean alway, come to us. Evey' ting' gone be fine."

Samuel came from around the back of the wagon and gave Gracie another big hug. "Don' wary bout' nuttin' no mo'…God got dis."

He climbed up on the buckboard and started the mule forward. When they reached the road to turn North, David Connally and his sons blocked their path.

"I gots no quarrel wit you, suh," Samuel offered but Connally ignored.

"Samuel and Margaret, seems the reports of your death were greatly exaggerated, were they not?" David grabbed the mule near his bit and held tightly.

Samuel just stared at him, "I'd trouble ya tuh let me on da' way, suh."

"I got grave markers on my farm with your names on them – care to explain?" Connally put his hand on the revolver at his hip to terrorize them. "Surely something ain't legal about that, now is there?"

"A man gots ta do wat needs be ta 'scape tha' bonds he gots."

"I see that table and chairs – and that blanket chest in the back. Them things don't belong to you – now do they?" Connally let go of the mule and rode around the wagon before coming to a stop next to Margaret.

"Gracie gift dem' suh."

"Those items belong to Summer House…please get out and carry them back inside."

Gracie slowly walked out to the road but stayed on her property. "What seems to be the concern here, Mr. Connally?"

"Besides the fact that these two dead slaves have returned from their graves to steal goods from me?" Connally twirled his horse around quickly in front of Gracie and a cloud of red dust filled the sky, causing Margaret to cough. "I don't take kindly to negro trickery, and I believe these two have more to hide. What do they know about the death of my cousin, Dewey?"

"You can ask his wife – she's in a pauper's grave over in Richmond," Gracie returned. "And those items belong to Summer House – which belongs to me."

"Don't smart off to me, girl!" He raised his hand as if he would backhand Gracie then he lowered it.

"There's two more chairs goes with that set in the house," Gracie turned and walked back toward Summer House. "I'll go an' fetch them for you."

"And …I'll have the boys get the other items from the wagon," Connally turned to his sons, "get off them horses and unload that buckboard."

The two boys climbed down off their horses and handed the reins to their father. One boy of about ten, who would grow up to be James Connally's grandfather, quickly covered his head with his arms and started screaming when Gracie let loose the first barrel of Thomas' double barrel shotgun over his head from ten feet away. She cocked back the second barrel and trained it on him – then she looked at Connally, "The next barrel puts your murderous boy where he put mine."

Connally pulled his pistol and pointed it straight at Samuel, then he slowly moved his arm and pointed it at Margaret from fifteen feet away. "Get down off the buckboard, boy."

"Samuel, you go on home now…it'll be dark soon," Gracie steadied her grip on the shotgun and took another step toward the boy. "You won't recognize him," she said.

Connally lowered the pistol and slid it back into the waistband of his trousers. "Which way you headed, boy?" he asked Samuel. Samuel didn't answer. "I'll find you," he said.

"Get gone, Samuel!" Gracie said. Samuel tapped his mule with the reins, and they headed off up the road toward the Mercantile in a cloud of hot summer dust.

"Get your damned gun off my boy – now!"

"When the sun goes down over the upper pasture…not one minute before," Gracie leaned back against the two-rail fence in front of Summer House and cradled the shotgun against her hip. "That man practically built the farm you live on with his own bare hands…the very least he deserves is a wobbly old table and chairs and a blanket chest that smells like moth balls and has holes in it."

As the sun slowly sank on the Western horizon Gracie turned the shotgun on David Connally. "You boys, mount up and go home to your mama." Connally nodded at them, and they headed back up the hill. She waited until they were out of earshot before she began to speak slowly and succinctly.

"You sir are a liar and a thief…but your skin color gives you power over the likes of me, and you know I have no re-course in the law of this state. But you will know this – I have nothing left to lose since you took my home… and killed my boy – and if you so much as step foot on my deeded land I will deliver a bullet to your skull…and then to your boy's after I drop you in the river."

"You don't have the guts to kill a man." Connally sneered.

"And you have me confused with some other poor little negro girl who was done wrong."

The look in her eye was terrifying and the coward Connally knew she was telling the truth. He turned and rode his horse straight up the hill and out of sight – and he never did step foot on Gracie's land ever again.

The bright moon soared high overhead and the mountain breeze provided a great respite to the day's summer heat as Samuel and Margaret crossed the Virginia line and into West Virginia near Pearisburg around midnight. The clear night sky was perfect for travelling – and making distance between them and the Connallys. Margaret looked up at Samuel and smiled, then she kissed him on the cheek, "I think I nee' a nigh' shawl…it's gettin' might cool," she said.

"You wan' I stop hea,?"

"No – keep gone."

Margaret turned and reached out to the blanket chest and unlatched first one latch and then the other – then she raised the lid.

"Praise be! Sam – loo' wha' in hea'"

Margaret reached into the back and pulled a bundle of blankets from the trunk into her lap. Then she peeled back one layer at a time until she saw two eyes peering up at her.

"You done fine," she said, "you done fine."

Tears trickled out of both beautiful blue eyes that night as Elijah Summerlin became Eli Montgomery.

# 69

Luke smelled oil…or was it gas? What was that humming sound…a helicopter? An airplane? It was an airplane – he was sure of it. He tried to open his eyes, but they wouldn't move. It was like that nightmare he used to have as a kid about being lost in the deep dark woods with peering eyes all around. He knew he needed to open his eyes – it was all a dream – but the harder he concentrated, the harder it was to pry them open. There was something holding his eyes closed…a cloth?…tape?…wait…had he been captured? Was he in a prison camp? He tried to call out for James – nothing came out – at least nothing that was audible to him.

Then his father was there. He wasn't saying anything – just leaning against the green wall of the hallway of his old high school staring at him with gray, sullen eyes. He wore his dirty overalls straight from the mine – just like he had for Luke's high school graduation in May of 1960. Luke was just glad he made it. Then he smelled fish and rice…and cold jungle rain…and then the frogs were back…so many frogs. It was deafening…so loud…too loud…then darkness again.

Luke was on the move. He could hear and feel the wheels turning underneath him. He wanted to open his eyes, but fear held him back. He tried to reach for his eye with his hand to pry it open – but he couldn't move his arm. Slowly he opened his right eye just enough to see his own eyelashes blocking his view. Then he saw bright overhead lights…fluorescent…and tubes – lots of tubes. He closed his eyes again when he realized he was in a hospital…and they were speaking in Dutch? No, German? He was in Germany.

Luke's chopper had taken heavy fire after he went down in the doorway, in fact both pilots including Captain Allan Osbourne sustained injuries – Osbourne's proved to be fatal. The 86th Airlift Wing flew Luke out of Seoul, South Korea and delivered him to the Landstuhl Regional Medical Center near Ramstein Airbase in Germany where he underwent his second surgery in three days. His chest had to be cracked to remove the bullet that had pierced his breastbone, and missed his heart by less than one inch. His shin was shattered, and the lower part of his right leg sustained heavy blood loss…he was probably looking at an amputation below the knee.

Luke opened his eyes again…was this another dream? The room was pale green, and dim buzzing yellow lights hung along the sides of two walls. He felt flannel on his arms – wasn't he allergic to flannel? Why didn't his mother tell them he was allergic? Or was it wool he was allergic to? He couldn't breathe – there was something on his chest and he needed to get it off – it was too heavy. He tried to call for help – but didn't make any sound. There was a woman now and she was putting a cold cloth to his forehead. Another one was injecting something into the tube in his arm. He went black again.

The humming sound was back…an airplane? His ears were hurting now. Need to pop my ears he thought. He tried to reach to pinch his nose so he could blow out and clear them – like he did when he went way up in the mountains with his father hunting. Something was holding his arms, so he pulled harder…then harder. Something popped and he heard the woman calling out for help. This time he heard the word "morphine"...no more please – his head was swimming and he closed his eyes again.

His father was there again – and this time he put his arms around him and held him close. "Am I dead?" he said to no one in particular. The hug was a long one and Luke buried his head into his father's shoulder and pulled in the sulfuric smell of the coal mine...deep into his nostrils until he thought he might choke on it. Then the smell got sweeter...at first like the smell of fresh cut grass...then flowers – maybe honeysuckle? Lilac?. He heard his name – was that his mother? The flowers came back – stronger this time. He felt pain – and stinging tears rolling from the corners of his eyes. Pain – then someone was holding his hand. His mother? No...he had held this hand before...had kissed this hand before...the flowers came back again...and Luke Montgomery finally re-opened his eyes and swam straight into the beauty of Emmaline Foster.

# 70

Gracie Henry-Summerlin and Katherine Draper had become the best of friends over the years, and they spent most of their days together either at the Mercantile or at the Negro Orphanage and School in Christiansburg. The Reverend Robert Johnson kept true to his word to come check on Gracie – an action which he performed all too frequently. Gracie and Robert became friends. He would visit her in Christiansburg, and she would attend his church most Sundays – and because she was one of the few who could read, she was called upon to recite the scriptures at every service. Gracie found a home in Robert's congregation, and the sheer amount of travel and activity she had had kept her extreme loneliness from completely overwhelming her. She missed the boys every day, and the few times she was able to sneak off to West Virginia to see Elijah made her very nervous and unsettled that she was being followed. She knew in her heart he would have a good life with Samuel and his family. They had asked her to move there with them, but she knew Connally watched her every move – it was better this way…at least for Elijah it was.

It was the nights that were the worst. She'd still sneak up to Thomas' grave sometimes – and she could see Mrs. Connally watching her from the kitchen window, but she had left her alone since the first nightly encounter. Gracie ached for Thomas…she was still a young woman…and her body still longed for his touch. Some nights she would wake up soaking wet from the dreams she had of him. Their days in the grass of the upper pasture…their first time in the darkness of the cave with the sliver of moonlight shining into his deep blue eyes. On those nights she would eventually find herself out on the swing under the oak alternating between sobbing and laughing as she thought of him. She thought her heart would never mend. With the boys gone now and her barely finding the ability to travel to Elijah, her life had become a pit of loneliness. Sure, she had Katherine and the children at the orphanage and her church, but still her nights were silent and dark.

Reverend Johnson was very kind to her, and often asked her if she was okay. One beautiful Spring day in 1878 as she was leaving the church, Robert asked her if she would like to join him for a picnic that afternoon at the river. She was quite reluctant, and had turned him down many times before, but this time she said "yes". Their first picnic turned into once-a-week dinners at Summer House and Sunday afternoons at the church or in Christiansburg. In 1880 the reverend asked Gracie to be his wife for the first time. She turned him down, but they continued their relationship. When Gracie got pregnant with Lynette later that year, he asked her again. Her response was, "I am married already." In 1883, Gracie gave birth to their second daughter, Beatrice, and he asked her again, telling her it was no longer appropriate for them to carry on out of wedlock. As the preacher he had a reputation to uphold, and she was impugning it. She told him she would consider his proposal. She considered it for six months, until he came to her and told her that he was offered a position at a large AME church in Washington and wanted to move his family there – he felt like he was "called". Gracie told him that she couldn't leave her home…or Thomas. In the early Winter of 1885, the Reverend Robert Johnson left behind Gracie and his two young daughters and moved to Washington. He came back to Summer House in the Spring and asked her to marry him one last time. Robert left Pulaski County two days later, and Gracie and the girls never saw him again.

Beatrice and Lynette became Gracie's life. Their upbringing was not an easy task. There were times in the cold harsh winters of the Virginia mountains that they struggled to eat and stay warm. But still, Gracie raised them well and taught them to read and write and do mathematics. As they grew older, they helped her at the orphanage in Christiansburg and she taught them along with the other children in the school. Still a huge part of their life was the church and she taught them both to be fierce God-fearing women. But Bea and Lynn couldn't have been more different. Bea met a man who was a school janitor in Blacksburg when she was twenty-two, and she got married. The new couple lived at the Summer House with Gracie, and she found Bea's new husband, Nate, to be quite helpful around the house. After a miscarriage and a still born baby, Bea and Nate had a healthy baby girl in 1905 and they named her Mathilde.

On the other hand, Lynette was carefree and longed to leave the "boring" mountains to see the world. While working for the Draper's at the Mercantile, she met a young white couple who were passing through with their two young children during a move from Knoxville to Richmond. They offered Lynette a job as a live-in nanny, and she left Gracie and Bea behind to go to Richmond in 1898. Gracie saw the first signs of problems when Lynn came back to visit for the first time. She could see the bruises on her arms, the healed black eyes, and the limp she had developed. Gracie begged her not to return to Richmond on her last visit home in 1903, but

Lynn told her everything was fine, "I just sometimes don't do things right and Mr. Stephen has to set me straight – I'll be okay, Mama." In the Fall of 1903, Lynette's body was shipped back to Pulaski by train with a note of regret that said she had "taken a horrible fall down the stairs and never recovered." Gracie and Beatrice buried her in the AME church cemetery in Christiansburg where her father had been the preacher.

Just after Thanksgiving of that same year, Gracie announced she was taking the train to West Virginia to visit with Elijah. Beatrice and Nate would stay behind to tend to the house, the school, and the Mercantile. She was gone nearly a week before she returned to Summer House. On Christmas Eve two men in black suits arrived under the oak tree out front as Gracie was watching from the kitchen window.

"Who are they, mama?" asked Bea.

Gracie turned and held Bea's arm just above the elbow. "You tell them I've been sick with the fever since Thanksgiving - and in bed the whole time. If they need to see me, they can come in…but they might leave sickened."

"What about your trip to see Elijah."

You tell them exactly what I done told you, girl – nothing more," Gracie moved toward the bedroom in the back of the house.

Bea spent over an hour with the two men outside before watching them ride away as the sun began to set. She came back into the house to find her mother seated at the kitchen table with a glass of cider.

"Well?" Gracie asked.

"The man – the one that Lynnette worked for – somebody shot him down in cold blood outside a bar in Richmond a few weeks back," Bea sat down across from Gracie.

"What they want with us?"

"Asked where you been."

"And..?"

"I told 'em just like you said."

"Now I need you to take some supper up to Nate at the school…and you tell him the exact same thing I just told you."

Bea started to do what her mother asked and as she left the kitchen to go to the door she stopped and opened the Martha Washington cabinet.

"Where's Thomas' gun, Mama?" she turned and looked hopelessly at Gracie.

"I lost it when I went to see Elijah."

"Mother…really?"

"Beatrice…mind your mother and get that supper on up to your husband."

"Yes, ma'am." Beatrice went out the front and the screen door slammed back behind her.

Gracie pulled the bible from the middle of the table and clasped her hands together on the top and closed her eyes. Then she began to speak very softly.

"I'm so sorry, Thomas… not for what I done…but for throwing your daddy's Colt in the James River."

# 71

"Am I – are we in Germany?" Luke tried to raise his hand to his forehead but was restricted by I.V.s. "Why are you in Germany?"

Emmaline glanced over him to the other side of the bed, and he rotated his head to see his mother's face – she had been crying…he could see it.

"Sweetie, you are in the Walter Reid Medical Center in Bethesda, Maryland," she put her arm on his.

"What? How? Where's James? Where's my team?" Luke tried to force himself up but the pain from the waist down was excruciating. "Emmie – what are you doing here?"

"Slowly," she said. "it's been three weeks since the incident." Emmie put a cold cloth on his forehead. "I need to go get the doctor and tell him you are awake. He doesn't care for me much because your mother had to really pressure them to even allow me to care for you. She's a saint."

Emmaline stood up and Luke noticed for the first time that she was wearing a white nursing outfit with white socks and black shoes. "She did it," he thought to himself. Then he turned back to his mother. "What's going on with me, mother?"

"The doctor told us not to tell you anything if you awoke."

"If? – was there a chance I wouldn't?"

"It's been touch and go for the last ten days that you've been home – well here at the hospital." Addie Montgomery smiled at him.

"And...Emmie?"

"Been by your side since they finally allowed her inside six days ago. Been changing your bandages and putting poultices on your infection – I think it's something she has, like a home remedy or something. The doctor told her she could put it on your wounds since it was a last resort."

"My wounds? Where?"

"Your leg is the main one now – chest is healing – they stapled it. Or some such."

"I'm confused how I got here."

"The story we have is one helicopter and two planes. They really won't tell us much about where you were when this happened...I'm just so glad you are alive." She put her head on his shoulder, and he could feel her sniffling – he didn't care.

Luke finally got a chance to look around and he realized he was in a huge open area that almost looked like half of a basketball arena. Huge glowing yellow lights glared down from twenty-five feet up, and he could just see a few high windows shrouded by darkness which told him it was nighttime. His hospital bed was a cot with a metal frame and two mattresses stacked – a thin white sheet and pale green blanket covered him from his toes to the middle of his stomach. He felt like skin and bones with tubes hanging out of his arms. Then he heard two sets of steps coming out of the shadows – Emmaline emerged, and another woman walked next to her – her mother.

"Doctor is gone for the night," Emmaline sat back down next to him. "I'm going to see if I can scrounge you up some soup and something to drink now that the chest tube has been removed."

"Hello, Mrs. Foster," Luke said like he was just arriving at her house in Richmond. "You didn't have to be here, but I'm glad you are."

"I'm glad you are awake, Luke," Mathilde said. "You came back, and our James didn't – so I guess I'm selfishly here to see if you know what happened to him. Please, just tell me the truth."

Luke closed his eyes for a moment – then he re-opened them and looked right at her. "We made it down the river… then we made for the rendezvous – we went into a firefight. I reached for him…but it went black on me," Luke felt tears coming. "I don't remember anything after that…I'm sorry."

"I don't understand where you were - we aren't at war?" Emmie was checking his pulse.

"Asia… that's all I can say…he looked around the cavernous room then looked at Mathilde again…Laos and Cambodia."

"Oh my God," she put her hands over her face and sobbed.

"Was he not on the chopper?" Luke drank some ice water from a cup that Emmaline held to his lips. "I never saw him get shot, Mrs. Foster."

"Why? Why were you there?"

"I can't tell you that – but it was mostly a recon mission."

"They won't tell us anything," she sobbed. "He's just gone…our James is gone."

"I'm sorry, everything happened so fast."

The room got silent as the group dealt with the news they got from the only firsthand witness they knew of. James was gone – he was missing…or more likely he was dead. Luke didn't want to think about that, so he closed his eyes again.

"They won't even say he's missing – they say he is deployed," Mathilde leaned into Luke's mother as she put her arm around her. "And then you come home barely alive, Luke."

"Mrs. Foster, your son is a great man and an even better soldier – he is resilient in the face of danger…I believe he is alive. I can feel it."

"Why won't they tell me then?"

"This country is on the verge of a war…where we were, and what we were doing there…I just can't. I'm sorry." Luke squirmed on the bed as the pain began to hit him harder.

Emmaline held his hand, "I can get you some morphine – without the doctor being here – he prescribed it."

"No Em – I need to stay awake now – if I can," he looked into her eyes – those eyes, "can you at least tell me what's going on with what's left of me here?" he tried to smile but knew it was crooked.

Emmaline smiled back at him, "The doctor will be 'round in the morning…best he tells you – after he looks at you."

Luke thought about protesting, then he realized he didn't want to put that burden on Emmaline…he was just so thankful to see her face again…his feelings for her all came rushing back in an instant. She was the only person in the room to him. Then his mother spoke again.

"We should let you get some rest, son."

"Are you in a hotel?"

"Heavens no – the hospital has given us some cots in another room – and a place to bathe. I've been to Richmond with Mathilde a couple times. They have a lovely home there – and I love their church family, they have been so supportive." Addie stood up and placed the back of her hand on his cheek. "Still feverish, Emmie – take care of him tonight."

"Wait you're not going too?" Luke looked back at Emmaline. "I'm sure you need rest too."

"Poor thing won't leave your side," said Luke's mother.

Emmaline pointed past Luke and he glanced over to see another hospital bed ten feet from his. "That's me…" she said.

Luke felt his tears coming again and he couldn't stop them this time. His mother wiped them away with a soft cloth.

Emmaline smiled at him, "you are the only one who might know where my brother is – I have one goal here – keep you alive."

"Thank you," said Luke.

"Goodnight, Luke," said Mathilde as she touched his arm.

"Good night."

The ladies disappeared into the darkness of the hall beyond, and Emmaline sat back down next to Luke on a small green metal chair. She wiped his face again and then dipped a clean cloth in cold water, folded it in a rectangle, and put it on his forehead.

"So, you graduated? Congrats!"

"Well, I got my certificate." Emmie frowned.

"Yeah – your certificate – sorry."

"I'm not – I got my certificate."

They both laughed until Luke had to stop because his ribcage felt like it had an anvil dropped on it.

"It's so good to see you – I couldn't believe it when I opened my eyes," Luke struggled to regain a position which didn't make him feel like a gutted fish.

"I'm so glad you are okay."

"I've missed you so…" Luke reached for her hand, and she let him take it. "I love you, Emmaline Foster."

She looked back in his eyes and smiled, "I know you do – I really do."

Wasn't the answer he wanted, but at least she didn't run away like the last time. She went to work doing nursing things like checking his IV's and tucking his sheets and pillows for him, and he just laid there and watched her for a while. Watching her move probably made him feel better than anything else she may have done for him.

"I have a lot to tell you – you remember Joe Millstone… of course you do," she lifted a cup of water with a straw to his lips.

"Oh my God – is he okay?"

"Yes-yes…not everyone goes around getting in shootouts like you do," she smiled, and he loved her more, but he could see the grief of James in her eyes. "I asked him to look into something for me that I read in Gracie's diary."

"Are you…seeing him?

"Really. You do realize that boy is even whiter than you are, right?"

Luke smiled, "tell me about the diary – we haven't talked about that in a long time, have we?"

"She makes mention of Elijah being her son, right?"

"I remember – I tripped over his grave marker at your grandma's house."

"Summer House…anyway the original diary talks about him, and it talks about his funeral when he was five," Emmaline placed her hands in her lap. "The pages we found in the bottom of the sewing cabinet mention visits to see someone named Eli Montgomery in West

Virginia. It also mentions Samuel and Margaret and their children."

"I don't know anyone named Eli in our family – never heard that name," Luke groaned and tried to turn on his side. Emmie propped another pillow under his arm.

"The graves at Waverly – two of them said Samuel and Margaret. They must have travelled with your great-grandfather John up from Pulaski into West Virginia. They didn't die at Waverly."

"I think I know what you are thinking…but go on. I love to hear your voice."

"Oh, stop," She smiled. "Anyway, Gracie talks about Eli's blue eyes in these pages. I think he was Thomas Summerlin's boy. I think the Connally's knew that."

"Okay…"

"I think Gracie held a fake funeral and sent him North with Samuel. Your father may have even known him."

"That's…crazy."

"I don't think Elijah died at five," Emmaline moved over to her own bed and sat on the edge. "I asked Joe Millstone if he could help me find out – you know – being that he is going to be a lawyer and such."

"I didn't know you knew Joe all that well," Luke turned his head so he could see Emmaline.

"Confession time I guess."

"Oh, no – here it comes."

"Again – no. I saw him at TPs one night and I asked him if he had heard from you," Emmie took off her shoes, laid down on the pillow and cut off the standing lamp next to her bed. "We sat and talked about you for a while – and we met a few times after that, once I started getting news from my brother."

"And he's looking for a boy who would be Gracie's son – Bea's brother?"

"Half-brother," Emmie took a deep breath. "Joe's coming up here to see you tomorrow from Blacksburg. I hope he has news for me. Don't mind the ticking of my alarm clock – I need to get up every couple of hours to check on you."

"Emmaline?" Luke said in the darkness.

"Yes?"

"Good night, beautiful."

"Good night, Luke."

The next morning Luke was stirred awake by Emmaline, and when he opened his eyes, he saw two men standing beside his bed.

"This is Dr. Cooper, who has been taking care of you… and this is…I'm sorry sir."

"Captain Westfield from the Pentagon, son."

"Wow – an audience," Luke rubbed his face for the first time and felt the sandpaper that was his stubble – it felt good to him.

Dr. Cooper began to speak, "The Captain needs to speak with you alone, but first I want to tell you the good news. You won't be losing the leg."

"That's great to hear – especially because nobody told me it was a possibility," Luke glanced at Emmie and gave her a dirty but playful grimace. She grinned back.

"Thank you, sir – I can't thank you enough."

"Don't thank me…I was ready to take it eight days ago," Dr. Cooper looked at Emmaline. "That was until your mother talked me into letting this young lady tend to you around the clock. She saved your leg – not me."

"I don't know what to say," Luke looked long and hard at Emmaline who was folding up the bedlinen she had just changed.

"Nurse Foster, can I get you some coffee while the captain speaks to Sergeant Montgomery for a few minutes?" Dr. Cooper started out and Emmaline followed him. Luke watched until they disappeared.

"Sergeant, sir?" Luke tried to sit up and made a little better effort of it this morning. "Ya'll must really want me back in that jungle."

"On the contrary, son. We promoted you for your heroic service to this country…and now we are discharging you, honorably with disability pay," the captain sat in the chair next to him.

"What happened to Corporal Foster and the others?"

"Two dead – one missing," Westfield seemed to sigh but it was barely audible.

"James Foster?"

"Never got on the helicopter and we have had no contact with him since."

"What did you tell his family?"

"You know what your mission was about, Sergeant. We can't tell them anything that can get to the press or to any civilian for that matter."

"So, what did you tell them?"

"He went missing during a training mission at sea."

"So, they think he's dead."

"We think he's dead too."

"You don't know that."

"He fell from a chopper in the middle of an intense firefight, son. He's dead."

"Is there anything else, sir."

"No, just remember your oath and allegiance to the United States."

"You already have my word on that."

"I'll send papers around for you to sign once you are discharged," Captain Westfield stood up to leave. "You know, I think you should get a Purple Heart for saving that private and performing a dangerous mission successfully – but you won't. Just remember that your work will save numerous soldiers' lives once the war starts."

As the captain walked away Luke really started to feel the pain in his legs and chest and called out for Emmaline. She was back by his side within a minute. He closed his eyes and couldn't force himself to look at her. He wept inside for his friend James.

Emmaline Foster didn't waste any time, she got Luke all cleaned up for the day – she even gave him a shave, which he greatly enjoyed. When she changed the poultice on his leg, she explained that the bullet had gone all the way through his shin bone and out the back of his leg – basically flaying open his calf muscle. By the time they had gotten him to Germany it was badly infected and probably had parasites from the Cambodian jungle still hanging on. It was the least of their worries, because the bullet in his chest was still lodged within a quarter inch of his aorta. They had tried to keep it clean and were running antibiotics into his system at a steady pace, but even when he was sent back to the states the doctor's message from abroad was to consider amputation before it killed him. Emmie cleaned his wound four times a day, and kept a poultice of tea tree oil, sulfur, and calendula on it around the clock. By the fifth day the skin had started to heal around the wound and by day nine the doctors sewed it closed.

Their mothers, Adrienne and Mathilde, arrived first in the morning, and appeared to be becoming close friends during this time of strife. They came in carrying Styrofoam cups of coffee and sat on Emmie's cot to finish their morning conversation as she finished taking care of Luke. Another older white nurse came by pushing a cart and handed a tray to Emmaline as she went by, without making eye contact or saying a word. Emmaline sat on the edge of Luke's bed and spoon fed him a small bowl of tepid oatmeal. It was the first thing he had had in his mouth in weeks and swallowing it was a battle. She helped him wash it down with a cup of milk, which was unfortunately tepid as well.

"Now that you can eat, I'm going to smuggle you in something worth chewing," said Luke's mother.

Luke smiled and said, "Good morning", but his entire focus was Emmie. Having her hand feed him seemed very intimate to him, and he hoped she felt the same. Her long shiny black hair was buried beneath her nurse's cap in a bun, and he longed to see it flowing around her shoulders again. She had given him some pain medication through his IV and he could feel it beginning to kick in. Shortly after he ate, he began to doze off.

A little after noon Luke was brought out of his nap by the sound of men and women speaking. He recognized his mother's voice, but not the man's. He waited until he felt coherent enough to open his eyes, because he was sure it was another Marine. But he was wrong. There were two men sitting in green metal chairs across from him and he immediately recognized Joe Millstone. They shared a smile before Joe spoke.

"You look a little worse for wear there, Lucas."

"You know me – I play through the pain," Luke responded.

Joe shook his head, and his expression became solemn, "I'm so glad you are okay, Luke. When Emmaline told me what happened I feared the worst."

"I'm sure I'm even more glad to see you, my friend," Luke leaned up on one elbow before he realized the ladies were all seated behind him on Emmaline's bed.

"Joey told me about your service, son – I was in the Navy during World War II. I appreciate your sacrifice," the man seated next to Joe spoke.

"Oh, Luke – I'm sorry, this is my father Joseph Millstone the third," Joey said.

"Boy, ya'll just line 'em up and give 'em numbers over there in Draper," Luke smiled. "I really am happy to see you again."

"What happened? Where were you?" Joey asked.

"I can't really say…but I can tell you things are going to get worse, but I'm being discharged – so it's somebody else's fight now."

"Southeast Asia appears to be a real hotspot right now," Joey's dad said.

"I hate to discount the visit, but I also came up here to see Emmaline – I have some news for you," Joey looked over at Emmie who was catching a break on the edge of her cot. "It's about Elijah Henry."

Emmaline looked at her mother who gave her a sharp look that Joey never saw.

"Really?"

"Turns out you were right...he didn't die in Draper. He was raised by the family of Samuel and Margaret Montgomery in Bland, West Virginia. Went by the name of Eli Montgomery until his death."

"That's amazing...thank you, Joseph," said Emmie.

"What did you do, girl?" asked Mathilde. "You need to leave things where they lay."

"It's Grandma Bea's brother, Mama, your uncle I believe," Emmaline turned back to Joey. "What else?"

"Looks like he may have had a family, but I don't know the details," he looked at his father. "Here's something funny I just stumbled on too – there's a colored elementary school not far from Bland that bears the name "Eli Montgomery" – they call it Montgomery Elementary School up there."

Luke and his mother looked at each other when the Montgomery name was brought up.

"My God, mama? Did you know any of this?"

Mathilde turned to her daughter and placed her hand on her arm, "You need to understand something, honey – your great-grandma – she hid Elijah away from Draper to protect him."

"From what?"

"From that God forsaken family up on the hill."

"The Connallys?"

"Why do you think they ran you off when they found out who you were?"

"There's something else you need to know," Joey looked at his father.

"You can tell them...you found it."

"What is it?" Emmaline stood up and walked toward Luke, then she sat down beside him on the bed. Joey started to speak.

"Dad's moving his office to Blacksburg, so I've been helping to clean out the cellar – you know all the old case files and documents and such. Anyway – I found a metal locker box marked Waverly/Summerlin, so I started reading through the stuff. It was mostly about Connally's inheritance of the property by being the only known surviving relative. There was also a document about the Summer House being given to Grace Henry for her "service to the family" it said. I pulled everything out of the box and placed it all in a new cardboard box because of the rust and what not."

"Okay – we know all of that I think," said Emmaline.

"Well, I carried the old box to the dump in the back of my Dad's truck and I guess the wind did it – but when I was unloading stuff I noticed the leather lining in the lid was peeling back and there was a leather woven pouch sticking out. I pulled the leather off and opened the pouch, which was tied with twine. There was a letter from my great-grandfather inside – it has his seal on it – and the local magistrate's seal from 1873. I'd like to read it to you if I can." Joey removed a piece of paper from his satchel and unfolded it slowly as if it might break or burst into flame.

The group was looking around at each other except for Joey's dad who held a slight grin. Joey held the letter toward the light and began to read.

***On October 5, 1873, this officer of the court for the State of Virginia and the county seat of Pulaski did hereby violate his oath to uphold the laws as written and defined.***

*In the specific matter of the awarding of the property known as Waverly Plantation to the Connally family of Roanoke, I have superseded and ignored the wishes of the last surviving member of the Summerlin family, that being Thomas Warren Summerlin. I take no pride in discounting the last will and testament of a man, but circumstances and promises for retribution brought upon my family by a very powerful state senator were enough for me to ignore the negro wife of Thomas Summerlin – Mrs. Grace Henry-Summerlin, who's marriage to Thomas was done lawfully and under the eyes of God. I see no chance of Grace winning anything in court in the State of Virginia as it stands now. As a selfish, but God-fearing man I am certain that my actions will one day lead to punishment by my Maker. To Grace Summerlin I would offer my apologies for rendering her inheritance non-binding. May God find mercy for me at my judgment.*

*Joseph h. Millstone – Esquire – Sealed and Stamped*

The group sat stunned, and nobody offered a word until Mathilde Foster decided it was her place to speak.

"You think that my family hasn't known this entire time that the farm at the top of the hill was stolen from us?" Mathilde got up and walked toward the Millstones. "You aren't telling me anything we don't already know – why do you think I got as far away from that place as I could?"

Joseph Millstone III stood up and walked over to Joey's satchel, where he reached in and removed a folder with another document inside. He pulled it out and the group could see the yellowed document had been sealed with a family crest.

"There was one more thing in the lining of that box," Millstone swung the document around for the group to see. "It's the last will and testament of Thomas Warren Summerlin leaving everything – and I mean everything – to Grace Henry-Summerlin."

The group stood silent again and Emmie reached out to Luke and found his hand – she clutched it tightly.

"Just more paperwork that says the farm was stolen from my family with the help of your family," Mathilde looked at Emmaline as Joey walked up to her and looked into her eyes. "It's been almost a hundred years."

"On the contrary, Mrs. Foster – with your mother being incapacitated you are the only known surviving heir to her estate," Joey held up the letter. "With these two documents, and your permission, my father feels almost certain he can take that farm back."

# 72

Mathilde had just turned seven when she and her mother's lives took a dark turn. Caroline German was a beautiful, blonde, fifteen-year-old who was the pride of her Christiansburg family. Her father was the mayor, and her mother was the head of the Women's auxiliary at Christiansburg Baptist Church. They were Christiansburg. In the mid-summer of 1912, Caroline's mother noticed a change in her daughter's habits and morning routine, and it did not take her long to realize that Caroline was going to have a baby. When confronted, Caroline panicked, and instead of revealing the true father of the child, she accused Nate the "negro janitor" of raping her one afternoon after school. She recanted her story a few days later, but the damage had already been done. After the accusations were made public, Nate was jumped by a group of men on his way back to Summer House one night and beaten to death. Beatrice found him about a half-mile from the Mercantile after she noticed he was late. Nobody was ever charged – and Beatrice never remarried.

In early 1922, Mathilde was in Blacksburg buying supplies for the school when she slipped from the buckboard and landed in thick orange mud. Anthony Foster helped her get cleaned up, and then escorted her back to Christiansburg and then on to Summer House in what was now being called Draper's Valley. Gracie and Beatrice served him a nice venison stew, and as he was leaving he asked Beatrice if he could come see Mathilde when he came back through these parts.

Bea looked at Mathilde who offered a sheepish smile – and she said that she thought that would be perfectly fine. Turns out Anthony came through these parts quite a bit…or more likely went out of his way. In 1925, Anthony and Mathilde were married, and she moved with him to Roanoke to start a family. As the Great Depression took hold of the country, the Foster's postponed having children until the early 1940's when James was born…and he was soon after followed by Emmaline.

Beatrice lived with her mother…for her entire life. She didn't regret it – she loved her mother more than anything in this world. They were best friends. Beatrice recalled once in 1898 when two colored men came riding up on horses. Gracie told her they were her brothers – and they stayed for almost a month. Tandey looked the worst for wear as he recounted numerous cattle drives he had been on with Cozy. Cozy had a limp when he returned and when Gracie asked him about it, he just simply laughed and said, "I finally met me a Commanche, Mama." Rhett had gotten married and parted ways with the boys many years back – he was now a cattle farmer on the coast of California. At the end of their stay, Cozy and Tandey Summerlin rode West one last time – "maybe to Latin America" they said…and Gracie and Bea never saw them again.

In the late Summer of 1916 came the news of Elijah Summerlin's death in Madison, West Virginia. Gracie sat on her swing for two straight days after returning from his funeral. At the age of seventy-four Gracie marched straight up the Connally's drive and strode through the pasture to Thomas' grave where she fell on her knees and sobbed. Then she placed honeysuckle and lilac on the grave and went to make her way back down the hill. She ran into the Connally's son James standing in front of the house.

"Why are you here, Gracie?" he said.

"Paying respect to my husband, Thomas."

"Your husband? That's funny."

"I also told him his son Elijah had passed on."

"Took you long enough to tell him – didn't it."

Gracie walked up to within two feet of James Connally, "Sir, your aim with your words is just as bad as your aim with a damned slingshot – way off the mark."

Connally raised his hand to back hand her, but his wife caught his arm.

"Don't come back up here."

"Everyone in your family will answer to God Almighty at Judgment Day – you don't concern the likes of me no more," Gracie pushed off down the drive and walked back to Summer House.

In the Spring of 1929, Gracie Henry-Summerlin got out of her bed at daybreak and made herself some Jasmine tea. Then she went barefoot out to her garden and picked a bunch of lilac. A short walk to the fence gave her the honey-suckle vines she needed to wrap the lilac into a bundle. Then she sat on her swing and waited. She never saw Beatrice come outside…never heard the words "Are you alright, Mama,", never felt her daughter's hands as she shook her shoulders back and forth. At 8:30 a.m. the tiny teacup in her right hand fell to the ground with a clink and her tea ran down through the roots of the oak and sank into the Summerlin soil. A minute later she stretched out her right hand over her daughter's shoulder – then she smiled, closed her eyes, and took Thomas' hand.

# 73

August 9, 1916, began as an abnormally warm summer day in Madison, West Virginia. Eli Montgomery, along with his wife and two daughters, were joined by four other children at the schoolhouse on Little Cabin Creek just Southwest of the small town. The area was characterized by sharp rising ridges with narrow valleys dispersed between them. Cattle and crops were the local economy. The school was a small, mostly dilapidated wooden structure with a very rusted metal roof that used to be red. Now it served as a negro schoolhouse with a curriculum designed and delivered by Eli and his wife Roberta. The windows were all raised, and the children were cleaning vigorously in preparation for a new school year. The Montgomery's had been operating the local school for twenty years now, and it was one of the best in the state. They planned to work all day and into the evening.

In the small town there was a single constable who ran a courthouse and a two-cell jail. At 6:30 pm the telephone began to ring in that office, but there was nobody there to answer it...and it was the only phone in town. If the sheriff had been there to answer the telephone, he might have been able to warn folks of the edge of the remnants of a hurricane that was wrapping around from the Northeast. Instead, there were no warnings – and the full force of the torrential rain and high winds began to pummel the mountaintops above Madison – and then it swept down into the valley and slowed down. An estimated ten inches of rain fell over the next few hours.

Eli and Roberta saw the dark clouds approaching and determined it to be a regular afternoon summer thunderstorm. They had the children close all the windows, and they all sat on the floor in the middle of the room to let it pass. The storm persisted as night fell. The winds sounded as though they would rip the old metal roof right off the building. One seam split and the attached panels began to bang loudly from above. Two of the children began to cry and Roberta gathered them in her lap and wrapped her apron around them. The group sat huddled in the darkness as the old building began to shift and groan. Eli knew this was no ordinary storm, but he was not prepared for the side door next to Little Cabin Creek to come flying inward and off its' hinges with two feet of water behind it. When it did, he felt the brick pier foundation of the building beginning to give way – and one corner of the schoolhouse started to crumble into the creek. Now the group was standing up in two feet of muddy water and everyone was screaming. Eli told his wife that they had to get out and move up the hill to higher ground. They moved the children to the side of the building farthest from the creek and Eli slammed open the window. It was dark, but his eyes had adjusted enough so that he could see the swift moving water pouring past the building. He sat on the sill and then dropped himself into the rising creek. Immediately he was struck by a log and almost knocked off his feet. The water was between his knees and his waist, and the roaring sound of it screaming through the valley was deafening.

He yelled to Roberta to lower the children to him – and one by one he transported them through the swift current, put them up on a rock outcropping on the hill, and told them to run straight up the mountain as fast and far as they could. Each time he returned to the schoolhouse the water was higher – until it was almost at his chest. Five children were moved, and it was time for his oldest daughter, Rose, to be transported. She crawled through the window and sat on her father's shoulders as the water pounded and swirled around them. Then another bigger log knocked Eli off his feet, and he lost his grip on Rose's leg as she disappeared into the darkness of the flood. He held his breath for a moment as the log pushed around him and headed south, then he heard her calling out for help in the darkness. She was somewhere below the schoolhouse hanging on to something. Eli argued with Roberta, but she eventually gave up her fight to save her daughter and crawled out into Eli's arms. He got her safely to the bank and told her to run as she screamed at him to save Rose.

Eli Montgomery plunged headfirst back into the raging floodwaters, and Roberta never knew that he reached their daughter and that they both clung to a large sycamore branch, and each other as the schoolhouse finally gave up its' anchorage, crumbled, and swept them both down Little Cabin Creek and into the dark wilderness beyond. Ten days later they were found twenty feet apart five miles downstream.

There was no parade or fanfare for Eli Montgomery, but twenty-two years later his widow, Roberta, oversaw the opening of the Eli Montgomery Provisional School outside of Madison, West Virginia. His legacy as an educator, a hero, and a good man, was sealed in the tiny mountain town forever.

In late August of 1965, Emmaline Foster and Luke Montgomery pulled into Madison in Luke's father's old green pickup truck. It wasn't a long trip over for them from Beckley, but the pickup still struggled mightily with each hill it climbed. They stopped at a Marathon station on the way into town, and each got an RC Cola and a Moonpie, Luke's favorite meal to share with Emmie. They laughed together as they continued the next mile and a half before pulling into the gravel parking area of the Eli Montgomery School. There were three other late model cars in the lot, and they sat there in the pickup as they finished their late lunch. As the pair exited the truck a colored woman came out of the building wearing a peach-colored dress – she carried a small cardboard box with rulers, pencils, and notebooks inside. She stopped to speak with Luke and Emmaline as they were walking toward the plaque on the wall at the school's entrance.

"Good afternoon…may I help you in any way?" she asked.

"I just wanted to stop by and…well pay my respects to the namesake of the school – I don't know much of him really," Emmaline faced the woman and gave her a small grin and maybe a shrug.

"He was my father…and he gave everything to give the colored children of this community a better life," the woman smiled. "I try to fulfill his legacy every day."

Emmie glanced at Luke who was smiling back at her from the single crutch that supported his quickly healing leg. "He seemed like a great man – I'm sure he's missed."

"Been gone near fifty years now," the woman stepped closer as if to get a better look at Emmaline. "Why the interest if you don't mind my asking, child."

"I don't mean this to come as a shock, but I'm pretty certain that your father was my grandmother's half-brother." Emmaline lifted her eyes and looked at the woman.

"I see it now," she said. "You're Bea's granddaughter – your mama is Mathilde."

Emmie looked at Luke with shock on her face, "You knew of my mother?"

"Knew of her?" the woman laughed. "Spent summers with her many times – your grandmother and her mother Gracie would come for a nice long stay…less after my father died."

"My mother never told me of you…neither did my grandmother…she gave me a diary, but it didn't mention you."

"She was very protective – that's certain."

"Protective?" Emmaline looked puzzled.

"We were never allowed to go to Summer House – I think they called it," the woman reached out and put her hand on Emmie's shoulder. "I always dreamed it was some big mansion in the rich farmland of Virginia – seemed to be very secretive about it."

"So, your father wasn't buried at Summer House?"

"Heavens no, child – he's buried right yonder at the church," she pointed across and diagonally down the street. "Next to my sister, Rose."

"I-," Emmie didn't know what to say next.

"I was Ruth Montgomery – now I'm Ruth Adams," Ruth smiled at her. "You need to follow me up to the house – I know Mama would love to lay eyes on you."

Emmie looked at Luke, "Is it okay?"

"You're kidding right?" Luke opened the pickup door for her. "This is why we came."

They followed Ruth in the creaky old truck until they were just a couple of miles outside of town, when she slowed to turn on a brown dirt road that was speckled with white, yellow, and brown river rock. A small cloud of dust rose as they followed. Not far up the road they pulled into a circular drive which curled in front of a little white house with green shutters. The front porch had a green wrought iron railing, and an aluminum chair and glider completed it. Luke and Emmie got out of the truck behind Ruth.

"My husband Ernie is working in the field up behind the house…I can see the dust from the tractor. But Mama is inside with a lady named Annie Jones who stays with her during the day," Ruth started up the three red brick front steps.

"Do you have children. Ms. Ruth?" Emmie asked.

"Benjamin – he's in the Army – scared to death for him right now, and Agnes – she's at Howard studying the law," Ruth pulled open the screen door and turned around.

"My brother is in the Marines," Emmie choked up saying this, then added, "he's missing in Southeast Asia."

"I'm so sorry Emmaline – that must be James."

Emmaline grabbed Luke's arm as if she needed to be steadied. "I didn't tell you my name."

"Come inside, dear," Ruth pushed the dark brown oak front door open. "You need to know that Mama has senility – some days she don't even know me."

They walked into a small living room with hardwood floors and a brown and tan throw rug under a walnut coffee table in front of a plastic covered sofa. But it was all the pictures on the walls that floored Emmaline Foster. Her great-grandmother, her mother and father, and finally her Grandma Bea sitting with two young children on her lap – her and her brother.

"My God," she said as tears filled her eyes…and she didn't try to stop them from running down her beautiful face. Luke reached into his shirt pocket and handed her his clean handkerchief, not the one he kept in his back pocket. He wanted to take her in his arms, but nothing had changed in their relationship, and they remained "very good friends."

Ruth reached out and took her by the hand to lead her through another doorway and into a bright kitchen and den with a great Southern facing exposure looking down over the farm fields in the small valley below. An older colored woman sat on the edge of a brown wool covered sofa holding a glass, as an even older lady seated in a green recliner leaned forward to drink. The woman in the recliner wore wire glasses that hung at the end of her nose with a chain that went back over both ears and around her grey hair in the back. She had a heavy Afghan across her lap. The woman slowly looked up as the three walked into the room. Ruth walked over to her.

"Mama, I want you to meet some folks," Ruth put her hand on Roberta's shoulder.

"I'm Luke Montgomery, ma'am," Luke thought he would get his introduction out of the way since it was of little importance in this moment.

"My heavens," Roberta spoke slowly and pushed her glasses up on her nose. "Lucky Luke's boy – how is Lucas?"

Luke's jaw dropped and he started to speak – to tell her of his father's death – but then he just stopped and looked at Ruth. His grandfather was the only person he had ever heard call his father "Lucky Luke."

Ruth took Emmaline by the hand and pulled her closer to Roberta Montgomery, but she didn't get a chance to speak.

Roberta pulled herself to the edge of her chair and reached forward to take both of Emmaline's hands in her crooked boney fingers.

"I always said you never aged a day in your life – more of a beauty than yesterday," Roberta pulled Emmie closer and kissed her on the cheek then she pushed her back up. "Let me get a good look at you," she grinned a broad smile with no teeth.

"My beautiful Gracie..."

# 74

Emmaline and Luke rolled into Richmond around eight-thirty after their long drive back from West Virginia. Their conversation revolved around the next steps in their young lives, and much to Luke's chagrin their continued "friendship". Emmie had traveled to Walter Reed at the request of Luke's mother. The doctors and staff had fallen in love with her and asked her to move there to take a position at the hospital – to treat colored patients of course. She had considered it, but felt like her calling was within her community, so she intended to return to Richmond to start her nursing career at Sarah Baker Hospital. She also wanted to stay near her parents in case there was any word about James. Luke was a wild card since he had been discharged from the Marines. His leg felt good now, although some mornings the pain behind his knee and down through his ankle caused him to hobble for the first hour or so after he got up. He told Emmaline he was thinking of taking his mother to Kentucky, where he could get a job training racehorses at a large Thoroughbred farm where he knew the owner. Emmie acted as if she was very excited about the next act of his life, but she couldn't control the ache in her heart. She found herself staring out the window of the truck to hide her sadness that he was probably leaving her…and maybe for the last time. She still tried to convince herself it was for the best. Luke was hoping she would beg him to stay, and his disappointment in her reaction was spread across his blank face. This drive felt like a goodbye.

But not one thing they talked about ever happened.

They entered the front door of the Foster's Church Hill home to find Anthony and Mathilde seated at the breakfast table with a piece of paper laying between them. After a quick round of hugs Anthony asked them both to sit down, then he began to speak.

"We got a phone call this morning from Joe Millstone… and then a man delivered this document to the door a few hours ago," Anthony picked up the paper to read it.

"Oh, God, is it James?" Emmaline leaned forward in her chair.

"No, Sweetie, there's still no word," Mathilde put her hand on her daughter's.

"This is a court order from Pulaski County - I'll read it as best as I can…got some words I ain't seen before," Anthony rustled the paper and pushed on his readers. He read it slowly "Based on the recent revelation of documents that were either hidden or destroyed by David and Rosemary Connally and the attorney Joseph Millstone in or around August 13, 1873, this court orders the rightful return of the property as stated below to the heirs of the lawful wife of Thomas Warren Summerlin, that being Grace Henry-Summerlin. The heirs of David and Rosemary Connally have as of this date been notified to vacate the property within thirty days of the date of this order. The land has been ordered turned over to Mathilde Foster, granddaughter of Grace Henry-Summerlin and eldest living blood relative with no encumbrances and in its current state with no taxes owed. All buildings, property, and assets previously on the plot described below are to be left as is. Only personal items may be removed "

There was a definite air of shocked silence that fell over the table. The group looked at each other until Luke smiled at Emmaline and she forced out a question.

"What does all of this mean?"

"It means we own a two thousand- and twenty-six-acre farm in the Virginia mountains," now it was Mathilde's turn to smile

"This came with a note from Millstone," said Anthony. "Connally wants to meet with us at Waverly tomorrow afternoon - Joe says he wants to offer us money to walk away."

"What are you gonna do?" Asked Luke.

"Since neither of us know anything about farming…I guess we'll go hear what he has to say," said Anthony. "Luke, I'd really like it if you would come since you have worked there - we don't know what to expect."

Luke glanced at Emmaline then looked back at Anthony. "I would be more than happy to sir. Can I sleep on the couch?"

"I made up James' room for you, Luke…family don't sleep on the couch if I can help it." Mathilde smiled at him. "Ya'll hungry? Got some left over beef stew I can put back on the burner."

"I would love that, ma'am, " Luke looked back at Emmaline.

"We are all blessed to have you in our lives, son," when Mathilde said this she directed her eyes at Emmaline who quickly looked down at the table.

"Luke, you can follow us in your truck. Planning to leave by nine," Anthony got up from the table. "I'm gonna hit the hay – got a feeling tomorrow will be a long day and I need some sleep…I already called my guys at the store to tell them I won't be in."

Luke devoured two helpings of Mrs. Foster's beef stew then joked about hoping Emmaline could cook this well for him someday. Her reaction was a smirk as she stomped off to bed. Mathilde told him to "stop poking the bear." Then she told him to put his bowl in the sink because she was off to bed.

Despite the anxiousness that swirled through Luke's stomach when his head hit the pillow, he slept well through the night, and morning came quickly. The first smell of bacon and eggs brought his feet to the floor with a smile on his face. The realization that he was sleeping in his missing friend's childhood bedroom quickly overwhelmed him and his smile faded...until Emmaline tapped at the door and told him to get up. They made quick work of breakfast and clean-up, and found themselves on the road earlier than they expected. Emmaline rode with her parents until they stopped for gas, then she switched over to Luke's truck.

"Came back where you belong, I see," Luke said.

"My mother said you looked lonely, and I said I didn't care – so she ordered me to ride with you," Emmie looked especially beautiful this morning with her long dark hair swirling over one shoulder and down to her waist. "Stop trying to butter-up my parents – I'm not theirs to just give away."

"So, they do like me," Luke laughed. "It's working just as planned."

Emmaline punched him hard in the arm and he pretended to lose control of the wheel long enough to make her gasp.

"I'm scared about today," Emmie looked at him. "I still think this man tried to either scare us away or kill us – and there's no doubt his grandfather thought he killed Elijah."

"We are meeting Joe and his dad at the Mercantile and following them up – I called him last night and asked him to call in a favor. The sheriff will be with us."

Emmaline put both hands on Luke's forearm and said, "Oh my God, thank you…that makes me feel so much better that you got the sheriff to come who didn't believe us in the first place." The feel of his arm almost caused her to not complete her smart retort.

"Joe told me he was planning to come anyway to serve some papers, or something related to this."

"We'll see…"

They arrived at the Mercantile early and they all went inside for some great iced tea and sandwiches. The Draper's great-granddaughter served them again and expressed how happy she was that they were back in town for a visit. Anthony seemed surprised at the warm welcome they received and told Luke in the bathroom that they had never stopped here when they came to pick up Beatrice because he thought it was a white folks place. "They are just good people" was Luke's response.

Around two o'clock the Millstones pulled into the gravel lot and told them to follow in one car. They drove past Summer House which was now badly overgrown with weeds from the neglect since Beatrice had left. Then they turned up the long dirt drive and under the archway leading to Waverly. Emmaline could tell her mother was very nervous, and she put her hand on her shoulder from the back seat. Mathilde met her hand with her own then put her cheek on top of both. They pulled up in Anthony's car behind the Millstones, who parked next to the sheriff's vehicle. The Connallys were nowhere in sight. The group got out of their respective rides as the sheriff walked over.

"Afternoon, folks," the sheriff tipped his hat slightly – mostly to the Millstones. "I was instructed to place these fine folks in the parlor whilst you lawyers meet with the Connallys in the living room first. Mr. Connally says he don't negotiate with this type."

Joe Millstone II stepped forward and said, "I will speak with them prior to whatever proposal they have for these folks – but you need to tell them that this is not a mediation…they can make a valid and fair offer that the Fosters have every right to either refuse or accept. Right now, they have twenty-nine days to vacate. You can also tell him that I can't be bought or threatened over this matter. This is as personal for my family as it is for my clients."

"Whatever you say, Joe," the sheriff turned to lead them into the house, then he stopped to kick mud from his shoes before going up the steps. "They want you folks to remove your shoes before coming into the home."

Mathilde could see the anger rising in her husband and she took him by the hand. "Sheriff – you tell James Connally that this is the only time I will ever take my shoes off to come into this house – and that his feet will never touch the floor in here again twenty-nine days from now."

"Yes, ma'am," the sheriff chuckled, and the group followed him inside where he stopped to open a twelve-foot-tall set of pocket doors which opened to a magnificent room filled with antiques, and skirted by wainscoting. "The Foster's and their boy can wait in here." He closed the doors behind them.

"This don't feel right," said Anthony.

"I don't trust any of these folks," said Mathilde.

"The Millstones are good people – I think you have to let this play out a little," Luke walked across the room and started looking at family portraits on the wall.

"James Connally is not a good man, Mama," Emmaline walked toward a writing desk and opened the top drawer as though she was checking the age of the piece. She closed it back then opened the glove drawer on the right side of another piece.

Mathilde sat down on the edge of the overstuffed Eastlake couch and Anthony stood by the doors to see if he could hear anything from the other room. They could each individually hear their own hearts beating in their chests. An eternity later led to the doors creaking open and the two Millstones stepped inside then closed the doors behind them.

"I'm not going to waste any time – they offered you $25,000 to be paid over five years if you walk away from this matter," The senior Millstone looked at Mathilde.

"What's land worth up in this part of the state?" asked Anthony.

"Honestly?" Millstone glanced around the room. "More than ten times that."

"Then why should we take it?" asked Mathilde.

"You don't have to…but do you know anything of horse and hay farming?"

"I guess, rightly so, I don't." Mathilde sat back on the couch. "What do you think, Luke?"

Luke shook his head. "I'd turn it down and see what they are actually willing to pay."

"They will drag this into court, Luke," said Joey.

"Will they win?"

"Depends on the judge…but its fifty-fifty."

"Will you represent them?" Luke looked at the Fosters.

"We will," said the senior Millstone. "Pro-bono."

Anthony looked confused.

"For free," said Luke.

"That's a lot of money, Luke," Emmaline walked back over from the desk.

"When I was working up here, I watched him sell one horse for more than that…several times," said Joey.

Mathilde looked at Luke and then Anthony, "Tell him we don't accept," she said.

"Do you want to offer them a number?" asked Millstone.

"No, just tell them we don't accept," Mathilde started toward the door. "You can also tell them we will be leaving now."

"Mrs. Foster, just wait right here and I'll be right back." Millstone walked out the pocket doors and closed them again. Joey stayed behind.

"What you think, Joe?" asked Luke quietly as he pulled him to the side.

"I think this poorly run farm is worth a goldmine if you want my opinion."

It wasn't long before the elder Millstone returned. "$100,000 – paid over ten years," he said. Then he waited for Mathilde.

"That's a lot of money," she walked over and took Luke by the hand, then she looked at Anthony who just smiled at her and nodded. "Luke, Anthony and me – we don't know anything about horses and farming…but you do. If we take this farm back – will you bring your mother here and run it for us?"

"Mother – what are you doing?" Emmie looked at her father. "Daddy?"

"I – I don't know what to say," said Luke.

"Well, you'd better say something, son," said Anthony. "We make this decision right here – right now."

Luke looked at Emmaline who glanced down at the floor. His heart was pounding into his ears. "Yeah – yeah, I can run this place – and make you a lot of money I think."

"Tell him we will not accept any offer, Mr. Millstone," Mathilde said.

"He will fight this in court," said Millstone.

"Then so will we," Mathilde turned to Luke and took his hand once more. "Firstly, I want you to move my grand-mother back up here to be buried by her Thomas. We will have a family ceremony."

The pocket doors flew open, and James Connally stormed into the room with the sheriff just behind him, and his wife with her arms crossed standing in the doorway. Emmaline could tell the woman had been crying all night…or were those bruises covered in make-up. Either way she looked very distraught.

"Hate to break up your little fairytale in here – but here is what's going to happen!" Connally made his way into the center of the room and stood in front of the group. "You will take the first offer and get the hell off of my property – or I will see you all penniless and living on the street!"

"We already penniless, sir," Anthony took a step toward him. "Ain't nothin' the likes of you gon' do to make that no worse."

"You stole this land from my family – and we are taking it back," Mathilde stood up next to her husband.

"Get your inbred, negro ass off my property!"

Luke stood between them and clinched his fist. Emmaline put her hand on his arm, and he felt his anger and tension wane – but just a little. Her voice of reason saved James Connally from a broken jaw yet again.

"That's enough, James," the sheriff moved further into the room and Connally took a step back. "The paper's been served, and you need to comply – call your lawyer."

Connally took another step back, reached behind him, and opened the little glove box on the desk. A small snub nosed .38 appeared in his hand and he pointed it straight at Emmaline's chest from eight feet away. Luke stepped in front of her.

"No Luke!" she screamed.

"Drop the gun, James!" the sheriff pulled his service revolver and pointed it at Connally.

Connally squeezed the trigger and Luke waited for the all too familiar flash of gunfire – and he expected to feel his chest explode in pain once again. But…there was a click…then another…then two more in succession…then Emmaline glanced around from behind Luke and smiled.

"You stupid little colored whore!"

Luke clinched his fist again and started to raise it. Then he stopped and looked into the beautiful eyes of Emmaline Foster who just gave him a little shrug of one shoulder.

The punch was two years in the making…the threats to Beatrice…the fire at Summer House…the loss of his scholarship at UVA…the full coiled up ferocity of Luke's fist came crashing into the jaw of James Connally as two teeth flew in one direction…bone crunched like a cracker… and the bastard stumbled backward into a heap on the floor.

The sheriff was on Connally then and quickly had handcuffs on him as he lay on the floor writhing in pain. As he was being charged with attempted murder, Emmaline slowly made her way over to him and he stared up at her with one eye already turning a deep purple color.

Emmaline Foster raised her clinched fist above James Connally and as her fingers slowly opened one bullet after another dropped to the hardwood floor next to his head with the clatter of a tap dancer.

"Close your ears, mama," said Emmaline. "Mr. Connally – get… the fuck out of my mama's house."

As the commotion of the day spilled out into the yard, a group of mares in the small upper paddock got very agitated and began to gallop in increasingly dangerous circles along the fence rail. Another mare in an adjacent field began to paw at the fence and turned to kick it a few times. Luke moved toward the paddock and climbed through the bottom two fence rails. The mares took another lap around as Luke held out an open palm to them. One by one they slowed down and walked toward him until he was scratching their heads with both hands. The other mare lost interest and moved back out into the grass.

"He does seem to have a way with them," Mathilde walked up behind Emmaline who was watching Luke from across the yard.

"Really, Mom, I think Luke will do a great job for you here." Emmaline smiled without looking back.

"No – he won't."

"Look at him – are you crazy?"

"Emmaline, my sweet angel, your father and I want you to have the farm…Luke works for you."

# 75

The Fosters didn't stand over the Connallys while they had their personal items removed from Waverly. The judge ruled that because the lineage of the Thoroughbreds was easily traceable back to Thomas Summerlin that any animal with any link to *Midnight* must remain as property of the farm. This was most of the horses except for a draft horse, a couple of quarter horses, and Rosemary's minis. The Connallys decided to have those auctioned in Blacksburg and Luke bought the lot of them, and brought them back home. James Connally was able to post bail easily on the attempted murder charge and he was ordered to stay at least five miles from Waverly House. While he was incarcerated, another inmate named Emile Rodriguez saw him and began to brag that he used to work for him. One night Emile told his cellmate that James Connally had paid him to "burn that house to the ground with those bastards inside." With the coaxing of his cellmate Emile was able to get his sentence reduced for his testimony. James Connally was re-arrested and charged with arson and attempted murder, and the judge ordered him held without bail. Still, he sued to get the farm back.

The District Court of Appeals upheld the lower court decision returning the property to the Summerlin heirs. Connally appealed to the Virginia State Supreme Court where the claim was again denied. An attempt to take the case to the U.S. Supreme Court was met with such resistance that it was immediately refused. The United States had gone from the Civil Rights Act of 1964 into full blown racial tension.

Riots occurred in Watts, Newark, and Detroit in 1965 and 1967, and in 125 different cities after the assassination of Dr. Martin Luther King Jr. in 1968. The U.S. Supreme Court had no appetite to hear the case of a white man's family who had stolen the rightful property of a widowed woman of color in the rural South. In late 1967 James Connally was sentenced to 25 years in prison for his crimes – unfortunately for him his ex-wife Rosemary corroborated every accusation against him. In February of 1978 James Connally died in a Virginia State penitentiary, and he was buried in a pauper's grave when no one claimed his body.

# 76

Emmaline Foster stood staring out the kitchen window at Waverly on a warm morning in the late Spring of 1966. She had just filled a kettle to make iced tea and was waiting for it to boil. She twirled two fingers through the ends of her long black silky hair as the sun reflected an almost orange glow around her face. Her other hand was clutched at her chest. This was, she thought, one of God's most magnificent mornings.

"Ms. Emmaline – Ms. Emmaline…does you needs to me to go start you an icy cold shower? Does you?" hearty laughter rose from behind her as Samantha Morgan entered the kitchen. Sam was one of Emmie's greatest friends from back in Richmond, and had come to stay for a few weeks.

"Very funny," Emmie said without turning around.

"Give me a chance to look too then – since you don't seem to have any horse in this race so to speak." Sam pushed up to Emmaline by the sink and joined her in staring out the window.

Two colored men were throwing bales of last year's hay up onto a flatbed trailer to a shirtless man who was stacking it four high. The plan was to take the hay to the new herd of Black Angus the Foster's had procured by selling a few horses. Sweat rolled down the man's back and his muscles rippled golden and tan in the bright morning sunshine.

"Lucas!" Sam yelled and stepped away from the window.

"Oh, hey Em – good morning…how are you?" Luke glanced back at her and the pause he took to catch her gaze caused him to miss the next bale, almost knocking him from the trailer.

"Just saying good morning," Emmaline kicked Sam in the ankle and walked away from the window to check on her kettle.

"You ain't fooling anyone but yourself."

"It's not fair to him – he needs to get married and settle down."

"What's not fair, my friend, is to see the pain in his eyes every time he looks at you," said Sam.

"What pain?"

"A young strong strapping man like Luke has needs."

"Oh my God, stop it."

"Are you that blind? He loves you, Emmaline."

"So, he says…"

"And you said he was going to take a bullet for you? A man doesn't do that for someone he doesn't care about."

"He's a soldier – it's instinct to him," Emmaline turned the heat down on the pot and floated ten tea bags in the water, then she dumped in a cup of sugar and put the lid on.

"That man would do anything for you…you're killing him."

"Don't I need to get you to the train station?"

"Do you dream about him? Be honest."

"Sometimes – but we are always around each other now."

"Emmaline, I love you…but you are a stubborn mule."

"Have you packed? Need some help?" Emmie walked out of the kitchen and back into the living room.

Three weeks had passed since Samantha Morgan went back to Richmond, and Emmaline had been working alternating night and day shifts at the Altamont Hospital in

Christiansburg, while sometimes traveling overnight to assist at Burrell Memorial in Roanoke. Luke had been working his regular seven day a week sunup to sundown shifts at the farm. At Luke's insistence he and his mother had been living at the Mercantile boarding house despite the Fosters offering up Summer House, and he rarely saw Emmaline for more than a few brief moments. Luke had resigned himself to running the farm for the Fosters, and Emmaline seemed to love living in the country. She had even learned to ride – with the help of a hired instructor…not Luke. Luke had built her a chicken coop, and she planted vegetables in the yard – very close to where Gracie's garden had been. Grace Summerlin's body had been exhumed and re-buried next to Thomas outside the upper pasture. Emmaline planted Lilacs around the cemetery and let the honeysuckle grow wild up there along the fence and into the oaks. She also moved Grace's swing back to its' original tree in front of Waverly. Everything was going smoothly for the two of them…until one warm evening when someone pounded on Luke's door at the Mercantile.

"Mr. Luke! You need to come quickly – there's a problem with Ms. Emmaline's horse, *Whinny!*" It was young Samuel Jenkins who was the son of one of the assistant caretakers at Waverly. His family lived in one of the old white houses that had been completely renovated and turned into a modern cottage complete with running water and appliances.

Luke grabbed Samuel a drink of water after his long run and helped him up in the old pick up for the ride up the hill. He could see the lights on in the barn from the road, and he didn't waste any time reaching the paddock gate. He sent Samuel home and walked into the barn to find Emmaline kneeling before *Whinny,* who was lying down in the center aisle.

"What have you done now, Ms. Emmaline?" Luke said.

"This isn't funny, Luke – she won't stand up!"

"Let's get her walking."

Luke dropped to his knees beside the mare and clipped a lead rope to her halter, then he put his hand on her head and stood up. As he stood, he gently pulled the mare to her feet, and she wobbled back and forth a couple of times – then she bit at her side once and looked at Luke with wide eyes.

"She's got good energy – go in the tack room and bring me the stainless-steel bucket hanging on the wall with the tubing in it…and grab the mineral oil."

Emmaline moved without saying a word and quickly brought what he needed.

"Fill the bucket halfway with water – then pour in mineral oil until I say stop," Luke unrolled the one-inch tubing with one hand as he clipped the mare into a set of crossties.

With his hands free he put his hand under the mare's neck and slid the tubing into her left nostril while blowing on one end until only four feet was left hanging out, then he attached the hand pump to the tube and pumped the oil and water mixture into *Whinny's* nostril. Then he sucked on the hose and began to siphon out green globs of hay mixed with feed. When he was done, he pulled the tube back out of the mare's nose.

"What is happening?" Emmaline finally spoke.

"Colic – um, impaction - wasn't too bad and I don't think she's flipped. We can have the vet out tomorrow. Can you walk her around for about thirty minutes and then put her in the stall with no hay," Luke picked up a rag and wiped his hands. "I need to go get cleaned up."

"Can you come back?"

"It's late, Em."

"Please, Luke."

"You walk *Whinny.*" Luke smiled at her and nodded.

"Deal."

Luke went back to the Mercantile and took a shower, then he put on a pair of tan work pants, a white button down, and his better pair of boots. He was back at the barn in twenty minutes and arrived just as *Whinny* was getting settled in for the night. Emmaline turned and met him in the aisle and gave him a hug.

"Thank you, Luke."

"I think she will be okay, but we should call Dr. Martin in the morning," he held onto her hug a little longer than a friend should have, and as he let her go, he took a deep sniff of her hair. She smiled to herself.

"There's a beautiful full moon tonight." Emmie said.

"Yes – it's bright out."

"Will you take me for a ride."

"In the truck?"

"No, Luke – on horseback – let's go down to the river."

"I'll have to tack up…"

"Bareback – we can take *Silver Queen.*"

Luke nodded his head and took the young mare out of her stall. Then he tied a rope bridle in place and climbed up on her back and reached an arm out to pull Emmaline up.

"Just a minute, it might get chilly."

Emmaline ducked into the tack room for a minute and came back with a bag slung over her shoulder…and wearing a dressage riding jacket.

"I didn't know this was a formal event," Luke laughed.

"Just pull me up."

The pair headed up the drive and turned out into the lower pasture. A few of the cows grumbled their discontent at being disturbed so late at night, but most just played dumb. They entered the woods on the other side and started down the old stream bed toward the New River. As they approached the huge rock outcropping Emmaline tightened her grip around Luke's waist.

"Let's climb up there and watch the moon set over the mountain."

"I thought you wanted to go to the river," Luke was trying to be cool but every nerve in his body was tingling.

"It will be fun – tie her to that small sycamore – she'll be fine for a few minutes."

Luke climbed down from *Silver Queen* and looped the hand tied bridle around the small tree, then he helped Emmaline down.

"If she gets loose, we'll be walking in the dark."

"Or we will have to stay on top of the rock until sunrise – always a pessimist lately," Emmaline laughed and started to climb with the bag slung over her shoulder.

The top of the rock provided an unprecedented view of the valley below, and of the farm above. They could even see the lights of Draper and the Mercantile five miles away. Even with the wind sifting softly through the new leaves of Spring, they could still hear the rushing of the icy river a hundred feet below. The bright full moon was cutting an arching path across the clear night sky, and stars fought for recognition in its wake. A lonely train horn groaned from the distance as it wound through the majestic Virginia mountains. It was the perfect night…and Emmaline couldn't have ordered one better.

"It's so beautiful up here, Luke."

"Yes, it is," Luke was staring at Emmie.

"No, Silly – the mountains."

They sat in silence for a while just listening to the lonely sounds of the forest around them.

"I've missed you," Emmaline looked at Luke just as his blue eyes reflected the moonlight back into hers. She almost gasped – and she definitely sighed.

"I've missed you too."

"I brought a blanket for us to sit on – sorry I forgot…is it okay?" Emmaline opened her bag and pulled out a flannel blanket.

Luke helped her unfold it and they sat back down.

"That's actually more comfortable than just sitting on rock," Luke laughed.

"I've missed you."

"Are you okay, Em?" Luke turned toward her, and he wanted to take her hand, but he didn't dare.

"I've been meaning to give you something," Emmaline turned away, unbuttoned her riding jacket, took it off, laid it on the rock, and turned back to Luke. "Well, to give you something back – I mean."

Luke immediately recognized his basketball sweatshirt, "I gave that to you – please don't give it back to me…it would break my heart."

"Well, it's never been washed so…"

Luke laughed, "But by now it must smell like you – maybe I do want it back."

"I felt you…when you smelled my hair…it's okay."

The train was getting closer, and a single wispy cloud passed by the moon.

"You're my world Emmaline."

"Luke, I want to give the shirt back to you."

"Em…"

Emmaline raised her arms and pulled the sweatshirt over her head as her beautiful black hair fell back to her bare shoulders. She placed the shirt to the side and pulled her hair back behind her. She took Luke's hand and pulled him toward her.

"Em…I-" Luke was stuck on that, so she spoke for both.

"Luke Montgomery – I love you…I have always loved you…I can't go one more night without being with you… without holding you in my arms…I -"

"Stop talking…" Luke put his hands on her cheeks, rose to his knees in front of her, and kissed her.

She unbuttoned his shirt and let it fall away as she fell into his eyes.

He kissed her again – this time longer…but softer.

She pulled him closer, and their bodies touched for the first time.

The train entered Draper Valley below them with a long blare of its horn at the distant road crossing in town.

Luke sat back on his heels and just stared at Emmaline. Tears were coming and he tried to stop them…it had been so long…but so worth it.

"I love you so much, Emmaline."

Emmaline stood before him and dropped the rest of her clothing, then she helped Luke remove his.

"Don't ever leave me again…" she whispered in his ear as she pulled him to her and onto the blanket.

"Never, never..." Luke didn't finish his thought as his lips met hers, and their bodies became one under the bright Virginia moonlight... as the train came around the river bend in the darkness… and the mighty rock began to tremble on the Summerlin Farm.

# 77

The staged handiwork of Gracie Henry-Summerlin was laid out forty-seven feet below the young couple… in a small cave with an entrance that was all but obscured after a mysterious rockslide blocked it from view in the late 1870's. Inside it appeared there had been a gunfight after a Union Captain and his corporal surprised a couple of vagrants or deserters – who would ever know? The captain was hit in the head by a rock wielded by the first man, who was then shot by the corporal. Another man in the cave fired a shot into the stomach of the corporal and ended his life near the entrance – then he finished off the captain with one shot to the head. The battle going on outside appeared to cause rocks to fall and seal off the escape of the fourth man. A man whose skeleton was eventually found with a mug in one hand and a pistol in the other. When he was discovered in the dim light of the cave a hundred years later, it almost appeared as though he was moving, but as the observer got closer, he found an eight-foot rattler coiled up tightly in the ribcage of the man – a man who was once known as the Gettysburg Ghoul…

…and then,

## June 18, 1967

Joe Millstone arrived at the Summerlin Farm in the early morning. Emmaline and Luke were already out in the barn with the farm staff having a brief morning meeting. Joe walked into the barn with a folder in his hand and walked right up to the young couple.

"I have some news from the court," said Joe.

"Pease don't tell us Connally has filed another appeal," Emmaline climbed down from the stool she was perched upon.

"This is from the U.S Supreme Court."

"I thought they wouldn't hear it," said Luke.

"It's not about Connally! You might want to sit back down."

"Just give it to us," Luke said.

"Have you heard of a case called Loving vs Virginia?"

"No," Emmaline leaned back on the stool.

"Richard and Mildred Loving are a married couple that moved to Virginia in 1958. He's white and she's colored. The State police arrested them, and they were sentenced to a year in jail. They sued the State of Virginia, and the case finally reached the Supreme Court." Joe was smiling now.

"Okay…," said Emmaline.

"The Supreme Court declared the laws of Virginia to be unconstitutional." Joe looked at them both.

"What does that have to do with us?" Luke said.

"Do you really think you guys have been fooling anyone for the last five years?" Joe laughed as young Samuel Jenkins ran up to them.

"It means you guys can get married for real!" Samuel yelled.

There was silence in the barn aisle as Luke and Emmaline looked at each other. Then Luke looked at Joe and then back at Emmie. Then he dropped to one knee to a collective gasp from the group. Then Emmaline dropped to her knees in front of him.

"We do this together…always together…will you marry me, Luke Montgomery?"

"Yes of course - will you marry me, Emmaline Foster?"

"Yes! Yes! the answer will forever be yes!"

On December 23, 1967, Luke and Emmaline said "I do" on the porch at Waverly House.

## March 9, 1972

Young Grace Abigail sat on the porch floor at her pregnant mother Emmaline's feet, playing with a small sack of marbles. As they inevitably rolled away from her, she would scramble in a huff to retrieve them. The late winter breeze coming down from the upper pasture was cooling, but not enough to keep them inside. Luke approached from the barn where he was undertaking a huge expansion that was doubling the size of their equine facilities. Their business had grown on the Thoroughbred side, but they also now dealt in Warmbloods and did Dressage training. They had two full-time instructors, and their clients came from all over the country. Luke stepped onto the porch and gave his wife a long kiss. Little Grace rolled her eyes and went back to her marbles as Luke kissed her on the top of her head.

"Got a slight issue outside the fence we took down."

"Where Gracie made the grave markers?" she knew they had moved the markers up into the family cemetery on the hill – as a symbolic gesture of course.

"Yes – the backhoe hit something where Samuel was supposed to be buried."

"What is it? Roots?"

"It's a large pine box – size of a coffin."

"Oh, my God."

"It can't be Samuel – he's buried in West Virginia for sure. Maybe it's one of the soldiers that was here."

"I'm having it lifted from the ground with a chain. We are going to open it."

Emmaline stood up and picked up young Grace, who protested at leaving her marbles behind. She followed Luke into the yard and up the hill to where the workmen had set the box. It certainly looked like a coffin – worn pine or ash about six feet long and three feet wide with no discernible markings. Luke retrieved a crowbar from his truck and met Emmaline next to the box.

"You don't have to see this – neither does Grace."

Emmaline nodded and walked with Grace about twenty feet away. She heard a squealing sound from behind her as Luke pried the box open against the protest of the old steel nails. She heard the lid hit the ground.

"Oh, my God!" Luke said and then laughed. "Em – come look at this!"

Emmaline came back with Grace in tow and when she looked in the box, she slowly lowered to her knees on the ground.

"It looks like your great-grandmother was the smartest person in the world," said Luke.

Inside the box…was silver…silver urns and chalices… silver plates…silver flatware…and four paintings.

"Her diary was a lie – the troops never stole the silver!" Emmie started to giggle. "She hid it where nobody would ever look."

"Killed two birds with one stone."

"Wait – the diary – watch Gracie." Emmaline turned and ran back to the house -she returned within three minutes and began leafing through the pages. Then she began to read – "Samuel was my silver knight in shining armor…she left us a clue."

Emmaline and Luke looked at each other incredulously.

"There's more," she said and began to read again. "There was never a shining star brighter than John, who shown like a diamond in the night sky," she looked at Luke and smiled. "Gunther was my hero. He was like a powerful cannon capable of fending off armies."

Luke looked back at the backhoe operator and picked up Grace.

"Keep digging – carefully along this straight line."

At the end of the day Luke and Emmaline had dug up the coffins in John and Gunther's graves...uncovering all the Summerlin family jewelry from John's and an arsenal of old guns from Gunther's. The first letter of each name even corresponded to what was inside.

"The page is torn, but it says something about the children keeping our lives full," said Emmaline.

A little more digging where "the children" were buried revealed another box – this one full of Mrs. Summerlin's fine china.

The following Thanksgiving the family used the china for the first time in one-hundred and twelve years in the Waverly dining room.

A few nights later Emmaline awakened Luke in the middle of the night.

"I had a dream."

"Are you okay?" Luke sat up.

"I went back and was looking at the diary again yesterday and I read the passage about Grace burying her son...it said, "Today I bury the second most important thing that ever happened in my life.""

"Okay."

"We know Elijah didn't die that day...and as much as I love you, Luke, I would never say one of my children was the second most important thing in my life."

"So, there's something else there....?"

"Maybe?"

"The marker was behind the house laying in the grass."

"She writes that he was buried under the oak."

"Be like a shot in the dark," Luke smiled in the darkness.

"You miss the shots you don't take – sorry for the basketball reference." Emmie laughed.

Luke started with an auger attached to the back of his tractor the next morning drilling holes in a pattern under the oak at Summer House. When he hit large roots or rocks, he stopped and moved over. Around four o'clock in the afternoon he hit something that sounded odd. He pushed a piece of long rebar down the hole and a hollow knocking sound came back.

"Let's start digging," he said.

By five they had the small pine coffin lying on the ground and Luke began to pry the box open. Emmaline turned away with Grace again.

"It's got a leather pouch inside it tied with string."

Emmaline turned and Luke handed her the pouch – it was her family after all.

Slowly Emmaline removed a wrapped bundle of paper and slowly untied it.

"Last Will and Testament of Thomas Warren Summerlin – leaving everything to Grace. It is identical to the copy the Millstones had."

## October 11, 1975

As Grandma and Grandpa Foster rolled up in front of the house Grace ran, and her little brother TJ waddled, toward the car. Emmaline came out the front door with an apron on, closely followed by her mother-in-law Adrienne who was working to get flour off her hands with a dish towel. It was a cool overcast day and it felt like snow was in the offing, but it wouldn't come for another few weeks. As Emmie stepped down off the bottom step Grace stopped in her tracks ten feet from Anthony Foster's car, then turned and ran behind her mother to hide. TJ climbed into Grandpa's arms, and they began to walk around the front of the car as Mathilde slowly got out of the front seat and closed the door. Emmaline met Luke coming from the barn and they walked toward the car. When they got within twenty feet the back door swung open and two black children climbed out and stood next to Mathilde. Emmie looked at her puzzled.

"This is Sovay, and he is eight, and this is Nimo, he is six," Mathilde was grinning from ear to ear.

"Have you adopted?" asked Emmie. Then a pretty Asian woman with long black hair got out of the car.

"This beautiful lady is Ponnleu, their mother, "said Mathilde.

"Hello, it's nice to meet you?" Emmaline gave her mother another funny look.

The boys stood on either side of their mother and she put her hands on their shoulders.

Emmaline walked closer to her mother, "And…who are they?"

"These are my grandchildren," Mathilde had tears streaming down her face now - and before she could say "they are your nephews", Emmaline was hit with an awesome realization and she dropped to her knees in front of the children.

A man got out of the car behind them.

"Hello, Ems…"

Emmaline Montgomery got to her feet and rushed into the waiting arms of her brother James.

## June 19, 1998

Beatrice Lynnette Montgomery came home from Chapel Hill to Summerlin Farm for a few days for a family reunion, she also took the occasion to announce to them that she was engaged to her long-time boyfriend Brooks Harrison, who had proposed to her the day after they graduated from undergrad. She was accepted at Georgetown Law School and the couple planned to move to Alexandria later in the summer. Brooks was starting work as a clerk for Representative James Clyburn of South Carolina.

The whole family was at the farm for this celebration, which was just made so much more special by the couple's announcement. The entire front yard of Waverly was filled with friends and family. Lynn decided to sit on her great-great grandmother's swing, and she slowly moved back and forth with just her toes on the ground. Emmaline decided this was a great photo opportunity and she told Lynn to get up and let Brooks sit down and then sit back on his lap. Emmie took a few photos before the entire yard heard the loud popping crack that was the two boards of the swing finally giving way after all these years. The young couple fell to the ground to rousing laughter.

Brooks hopped up and pulled his fiancé back to her feet, then he turned to look at the broken swing.

"There's something leather sticking out from between these boards," he said.

Emmaline walked over and gave a tug on the pouch, and it slid right out. It was identical to the pouch they had found in Elijah's grave twenty-five years earlier. She called Luke over.

She gently untied the twine and opened the pouch and a small silver ring rolled out and hit the ground. Emmaline picked it up and handed it to Luke who put his reading glass-es on.

"It's engraved – looks like a wedding ring – says "Madeline Gracie."

"No," Emmaline said, "it says "Madeline and then it says Gracie…this was Thomas Summerlin's mother's ring that he gave Gracie."

Emmaline twirled it in her fingers and looked at Lynn, "I think we can fit Lynn inside the ring."

"Can we fit "Bea" also," Lynn asked.

"I'm almost sure of it."

Emmaline looked back at the pouch and saw a document tucked deep inside.

She carefully unwrapped the document and the tears appeared instantly. She handed it to Luke who began to read.

"State of Virginia, County of Pulaski, Official Marriage License and Executed Certificate of Grace Henry and Thomas Warren Summerlin". It had wax seals of the Summerlin family and the Drapers…and the signatures of both Thomas and Gracie at the bottom.

# Epilogue

May 9, 2016

**University of Virginia**
**Commencement Ceremony**
**Charlottesville, Virginia**
**Commencement Address by The Honorable Dr. Lucas Montgomery Ph.D.**

It amazes me to see all the faces in robes and hats and tassels staring back at me. I'm not amazed by your achievements, that was expected. I have heard that you simply are the most diverse and talented group to walk the halls in Charlottesville history. No, what amazes me is that I see Black and White, Asian and Hispanic, men…and women. I was so humbled to play basketball for the Cavaliers from 1960 through 1963. The memories I have are simply unforgettable. The friends I made - the wonderful wife I met. I would never give that up. But…there was a dark side to the school even before the 1964 Civil Rights Act…which was largely ignored. As our family developed our equine business and grew our Black Angus herd through nutrition and well…grass, I was contacted by UVA to assist in the curriculum development for their graduate Biological Sciences program due to my work at Virginia Tech - no boos please, and then Ohio State, Cornell, and the University of Georgia in their veterinary sciences programs. I turned UVA down…three times. I also turned them down for an honorary doctorate twice. So now the story becomes - Why am I here today?

Let's go back to 1962 when I met my beautiful wife, Emmaline, who is seated right down front here with our daughter Grace Bryant who is a fantastic elementary school teacher in Raleigh, our youngest daughter Beatrice Lynn Harrison, who is just about the best Civil Rights attorney on Capitol Hill, and our son, TJ, who you might all have fond memories of during his days as a Tarheel under Dean Smith - again no booing please. They have blessed us with seven grandchildren. Today my story is about one person and her family. A person who represents the struggle for many. The person who is the reason I have always refused to come back to Charlottesville even though she has always urged me to do so. She has adored this place just as much as I have resented it for so long. She is a much better person than I and should probably be the one up here now. My wife, Emmaline Foster, daughter of Mathilde Foster and Anthony Foster, granddaughter of the fantastic Beatrice Henry-Thompson, great-granddaughter of Gracie Henry-Summerlin - who I would have given anything to have known. Gracie may have been the strongest woman who ever lived...before Emmaline Foster came along of course. This story doesn't belong just to my Emmie though. This message belongs to humanity. It's not about acceptance...it's about equal footing. When Emmie came to Charlottesville in 1962, she wasn't allowed in the dorms, the library, the fieldhouse, or any other school building. She was allowed to come to the UVA Hospital, where she was taught nursing classes with 19 other black women in the basement. She lived in a small building behind Tail Pipes Drive-in - where she worked every single day. When she walked from the Drive-in to the hospital each day, she was subjected to being called names, and she was even hit on a few occasions with mud and at least once with an egg. But… she got up every day, and she went to work, and she went to school. Imagine sending your children off to college to a life like that. You wouldn't. When we first met in 1962, she wouldn't agree to see me - even though I could tell she wanted to. You see, in 1962, interracial dating was illegal- as was interracial marriage in the state of Virginia. I always thought she was just scared to date me. I was wrong. It wasn't until after we were married that her father Anthony told me that she loved me too much to watch others treat me the way they treated her. She is the bravest person I've ever known, and I am damn lucky to be with her – it is my greatest honor in life.

This isn't just another woke social justice speech that causes half the people to want to jump up and down and declare themselves warriors while the other half just rolls their eyes and tunes out. This story is about history, struggles, and the interaction of human beings who love and support each other for no other reason than that is their heart's desire. Emmaline's grandmother Gracie Summerlin was born a slave in Maryland in the 1840's. She was half Black and half Iroquois. The very definition of our "melting pot". She endured the Civil War and did unimaginable things to keep her true love Thomas alive, and her family safe. She fought the Rebels and the Yankees, and raised and cultivated crops by herself. She was well educated when she could be … and acted like she could hardly speak English when she needed to be just another negro. She married Thomas, a white landowner who survived for ten years after being injured at Antietam in 1861.

When Thomas died, an obscure relative stole the land from Gracie and their son. She lived out her life on an adjacent property devoting much of the rest of her life to educating and housing young orphaned or lost black children. She protected these children from the Virginia Vagrancy Act that was designed to put them back in chains. And she was my Emmie's great-grandmother. One hundred years is three or four generations. Thats how long it took the US Congress to grant African Americans freedom after the Emancipation Proclamation and the end of the Civil War.

Negroes became colored and then black and then African American. But their rights never came. Politicians talked and argued and finally passed the Civil Rights Act in 1964. Then they went home and wiped their hands of the race issue. They poked a hornet's nest. States fought to undo everything the Act stood for. Discrimination ran rampant throughout the country and a generation of colored gave birth to an angry generation of blacks who were tired of false promises. Riots erupted, schoolchildren were denied education, young black men were incarcerated…and Dr. Martin Luther King jr. was murdered.

Now where are we? Another group of whites claiming to support the African American community when they are actually just following the crowd, and not making real change, while the other half stands around in full blown resentment. This is not progress. Progress was so close when my Emmaline came to UVA. It was so close…and it slipped away. Anthony Foster was Emmaline's father, and God rest his soul, he may have been the wisest man I have ever known. The first thing he told me was to never give up on Emmaline. Best advice I ever received.

Anthony and I used to take long walks together through the woods and mountains of Southwest Virginia. One time we were meandering along the New River, and I asked him why the black community was so adamant about demanding respect. He told me this - and I wrote it down that very evening. So, I quote Anthony Foster here - "No black man I've ever know has demanded respect. We understand that respect cannot be demanded- it can only be earned. When the opportunity to earn that respect is held away from a man for too long he becomes bitter." Anthony Foster spent his life doing the right things while constantly being overlooked because of the color of his skin. His ancestors were told to assimilate and then they were never even dangled a carrot. Another time I asked Anthony if it bothered him that I was white. He said does it bother me that his daughter is black. I just stared at him, and he said "what bothers me is that my daughter wanted a happy life and she decided she can't have that without you by her side. I honor and respect you for the gift you give her each day. The color of your skin makes no difference in that does it? "

That's what's missing today. Not another television commercial with a white father and a black mother. The opportunity to earn that respect must be born in this country because it has never existed. We need to get back to where all sides have the desire to both offer, and earn, respect for one another in every aspect of our lives. I never graduated from UVA, so I don't really deserve an honorary degree - and I have turned that down again this time. This day is about all of you getting to share the stage with my wife. Emmaline Foster earned the same Nursing degree that the hard-working white women did in 1965. Only, instead of walking across this stage and receiving a diploma, she was handed a certificate on her way out the back door of the UVA hospital. That, my very young friends, is why I am here today. Fifty-one years later my wife - who has a hall at Virginia Tech named in her honor by the way - will finally walk across this stage and be granted the very diploma she earned and that she deserves. Make her shining resilience one of the messages you take from this wonderful day that marks the beginning of the rest of your lives. Remember to not only earn, but also offer respect in every aspect of your life every day, to every person – no matter the color of their skin.

*If one minute's freedom had been offered to me...I would have taken it - just to stand one minute on God's airth a free woman.*

*Elizabeth Freeman*
**Circa 1800s**

Made in United States
Troutdale, OR
11/23/2024

25159153R00311